LUSAM

THE DRAGON MAGE WARS
BOOK THREE

by

DEAN CADMAN ©2016

www.deancadman.com

Dean Cadman

First published 2016

This edition published 2016 by Dean Cadman

ISBN-13: 978-1534774865

Copyright © Dean Cadman 2016

The right of Dean Cadman to be identified as the

author of this work has been asserted by him in accordance

with the Copyright, Design and Patents Act 1988

Visit www.deancadman.com to read more about the

authors publications and purchase other books by the author.

You will also find features, author interviews and news about

forthcoming books and events. Sign up to the mailing list so

that you're always first to hear about any new releases.

Chapter One

For the past twelve days Lusam and his party had been relentlessly pursued by the enemy agents they had first encountered outside Stelgad. Not long after Lusam had managed to guide them safely out of the fog covered valley, and they had accidentally discovered the possible existence of another Guardian book hidden somewhere in the mountains ahead of them, the agents of Aamon also emerged from the fog behind them. Fortunately Neala and Alexia had spotted the enemy agents almost immediately as they had emerged, giving them a crucial head start through the sparse trees on the west side of the valley.

They had also been exceptionally lucky that first day, when they had managed to trick their pursuers into following a fake trail laid by Alexia. It had gained them a few precious hours' distance between themselves and the agents. Up until that point they had been forced to travel in single file, with Lusam at the rear, using his magical shield to protect the others as best he could. The flat valley floor had been strewn with huge boulders, some the size of a small house. In one way it made it easier to gain some cover from the multitude of magical-missiles constantly being fired at them, but it also made it very difficult for Lusam to maintain his shield around everyone as they dodged in and out of the boulders. Both Renn and Neala had sustained minor injuries during that first day, but fortunately neither injury was serious enough to slow them down much.

The valley floor they had travelled through was flanked on both sides with an almost vertical rock face, making it impossible to climb—not that they could have even tried while being pursued as they were.

When they reached the far end of the valley they were faced with a stark choice. Directly in front of them the ground had ended suddenly, plunging several thousand feet down a sheer precipice to a valley floor below. They found two paths, one leading west up the mountain where they needed to go, and the other path ran east, possibly to the valley floor below, but they couldn't be sure because it was hidden by trees a little further along.

The path leading up the mountain was completely exposed, with no cover whatsoever. If they had gone that way they would not have survived long once the agents had a clear view of them. They had quickly decided the only possible option was to follow the path to the east, and try to lose their pursuers first, then try to find another way back up the mountain later.

They had followed the easterly path for only a short distance when Neala had noticed a small cave in the rock face below. They quickly came up with a plan for Alexia to create a fake trail, while Lusam levitated the rest of them down the sheer rock face and into the cave below. Neala had been petrified at the thought of stepping off that precipice, but Lusam had convinced her it was the only way, and so she had reluctantly agreed. Alexia had somehow managed to cause a small rockslide, which sent dozens of boulders crashing down the steep path and through the trees below. Later when Lusam had asked her why, she had told him that it would have made it almost impossible for the agents to tell if they had indeed travelled that way or not with all the broken foliage the rocks would have caused.

When Alexia signalled her return to Lusam, he quickly levitated her down the rock face and into the cave before she could be seen by the pursuing agents. Fortunately the cave had been deep enough to hide their presence from the agents, and they had passed them by without discovering their hiding place. It had been difficult to decide how long to stay within the cave. If they tried to leave too soon and were spotted, their lead would not be significant enough to safely allow them to climb the western path. But if they stayed too long and the agents discovered their ruse too early, they might lose any advantage they already had, or worse, they might even be discovered within the cave with no way to escape.

They agreed amongst themselves that the agents would likely need at least two hours to discover their deception. They waited within the cave for an hour, then levitated back up the rock face and put as much distance between themselves and the agents as possible.

They had managed to climb the exposed western path before being discovered once again by the agents. Thankfully the agents were now over half a day behind them on the winding path up the mountain, and because the path switched back and forth so much as it climbed higher, it also gave the agents far less opportunity to fire randomly at them from below.

That was nine days ago, and since then neither side had gained much ground on the other.

***

The light was fading fast as they continued to climb the mountain path. A path leading to where, none of them knew —but it was the only option now available to them. They had been running on and off for almost two weeks now, and they were all on the verge of exhaustion. However, if it hadn't been for the keen eyes of Alexia, who had managed to kill three rabbits with her bow, things would have been a whole lot worse for them by now. Along with the rabbits, they had also managed to collect a fair number of berries as they climbed the ever steepening mountain path.

For the first two nights, while climbing the mountain, Lusam's party were forced to travel all through the night. The agents following them had refused to stop for the night, and that had forced Lusam's party to also keep moving. As the lack of food and rest took its toll on both parties, there seemed to be a mutual acceptance to stop for the hours of darkness. Only once did the agents try to gain ground on them during the night, but they were easily spotted by their bright auras moving in the darkness below, and all it achieved was yet another night of no rest for both parties.

It soon became apparent that Lusam's party had one big disadvantage over their pursuers. Only Lusam and Renn were able to see the agents' auras, which meant one of them had to always be acting as lookout during the night, just in case the agents tried to gain ground on them once more. This meant that both Lusam and Renn were becoming more and more exhausted with each day that passed.

Over the past several days it had become almost like a game between the two parties. Lusam's party would find a spot to camp before full darkness, making sure the agents could see them clearly, and when the agents were happy they had stopped, they also made camp. Only on two occasions were Lusam's party fired upon after they set up camp, both missiles harmlessly impacting on Renn's blessed shield as he acted as lookout. After that night no other attacks came. Neither party wishing to waste energy they simply didn't have.

Tonight it was Renn's turn to take first watch, and he took up his position while the others tried to make themselves as comfortable as possible. Neala had picked up a small branch, and was busy whittling it with one of her knives when Alexia broke the silence. "You never did tell me about those enchanted knives of yours. What exactly do they do anyway?" she asked, nodding towards the knife in Neala's hand.

"Oh, Lusam made them stronger, so they would always stay sharp and never corrode," Neala replied, turning the knife over in her hand, as if only just now noticing she was holding it.

"Ah, okay. That's certainly very useful. Does the enchantment make them fly any further?" Alexia asked. Neala was about to answer her, but was interrupted before she was able to.

"No, it doesn't make them fly any further. I never thought about that when I enchanted them to be honest, or I probably would have tried to add that too," Lusam replied, almost collapsing next to the two girls through his exhaustion.

"Really, you could do that?" Alexia asked.

"I think so. Why do you ask?" Lusam replied.

"Maybe if we make it out of here alive, you could enchant my bow to make it shoot further?" Alexia asked hopefully. Lusam nodded absent-mindedly at her request, then realised that given the small amount of food they had left, maybe enchanting Alexia's bow wouldn't be a bad idea at all. It would take very little effort to enchant the bow, and if they *did* happen to see any more game animals on their way up the mountain, it would give them a much better chance of gaining some more food.

"Give me your bow," Lusam said, sitting back up and holding out his hand.

"No, I didn't mean for you to do it now. You need to save your strength. You're not getting enough rest as it is, always having to stay awake half of the night on lookout duty. I wish *I* could see them, and take my turn. I feel so useless not being able to help out," Alexia said.

"Yeah, me too. I'm sick of all this running. We're all exhausted, not to mention almost starving. I wish we could just fight them," Neala said, looking back down the mountainside towards where she guessed the agents were now camped.

"There are too many of them to fight right now. Our only chance is to find that book. Maybe I can learn something new that might help us defeat them, or at least slow them down a little. But in the meantime, let me enchant your bow. It would be a real shame to miss the opportunity of some easy food, just because it was out of normal bow range, don't you agree?" Lusam said smiling.

"I do, but surely you could use your magic to kill any animals we come across?" Alexia replied. Lusam laughed, but it was a humourless laugh.

"Normally I would agree with you, but as you've seen, each time I use my magic they attack us. They can't see my aura, but they can see me when I use my magic. I'm not sure if I could protect us all with my magic shield against another sustained attack. There are at least twelve of them down there, maybe more. And each time they attack, I have to use at least twelve times more energy than each of them do. I have been wondering why they haven't pushed us more over the last few days, and I think I may have worked out why," Lusam said wearily.

"What do you mean? They have been matching our pace ever since we started climbing this mountain path," Neala said looking confused.

"Yes, they have been matching our pace, but for the last few days that's all they have done. At first I thought they knew something we didn't about what lies ahead of us, maybe a dead end or something worse, but I think I finally worked out what they are doing. They are simply trying to exhaust us, or more precisely, me," Lusam said.

"But I thought we agreed that they were even less prepared for this journey than we were. They must be in just as bad shape as us, if not worse," Neala said, again looking down into the darkness towards where their enemy would be.

"Maybe at the start of this journey we *did* have a slight advantage, but no longer. I have been watching them closely today using my mage-sight, and what I saw will certainly swing the advantage back in their favour very quickly. As you all know, during the day while we're travelling I have to position myself within our group so that my shield will protect our vulnerable spots. At first the lack of missiles coming from them was a welcome relief, but keeping my shield active all day while travelling is extremely tiring in itself. Although I began to notice a while ago, that when I use my magic more often and push myself, I seem to be able to do even more later without feeling as tired. A bit like when you overuse your muscles, it hurts while you are doing it, but later you're stronger for it. The problem is, I don't have enough time overnight to fully recover my energy reserves, so each day I grow weaker and weaker.

"Today I noticed that none of the agents were using a magical shield any more. They are rebuilding their magical reserves, albeit slowly without food, but the result will still be the same. At some point there will be at least twelve magi who have full power reserves, and myself with a very depleted one. I'm sure they intend an all-out assault on us within the next day or two, and I'm also sure it's going to be a very one-sided battle when they do," Lusam said in a very sombre voice.

"Then we better convince them to start using their shields again lad," Renn said, obviously paying attention to their conversation, whilst keeping a lookout for any activity below.

"I thought about sending a fireball or two at them today, but I decided against it. I figured it was just a pointless waste of energy. Whatever I sent their way they would see in plenty of time to erect their shields and block it. It would only weaken me, not to mention they would surely fire back at me, sapping my strength even further."

"I see your point lad. I guess if you tried to drop your shield during the day they would more than likely send another missile at you, forcing you to use it, or killing you if you didn't," Renn said.

"Then we need another way to persuade them that not using their shields is a bad idea. Alexia, could you hit them from this range with an arrow?" Neala asked.

"No, I'm afraid not. I've been watching them closely, and they have never come within my bow range. That was one of the reasons why I asked if your knives would fly further, but then I remembered they had shields anyway, so I never mentioned it," Alexia replied.

Lusam sat up straighter as he thought about the

possibility of enchanting Alexia's bow for increased firing range. He knew he could enchant the bow easily enough, but he was also considering the arrows. If he could increase the range of both the bow, and the arrows, it should be enough to make the agents of Aamon use their shields at all times. If they didn't, and they dropped further back out of range instead, they risked losing sight of Lusam's party altogether, and he doubted very much that they would want to do that.

"Alexia, did you see where the agents set up camp tonight before we lost the light?" Lusam asked.

"Yes, I always look, just in case they did come close enough for me to take a pot-shot at them. Why do you ask?"

"Tell me, if I enchanted your bow to reach their camp how many arrows could you get into the air at once?" Lusam asked. Alexia looked back down the hillside, as if judging the distance to where she last saw the agents before the failing light had hidden them from view.

"I think four or five, but in the darkness I probably wouldn't hit anything," she replied still looking in the direction of the agent's camp.

"Hmm, I'm sure you wouldn't, but if we attacked them at first light we might just kill or wound enough of them to even the odds a little. As soon as they realise what's going on they will resume their shields immediately, but maybe we can thin them out a little before that happens. If I enchant both the bow and the arrows, it will vastly increase their range and killing power. If I can increase the range of your weapon enough so that it makes it impossible for the agents to remain out of its range, whilst at the same time maintaining sight of us, they will have no choice but to use their shields at all times, even while they sleep," Lusam said.

"That might just work lad, but you can bet they will likely send an awful lot of missiles our way when they realise their current plan will no longer work. Are you sure you can handle such an onslaught in your condition?" Renn said, sounding a little concerned.

"No, I'm not sure I *can* handle it. But the alternative will mean certain death for all of us if we just continue to wait and play into their hands. At least this way we get to choose when and where to make a stand. Besides, every one we kill is one less that can fire at us later, and any that are injured would either have to be healed or left behind. Healing someone takes a lot of energy, so if they did heal any of their wounded it would also weaken them further. A win-win situation if you ask me," Lusam replied. The others remained silent for a few minutes, each obviously playing out the various scenarios in their minds, and the lack of alternatives available.

"If we can survive the initial retaliation I think we might have a chance," Renn said breaking the silence. "We need to plan our departure from here carefully though. Every wasted missile from them is good for us, but any that find their mark will reduce our chances of surviving tomorrow. Lusam, could you erect your magical shield around me, but leave my shield outside your protection?"

"I don't see why not, but what good will that do?" Lusam asked.

"I propose a two stage retreat after we attack tomorrow. As soon as the arrows find their targets, the two girls will run as fast as they can, and put as much distance between themselves and the agents as possible. I will face the incoming missiles with my shield, hopefully neutralising most of them before they even touch your magical shield. If we stand back to back so I can see the incoming missiles, you can guide me backwards along the path as we also retreat. Hopefully the agents will waste a lot of energy before they realise the futility of their attacks," Renn said.

"I'm not running away and leaving Lusam alone," Neala said firmly.

"No, it's okay Neala. I think Renn's plan might actually work. Especially if I expose my aura to them. It would be like waving a red rag to a bull. I'm sure they wouldn't be able to resist a chance to finish me off, and hopefully waste a lot of energy in the process. In fact, if I stayed very close to Renn and projected my aura just in front of him, I doubt they would even be able to tell that Renn was even there, and if they thought it was just me with my magical shield, they would likely throw everything they had at me," Lusam said, grinning at the imagined looks on the agents' faces when they realised their costly mistake.

"Yes, you might be right lad. If you did project your aura in front of me, it should be more than bright enough to blind them to my lesser aura. Like I said, I'm sure they will throw everything they have at us once we attack them, especially after they realise their original plan has failed. It would have been nice to know how exposed we will be further up this path before we made our move though, but I guess we can't have everything," Renn said.

"Maybe we can," Lusam replied grinning.

"I don't see how. If we move they will see us and think we are attempting to escape. All that would achieve is another sleepless night for all of us," Renn said.

"Not necessarily. I've been partially hiding my aura since we entered these mountains, so the agents couldn't tell from a distance who I was. I could hide my aura completely, then go alone to scout the path up ahead without being seen easily enough," Lusam said.

"It would certainly help knowing what we're likely to come across tomorrow before we commit ourselves totally. But it might be too dangerous for you walking on this narrow path in full darkness," Renn said.

"Don't worry about me. Even if I fell over the edge I would just levitate myself back up again," Lusam said laughing.

"That's not what I meant. I was referring to any night-time predators out there, like mountain lions or wolves. You can't use your shield because you would be seen leaving. In fact, now that you mention it, if you did fall over the edge and levitate yourself back up again, the agents would see you the instant you used your magic, and likely fire at you with everything they had. You would have to be very careful out there lad," Renn said.

Chapter Two

Lusam wondered to himself just how likely the threat of an attack by a predator actually was this high up in the mountains, but he realised that he didn't have enough experience in this type of environment to make an educated guess.

"Lusam, do you mind if I ask you a question about your aura. I've been meaning to ask you this for a long time, but never seemed to get the chance," Neala said, breaking the silence.

"Of course not. What did you want to know?" Lusam replied.

"You told me that everyone has an aura, and certain people like you and Renn can see them in others. I also remember you telling me of your promise to your grandmother, to hide your aura at all times," Neala said, trailing off into silence.

"Yes?" Lusam asked, prompting her to continue.

"Well, if you always hide your aura from others, doesn't that make you very conspicuous? What I mean to say is, if you don't have an aura, but everyone else around you does, surely that would make you more of a target and easier to find in a crowd," Neala said.

"Yes, you're right, that would make me very conspicuous. My grandmother also realised that potential problem when I was young, and had me adjust my aura so that I appeared no more powerful than a normal person, instead of hiding it completely. The best way I can describe it is like a shutter on a lantern. Normally I leave a small amount of light visible to others, but hide the full strength of my aura behind a barrier, so that nobody can see my full magic potential," Lusam replied.

"Ah, that explains a lot then. I was wondering why that agent we first came across in Helveel didn't confront you," Neala said. Lusam was about to announce he was ready to go and scout the path up ahead of them, when Renn spoke first.

"I was also there when you encountered that agent. I was secretly observing him from a window above, when I saw you both walking up that cobbled street holding hands. I checked your auras and found you both devoid of any magical abilities, so I continued to observe the agent instead. What you don't know is that when you left the street, he reanimated the corpse that had its throat cut. Then he sent the abomination out into the streets to find and kill you. Of course, at the time I didn't know it was you, but luckily I was able to find it and destroy it, before it did any harm."

"Thanks, I'm glad you did. He was creepy enough while he was breathing. I'm glad I never had to meet him face to face when he was dead too," Neala said, shuddering at the thought.

"Yeah, thanks Renn. Meeting him once was enough for me too, but how can anyone reanimate a dead person though?" Lusam asked curiously.

"It can only be achieved through the use of necromancy. A vile and dark magic known only to the followers of Aamon. Its very existence is an affront to Aysha and all that she represents. It's the main reason why the paladins were created, to fight the evil of Aamon's followers, and their undead minions," Renn replied.

"How can you kill something that's already dead?" Alexia asked, with revulsion clearly evident in her voice.

"It's almost impossible for a non-blessed weapon to kill an undead minion. Fire of course will eventually burn it away to nothing, but regular steel weapons are almost useless against them. If you cut away a hand, it will still grasp at you. Remove a head, and the body will continue to advance on you. They have little intelligence, but they do possess great strength and can easily kill a man. If you're ever unlucky enough to be confronted by such an abomination, my advice would be to run. They may be strong, but they're not fast, and you can easily outrun them. Just remember they don't ever need to eat or sleep, and they will never give up chasing you until they are destroyed, or you are dead," Renn replied.

"Are you guys trying to scare me to death before I go out into the darkness alone or what?" Lusam said, sounding rather nervous. Renn laughed loudly startling them all a little.

"Don't worry lad, you're not likely to come across any undead up that path, but if you do, try not to bring them back here with you. I'd like to get some sleep later when you get back so I'm fresh for tomorrow. I can do without fighting any undead tonight," Renn said still laughing. The two girls also laughed at his comments, but Lusam didn't seem to find it quite as amusing for some reason.

"Okay, I'll go and leave you guys to have some more fun," Lusam said sarcastically.

"Wait," Renn said. "You can't just vanish into thin air, the agents are bound to have a lookout, and if they see your aura vanish they will know something is amiss. Come and sit behind me, but do it slowly so whoever is watching down there can see you disappear behind my brighter aura. Once you're sitting down reduce the strength of your aura gradually until it's completely gone before standing up. Also, when you leave camp don't walk in front of anyone else and block their aura either, or it may give away your position,"

"Oh, I'd never have thought about that," Lusam said, moving slowly to Renn's position and sitting down behind him.

"I've spent far too much time observing enemy agents from a distance to overlook things like that lad. I'm sure they will also be trained in such tactics, so let's not give them any more help than we have to," Renn said. Lusam grunted his agreement and started to gradually fade out his aura from sight. Once he had completely hidden his aura he stood up and moved to the back of their camp. He said his goodbyes and quickly left their camp behind, making sure not to walk in front of any of the others as he did so. He then headed up the path to scout out what lay ahead of them for tomorrow's crucial retreat up the mountain.

After Lusam left nobody spoke or moved for a long time in camp. Renn was busy carefully watching for any signs of movement in the agent's camp below, and even though neither Neala or Alexia could see their camp, they too found themselves staring in that direction. After several minutes Renn heard movement from behind as one of the girls stood up. A moment later Alexia appeared at his side and knelt down beside him.

"Renn, may I ask something of you please," Alexia said quietly by his side.

"Sure, what is it?" Renn replied, never taking his eyes away from the enemy's camp below.

"I've never met a paladin of Aysha before, but would it be appropriate to ask for a blessing from you in preparation for tomorrow's battle?" she asked sheepishly. Renn was surprised by her request, and didn't really know how best to respond. He had never been asked for a blessing before by anyone, let alone given one. As a paladin he was a solider of Aysha, not a priest who dealt with the spiritual needs of people. He considered her words carefully, and what his response should be for a few moments before he replied,

"I'm honoured you would ask me, but I think the best person to request a blessing from would be Aysha herself. I would be more than happy to join you in prayer in this regard," Renn said.

"Thank you Renn, I would really appreciate that," Alexia replied. Neala watched as Renn removed his sword and took to one knee in front of it, head bowed in prayer, while Alexia knelt beside him also in prayer. Neala felt strange mixed emotions. She had never been a religious person, but for some reason right at this moment she felt left out, as if she were missing out on something important. She found herself also praying for their success in the coming days, but still felt a tinge of jealousy that Alexia had prayed alongside a paladin of Aysha for some crazy reason.

When Alexia and Renn were finally finished praying, Alexia returned to Neala's side and sat quietly in the darkness.

"I didn't know you were the religious type Alexia," Neala said quietly.

"Yes, I always have been since I was very young. We had a priest of Aysha join us in the forest when I was a young girl. He came to try and convince our band of thieves to change their ways. Although no one there would have caused him any harm intentionally, at first he was ridiculed for his beliefs and views of the world by many. Not long after he arrived in camp we were viciously attacked by a roaming patrol and took heavy casualties. He saved many lives that day, and the respect the other members of our band gave him from that day forward helped cement his place among us. He came to understand the injustices we faced on a daily basis, and apparently decided to make our 'godless band of men and women' his personal mission. He started conducting sermons within our camp soon afterwards. At first his congregation was made up of only a few people.

"As time passed, either through luck, coincidence, or his direct intervention with Aysha, no one knew, but our luck changed for the better. Patrols lessened, injuries and deaths decreased dramatically, and there was a new found prosperity in our camp. I think the real reason for the change was the fact that the priest had convinced our leaders that they didn't need to kill people in order to rob them. Traders and travellers were no longer killed or harmed as long as they didn't resist too much, and as a result the local authorities simply posted warnings not to travel through our forest. Of course, many did as it saved a lot of travelling time in comparison with travelling by road, but the authorities deemed it their own fault if they were robbed, due to ignoring their advice in the first place, and we were left alone for the most part.

"The priest became almost talisman-like, and everyone

wanted his blessings. His congregation grew rapidly, and I became one of his young followers. He taught me and a few other youngsters many things about life outside the forest, and instructed us all in the ways of Aysha. Many years later he was killed during one of the many raids sent by the Duke of Oakedge. He was trying to protect one of our elderly women, and was viciously cut down as he did so. They left him there to bleed out, ignoring his pleas to spare the women and children. I was there when he died. He asked me to promise him that I would not stray from the path of Aysha after he left this world. I freely made him that promise, and from that day on I have put my complete faith in Aysha for all things, and I will continue to do so for as long as I draw breath," Alexia said quietly.

"What was the priest's name?" Renn asked from the darkness.

"His name was Sigmond," Alexia said quietly.

"I know of whom you speak. He was a good man, and it saddens me greatly to learn of his passing in that way, but his mission was as you guessed; to spread the word of Aysha to any and all non-believers. It seems he achieved his goals. He would have considered even one saved soul worth his life, and from what I just overheard he certainly achieved that," Renn said. "Come, let us thank Aysha for our mutual friend, and his successful life." Alexia didn't reply, but gladly accepted Renn's offer and rejoined him in prayer for her old mentor and friend.

Chapter Three

Lusam slowly and carefully followed the path, making sure his footing was good before taking each step. It was slow progress, but he knew how important it was for their plan to remain a secret from the Empire agents below.

After about an hour the path widened and became much less steep, levelling off into a small plateau. He couldn't see above or below, but he felt sure it remained almost vertical on both sides of him. The wide flat path would make it much easier to run, but it would leave them extremely exposed to the magical-missiles coming from the Empire agents who would be chasing them tomorrow. A few minutes later Lusam stubbed his toe on a large rock sitting in the middle of the path. After hopping around on one foot and quietly cursing to himself for a while, he felt sure he hadn't broken anything and resumed his exploration, albeit with a little more care. It became increasingly apparent that this part of the mountainside was unstable, as more and more rocks littered the path the further he travelled.

His worst fears were confirmed when a few minutes later he found the path completely blocked by a rockslide. He couldn't see how high the blockage was in the darkness, or how far across the path it stretched. He needed to use his mage-sight to check, but he wasn't sure if he would still remain unseen, even whilst his aura was shuttered. He made a mental note to ask Renn later if he could detect any signs of his magic, when he used his mage-sight and had his aura completely shuttered. For now he needed to err on the side of caution though, just in case he could be spotted in the darkness by the Empire agents. He needed something to block their line of sight to him, so he started to carefully feel his way around the area, looking for anything large enough to hide behind, but found nothing.

He made his way back to the safety of the rock face and away from the edge of the dangerous drop-off, before leaning against the wall to think for a moment. He leant back against the wall, but instead of finding a solid wall behind him, he instead found himself falling. He was about to initiate his levitation spell, when his fall came to an abrupt and painful halt, as his elbows met the hard unforgiving rock-strewn floor, quickly followed by the rest of him with a solid thud.

"Ouch!" he said, wincing at the pain in his elbows, and the lump now forming on the back of his head. Carefully, he knelt up and reached out with his hands, trying to work out where he was. He could feel a smooth wall to his right and traced it upwards, making sure there was enough room to stand up there, as he didn't want to add another lump to his now throbbing head. When he regained his feet he followed the smooth wall to where he expected to find the path again, and was quickly rewarded with just that. Realising it must have been some kind of cave he had discovered, he returned to the entrance and gingerly stepped back inside. Knowing the Empire agents could no longer see him, he quickly slipped into his mage-sight so he could finally get a proper look at his surroundings. The cave wasn't very deep, in fact, it wasn't really a cave at all, it was more like a scoop of missing rock from the mountainside. It was only about five paces deep, and just about high enough to stand upright near the entrance, with the roof becoming lower the further back you went.

When Lusam saw the extent of the rockslide his heart sank. It was at least three or four times higher than he was tall, and stretched all the way across the path to the drop-off at the far side. There was no way they would be able to safely climb over such an unstable obstacle, and certainly not while under constant fire from the Empire agents. One sudden movement, and the whole pile of rocks could easily slide over the edge taking them all with it, to their deaths far below. He also knew he could not possibly levitate everyone over the rockslide all at the same time, not in his current weakened state, and not while he was under constant bombardment from the Empire agents. Feeling totally dejected he sat down to contemplate what options still remained to him, but could only think of one: stand and fight. He knew very well how that would end, and it wouldn't be good for any of them.

Lusam had lost track of time as he sat there in the dark cave entrance. He knew he should return to camp soon, but he had no idea how he would tell them all of their impending doom, especially Neala. The weather seemed to be worsening too. The wind had grown gradually stronger since he had left camp earlier, and was now whistling around him in the cave entrance. It was then he realised that the whistling noise of the wind was actually coming from behind him, from within the cave itself. He followed the whistling sound to the rear of the small cave, and found what looked like a pile of rubble. When he looked closer, he realised it was actually made up of debris from the rockslide outside, and not a solid wall as he had first thought. He began to clear the rubble using his hands. As he did so, he felt the wind coming through the widening gaps strengthen, and he instinctively knew it would lead him to the far side of the rockslide. Several minutes later and he was proved correct, when the last of the debris fell in on itself to reveal a small tunnel that led around the rockslide outside. He squeezed through the gap and crawled for a short distance, before emerging on the opposite side of the rockslide.

While standing close to the rockslide, Lusam used his mage-sight to check the path further along. For as far as he could see the path was clear, but it turned a sharp corner and disappeared from view about half a mile in the distance. He wished he had time to check the path further ahead, but he knew he had to return to camp now if they were to have a chance of attacking the Empire agents at first light. He crawled back through the cave, returned to his normal-sight, and exited back out onto the path at the other side of the rockslide. Happy with his discovery, and the fact that he could now deliver much better news, he started to retrace his steps back to their camp further down the mountain path, this time being much more careful not to stub his toes again on any large rocks.

***

Zedd's patience was wearing thin, but he knew his plan to exhaust the boy-mage would work eventually. He had tried to physically chase them down, but without supplies he had found it impossible to maintain the pace necessary to close the gap between them. He had tried a direct magical assault, but at this range it had also proved ineffective. He had been fortunate that amongst the men he had acquired there was a summoner. Summoners were magi who specialised in summoning magical items, and one of the things they could create was a type of bread. It was created using the magical reserves of the summoner, and although it sated the hunger of the men, it held little in the way of nourishment. One thing a summoner was able to do however, was to summon real water from the ground, or even the air, which meant at least no one went thirsty.

Zedd had noticed the boy-mage always used his magical shield while they pursued him, and had given strict orders to fire on him should he attempt to drop his defences. He knew only the boy-mage and the paladin were capable of seeing them in the darkness by their auras, so he knew one or the other had to always be on lookout duty each night. At first he had issued orders for all his men to maintain their shields at all times, just in case they were fired upon, but after a couple of days Zedd had noticed his own magical reserves depleting. There simply wasn't enough time overnight to recoup the energy used during the previous day, and so he had issued new orders not to use their magical shields, unless fired upon first. He had seen first-hand some of what the boy-mage was capable of, and refused to underestimate him again. Anyone else, and Zedd would have already ordered an all-out attack, but he knew this boy was far more powerful than an average mage, and he needed to be weakened enough in advance for his attack to succeed.

Zedd glanced up at the enemy's camp and counted only three auras visible. "Report!" Zedd commanded the man on lookout duty.

"No movement sir. They seem to be sleeping, or at least resting for now," replied the lookout.

"Why are there only three auras visible?" Zedd asked.

"One is sitting behind the paladin sir. I saw one of them move and sit down behind him earlier, and now the paladin's brighter aura is blocking the view of the fourth person,"

"I see," Zedd replied still looking up at the enemy's camp. "Wake me if they attempt to move, or anything out of the ordinary happens."

"Yes, sir," replied the lookout.

Zedd turned to find Cole following him like a faithful hound dog as usual. He had considered distancing himself from Cole several times since they had first entered the mountains, but he had somehow taken on the role as an unofficial second-in-command in the men's eyes, and so now they pestered him with any minor concerns, instead of Zedd; and that alone was worth keeping him around for.

"Sir, all the men report that their magic reserves are fully restored. All except the summoner that is," Cole said.

"Good. Then we shall attack them tomorrow at the first opportunity we get. Inform the men to prepare for battle. Tomorrow we end this chase, once and for all," Zedd said, and he started to walk away before Cole had a chance to reply.

"Yes-sir," Cole replied to Zedd's back as he disappeared into the darkness.

Chapter Four

"I was beginning to wonder if you'd got lost, or fallen off the cliff lad," Renn said quietly as Lusam re-entered their camp.

"Sorry, I didn't mean to take so long. It looks like neither of us will get any sleep tonight. It will be starting to get light soon and we need to prepare for our attack," Lusam half-whispered, not wanting to wake up the girls.

"Before you fill me in on any details lad, come over here and sit down behind me again. You'll need to slowly reveal your aura again, so our friends down there don't get suspicious. I haven't been able to move since you left, and this rocky floor isn't exactly comfortable you know," Renn said, fidgeting a little on his bottom. Lusam smiled to himself, but decided it would be best if he kept his humour hidden from Renn. Lusam did as Renn asked, and a few moments later he stood up from behind Renn with his aura now clearly visible to anyone watching their camp from below.

Lusam sat back down on the ground and left Renn to stretch out his stiff legs, before telling him what he had found further along the path. While he was up Renn woke Neala and Alexia, so they too could hear what Lusam had to say about what lay ahead of them in the hours to come. Once everyone was ready, Lusam began to describe what he had found. He told them all about the rockslide blocking the path, and the small cave he had accidentally discovered at the side of it. He explained how he had dug out the loose rocks at the back of the cave, and how it had revealed a small passage through to the other side of the rockslide. When he had finished describing what he had found further along the path, he fell silent, and waited for any questions or concerns they might have, but he didn't have to wait too long.

"It sounds to me like we may have just got lucky for a change," Neala said yawning and stretching.

"It certainly could have been a lot worse by the sounds of it," Alexia agreed.

"Maybe, but that large flat section of path will leave us very exposed. You two girls will have to make it to that cave before the Empire agents arrive at that part of the path. If you don't, and they gain line of sight of you, you'll both become a target for sure," Renn said, sounding a little concerned.

"Neala, I need you to promise me, that you will run as fast as you can to that cave, and not stop for anything, no matter what you see or hear behind you. I can't protect you or Alexia once you start running, and I'd never forgive myself if anything happened to you," Lusam said leaning over and taking Neala's hand in his.

"I'll be fine, it's you I'm worried about. You're not strong enough at the moment to defend yourself against so many Empire agents, especially if anything should go wrong with your plan. How can you expect me to live with *myself* if something happens to *you*, and all I did was run away?" Neala replied quietly.

"Neala, you know as well as I, that even if our plan fails and I'm killed, there would be nothing you could do against the Empire agents, they would kill you and Alexia far too easily. Promise me, you will run, and not look back," Lusam said squeezing her hand gently.

"Only if *you* promise to stay alive too," Neala whispered leaning in to kiss him.

"Oh, I think I'm going to throw up," Alexia said, feigning revulsion at their kiss. "Don't worry lover-boy, I'll make sure she gets to that cave alive. She'll be right in front of me all the way there. I'll look after her, and Aysha will look after us both, you'll see."

"Thanks Alexia, I appreciate that. Now, I suppose you

better give me that bow of yours, and the quiver of arrows, so I can enchant them for you. We wouldn't want you falling short of your target after all our planning," Lusam said teasing her.

"It's still a long way to shoot an arrow, there's no guarantee I will hit them from this range, just so you know," Alexia said nervously as she handed over the bow and quiver to Lusam.

"Oh, don't worry about hitting them too much. As long as you're close the arrows will find their targets once I'm done with the enchantments," Lusam replied smiling.

"How can you be so sure? What exactly do you intend to do?" Neala asked curiously.

"Well, the bow enchantment is simple enough, it just needs to be made much more powerful. I can easily make it shoot three or four times further, and give it much more force behind each arrow, without making it any more difficult to draw back the bow. It was the arrow enchantments that took me a while to come up with, but I think I have the answer now. I will actually put two enchantments on those. One to make them fly truer, and not be influenced by any wind, but the second enchantment should make them very deadly. I will make them magically attracted to the sound of a beating heart. If you get the arrow within five paces of an agent, it should find its own target, with deadly accuracy," Lusam said grinning to himself.

"Whoa! You can do that?" Alexia asked in amazement.

"Yes, I'm pretty sure I can, but there's only one way to find out for sure I guess," Lusam replied. "Renn, I shouldn't have to use very much magic at all on this, but it may be better if you sit in front of me again to block their line of sight to me, just in case they can detect the slight increase in my aura when I perform the enchantments."

"Okay," Renn replied, and quickly came to sit in front of Lusam.

Lusam took less than fifteen minutes to enchant the bow and quiver of arrows. He had Renn watch the agent's camp carefully for any sign of movement, just in case his activities drew any unwanted attention from below, but all remained calm.

"Lusam, I have an idea which may help you a little," Neala said.

"What's that?" Lusam asked curiously.

"I know how tired you are, and how low your magic reserves are right now. I know I don't have a lot, but I want you to take some of my reserves, like you did with Lucy at the book shop when you healed her. Even if it's only enough to survive one extra attack, it has to be better than nothing," Neala said.

"We've no idea how that would affect you Neala. For all we know it could make you sleep for hours. I don't think it's worth the risk, but thanks for the offer," he said squeezing her hand again.

"I'm sure it wouldn't affect me at all. After you lost consciousness healing Lucy she awoke almost immediately afterwards. All she complained about was a headache, and I'm sure I can put up with a mere headache, especially if it gives you a better chance of coming back to me in one piece," Neala replied. Lusam hated the thought of draining Neala's magical reserves simply to replenish his own, but he had to admit he wasn't looking forward to the coming battle in his current state, and even a small amount of magic could make the difference between success or failure. So reluctantly he accepted Neala's offer.

"Okay, but if you start to feel tired, or weak in any way, tell me to stop," Lusam said.

"No problem, but I'm sure I'll be just fine," Neala replied.

"Hey, lover-boy. As long as your girlfriend doesn't mind too much, you can take some from me too. Whatever it is you're taking," Alexia said.

"Me too," Renn said.

"Thanks, both of you, but don't you need yours Renn?" Lusam asked.

"No. I've already told you lad, I'm not a mage, I'm a paladin. Our power comes from our weapons, not our own magic reserves like yours," Renn replied, then after a moment he added, "I take it you've done this before Lusam?"

"Yes, twice. Once on a woman called Lucy, and a second time on the dire wolf in the forest. Both times I used their own magic reserves to help heal them," Lusam replied. Renn almost choked on his words as he tried to get them out too fast.

"You stole magic from Aysha?" Renn said incredulously.

"Not really, I just used it to heal her wounds. I think it was some kind of test. She tried to stop me from tapping into her magic, but when I bypassed her barriers she appeared to us in her true form, and the rest you already know," Lusam said defensively.

"You do realise that taking someone else's magic is supposed to be impossible don't you lad? Then again, I guess you've heard me tell you other things that you do are supposed to be impossible too, but somehow you're always able to achieve them. I'm not even going to ask how you manage to do it, not that I would understand it even if you told me. You really are special Lusam. No wonder the Empire wants you dead so much," Renn said, shaking his head slightly.

"Talking of the Empire, I thought they shared magic with each other? Isn't that how they manage to maintain such strong magical shields?" Lusam asked confused.

"You're correct, but they share magic through their Necromatic rings. Apparently they undergo an initiation ceremony that links their rings directly to their own magical reserves. It also enables any higher ranking agent to draw magic directly from any nearby subordinate agents. Currently our best intelligence tells us that the magic only travels one way, from low rank to high, and not in the opposite direction. No one knows for certain how the rings work, but our best guess is that a conduit to the wearer's own magic reserves is somehow formed during the ceremony, forcing open a permanent link between their magic reserves and the outside world. With only the ring acting as a way to control the outflow of magic, if you remove the ring, you also remove the ability to stop the flow of magic, and as a consequence they die when their magic reserves run dry. It sounds like what you can do is very different though. You tap directly into the magic reserves of a person without the aid of any pre-made conduit, and as far as I know, that shouldn't be possible to do," Renn said.

"I get the feeling my magic skills may be unique now, but it's only because the knowledge has been lost over time. Almost everything I know about magic I learned from that Guardian book, and I'm hoping the book we seek now will give me something useful to use against those Empire agents down there. If it doesn't, we might never leave these mountains," Lusam said, placing a hand on Renn's shoulder and draining some of his magical reserves into his own. He felt better almost immediately, and by the time he had taken some of Neala's and Alexia's magic too, he felt better than he had in days, and much more prepared for the battle that was to come. They quickly ran through their plans one last time, then sat back and waited for the first light of dawn which would signal the start of their attack.

Chapter Five

Zedd awoke to the unmistakable magical pulse-of-power that follows the death of a mage, quickly followed by three more, and then a fourth moments later.

"SHIELDS!" Zedd shouted at the top of his lungs. All around him sleep-dazed men were scrambling for whatever cover they could find. Zedd saw several of his men return fire, aiming at what looked like several of the enemy fleeing up the mountain path, and disappearing from view once they crested a small ridge. One solitary figure remained. Zedd was about to check their aura, but it wasn't necessary, as his identity was confirmed almost immediately by several incoming magical-missiles.

"Hold your fire!" Zedd commanded. Only moments later the magical-missiles impacted harmlessly on their shields. Zedd knew the boy-mage must be weak by now. It seemed that he too had realised he was becoming weaker day by day, and had decided to mount a challenge against Zedd and his men while he was still able to do so. Zedd instinctively slipped into his mage-sight, and was truly shocked by what he saw. The boy-mage had an aura more powerful than any he had ever seen before. He had no doubt that he would lose a one-on-one battle with this boy should it ever come to that. Fortunately he had fifteen men at his disposal, then he suddenly remembered, five had just been killed. Now he only had ten men. Anger coursed through him at the loss of a third of his men. Men he had ordered not to use their shields. `It was a big loss of course, but at least they *were fully rested, unlike the boy-mage, who by now should be almost magically exhausted,* he thought to himself.

His men awaited their orders, and the boy-mage stood his ground further up the mountain path. *The boy was arrogant to think he could withstand the combined force of ten fully rested magi and me,* Zedd thought to himself. He would make him pay for that arrogance, and the death of his men.

"Target the boy-mage, and fire at will. I want him dead!" Zedd commanded his men. Each man sent missile after missile at the figure standing before them. One after another the magical-missiles found their target, but he didn't falter. On a couple of occasions several missiles came back their way, only to be easily absorbed by their shields.

"Increase the power of your attacks!" Zedd half-screamed at his men. They did as he asked, and the air around them almost sizzled with the intense magic now emanating from the hands of each man in their camp. The boy seemed to stagger a little, but still held his ground. Then he started to slowly walk away, as if in no great hurry at all.

"Don't let him escape. Send everything you have at him. NOW!" Zedd shouted above the noise. Again the boy simply carried on walking away, as if they were hitting him with nothing more than rotten tomatoes. Zedd couldn't understand it. Something was wrong here. Why would the boy-mage simply stand there and take all this punishment? His magic reserves would be devastated absorbing all their attacks, and why does he only send weak missiles to attack us in return? Maybe he was simply trying to give his friends time to escape?

Zedd noticed that ever since the boy-mage had started his slow retreat, some of their missiles were now missing their target. They needed to get closer, so every shot would count.

"Cease fire!" Zedd commanded. His men gladly followed his orders. In the short time they had been attacking, most had used well over half of their magic reserves, and were now feeling the effects of using so much, so rapidly. "Everyone, maintain your shields. I want one man on point, firing at the boy every five seconds. When you have fired ten times, switch with another man. We must keep up the pressure while we make some ground on him. Now move!" Zedd commanded his men. His men formed up into a tight line, and they started running towards the boy-mage, with the man on point firing magical-missiles every five seconds as instructed. The boy kept absorbing their shots without apparent effect, but he didn't seem to be in any rush to escape, simply maintaining his almost casual walking speed away from them.

Only once did they lose sight of the boy-mage when a small crest blocked their view. Zedd expected him to have taken advantage of the momentary lack of incoming fire by increasing his speed, but when they once again could see him clearly, he was no further ahead than his previous walking speed would have carried him. Something strange was going on here, and Zedd needed to figure it out fast.

After another twenty minutes of hard running they had closed the gap to the boy-mage, but nowhere near enough. The path switched back and forth across the mountainside, each time rising higher and higher above them, and the boy-mage was still several levels above them. Zedd needed to catch the boy-mage at a much faster rate, especially if his men were going to be in any fit state to fight once they got within range of the boy. Zedd had been studying the way the mountain path had been constructed. He could clearly see a dip in the path up ahead of the boy-mage, and felt sure they would lose sight of him again for a short while until he later re-emerged further along the path.

"Hold your fire!" Zedd shouted. The man on point ceased firing, and they all came to a stop to await fresh orders from Zedd. "If any man here can not levitate, raise you hand now," Zedd said. Three men including Cole raised their hands, which was far better than Zedd had expected. The last thing Zedd wanted, was to be a ferry service for someone else incapable of levitation, but he also understood how exposed they would be in the air, and he also knew he could tap Cole's magic if he needed it.

"Cole, you're with me. You two, pair yourselves with someone who can levitate your worthless hides up the mountainside, and make sure you shield them on the way up. When the boy disappears from view again we move fast. I suggest you make it to the path he is on as fast as you can. You wouldn't want to be still in mid-air when he can see you again," Zedd said, grinning at the terrified looks on some of his men's faces. He knew that it took a very powerful mage indeed to be able to levitate and maintain a shield of any kind at the same time, let alone one strong enough to withstand an assault from a mage as powerful as that boy. Zedd sent another couple of weak missiles towards the boy-mage while they waited for him to disappear from view again, not wanting him to become suspicious of their sudden ceasefire. As he approached the part of the path that would conceal him from them, and vice versa, Zedd sent one last missile his way.

"Get ready," Zedd said watching the boy as he vanished from sight. He waited a few moments longer before issuing the order. "GO!" Zedd shouted, and before anyone else left the floor, he and Cole were on their way.

***

Renn stumbled backwards a little as the magical-missiles intensified in power and numbers. Several had impacted on Lusam's magical shield, but the vast majority had been harmlessly absorbed by Renn's blessed shield. They had stood still in the beginning, offering the Empire agents a target they couldn't refuse, or miss. Lusam had projected his aura just in front of Renn to mask his presence, and their plan seemed to be working even better than they had imagined. They had expected the Empire agents to advance on their position immediately, but instead they had fired hundreds of missiles at them from their current location. A few moments ago the missiles had greatly increased in strength and number, and Renn now struggled to maintain his balance and accuracy intercepting them. A handful of missiles struck Lusam's magical shield, and he too stumbled a little at the force of their impact.

"We have to start moving Renn. I can't absorb many more of those impacts, and if you're knocked over they will see through our ruse when they spot two auras instead of just one," Lusam said desperately.

"Aye lad, you're right. Let's see if we can't make them miss a little. I'm getting a little tired of being a punch bag anyway," Renn replied as he took another dozen blows in quick succession. They both began their slow careful retreat, making sure to stay close enough to each other so they would appear to be only a single person from down below. Luckily they were still in the dark shadows of the mountain, otherwise their deception would never have worked so well, but they both knew that would change very soon now that the sun was rising fast.

They crested a small mound onto a flat section of path and momentarily lost sight of the Empire agents. Lusam took the opportunity to refine his shield around Renn, putting more power into the parts that had taken most of the strikes so far. Just as he finished the Empire agents once more came into view, and the missile bombardment resumed like clockwork.

"It seems like they want me dead pretty bad," Lusam said with a nervous laugh.

"Aye lad, that they do," Renn replied, bracing himself against the massive impacts. "At least some of their shots are missing us now."

"I know that's supposed to make me feel better, but somehow it doesn't," Lusam replied with another nervous giggle. Suddenly the bombardment from below stopped and the mountainside fell into an eerie silence.

"Renn, can you see what they're doing down there?" Lusam asked, still back to back with Renn and unable to see for himself.

"It looks like they've finally decided to come after us lad. They've started running towards us," Renn replied calmly.

"Well, I suppose that was inevitable. I suggest we keep moving, it's a long way to the cave at this speed," Lusam said, guiding Renn backwards up the mountain path. A moment later the magical-missiles resumed, but this time only single shots, and evenly spaced by five second intervals.

It continued that way for another twenty minutes, with the Empire agents slowly gaining ground on them. Renn kept Lusam informed on their progress, but neither of them were overly concerned at the speed which they were being caught by the Empire agents. The missiles once again stopped coming, but only for a short time, and were resumed moments later just before they lost sight of the Empire agents again.

"You better take a look at this," Renn said suddenly. Lusam spun around and looked over his shoulder. What he saw turned his blood cold. The Empire agents were levitating themselves up the mountainside, and were now almost at the same level as they were. Lusam mentally kicked himself for not thinking about that possibility. How could he have been so foolish not to have even considered that they might do that?

"I know you're weak, but now might be a good time to send a few missiles of your own," Renn said frantically. Lusam could see eleven agents in total; three groups of two, and five single auras, all levitating towards the path they were now on. Strangely, only the groups of two had shields activated, the other five agents didn't. Lusam wasted no more time, and sent powerful missiles directly at the five unprotected agents. One of his missiles missed completely, impacting the rocks further along the mountainside. Three of his missiles hit their intended targets, each one killing an agent on impact. The final missile also struck an agent, but not before he had created a magic shield around himself. Although the missile didn't kill him, a moment later he died anyway, as he struck the ground below, unable to re-establish his levitation spell in time.

"Well done lad, you got another four of them," Renn said grinning, "I think it's time we left now though."

"I think you're right, let's get out of here. Stay in front of me, and stay close so I can keep you inside my shield," Lusam replied, just as the first missile struck his shield with such force it sent him sprawling to the ground.

Chapter Six

Zedd watched, as the first missile narrowly missed one of his men, and instead impacted on the mountainside behind them. Then a moment later three missiles found their targets, killing another three of his men. Then a fourth man all but killed himself, when he fell from the air and landed with a sickening crunch on the rocks below, only because he had tried to erect a shield for protection, and was unable to reactivate his levitation spell before he hit the ground. Zedd let out a scream of frustration and rage. Frustration that he was surrounded by weak fools, and rage because he considered the men to be his, and no one but he had the right to kill them, least of all this boy. Now he had only six men at his command.

Zedd gathered the few men he had left and started the hunt. It only took a moment to reach the flat part of the path and regain sight of the boy-mage. What he saw enraged him beyond anything he had ever felt in his life. The boy-mage wasn't alone, the paladin was with him. Suddenly it all made perfect sense. How could he have been so foolish? No one could have survived that amount of magic thrown at them. No one except a paladin that is. Zedd roared an almost primeval scream of rage towards the boy-mage and paladin, then sent forth his wrath in the form of a series of magical attacks. The first missile struck the boy-mage with such force it actually lifted him clean off his feet, and sent him crashing to the ground in a cloud of dust. The paladin must have heard or felt the impact, as he turned around just in time to avoid the second missile hitting him square in the back. Instead he took it cleanly in the centre of his shield and staggered backwards with the force of the impact.

Zedd's head felt light with the huge amount of magic he had just used against the boy-mage and paladin, but there was no way he was about to let them escape again.

"Fire at will. I want them dead!" Zedd roared at his few remaining men. Each man started to send their own missiles towards the boy-mage and paladin, who by this time were now back on their feet and fleeing for their lives. There was still maybe a quarter of a mile between the two groups, but they were certainly much closer than they had ever been since leaving the outskirts of Stelgad.

The boy-mage seemed to be protecting the paladin with his magical shield as they both ran for their lives. `Foolish,` thought Zedd, `that would only expedite his exhaustion, and play right into his hands.` He couldn't believe how many shots the boy-mage had taken, and yet he not only drew breath, he still had the energy to run. `If he had been born in the Empire, he would surely have become a member of the Darkseed Elite,` Zedd thought to himself begrudgingly.

***

Lusam could hardly stand, but he knew he must. He had to, or Renn would die too, and he had also promised Neala that he would return to her alive. *I must make it to the safety of the cave*, he kept telling himself. Deep down he knew the cave no longer offered any of them much protection. It was now little more than an inconvenience for the Empire agents pursuing them, now they were so close behind them. Once they had passed through the cave, they would once more be able to attack Lusam again at will, except this time he would have to protect Neala and Alexia as well—something he knew he could no longer do.

Renn was now at Lusam's side, attempting to run backwards whilst blocking as many incoming shots as he could with his shield. It proved quite ineffective, as he found himself stumbling backwards over the many unseen rocks littering the path.

"How are you holding up lad?" Renn enquired breathlessly.

"I've been better," Lusam replied, just as another two missiles struck his magical shield.

"You're taking far too many hits lad, we need to make them miss more. If we don't, you'll never make it to the cave alive," Renn said, almost stumbling over yet another rock.

"I agree with you. Any ideas?" Lusam replied desperately.

"I think so, but you'll need to be behind me, and shielding us both. Hopefully if my plan works you should have far fewer shots to block."

"I'm all ears," Lusam replied.

"Well, we need to see the incoming missiles to be able to avoid them, that's obvious enough, but me running backwards doesn't seem to be helping us much, because we are forced into running a straight and predicable path. What we need to be able to do, is see the missiles coming and dodge them by zigzagging down this path, that way avoiding being hit by as many as possible," Renn said. Before Lusam could reply he was struck by three more missiles, and once again Renn found himself lifting him out of the dirt and half-carrying him down the path. Lusam spat out his mouthful of dirt and gave a mirthless laugh.

"How can we run, zigzag, and see what's coming from behind us in time to dodge it if we are facing forwards?" Lusam asked confused.

"Because of this," Renn replied holding out his shield. He spun it over in his hands to reveal the inside of the shield, and Lusam could clearly see an almost mirror-like finish to the metal. "If I use my shield as a mirror, I should be able to see the incoming missiles in plenty of time to guide us in the opposite direction, but you will still need to shield me too, just in case I miss an odd one,"

"Okay, let's try it. Anything is better than this," Lusam agreed, taking yet more impacts on his shield. Renn moved in front of Lusam, and held up his shield so that he could see what was coming from behind them in its reflection. Almost immediately he saw two missiles heading their way.

"Move left!" Renn shouted, and Lusam complied. Two missiles went flying past harmlessly to their right.

"Nice," Lusam said, relieved to have dodged at least those two missiles.

"Right!" Renn shouted, and once again Lusam moved in time to avoid being hit. Their new tactics proved so effective that Lusam only had to absorb one impact from the next ten or twelve volleys, and Renn knew the Empire agents would soon also have to change their tactics. Renn had tried to put himself in the position of the enemy leader, and knew exactly what he would do in his place, so when it happened, he knew exactly what to do in response. Renn had surmised that the only option left to the Empire agent in command, would be to send a whole bunch of missiles at the same time, so as not to leave any room for Lusam and Renn to avoid them. He was right, and with a huge grin of satisfaction on his face he shouted,

"Down! Lie down!" Both of them hit the ground on their stomachs, skidding to a halt as seven missiles flew harmlessly above them. Renn quickly got back up and dragged Lusam with him.

"They won't like wasting seven shots at a time," Lusam said, laughing at the imagined faces of their enemies.

"I wouldn't laugh just yet," Renn said, "if I'm right, they will send another volley just like that last one, except this time it will be at ground level. Yup, just like that...Down!" This time Renn remained standing until Lusam was on the floor, then he quickly lay across the top of him, with his shield pointing towards the incoming missiles. One missile impacted on Renn's shield, and six others skimmed the ground, three each side of them. Again Renn was up and hoisting Lusam back to his feet long before the next volley came.

"It won't take them long to realise that each time we hit the dirt like that they gain ground on us, and the closer they get, the less time we will have to react," Renn stated.

"What are you suggesting?"

"You're not going to like it lad, but I think you're going to have to absorb one of those seven missiles until we get closer to the cave. I'll keep watching them, if they start sending single shots again we can dodge them instead. Do you think you can handle a few more shots?" Renn asked.

"I don't see I have any choice. The cave is another ten minutes away at least, and if we keep stopping they will be on top of us before we reach it."

"Okay lad, let's try and pick up the pace a little if we can, I know you're tired, but so are they," Renn said putting a hand on Lusam's shoulder for encouragement. Lusam nodded and braced himself for the next impact. He didn't have to wait long, as another missile impacted on his shield, and another six flew by harmlessly.

Five minutes later Lusam was on the brink of exhaustion, all thoughts except survival long since gone from his mind. He knew they were getting closer to the cave by the vastly increased number of rocks that littered the path all around them, and found himself absent-mindedly wondering how they had all got there. Of course, it was obvious once he thought about it: they had come from the mountainside above. Suddenly he found himself looking up at the rock face to their left, and could clearly see the huge number of unstable rocks perched on the steep sides of the hillside.

"Wait!" he called out. Renn stopped dead in his tracks and turned with concern clearly evident on his face, half-expecting Lusam to have collapsed behind him. "Shield me for a few seconds, I have an idea," Lusam said. Renn didn't waste time asking questions, he simply moved behind Lusam and prepared to intercept any incoming missiles. Lusam searched the hillside above them for any loose looking rocks, and quickly found a large area that looked suitably unstable. He formed a fireball in his right hand, adjusting the spell in his mind so that it would explode on contact, and sent it hurtling towards the unstable hillside.

"Run!" shouted Lusam, just before the explosive fireball found its target. They were both running at full speed when they heard the huge explosion and the rumble of sliding rocks that followed. Lusam chanced a quick glance back over his shoulder, and what he saw made him smile. The Empire agents had not only stopped their pursuit, they were now in full retreat, and running away from the potentially deadly rockslide. The rocks Lusam had targeted had rolled down the hillside, picking up many more along the way as they went. They now slid and bounced down the sheer hillside towards the path below, creating a huge echoing roar as they did so.

"Well done lad," Renn said clapping Lusam on the shoulder, "I'd never have thought of doing that."

Unfortunately the rockslide was over far too soon, and it had done little more than increase the number of boulders and rubble littering the path behind them, but it had allowed them to reopen the gap between themselves and the Empire agents a little. Lusam and Renn stalwartly pushed onwards, thankful for their small victory, but also acutely aware that the problem of the pursuing Empire agents wasn't any closer to being solved, nor would it be, even after they reached the cave.

Chapter Seven

"They should have been here by now. Something bad has happened, I just know it," Neala said worriedly.

"They'll be fine, you'll see. Aysha wouldn't allow one of her own paladins to fall against such evil men," Alexia replied confidently, bristling with faith in her own words. Just then they both heard a huge explosion in the distance, quickly followed by a rumbling sound that sent vibrations they could feel through their feet.

"That's it, I've had enough, I'm going to go find them," Neala said.

"No, wait. The plan was to wait here until they arrived. You know Lusam won't be able to shield us all in his condition, so if we go out there we're putting his life in jeopardy too," Alexia replied.

"That's just it! For all I know his life is already in jeopardy, and all I'm doing is hiding in this damn cave!" Neala half-screamed. After a moment longer Neala took a steadying breath and continued, "Sorry Alexia, I didn't mean to get angry with you, it's just that I couldn't live with myself if anything bad happened to Lusam. I love him so much."

"Yes, I know you do Neala. I've known ever since the first moment you spoke of him to me. I remember being in the darkness of my cell, and hearing the love and tenderness in your voice whenever you mentioned his name. And, I don't mind admitting that I felt more than a little jealous that you'd found love in your life, not least because it seemed at the time, that I would never get a chance to experience it for myself, especially after Shiva had done with me. I'm happy for you Neala, truly I am, but I know how devastated you would be if Lusam came to harm because he was trying to protect you. Please, stay here and wait for them," Alexia said quietly.

"Do you really think Aysha will watch over them both Alexia?" Neala whispered through her tears.

"Yes Neala, I really do. You know, there's nothing stopping us asking for her help anyway, if it would make you feel better," Alexia said winking at Neala. Neala let out a forced laugh, and nodded her head. Drying her eyes she took hold of Alexia's hand and thanked her for her friendship and faith, then knelt in silent prayer with her friend.

***

"There, I see it," Lusam said pointing at the rockslide in the distance that marked the cave's location. The Empire agents hadn't gained any ground on them since Lusam had created his own rockslide, but they hadn't lost any either.

"I don't see any movement up ahead, maybe the girls have gone on to scout further ahead," Renn said.

"I hope you're right. At least I won't have to shield them for a while if they have," Lusam said through gritted teeth, as he was struck by another missile. Ever since Lusam had caused his earlier rockslide, the Empire agents had periodically tried to use the same tactic against them. Luckily for Lusam and Renn the hillside here contained far fewer precarious boulders than where Lusam had chosen to cause his own rockslide earlier.

They were only several hundred paces away from the cave entrance when another explosion erupted above them on the hillside. Lusam glanced up to see several huge boulders gathering speed towards them, collecting many more smaller rocks as they came thundering towards them.

"Look out!" Lusam screamed, as a gigantic boulder literally bounced off the hillside and flew above their heads, before plunging over the edge of the path and disappearing below. Lusam's shield was peppered with small to medium sized rocks, each one impacting on his shield, and each one sapping their own portion of his now very much depleted power reserves. Stunned momentarily, Lusam lost his concentration and allowed himself and Renn to be exposed to the falling rocks. It was only for a split second, but it was long enough for a large jagged rock to smash into Renn's left leg with a sickening snapping sound. He was knocked clean off his feet—his left leg was now at an impossible angle, and he had a look of complete shock on his face as he hit the ground hard with a thud. It all happened so fast that it was hard to comprehend, and as time seemed to slow, it also seemed to take Renn a very long time to become aware of the pain in his now destroyed left leg. But when he did, the scream of pain was like nothing Lusam had ever heard before. He screamed in agony on the floor, clutching at his now useless left leg. Thankfully, the screaming didn't last for long, the pain being so intense that he simply blacked out from it moments later.

Buoyed by their sudden and unexpected success, the Empire agents immediately intensified their bombardment of Lusam's position as he knelt next to Renn trying to work out what to do next. He couldn't leave him here to die, but he didn't have the strength to heal him either. He couldn't make his mind work past the point of not leaving Renn behind, so he picked up Renn's shield with one hand, and with his other hand he grabbed Renn by his belt and levitated him off the ground. It must have been a very strange sight indeed for anyone watching, as he pulled a weightless Renn along at his side, dodging and weaving down the path towards the cave entrance.

When Lusam came within hailing distance of the cave he noticed Neala peering out from within, and his heart sank. He knew he was no longer able to protect even himself for long, let alone Neala, Alexia and, a now unconscious Renn; they would all die very soon, and there was nothing he could do about it. He staggered the final few paces to the temporary safety of the cave. Neala attempted to leave the cave entrance to come and assist him, but she was forced back inside by another barrage of missiles. Lusam carefully manoeuvred Renn inside the cave, then took the opportunity to see how far behind the Empire Agents were. What he saw didn't make him feel any better at all. They were now no more than five minutes behind him, and still running towards his location. The Empire agents had also noticed Lusam's stationary position, and tried to take full advantage of it by sending seven missiles directly at him. Lusam dived into the safety of the cave only a split-second before the missiles impacted on the rockslide outside the cave entrance.

"Get back!" Lusam shouted. There was a series of huge explosions just outside the cave entrance, and everyone inside tried to protect themselves from the flying debris as best they could. Temporarily deafened by the explosions, they could neither hear anything or see anything through the thick clouds of dust that now filled the small cave. Instinctively they all wanted to run from the cave and gain some fresh breathable air outside, but each knew their fate if they tried to do so.

"Is everyone okay?" Alexia asked, coughing through the dust cloud. A strained laugh came from the back of the cave, barely recognisable as Neala.

"No, I don't think I am okay," Neala replied weakly. Lusam's heart leapt into his mouth when he heard her words.

"What's wrong Neala? Are you hurt?" Lusam asked desperately. No reply came. "Neala!" he shouted. Still no reply. Panic gripped him as he struggled to think of a way to clear the air in the cave of dust. He had to see Neala and find out what was wrong with her. He tried to magically pull some fresh air through the cave from the other side of the rockslide to clear away the dust, but was unable to do it for some reason. Instead he chose to push out all the dust-filled air within the cave, allowing clearer air to take its place. When he turned to find Neala his world stopped. She was lying against the wall at the back of the cave unconscious, holding what looked like a stone dagger protruding from her chest. Blood pooled around her legs, and her face looked deathly pale.

"NEALA!" Lusam screamed.

"Oh Gods!" Alexia said seeing both Neala and Renn clearly for the first time. Alexia almost wretched at the sight of Renn's twisted and bloodied leg; she was sure she would have done if she had eaten more that day.

Lusam bolted to Neala's side, placing his hand on her, and instantly fell into his mage-sight to ascertain the extent of her injuries. She was very badly hurt, and if he didn't stop the internal bleeding immediately she would not survive more than a few more minutes. Lusam screamed loudly in frustration, then a heartbeat later he was laughing like a madman.

"What's so funny?" Alexia asked, unsure if he had actually gone mad or not.

"Look," Lusam said, pointing to the back corner of the cave. Where there used to be a gap leading to the far side of the rockslide, there was now a huge boulder blocking the way.

"Aysha have mercy on us all," Alexia whispered, instantly knowing the certainty of their imminent demise. Alexia watched helplessly as Lusam spent the last of his strength attempting to heal the one he loved. She witnessed the sharp stone seemingly eject itself from Neala's chest, and the wound close up behind it as it did so. A few moments later Lusam blacked out, and simply collapsed onto the ground at the side of Neala. Alexia was now alone. She had no idea how close the Empire agents were, or how long they all had left in this world. She swiftly went to the entrance of the cave and stole a glance outside towards the approaching Empire agents. They were no more than a few hundred paces away from the cave, and closing fast. One noticed her appearance and sent a missile her way, but she managed to retreat inside the cave just before it struck the wall outside.

Alexia knew her time in this world had come to an end. Strangely she felt no fear, only peace within. She calmly knelt down within the cave and thanked Aysha for her life, and the life of her friends beside her. She asked that Aysha would take their brave souls, and that their deaths would be as swift and painless as possible. Then she stood up, removed her bow, strung an arrow, and exited the cave to meet the oncoming Empire agents.

Chapter Eight

Lord Zelroth entered through the two huge doors that dominated the eastern wall of his immense throne room. Each door the height of ten men, and weighing more than a hundred. The chamber was huge by any comparison, and the vaulted ceiling   rose high above him, to impossible heights. Painted on the ceiling were works of art beyond anything else in the known world. Centuries of incredibly detailed work, by scores of now unknown men and women, their names long ago forgotten through the passage of time. As incredible as the ceiling was, it paled into insignificance compared to the artwork that adorned the walls of the gigantic chamber. The entire history of the world seemed to be recorded here, all in painstaking detail. Everything from the story of creation, to the final battles of The Dragon-Mage Wars.

One Mural however seemed to stand out amongst all the others. It depicted the God Aamon opening the great rift to the Netherworld, releasing its dark creatures upon his enemies, and his eventual imprisonment there. Next to this image there was a half-finished mural. A mural that depicted the re-opening of the great rift, and the release of the God Aamon. `Unfinished, but obviously a work in progress,` thought Tristan.

Tristan was one of two men recently captured by the Empire. He didn't know the name of the man in chains next to him, but he did know that he was also a fellow countryman sent from Afaraon to spy on the Empire. They had arrived at the fortress separately that morning, and had momentarily seen each other in the courtyard outside the main entrance. The man had tried to escape when his prison-wagon door was opened, and was brutally struck in the head as punishment by one of the guards sent to escort him. He had not regained consciousness since, nor did he show any signs that he ever would.

Lord Zelroth walked slowly towards his throne. A throne magically created from the bleached bones of dragons and men. It sat on a large solid gold platform at the top of three steps. Each step had intricately carved symbols set into it, none of which Tristan understood the meaning, but he could sense the power within the symbols even from where he was chained. At each side of Lord Zelroth walked five Darkseed Elite guards. Powerful and fearless magi, each in their own right capable of defeating even the strongest magi of Afaraon, but when combined, and their magic channelled through Lord Zelroth, they were unimaginably powerful. Tristan knew that if it were not for the defences in Lamuria, the capital would have fallen a long time ago to their evil.

Tristan knew he would not survive this day. He knew even before he volunteered for this mission that the likelihood of him returning to Afaraon would be very slim indeed. Spies sent from Afaraon were easily spotted amongst the general population, and were often captured long before they were able to gather any useful information about the Empire, let alone relay that information back to Afaraon. It was however the only way to gain intelligence about their enemy, and so, many brave men and women risked their lives to obtain such information, but most never returned home again. The reason the Empire found it so easy to discover the spies sent by Afaraon was simple: the Necromatic rings they wore were fakes. All it took was an inquisitive guard, or a member of the public, and they were discovered for what they were.

Tristan had spent all his life as a fisherman in a small coastal village south east of Lamuria. He had been very happy there with his wife and two small children, and knew, or cared, very little for the politics of Afaraon or the Empire.

That was until one day he arrived home from a long fishing trip, and found his entire village laid waste by Empire forces. Desperately he searched for his family, hoping beyond hope that they had fled the attack in time. It took him hours to find the bodies of his two children amongst the mutilated corpses strewn throughout the streets and buildings of his village. Charred beyond recognition, only the small doll clutched tightly to his daughter's chest gave any clue to her identity, and the charred copper bracelet on the wrist of her smaller brother, who still clung to his sister, even in death.

The scene Tristan discovered was enough to send any man insane with grief, but what he witnessed next, sent him further into insanity than any man should ever be able to return from. Lumbering slowly down the street towards him was a creature from his worst nightmares. Its shape, was that of a woman. No longer alive, but still moving, and still making a hideous sound as it moved towards him. It was obvious by her injuries and torn clothes, that she had been ravaged whilst still alive by the same men who had destroyed his village. Half of her clothes where charred to her skin, and half of her face blackened and blistered by fire. Tristan stared dumbfounded at the undead creature as it approached him, not knowing what to do. It wasn't until the hideous creature came closer, that he recognised it as his wife. He fell to his knees, all strength and desire to live fleeing him at that instant. He knew the creature before him was no longer his wife, but he could also clearly see the results of how she had been tortured before she had died, and that sent him over the edge.

To this day he couldn't remember what he had done to that foul creature, or for that matter, anything else about the following few days. Maybe that was for the best he had told himself many times, not wanting to remember his wife like that. He had no idea how many days passed before he was found by a travelling merchant on his way to Lamuria. He couldn't even remember agreeing to go with the merchant, but found himself travelling with him to the capital nonetheless.

It was shortly after he had arrived in Lamuria that he heard about the opportunity to become a spy against the Empire. It didn't take him long to decide, that joining their ranks would be a good way to gain revenge against the Empire for the brutal murder of his family. He enrolled immediately, and with single-minded determination, completed the training in record time. The risks to his life were never withheld, and he embraced the dangers with open arms.

Many things about the Empire had been discovered throughout the years, by sending generations of spies to Thule, but many things also remained veiled in secrecy. It was well known for example, that the Empire had the ability to read the minds of any spies they captured. Part of the training Tristan had received consisted of shielding his mind from such attempts, but truth be told, no one knew how effective it was, because anyone captured never returned to Afaraon alive.

None of the spies knew, but for the past few decades some misinformation had been given randomly to various spy recruits. If they were captured, and their minds successfully read, certain information would be obtained by the Empire that would make Afaraon seem more prepared for war than was actually true. Any information obtained by the Empire in this manner would have to be considered as truth, and therefore an intricate web of lies had been built up over a long period of time, all of which were aimed at gaining more time for Afaraon.

Tristan watched as Lord Zelroth slowly climbed the steps to his throne. The ten Darkseed Elite guards taking their positions, five either side of him. Lord Zelroth wore a long black robe edged in gold and silver around the hem, cuffs and hood. The hood of his robe covered his head completely, and put his face in total shadow, making it impossible to see anything of his features. When he reached the golden platform, he took his place upon the throne. Tristan couldn't see his face, but he could feel his stare burrowing into him, like a thousand insects in his mind, all trying to devour his brain.

The feeling subsided as suddenly as it arrived, and Lord Zelroth pointed to the man beside Tristan. No words were spoken, but one of the Darkseed Elite left Lord Zelroth's side and approached Tristan and the unconscious man in the middle of the giant chamber. Tristan no longer feared death, and almost looked forward to joining his wife and children in the afterlife, but he had no desire to be tortured before joining them. The Darkseed Elite stopped directly in front of Tristan, before stepping to the side and kneeling next to the unconscious man. He spoke several strange words of power, and light erupted from his outstretched hand, entering the unconscious man's body. Then—without waiting any longer—he simply stood back up, turned around, and returned to his position at the side of Lord Zelroth.

Tristan expected the questioning to begin shortly after the Darkseed Elite had returned to the platform, but instead the silence dragged on and on. No one moved, and no words were spoken. Ten minutes later the deathly silence was broken, when the man next to Tristan began to stir. At first he let out out a few strange groaning sounds, each one accompanied by a spasm of movement. Tristan watched as his body contorted with muscle spasms, eyes flickered open and closed, and strange noises came from deep within his throat. After a few minutes all movement just ceased, and the room was plunged back into an eerie silence once more.

At first Tristan thought the man was dead, but looking more closely he could see the gentle rise and fall of his chest beneath his tunic. It was then that the man suddenly opened his eyes, and stared directly at Tristan, as if trying to gain some insight as to where he was, and why. Noticing his chains for the first time, he sat bolt upright and looked around the room, his gaze finally coming to rest on the platform and Lord Zelroth at the far end of the gigantic room.

"Ah, glad you could join us," said Lord Zelroth in a deep clear voice. A voice that came from deep within the shadows of his hooded robe. "Let us begin by introducing ourselves. As I am sure you may have already guessed by now, I am Lord Zelroth, ruler of the Thule Empire, and soon to be ruler of Afaraon. And you are?" he said, gesturing to the newly conscious man next to Tristan. The man didn't answer, instead he spat towards Lord Zelroth. Lord Zelroth let out a crazed laugh at the man's response, then signalled to another of his Darkseed Elite, who nodded and started to approach the man.

"You are not the first man to respond in such a manner, nor will you be the last I'm sure, but let me assure you of one thing; you will give me the information I require, and willingly," Lord Zelroth said with an almost humorous edge to his words.

"Don't count on it," the man said defiantly, spitting once more towards the oncoming Darkseed Elite. Halfway between the throne platform and where Tristan and the man were chained, the Darkseed Elite stopped. He extended one hand towards the man, and spoke the incantations of a spell. Almost immediately the man started to scream, as one after another of his fingernails exploded from the tips of his fingers on his right hand, showering the floor in front of him with blood and small pieces of flesh. His sickening screams seemed to be amplified by the immense size of the chamber, and long after he had relented to a soft whimper, the echoes could still be heard.

"Now, shall we try that again? But, before you say something you might regret, know this – the Darkseed Elite standing by my side are not merely here as my guards. Each one has his own unique skills and methods of persuasion, and each one has had an awfully long time to hone their skills to what they are today. I can assure you both, that they could take you apart piece by piece, and still keep you alive while they did it. Then when they reached a point where you were about to die, one of them would heal your wounds, so they may start all over again.

"Now, I know what you are thinking, and not because I bothered to read your minds, but because I have heard it all countless times before. You're thinking you will somehow overcome the torture, or death will claim you early, saving you and the petty secrets you hold dear. Let me assure you, you are wrong. If I merely wanted the information you held, I could simply kill you here and now, then reanimate you and question you that way instead, but I want you to give me your information freely. That way I know you are beaten, and you will know it too before you die. So, with that in mind, do either of you have any questions, or shall we start over with our introductions again?" Lord Zelroth said casually, as if he were simply announcing the seating arrangements of a grand dinner.

"Go ... to ... hell!" the man said vehemently, spitting once more in defiance.

"Oh, wonderful. I do like a challenge. You know, before I revived you, I read the mind of your friend there, and I could clearly see he no longer valued his own life. He only wishes to pass from this world peacefully, and join his departed family. I was hoping you would provide me with more entertainment, and I'm happy to see you haven't disappointed me. Shall we begin?" Lord Zelroth said, nodding to the Darkseed Elite in the centre of the room.

Chapter Nine

Zedd was still reeling from the boy-mage's earlier success at causing a rockslide, and the time they had lost retreating back down the mountain path to avoid it. He had ordered his men several times to hit the rocks on the mountainside above the boy-mage and paladin, but each time the results had been less than desirable. In the distance he could see what looked like a huge rockslide blocking the entire path. He knew this could be his best chance to end the chase, once and for all. He had no intention of underestimating the boy-mage again, but he felt certain that even *he* couldn't levitate and shield at the same time after already being weakened so much. Trying to cross the rockslide would leave both him and the paladin totally exposed to whatever attacks Zedd and his men sent at them, with only the paladin's shield able to try and block their missiles, which Zedd knew would be next to impossible.

Zedd's mood lightened even further when he happened to glance up at the mountainside above the boy-mage and paladin. What he saw was dozens of large rocks, all loose, and just begging to be nudged in their direction. Grinning to himself, he knew this time he would be much more likely to succeed. Even if the rockslide somehow missed them both, Zedd and his men would still have some new cover of their own from which to fire when the boy-mage and paladin finally came up against the rockslide blocking their path. Zedd sent a missile at the loose rocks without another thought. When it struck its target, it exploded, and the whole rock face shifted, sending several huge boulders cascading down the mountainside towards the boy-mage and paladin below.

Zedd watched and held his breath as one huge boulder headed directly for the boy-mage. As it rolled and slid down the mountainside it collided with another large rock protruding from the ground and bounced slightly, making it pass harmlessly over the head of the boy-mage, missing him by no more than a few inches, before disappearing over the edge of the path, then plunging to the ground far below. Zedd let out his pent-up breath with a slight sigh, disappointed the boulder hadn't done the job for him. Seconds later his smile returned as he witnessed another large boulder strike the paladin's leg. Even from this distance he could clearly see the paladin's leg was broken, and the boy-mage stunned.

"Everyone, fire!" Zedd commanded, trying to take advantage of the situation. What Zedd witnessed next shocked him to his very core. The boy-mage levitated the paladin from the ground and ran with him, zigzagging down the path to avoid the numerous incoming missiles. That in itself was impressive enough, but when the first missile struck him, instead of killing him, it merely impacted on his shield; the boy-mage had somehow managed to levitate and shield himself simultaneously.

Zedd's jaw hung slack at the sight. How could an untrained boy command so much power? Zedd suspected he might be able to achieve two spells simultaneously given enough time to prepare, but not under constant fire, and on the run like he had just witnessed with the boy-mage.

No one knew for sure, but one of the prerequisites of becoming a Darkseed Elite was believed to be the ability to cast more than one spell at the same time whilst under duress. Zedd wondered why no one knew for sure, but when he thought about it, it became obvious; if you failed to hold your magical shield whilst under attack and performing another spell at the same time, you would be dead from the attack, plain and simple. That also explained the lack of failed Darkseed Elite recruits in society. It was a one chance deal, fail and you're dead.

Zedd watched helplessly as the boy-mage carried the paladin towards the blockade. He was about five minutes in front of Zedd and his men when something unexpected happened. The paladin seemed to just vanish into the rock face, whilst the boy-mage stood and watched. Realisation hit Zedd moments later and he swore out loud.

"They've found a cave. Everyone, fire at the boy. Now!" Zedd shouted, adding his own missile to the other six now heading directly at the boy-mage's location. Only a split-second before impact the boy-mage managed to dive into the safety of the cave, and narrowly avoided being hit by all seven missiles. Zedd screamed with rage. Both he and his men were almost exhausted, and no matter what they seemed to throw at this boy he was able to somehow thwart them at every turn.

"Take up positions behind those boulders," Zedd said, pointing at the remains of the rock slide he had caused only a few hundred paces from the cave. He had no intention of entering a cave he knew nothing about. He clearly saw the paladin disabled, but he also knew how powerful this boy was, and certainly wouldn't put it beyond his abilities to heal the paladin. The last thing he wanted to do was to walk onto a paladin's blade in the darkness of a cave, or have the roof brought down on top of him while he was inside.

Zedd watched as the huge dust cloud began to settle, running to take his position behind the largest of the rocks. A few moments later he saw another large dust cloud blown out through the cave entrance, and detected magic being used to achieve it. `Why would the boy-mage clear the cave of dust?` Zedd thought to himself a little confused. The only explanation Zedd could think of was that the cave was a dead end, and didn't have any other exits. If it did, surely they would have simply left via another route, he concluded. The grin returned to his face as he addressed his weary men.

"They're trapped inside that cave with nowhere to run, and no other exits but this one," Zedd said confidently. Just then a young girl confirmed his suspicions by momentarily poking her head out of the cave. One of his men fired at her, but the shot impacted on the huge pile of rocks outside the cave entrance.

"Halt! Take up your positions here," Zedd commanded as they reached the remains of the rockslide he had caused. Zedd thought about his next move carefully. He felt sure this would be his moment of victory, but he would take no more chances.

"You," Zedd said pointing at one of his men, "move towards that cave. I want a report of what you can see from the entrance." The man looked very nervous, but obeyed nonetheless. He stepped out beyond the safety of the boulder field and headed towards the cave entrance. He didn't get more than ten paces before the young girl they had just seen reappeared from the cave, and fired an arrow directly at him. Several of Zedd's men sent missiles of their own, but she managed to dodge them all, and sent another arrow in their direction before diving back towards the safety of the cave mouth.

The first arrow flared bright blue as it passed cleanly through the agent's magical shield and buried itself in his chest. The second arrow also flared blue and struck another agent standing beside Zedd. Both agents fell dead to the ground, and the death-pulse of both agents were clearly felt by the remaining men.

"No. It can't be!" Zedd whispered to himself, now crouching behind his large rock like a cowering animal. Rage built within him to a point where he thought he would storm the cave alone, but sense got the better of him moments later when Cole spoke to him.

"What happened? How did she kill our two men?"

"It seems she too is a paladin. Didn't you see her arrows as they passed through their shields?" Zedd replied, not really believing his own words, even as he spoke them.

"But, she can't be, she's a girl," Cole said, confusion written all over his face.

"Why don't you go and ask her then?" Zedd replied angrily. Cole remained silent, not wanting to be the next man who *volunteered* to storm the cave. Zedd knew that Cole had a good point though. Paladins were only ever men, but here he had just seen a young girl, not even old enough to be a paladin, firing a blessed bow and killing two of his men right in front of him. Now he had only four men under his command. Just as he was coming to terms with his new number of men, he lost another one. The death-pulse felt by himself and the remaining three men.

Zedd roared his frustration, but kept his head down. He had seen where the last man was when he was hit, and he had been showing no more than a glimpse of his body to the cave entrance. It seemed like the arrows were also charmed somehow to find their target, even if that target wasn't completely visible. They needed to get out of there right now, but there was nowhere to run. If they tried to run back the way they had come, they would be dead before they made it ten paces. The only way to escape was down.

"You," Zedd said pointing to a man cowering next to the two dead men, "remove those two arrows and keep hold of them." The man did as commanded, but made sure that he remained completely concealed behind the huge boulder. "We're all dead if we stay here much longer, we need to jump over the edge. Forget about your shields, they're useless against that paladin. On my command we will all fire at the cave entrance. When the first missile strikes, you better be running if you want to live."

"Sir, I can't levitate," Cole said nervously at his side. For the first time since meeting Cole he was glad of his inability to do something. Cole's magical shield would do nothing to protect Zedd, but Cole's body between him and the cave would do just fine, Zedd thought to himself. Smiling inwardly, he positioned Cole to his left side, putting him in a direct line of sight to the cave entrance once they broke cover.

"Fire!" Zedd commanded, letting one of his men break cover before he did. Fortunately there was no sign of the young girl, and no arrows came their way as they all to a man jumped over the edge of the mountain path.

Chapter Ten

Alexia sprang from the cave, arrow nocked and ready to fire at the distant Empire agents. What she found instead, was a single agent no more than fifty paces away in the open, and the remaining agents taking cover behind the freshly fallen boulders further down the mountain path. She let loose her arrow at the closest man, nocked a second arrow while she rolled to the side, and then released it at one of the exposed agents further down the path. She fully expected her arrows to bounce harmlessly off their magical shields, but instead she witnessed a bright blue flash come from each arrow as it passed cleanly through their shields, and a satisfying thud, as both arrows buried themselves deep in the chests of the Empire agents.

Alexia was so shocked by what had just happened, she barely avoided being hit by several incoming missiles sent by the remaining agents. She desperately dived for the relative safety of the cave, and just about made it inside as the missiles struck the giant pile of rocks outside the cave entrance, covering her with dust and debris once more. Her mind seemed to move in slow motion. She had fully expected to be killed when she attacked the Empire agents. She had only ever intended attacking them as a last act of defiance. Never for one moment did she expect her arrows to be effective against their shields.

Alexia waited until the dust settled a little before carefully approaching the cave entrance. She had to confirm for herself, what she thought she had just witnessed outside.

Creeping to the edge of the cave opening she gingerly looked out. She could clearly see the dead Empire agent lying on his back with her arrow protruding from his chest.

"How?" she whispered to herself, completely confused by her own success. She risked poking her head out a little further to see where the remaining agents were, and was relieved to see they were still hiding behind the various sized boulders, right where she had seen them last. She noticed that one of the agents had his arm exposed whilst trying to hide behind a boulder that was a little too small to fully conceal him. She nocked another arrow and took the shot. The arrow flew true until it came within inches of its target, then it seemed to whip around at an impossible angle and into the side of his chest, just under his right arm. It too flashed bright blue as it passed through the agent's shield. She heard a howl of rage come from one of the agents still hiding behind the rocks, and it made her smile.

Alexia listened intently for any movement outside, but heard none. She was about to take another look outside when four more missiles struck the rocks outside the cave, showering her in even more rocks and dust. She heard movement outside in the distance, and fully expected them to be storming her position, so she once again nocked an arrow and left the safety of the cave to meet the oncoming charge. She rolled to the side as she exited the cave, coming swiftly to her feet, ready to fire at the advancing agents. Instead of seeing agents charging towards her, what she saw instead was the last of them jumping off the edge of mountain path, and disappearing from view below. She froze in position, scanning the large boulders further down the path for any signs of movement, but saw nothing.

Alexia remained within easy reach of the cave entrance for another ten minutes before she dared move any further away from its relative safety. She fully expected it to be a trap of some kind, and once she had committed herself too much, they would surely come out of hiding and kill her. She moved further towards the edge of the path, giving herself a fresh angle from which to view the large boulders, but she could see no sign of any Empire agents behind them. Taking a deep breath, she silently approached the area she had last see the agents. She was convinced they were somehow hiding behind the rocks, but when she reached the boulders, she discovered nothing but two bodies. Relief flooded through Alexia, as she fell to her knees to thank Aysha for sparing her life, and those of her friends.

Alexia searched the two dead agents for anything useful, but didn't find anything at all. She noticed that both arrows had been removed from the dead agent's chests, and were nowhere to be found. It reminded her of how important her remaining arrows might be, and so she went to retrieve the arrow still embedded in the first agent's chest that she had killed. When she stood up after removing the arrow, she noticed movement out of the corner of her eye. In one fluid motion she whipped herself around towards the detected movement, and had an arrow nocked and ready to fire even before she faced her target. There, on the hillside above her, stood a mountain goat. It just stood there watching her, and she watched back, as if both of them were too scared to move an inch. Neither Alexia nor the others had eaten much that day, and even their water supply was beginning to run low. Alexia knew if it hadn't been for the fact it had rained several times since they had entered the mountains, they would all have died from dehydration a long time ago.

Very slowly Alexia drew back the bow, almost scared to breathe in case she frightened off her prey. Normally she would have aimed for the head of her quarry, but she knew full well how hard the head of a mountain goat was, so instead she aimed for its chest. She hated to kill such a magnificent creature, but knew if she didn't, none of them would survive for much longer without more food. She let her arrow loose, and it flew straight and true, killing the creature cleanly. Once again she thanked Aysha for her bounty, before retrieving her prize and returning to the cave.

Alexia checked on the others, and found that they were all still unconscious. Neala seemed to have more colour in her face, but Renn seemed to look even worse than he had before. She left the cave again in search of some firewood, and although not many trees grew this high up in the mountains, a few did cling stubbornly to the hillside here and there. The recent rock slides seemed to have taken their toll on some of them, and Alexia managed to find enough small branches scattered around on the path to make a small fire possible. She knew the wood wouldn't burn for long, so she decided to prepare the meat before lighting the fire.

It was hard work skinning a mountain goat, and in her current weakened state she found it even harder, but after two hours or so she had the animal skinned and butchered sufficiently to start the fire. Once she lit the fire and the meat had started to cook, she felt almost dizzy at the delicious smell that came from the fat-rich meat as it sizzled over the flames. It didn't take too long to cook, but to Alexia it felt like a lifetime as she waited to taste the cooked meat.

Neala awoke to the delicious smell of cooking meat. Instinctively her hand fell to her chest where only hours before a stone shard had impaled her. She looked around dazed and confused, but seeing Lusam unconscious by her side seemed to wake her up fully.

"Lusam!" she croaked, as she tried to stand up in the low cave, only to hit her head on the ceiling above. Rubbing her head, she knelt down next to Lusam, not even noticing Alexia outside the cave entrance. Alexia heard Neala inside the cave and went in to speak with her.

"Don't worry, lover-boy's fine. He passed out after he finished healing you, but he's still breathing," Alexia said smiling.

"I don't understand, why aren't we all dead? What happened to the Empire agents?" Neala asked confused.

"It's a long story. I have some food cooking, so maybe you would prefer to hear it while we eat?" Alexia said gesturing towards the food cooking over the fire. Neala almost passed out again at the thought of food, but managed to nod her agreement and make her way to the cave entrance.

"What about Renn?" Neala asked. "Has he regained

consciousness? He looks in a bad way to me."

"No, he hasn't woken up since he arrived at the cave. I was hoping Lusam might be awake by now to at least stabilise him, even if he can't fully heal him," Alexia replied, looking at the still and pale form of Renn lying deeper within the cave.

"I'm not sure how long Lusam will be unconscious for. When he attempted something similar in Helveel he was unconscious for almost five days," Neala said.

"Oh Gods! I hope you're wrong, I don't think Renn has five days," Alexia said with a worried look on her face.

"I agree, but we tried everything to wake him last time, and nothing worked. He simply woke up when his body was ready. We need to clean Renn's wound, but we have no water, or bandages. I did see some Calendula plants not far from here though."

"Calen... what plants?" Alexia asked looking puzzled.

"Calendula plants. The flowers can be used to stop bleeding and infections, they also speed up the healing process, but in Renn's case we only need to stop the infection and keep him alive until Lusam wakes up ... if we can," Neala replied.

"How do you know all that?" Alexia asked amazed at her knowledge of plants. Neala laughed and pointed with her thumb over her shoulder.

"Lusam taught me all about the use of various plants in the forest next to Helveel. We used to visit there every Seventh-day, and each time he showed me something new,"

"I'll bet he did," Alexia said winking at her friend.

"Hey!" Neala said blushing and swatting at Alexia's arm. Alexia laughed loudly and dodged Neala's half-hearted attempt at hitting her arm.

"What's so funny?" croaked Lusam from the back of the cave.

"Lusam you're awake!" Neala said excitedly.

"Shhh... not so loud," Lusam replied holding his throbbing head. "Is that food I can smell?" Neala rolled her eyes and shook her head.

"Oh, how silly of me. It seems I was mistaken Alexia,"

Neala said apologetically. "We didn't try *everything* to wake him last time in Helveel. It seems all we needed was the smell of cooking food to wake him up." Alexia burst out laughing at her friend's joke, but Lusam obviously didn't appreciate the volume of her humour. Holding his head he slowly made his way towards the cave entrance, then suddenly stopped half way.

"Where are the Empire agents?" he asked cautiously, trying to glance past the two girls sitting near the cave entrance.

"Dead, mostly," Alexia replied. "I was just about to explain to Neala what happened before you woke up." Alexia handed them both a chunk of cooked meat and took one for herself. Nobody seemed in any rush for an explanation whilst they were eating their fill, and Alexia was happy to remain silent while she ate hers. They each devoured several chunks of the delicious meat before Neala prompted Alexia once more to continue with her story.

It didn't take Alexia long to describe what had happened, and both Lusam and Neala were amazed by what she told them. Lusam couldn't imagine why his enchantment would allow the arrows to pass through their magical shields, nor could he offer any other explanation. At that moment it didn't really matter. The Empire agents were no longer an immediate threat. Their numbers were now diminished even further by the three Alexia had just managed to kill, as well as the five she had killed earlier, and the one who had plunged to his death whilst trying to levitate up the mountainside. Lusam didn't know how many Empire agents remained, but he did know it was far fewer than it had been the previous day.

"I need to take a look at Renn," Lusam said, feeling a little guilty he had spent time eating and talking before helping his friend. In truth he knew that without the food he would have been too weak to do much anyway, and he probably still was.

"Can you take any more magic from us before you try to help him?" Neala asked, worried that he was still far to weak to attempt any magic.

"I'm not sure how much magic you could have recovered since last night without any food or sleep, but I suppose we could take a look," Lusam said sceptically. Neala nodded and offered him her hand. Lusam easily located Neala's small reserve of magic, but as he expected, little of it had regenerated during the short time since he had last taken it from her. He gathered a small amount from her, then he did the same with Alexia. He felt a little better, but knew healing Renn's wounds would take much more magic than he currently had. `I'll have to do the best I can until I regain more of my strength,` he thought to himself, as he knelt by Renn's side and began to heal what he could of his injuries.

Chapter Eleven

Zedd and his remaining three men landed safely halfway down the mountainside, well out of range of the young girl and her deadly arrows. At first Zedd remained silent, unwilling to give further orders until he had thought through all of his options carefully. `They're certainly very limited now,` he thought to himself, incredibly frustrated at what had just happened.

He had started with fourteen men, now he had only three left. Fourteen men he had taken under his command without telling anyone else. Protocol dictated that he must inform another Empire agent of his intended mission, and also the number of any men he intended to take with him, and he had not done that. With their Necromatic rings the agents were able to communicate with each other easily over relativity short distances. If Zedd had followed protocol and informed another agent of his plans, it would have meant whomever was in charge locally would have become aware of why he suddenly had fourteen men missing.

Zedd's intention had been to capture or kill the boy-mage quickly, then return as a hero, and ultimately return home to the Empire and his family as reward. In reality with the losses he had already suffered, coupled with his disregard for protocol, he was more likely to be executed on his return, and his family forced into abject poverty. Fortunately for Zedd no one knew he had even arrived in Stelgad, let alone taken fourteen men under his command and entered the mountains to chase down the boy-mage. `And no one ever *would,*` he thought to himself smiling. Whatever the outcome, he fully intended to kill the three remaining men before he returned to Stelgad. He would secretly re-enter the Dark Forest near Stelgad, then emerge openly and announce his arrival to whomever was in command. He would report Cole's demise within the Dark Forest due to one of the Netherworld creatures, and no one would be any the wiser.

Zedd knew he had to continue up the mountainside after the boy-mage. If he didn't, and turned back towards Stelgad instead, there was a strong possibility he would be intercepted by his fellow agents, who would no doubt still be searching for the boy-mage themselves. They didn't know that the boy-mage had gone into the mountains, but they did know he and his friends had entered the forest, and with so many agents in Stelgad it wouldn't take long for them to expand their search into the surrounding mountains.

This time he would follow the boy-mage from a safe distance, and choose his time of attack carefully. Brute force hadn't worked when he had fourteen men at his disposal, so it was painfully obvious it wouldn't work with only three. He needed to be smarter and bide his time, then maybe an opportunity would present itself further down the road. At this point he had nothing to lose by following the boy-mage and his companions, and possibly much to gain.

"We need to find some food before we continue after the boy-mage again. I want you all to spread out and start casting tracing spells. Look for both animals and plant life, and don't forget to search underground for edible roots and vegetables," Zedd commanded.

"Sir, are you sure it's wise that we confront them again with only four of us left? Wouldn't it be safer to return to Stelgad and gather more reinforcements first?" one of the men asked.

"Are you questioning my command?" Zedd asked in a threatening tone.

"No sir," the man replied quickly, snapping to attention in front of Zedd and visibly paling.

"Good, then do as I command."

"Yes — sir," replied the man nervously, as he quickly moved away and began to search for food as instructed.

Zedd and his men spent the rest of the afternoon searching for food, and when they had done they had enough to last them several days. They created a fire and ate a hearty meal before continuing their trek up the mountainside.

Just before dark they arrived at their earlier camp where five of their fellow agents still lay dead. It was a stark reminder of how deadly the young girl and her bow was, and did little to improve the mood within the camp. There was no way to bury the bodies in the rock-hard rocky ground even if Zedd had felt the need, which he didn't. But neither did he want to leave them here to be discovered by any other group of agents that may be following behind them. It was strictly forbidden to reanimate a fellow agent, and doing so was punishable by death. It was considered very disrespectful, and only in exceedingly rare circumstances was it ever done. Zedd had absolutely no doubt, that if the five dead agents were discovered here like this, that it would be classed as one of those *exceedingly rare occasions.* He also knew that if one of them were to be reanimated and questioned, he was done for, and so was his entire family back in the Empire.

Zedd sat on a rock staring at the five dead agents before him. He felt no remorse or guilt for their deaths, only concern for his own future welfare. He knew he could burn the bodies using magic, but he could also use them as a weapon against the boy-mage and his companions. Even if the reanimated agents failed to kill the boy-mage or his companions, and instead they managed to defeat them all, it still wouldn't be a complete failure. Corpses could only be reanimated once, and that meant there would be no chance they could be questioned later should they be discovered by another party of agents.

Zedd knew that the body of the man who had plunged to his death after failing to re-establish his levitation spell would be in too bad a condition to reanimate, so he wasn't worried about him. The three who were shot from the sky whilst levitating were burned beyond recognition by the fireballs that hit them, and therefore would also be in a condition beyond reanimation. That only left the three men who died near the cave, and those he could deal with when they arrived there. Zedd stood up with an evil grin on his face. He would not reanimate them himself. If he did and the minion was intercepted by any fellow agents in the future it would lead them straight back to him. Instead he would command one of his men to raise all five dead agents, and as an added bonus when he eventually killed that man, it would automatically sever the spell that bound the undead minions, releasing them all back into death, and neatly tying up all the loose ends in one fell swoop.

"You," Zedd said pointing at the man who had earlier questioned him, "reanimate those five corpses." The man looked aghast at Zedd's command, looking to the other two men for support, but found none.

"But, sir – it's against our holy law to do that. I can't do it. I won't do it," he said with conviction. Zedd didn't even bother replying to the man's refusal to carry out his orders, he simply killed him where he stood, draining all of his magic through his own Necromatic ring. The man's death-pulse was felt by Zedd and the other two men even before he fell.

As he crumpled to the floor, Zedd smiled and said, "Very well, then you will serve me as a minion instead." Zedd considered asking Cole to reanimate the—now six—dead agents, but wasn't sure if he was capable of doing it, especially in his weakened state.

"Would you like to reanimate them all for me?" Zedd asked the remaining man, daring him to refuse. The man visibly paled and simply nodded mutely to his request.

Ten minutes later and there were six undead minions standing in the camp.

"Command them to remove the arrows from their chests. We don't want to be returning any ammunition to the young lady now, do we?" Zedd said flippantly. The man gave his command to the undead minions, and as one they all removed the arrow from their chests with a sickening ripping-of-flesh sound, and dropped them on the floor by their feet.

"What would you have me command them to do sir?" the man asked nervously.

"Oh, I don't know. Maybe go kill the boy-mage and his companions," Zedd said sarcastically.

"Yes – sir," the man replied. He repeated the order to his new undead minions, and the three men watched silently as all six disappeared into the darkness, heading up the mountain path in the direction of the boy-mage and his companions.

Chapter Twelve

Lusam managed to close the wound and control the beginnings of an infection in Renn's leg, before he was forced to stop, or run the risk of passing out again. The setting of the bones, and repair of the muscle would have to wait until after he'd rested a little. Alexia had already volunteered to watch the Empire agents while Lusam got some well needed sleep. At first Lusam kindly refused her offer, as he was concerned that Alexia wouldn't be able to see them or their auras in the darkness, but after she had pointed out that they were simply sitting around their campfire in plain sight, he quickly changed his mind, thankful for the rare opportunity to rest. Lusam retreated back to the relative safety of the cave, and fell asleep almost as soon as he lay down his head.

Neala came to sit by Alexia's side, checking out the Empire agents' position as she did so.

"Do you think they will attack us again tonight?" Neala asked nodding her head towards the campfire in the distance.

"I doubt it, they lost a lot of men today. From what I can see there are only a few of them left, and they don't look like they're in a rush to do anything at the moment," Alexia replied without taking her eyes off the agents' camp.

"I really hope you're right Alexia, we all need a break after what we've gone through the last couple of weeks, especially Lusam. I've no idea how he's managed to make it this far without collapsing." Alexia nodded her agreement, but said nothing.

"Alexia," Neala said quietly.

"Yeah?"

"Thank you, for what you did today. You saved all our lives. When I was hit by that sharp rock I knew I'd probably die, and that was fine — but I knew Lusam would try to save me no matter what the cost to himself, and that he too would probably die because of it," Neala said with tears in her eyes. Alexia finally took her eyes off the agent's camp below, and turned to face Neala.

"To be honest, I thought we were all going to die on this mountain Neala," Alexia replied in a hushed voice. "I even prayed that your deaths would be quick and painless, and that Aysha would take care of your souls. I never really expected to live through today, but now that I have, I have so many unanswered questions. At first I thought the enchantment on my bow had allowed me to kill the Empire agents, but Lusam said he didn't think that was possible. Nothing else I can think of makes any sense, but there they are … dead," she said, pointing towards the three dead agents still lying in the mud. Neala thought about it for a while, but found she too had no answers as to how it was possible.

"I don't suppose it matters how you killed them Alexia, only that you did, and we're all alive because of it," Neala said placing her hand on Alexia's, and giving it a small squeeze. Alexia smiled at Neala's words of encouragement, and nodded her head in reply.

Six hours later it started to rain again. Light at first, but becoming increasingly heavier as the minutes ticked by. Lightning flashed, and thunder boomed through the dark night sky above. Lusam woke to the sounds of thunder echoing inside the cave. At first he thought they were once more under attack from the Empire agents, but when his sleep-hazed mind started to work again, he realised it was simply a storm outside. He had no idea how long he had slept, but he felt much better than he had in days.

As Lusam made his way towards the cave entrance, he noticed Neala taking advantage of the storm outside by refilling their waterskins at a tiny waterfall. It had been created by the deluge of rain running down the rock face high above them, then it flowed into a small channel, where Neala easily collected it as it cascaded over a final rock, and onto the path where she stood. Neala offered Lusam a waterskin she'd already filled, and he accepted it gladly. It had been the previous day since any of them had drunk very much, and they had all been desperate for water.

Alexia remained on the edge of the mountain path, looking towards the agents' camp far below, never once showing any signs of being bothered by the violent storm above, or the rain that was soaking her to the skin. Lusam walked over to where she sat, and offered her a drink of water.

"Any movement down there?" he asked, holding out the waterskin to her.

"No, they haven't moved all night, but I'm not sure how long their fire will last in this rain," she said, taking the waterskin from Lusam and thanking him. Lusam slipped into his mage-sight and looked at their camp below. As he suspected they had erected a shield over their camp, protecting both themselves and their fire from the heavy rain, or any magical-missiles he might decide to send their way.

"Their campfire is protected from the rain by a magical shield, as are they. I need to finish healing Renn's leg, but after I'm done I can take over here for a bit, while you get some sleep if you like?" Lusam said.

"No, I'm fine thanks. You and Renn have been without much sleep for days acting as lookout, it's about time I took my turn," Alexia replied.

"Yes, me too," Neala said from behind them. "I'll take over from Alexia now, so she can get some rest. Once you've finished healing Renn's leg you should try to get some more sleep too, before the sun comes up. I don't think we should stay here any longer than we really have to."

"Yeah, I don't like being penned in by this rockslide either, but we need to wait until Renn is ready to travel again before we can move on," Lusam said. "I'll go see to his leg, then I'll try to get some more rest as you suggest."

When he reached the cave entrance he noticed Renn was already awake. He could see the pain etched on his face, and felt bad that he hadn't dulled it for him before leaving the cave earlier.

"Try to stay still, I need to mend that leg of yours before you start trying to move around on it," Lusam said kneeling by Renn's side. He placed a hand on Renn's leg and magically numbed the pain for him. Renn let out a grateful sigh of relief, as the pain first diminished, then vanished completely from his badly damaged leg.

"Thanks lad, you've no idea how much better that feels," Renn said, still a little out of breath with the earlier pain. After a moment Renn seemed to become fully aware of his surroundings, and asked, "What happened to all those Empire agents?"

"Alexia killed most of them somehow, but we're not sure how. The rest of them have retreated further back down the mountain. They seem happy to simply remain in their camp for the time being, but we've been watching them closely, just in case they change their minds again," Lusam replied.

"Your enchantment allowed her arrows to pass through the agents' shields?" Renn asked with a look of astonishment on his face.

"No, I don't think so, or at least I don't know why it should have." Renn was about to say something else, but his words were cut short when he gasped loudly.

"Quick, help me stand up lad," he said desperately. Lusam was about to argue with him, until he saw Renn's sword had started to glow with its eerie blue light.

"Oh, Gods!" Lusam said out loud, visions of Netherworld creatures springing into his mind. Neither he nor Renn were currently in a fit state to battle any Netherworld creature the Empire agents may have summoned.

"Come on lad, move!" Renn said, attempting to stand up alone, and failing miserably.

"You can't stand on that leg Renn, and you certainly can't fight on it!"

"Stop arguing, and help me up will you?" Renn replied angrily. Lusam did as he asked, supporting Renn's left side so he could hop towards the cave entrance. Renn's sword was now glowing very brightly, and sounds of battle from outside the cave reached them within. Lusam was terrified something bad would happen to Neala or Alexia whilst they moved so slowly towards the sounds of battle outside.

When they reached the cave entrance, what they saw outside shocked them both. Neala was engaged in battle with an Empire agent, her daggers moving incredibly fast as she dodged in and out of range. She scored hit after hit on her target, but no matter how much damage she caused, the agent kept advancing on her.

Lusam could see another agent emerging from the darkness further down the path, and he was heading straight for Alexia. Alexia hadn't noticed the approaching agent yet, as she was busy retrieving her bow from where she had been on lookout duty. Lusam didn't waste any time warning her, instead he sent a fireball in the direction of the oncoming agent. He fully expected the fireball to harmlessly impact on the agent's shield, but instead it exploded on his chest, fully engulfing him in flames. Lusam couldn't believe his eyes, as he watched the fire-engulfed agent continue walking towards Alexia, without showing any signs of pain whatsoever. Then realisation struck him like a thunderbolt; they weren't actually alive, they were undead minions, just like the ones Renn had described, and that was why Renn's sword was glowing.

Instinctively he knew the flaming undead-agent would not stop advancing on Alexia, and the fire would likely cause her far more problems than the undead-agent would have done by itself. He saw Alexia had already reached her bow and replaced her quiver, but the creature was closing fast. Lusam concentrated hard, and sent out a pulse of force towards the approaching undead-agent. It struck the undead-agent with such force, that it blasted it clean over the edge of the path and into darkened night sky beyond. It flew like a flaming meteor through the dark night sky, falling thousands of feet to the valley floor below, ending in a shower of sparks.

Alexia looked towards Lusam and nodded her thanks, then drew back her bow in one fluid motion, and released an arrow in the direction of Neala. Lusam held his breath as the arrow cut through the night sky, glowing brighter as it got closer to the undead creature. With a thud, the arrow ended its flight, now embedded deep in the skull of the undead-agent Neala had just been battling with. The undead-agent instantly ceased moving, and collapsed to the floor in front of Neala.

Lusam remembered that he was still supporting Renn by his side, and when he turned to see what Renn wanted to do next, he saw the look of complete astonishment on his face.

"Are you okay?" Lusam asked. Renn simply nodded his head, whilst remaining slack-jawed at the scene now unfolding before him. Neala had now dropped back to the base of the rock slide, knowing her weapons to be ineffective against the undead-agents. Alexia however, calmly stood in the centre of the path, and watched, as four more undead-agents lumbered their way towards her. She calmly removed and nocked one of her arrows, drew back her bow and waited. She remained motionless until the lead undead-agent came almost within touching distance, then one after another, in quick succession she sent an arrow at the head of each undead-agent, dropping them where they stood; each arrow glowing brightly just before impact, then returning to normal as the undead-agent fell.

Lusam released a breath he hadn't realised he was holding. He thought Alexia had frozen through fear, or some other unknown reason.

"What were you doing? Why didn't you just shoot them?" Lusam blurted out. Alexia was still searching the darkness further down the path for any more undead-agents, but Lusam knew there were no more nearby; all the weapons had lost their eerie blue glow. A moment later Alexia must have come to the same conclusion, as she inspected her now normal looking bow. Remembering Lusam had just spoken, she turned in his direction.

"I'm lazy, I didn't want to walk a long way to get my arrows back," she said grinning, as if it were the most obvious thing in the world. Neala burst out laughing, closely followed by Lusam, and then Alexia herself. Renn remained silent until they had all quietened down again, then he addressed them all.

"Now I know how Alexia managed to get through the magical shields of the Empire agents and kill them, and how she killed these undead-agents," Renn said, pointing towards the remains of the undead-agents all around them.

"How?" asked Alexia curiously.

"You are wielding a blessed weapon Alexia," Renn stated simply.

"That's impossible," Alexia replied, "I'm not a paladin. You of all people should know that only paladins can use a blessed weapon, and this is a bow, not a sword or hammer. No paladin I have ever heard of has ever used a bow. When Hershel gave me this bow, he said it was only a low quality hunting bow, used to kill game in the forest. You even heard him yourself."

"It's true that a paladin doesn't use a bow, and I have never heard of any using one either, but I just witnessed it with my own eyes..." Renn trailed off in his statement, eyes widening with sudden realisation. "Aysha be blessed," he whispered loudly. "When we were in The Sanctum of Light and Aysha visited us, she said she had blessed all the weapons in the temple. Your bow was inside the temple, as were your knives. They must have been blessed along with all the regular paladins' weapons and shields. Aysha must have known you needed a bow, and as with everything else in life, she provided what you needed."

"Wait..." Lusam said sceptically. "I thought you told me a blessed weapon only had power in the hands of a paladin, and even then its power was linked directly to the amount of faith the paladin had in Aysha?"

"That's right lad, but you heard Aysha tell the recruits that they didn't need to be fully trained paladins to wield her weapons. If I remember her words correctly, she said: *Fear not my young paladins, hold true to your faith, and your weapons will become powerful allies upon the battlefield.*

"I have seen and heard the evidence of Alexia's faith in Aysha, and I can tell you that I believe it to be absolute. Nothing I have seen or heard would make me doubt her ability to wield a blessed weapon, paladin or not."

Alexia somehow knew Renn's words to be true. She immediately fell to her knees and thanked Aysha for the blessing she had bestowed upon her. She felt humbled beyond words, that Aysha would allow her to wield such power in her name, and promised to use it for only good, and to help protect Lusam and the others on their journey, wherever it may lead.

"Come on, let's go fully heal that leg of yours," Lusam said, breaking the awkward silence a few moments later. Renn grunted and nodded his reply, obviously still deep in thought about what had just occurred. Inside the cave Lusam set about healing the bones within Renn's leg, then he repaired the damaged muscles and tendons. When he was done he slumped down against the wall at the back of the cave.

"You're awfully quiet," Lusam said after several minutes.

"Aye lad, I guess I am. You know, I never said anything outside, but Alexia being able to use a blessed weapon is troubling me somewhat. There has never been a female paladin before,"

"Why should the fact her being a girl bother you so much? Surely if Aysha allows Alexia to use her power, you should be happy about it," Lusam replied a little confused at Renn's reactions.

"No, you misunderstand me lad. It's not the fact she's a girl and can use a blessed weapon. It's the fact that the High Temple has only ever recruited men to become paladins in the past. It seems we've missed out on a golden opportunity to recruit female paladins too, and all at a time when our numbers have fallen to dangerous levels. It seems we've been very short sighted lad, something I intend to try and rectify as soon as we reach the High Temple in Lamuria, of that I can assure you."

Chapter Thirteen

Zedd watched impassively as the fireball streaked through the night sky, plunging thousands of feet to the ground below. He already suspected it was one of the reanimated agents he had sent after the boy-mage, but his suspicions were confirmed when he saw the agents' reactions as it finally hit the ground in a shower of sparks, severing its tenuous link with its master. Zedd smiled to himself, knowing it was one less dead agent he would have to hide should he be discovered here.

He never really expected the undead-agents to kill the boy-mage, or even cause them much trouble if he were being honest. Of course, he would be delighted if they had killed any of the boy-mage's party, but now the boy-mage was obviously aware of their presence, he could no longer hold out much hope of that.

Zedd felt confident that the boy-mage and his party wouldn't attempt to leave their camp tonight, not in the dark, and certainly not in a storm such as this. If all he had achieved by sending the undead-agents up the mountain after the boy-mage was to give them all a sleepless night, then he was happy with the results. A few minutes later Zedd's thoughts were interrupted by the agent who reanimated the dead agents.

"Sir—I thought you should know, all my undead minions were destroyed."

"That's okay, they have no idea how many more might be out there in the dark," Zedd said with a wicked grin. "I'm sure they won't be getting much sleep tonight. I, on the other hand, intend to take what sleep I can while it's still dark. Cole, you're on lookout duty. Wake me if they try to leave camp. Although I doubt they will until morning. Make sure you're both ready when they do leave camp, because as soon as they cross over that rock slide, we will be levitating back up there."

"Yes—sir," Cole replied, with his now usual worried look firmly in place.

***

The storm had raged throughout the night. That, combined with the possibility of further attacks, had kept them all from sleeping for most of the night. Even though Lusam had only managed a few disjointed minutes of sleep, he still felt far better than he had done in days. Coupled with the fact that they now had food and water to last for at least several days, Lusam felt that their situation also seemed much brighter, just like the weather outside, he thought to himself.

Lusam emerged from the dim light of the cave, and into the bright morning sunshine outside. He was keen to move on, now that they had rested a little and regained some of their strength. He saw Renn was still on lookout duty and went to sit with him while he ate some breakfast.

"How long have you been here?" Lusam asked.

"A few hours, that's all lad. I took over from Neala when their campfire went out. She couldn't see them in the dark, so she called for me to take over."

"Any movement down there?" Lusam asked between mouthfuls of meat.

"No, they seem to be content just staying put, for the moment,"

"That's what bothers me. I can understand them wanting to remain outside the range of Alexia's bow, but why just sit there like that? They're either waiting for reinforcements to join them, or they intend to attack us again. I never thought I'd say this, but I hope it's the latter. Either way, I think we should move, and sooner the better," Lusam said.

"Aye lad, I think you're right. I came to the same conclusion while I was watching their camp earlier, but, I think there's also a third possibility," Renn said still watching for movement.

"What's that?"

"Well, maybe they'll just try to follow us at a safe distance. Who knows what's up ahead of us? Maybe they know something we don't, and plan to take advantage of it later. At the very least, if they did follow us, and happen to come within communication range of any other Empire agents, they would still know exactly where to find us. After all, finding wherever the Guardian book is hidden is one thing, but we have to also leave these mountains, and there's no guarantee that there will be any route out, other than the one we've just used." Lusam thought about his words carefully before replying.

"I see what you're saying Renn, but it changes little. If they have reinforcements coming from behind, we should move forward quickly. If they intend to follow us at a safe distance, we should still move forward, and if they already have reinforcements ahead of us, we should move forward and engage them before we get trapped between them both. Whichever the case may be, it seems that the right thing to do, is move forward. Let's just hope we can actually find that second book, and it can help us somehow, or we may all end up dead on this mountain yet," Lusam said.

Renn turned to look at Lusam, slowly nodding his head. "Okay lad, let's get the girls and get moving. After all, the sooner we're done in these mountains, the sooner we can get you safely to the High Temple in Lamuria."

Lusam had almost forgotten about his promise to Renn with everything that had happened over the past few weeks. He knew he had to keep his word and return to the High Temple with Renn, but he wasn't looking forward to it one bit. But after everything Renn had gone through rescuing Neala with him, and now in these mountains, Lusam hadn't the heart to do anything other than agree with him.

Ten minutes later they had all gathered the few possessions they had, and regrouped outside the cave entrance ready to depart. Lusam took one last look at the agents' camp to check they hadn't moved, then returned to the others.

"If we stay close together I should be able to levitate us all at the same time. Even if the Empire agents fire on us, we should be over the top well before their missiles arrive," Lusam said. They all gathered close to one another, and Lusam began to quickly levitate them over the huge rock slide. Once they arrived at the other side, Renn went back to the edge of the path and checked on the agents below. They were now scurrying around within their camp like ants in the distance. One of the agents must have noticed Renn's aura visible at the edge of the path, because as one, they all ceased their scurrying around, and tried to appear relaxed once more.

"Looks like our friends down there noticed our departure. They all started rushing around as soon as we moved, but they've seen me watching them now, so they're all sitting down again, trying to make it appear like they don't know," Renn said chuckling to himself.

"I might have an idea," Lusam said. "Renn, just stay there a minute please, I'll be right back." Lusam moved over tight against the wall, and then began to follow the path for a few hundred paces. The path was wide here, and it curved to the left, making it impossible for the agents below to see him. He knew there was a switchback also to the left a little further along from when he had scouted the path earlier. Maybe he could fool the agents into thinking they had remained there longer than was actually the case, by using his old trick of projecting his aura. He returned to the others and explained his plan, exchanging positions with Renn and placing himself in the agents' line of sight. Once the others were at the switchback, he checked the agents' camp to make sure their ruse had worked, and then took a step back. He projected his aura at the place where he had just been standing, then carefully made his way to the others at the switchback. It got more difficult to maintain his projection the further away he got, but once they reached the switchback, it became gradually easier again as they travelled directly above where they were only minutes earlier.

Fortunately the path seemed to get wider the further they travelled, and staying away from the agents' line of sight was fairly simple. When they reached another switchback they stopped. They could clearly see that path here became much narrower further along, meaning they would be spotted easily if they attempted to go any further. It would only be an advantage if the agents levitated to the cave level. If they were spotted this high up the mountain the agents would simply bypass the cave level, and later come directly to where they were now. Lusam soon realised what they had done hadn't given them much, if any advantage at all. He was about to suggest that there was no longer any point hiding, but he suddenly had another idea.

"Everyone wait here, I'll be back in a minute," Lusam said getting to his hands and knees. He shuttered his own aura completely, but maintained his projected aura at the rock slide below. He crawled slowly up the path, to the point just before where he would have been seen by the agents if his aura had been visible, then stopped. He moved slowly to the edge of the path and peered over the edge. What he saw below put a huge smile on his face; he was directly above the cave. The reason the path here was so narrow, was because most of it had slipped down the mountainside causing the blockage outside the cave. One advantage however, was the fact that it now gave an unrestricted view of the immediate area outside the cave entrance, and surrounding path. It would be a perfect vantage point from which to stage an ambush, possibly ending their pursuit once and for all.

Happy with his discovery, Lusam moved back away from the edge of the path, and returned to the others with the good news.

"I think we may have a chance to end this chase right here," Lusam said, grinning widely. "Where I just looked over the edge, is directly above the cave. There's also a clear view of the area in front of the cave, and about twenty paces further down the path. I'm sure it would be an easy shot for Alexia to make from there."

Renn chuckled a little. "I like it lad. The Empire agents will think they're safe at the other side of the rock slide, but instead, it should be like shooting fish in a barrel."

"Even if Alexia missed them, it would put them on the back foot again. I'm guessing they would think twice before they came rushing headlong into any possible future ambushes," Neala said confidently.

"Oh, I won't miss," Alexia said seriously, eliciting good humoured laughter from the others around her.

Lusam eventually cancelled his projected aura at the rockslide, and they all hastily began making preparations for their ambush.

Chapter Fourteen

Zedd gave the order to move, and both his men scrambled around the camp gathering their possessions. A few seconds later Zedd noticed they were being watched from above.

"Stop!" he commanded. "Sit back down. We're being watched from above." The two men did as commanded, ceasing their movements immediately, and attempting to look as relaxed as possible to any onlookers.

`Whoever was spying on them, seemed in no hurry to leave,` Zedd thought to himself as the minutes steadily passed by. After thirty minutes Zedd began to wonder if they would ever leave, that was until his thoughts were interrupted by a strange voice.

"*Identify yourselves!*" the voice said inside Zedd's head. Zedd spun around in search of its owner, and was shocked to see four agents approaching their camp in the distance.

"Stay silent!" Zedd spat at his men, who evidently had also heard the request in their minds. "*My name is Zedd—who are you?*"

"*I am Vintenar Yeroth, and I command you to stay where you are.*"

Zedd voiced a few choice words. A *Vintenar* was a commander within the Empire, and usually commanded twenty men. This was the last thing he needed right now. If they had been regular Empire agents he would have simply assumed command of them as he had done the others, but this man was a *Vintenar*, and significantly more powerful than he was. If he should find out what Zedd had done, he would kill him on the spot, and his family would be forced to bear the shame back in the Empire.

Zedd needed to think of a plausible reason for being here, let alone recruiting men without permission.

"Sir, I was under Yeroth's command in Stelgad. They were *his* men you commandeered," the agent informed Zedd, barely hiding his amusement at how Zedd was now squirming. Zedd fumed with rage as the agent almost taunted him with his words.

"If you say a word to *Vintenar* Yeroth contradicting what I'm going to tell him, I will kill you instantly. He will kill me if he finds out what's happened here—but not before I kill you. Do you understand me?" Zedd growled at the man. The man's face went white at the choice he had: tell the truth and be killed by Zedd, or lie to *Vintenar* Yeroth, and die by his hand later. He didn't reply, he simply nodded his understanding. Zedd looked at Cole, and he also nodded his understanding, knowing he was far too involved now to do otherwise.

Zedd was good at thinking fast on his feet, but this time he knew he must be far better than *good,* – his story had to be perfect, or he was dead.

It felt like an eternity as he watched the four men approach their camp. He could clearly see the strong shield *Vintenar* Yeroth had erected around himself and his men – he obviously didn't trust Zedd. He could also see the strength of *Vintenar* Yeroth's aura, and he knew he was far outclassed there too. `Things don't look good,` Zedd thought to himself.

A few minutes later *Vintenar* Yeroth and his men entered their camp. He was older than Zedd, possibly in his mid-fifties, and he looked like he had never done a day's work in his life. He was short with a balding head that glistened with sweat in the morning sun. His large rounded belly made him look almost as wide, as he was tall, and the intricate tattoo on his forehead signified that he belonged to one of the larger noble houses in Thule. Although status in the Empire was dictated by a person's magical ability, it wasn't unknown for the nobility to buy their way into positions of power, and Zedd suspected this was one of those occasions.

"I will give you one opportunity to explain to me why you commandeered my men without my permission, or indeed informing anyone else you had done so," *Vintenar* Yeroth said threateningly. Zedd feigned innocence, eyes going wide, as if he were not guilty of the accused crime at all.

"Sir, I can assure you that I *did* send word back to Stelgad regarding the men I commandeered. I don't understand why you didn't receive word of it sir," Zedd said in his most subservient voice, and turning to the agent he had just threatened to kill. "What was that man's name I sent back to Stelgad, you know, the *fiery* one." As he said it, he moved his eyes through the sky behind the man, simulating the trajectory the fiery undead-agent had taken the night before. Zedd knew that was one agent *Vintenar* Yeroth was unlikely to ever see again.

"His name was Torl," the man replied begrudgingly.

"Ah, yes—that was him, Torl," Zedd said turning back to *Vintenar* Yeroth. "I sent him back to Stelgad shortly after we entered these mountains with word of our intended plans. I can't image why he never reported our intentions to anyone. I can only assume something prevented him from doing so, but what, I have no idea I'm afraid."

Vintenar Yeroth's gaze bore into Zedd, as if he were trying to determine the validity of his story. The reading of minds were not permitted between agents. Only the Inquisitors were permitted to do so, and of course, Lord Zelroth. But under the circumstances, if he chose to do so, *Vintenar* Yeroth could command Zedd or one of his men to submit to a mind read, and he would unlikely be punished for his transgression once he returned – something Zedd was very well aware of.

"Very well—then report to me why you are here, and where the remainder of my men are," *Vintenar* Yeroth said, still watching Zedd's reactions closely.

"Of course sir," Zedd replied with a disarming smile. "When the location of the boy-mage was discovered outside

Stelgad, my colleague and I were the closest to him. We gave chase into The Forest of Dannar, as did another larger group of agents. We formed into one larger party for increased effectiveness — as regulation dictates — and then pursued the boy-mage and his party through the forest and into the base of the mountains.

"At that point I was the highest ranking agent there, so I took command of the group. We felt sure we could capture or kill the boy-mage at first, but he and his party proved to be more, troublesome, than we anticipated. They entered the mist covered valley, which I'm sure you also passed through on your way here, and that's when I sent Torl back to report our position, and request further reinforcements."

Vintenar Yeroth remained silent for what seemed like a very long time to Zedd. He felt certain none of his story so far, would, or could be disputed, but he still felt a huge amount of apprehension about what he would surely be asked next.

"So, where are my men now?" *Vintenar* Yeroth asked, still staring intently at Zedd.

"We had been pursuing the boy-mage and his party for days, when I noticed that rock slide blocking the path up there," Zedd said, pointing up the mountainside. "I sent the men to attack them as they tried to cross the barrier. I had seen the boy-mage levitate from the city wall in Stelgad, so I felt it was necessary to remain here, just in case he tried to escape down the mountainside, instead of trying to cross the barrier. Either way, he should have been an easy target I felt."

"What do you mean, *should have been'?*" asked *Vintenar* Yeroth suspiciously. "Are you trying to tell me they *have* escaped?"

"The truth is, I don't know sir. The last report I received described a cave entrance next to the blockage. After that I've been unable to contact my men. I presumed they had entered the cave in search of the boy-mage and his party, and that was the reason why I couldn't contact them. We were about to go investigate when you arrived sir." Zedd replied, intentionally leaving out the small detail of the two paladins, one of whom was carrying a particularly deadly bow.

Zedd heard *Vintenar* Yeroth try to communicate with his men on the ridge high above them – but he knew no reply would be heard. Zedd realised that whoever had been watching them from above was now gone, but even more disturbing to Zedd, was the fact he could no longer see any trace of them. He didn't relish the prospect of going up the mountainside blind, not knowing where that girl and her bow were hiding.

"Then I suggest we go see where they are," *Vintenar* Yeroth said, indicating he wanted Zedd and his men to remain in front of him, where they could be easily seen.

"Of course sir," Zedd replied, bowing his head in deference. Zedd indicated that Cole should join him, and his remaining man fell in behind without question. `Not surprising now he had lied to Vintenar Yeroth, or at least not been forthcoming with the truth,` Zedd thought smugly.

Zedd could only guess where the boy-mage and his party were now. He intended to keep a keen eye open for them on his ascent up the mountainside, but he also wouldn't hesitate to use Cole as his own personal shield if he had to. Once they reached the sheer rock face Zedd began to levitate, taking Cole along with him, and once again his remaining man followed close behind. Zedd glanced back towards *Vintenar* Yeroth and his men, still on the ground far below them. `He's waiting to see if we're attacked in the air before he follows us,` Zedd thought, with utter contempt for the man.

Zedd scanned the mountainside for any evidence of the boy-mage's party, but he couldn't see any sign of them anywhere. When he reached the level of the cave he began to move towards the path, but instead of landing on the path, he momentarily levitated a little higher. That's when he saw it. The briefest flash of someone's aura high up above the cave. `They were waiting to ambush him and his men,` Zedd thought, anger quickly building within him. Then after a moment, his smile returned, as he realised he may be able to actually use this to his own advantage. He checked to see where *Vintenar* Yeroth and his men were, and was glad to see they had only just left the ground below.

"I suggest you stay near the wall if you want to live. They've planned an ambush for us in front of that cave. And don't even think about warning our friendly *Vintenar* about it, or the ambush will be the least of your concerns," Zedd said glaring at his remaining man. The man subconsciously glanced towards the cave, as if he were expecting to see the boy-mage and his party there, before turning back to Zedd and nodding that he understood.

"Good, now it's about to get interesting, especially when our *Vintenar* finds all those bodies," Zedd said quietly. Seconds later *Vintenar* Yeroth and his men joined them on the path. Once again *Vintenar* Yeroth insisted that Zedd and his men should lead the group, which he did, making sure he kept as close to the wall as possible.

When they came within view of the rockslide, they could also clearly see the bodies of the dead agents strewn across the path. Eight bodies lay in the mud, five of which had already been reanimated once, but three still remained viable minions.

"How could one boy possibly kill so many of our agents?" *Vintenar* Yeroth asked, shocked at the scene before him.

"I have no idea sir," Zedd replied, pretending to be equally shocked. "I think that must be the cave they're hiding in sir," he said, pointing to the opening. He watched the *Vintenar's* face pale at the thought of entering the dark cave. A cave where someone powerful enough to cause the deaths of so many agents may be lying in wait for him and his men. Zedd smiled inwardly, knowing he could use the uncertainty of this man against him.

"Sir ... I feel responsible for the deaths of these men. It was my orders they were following when they died, please, allow me and my men to check the cave. If they're still inside, I will bring them to swift justice for what they have done here, that I promise," Zedd said passionately. It didn't take

Vintenar Yeroth more than heartbeat to accept Zedd's offer—just as Zedd had expected it wouldn't.

"Very well, I will allow you to avenge their deaths on my behalf," *Vintenar* Yeroth said, waving his hand as if he had just granted Zedd a great privilege.

Zedd had to swallow his anger for the man before he was able to calmly reply, "Thank you, sir." Zedd turned to Cole and his remaining man, signalling they should join him inside the cave, then began walking towards the cave entrance.

"Oh, I almost forgot sir," Zedd said stopping mid-stride and turning to *Vintenar* Yeroth, "One of the boy-mage's party dropped a pouch full of gemstones. There was also a map showing the location of what looks like a new training facility here in Afaraon. I had one of my men carry them for safe keeping ... sorry, I mean *your* men sir," Zedd pointed in the general direction of the dead bodies, then continued towards the cave entrance, his smile growing wider with each step he took. It was common knowledge amongst Empire agents, that Lord Zelroth had suspected the existence of an unknown training facility here in Afaraon for a long time, but none had ever been found. Zedd knew that anyone who brought such knowledge to Lord Zelroth's attention would be rewarded handsomely indeed, and he was equally sure *Vintenar* Yeroth knew that too.

When Zedd reached the cave entrance he paused, taking a moment to check if his ruse had worked. It had. Behind him he saw *Vintenar* Yeroth and his men begin searching the corpses one by one for the fabled map and gemstones. `Now I just hope that girl is paying attention,` Zedd thought to himself. He didn't have to hope for long. Even before he entered the cave he heard the arrow thud into someone behind him, then felt the first death-pulse as the agent died. He turned just in time to see the look of complete shock on *Vintenar* Yeroth's face, as the second arrow struck him squarely in the chest. *Vintenar* Yeroth stared unbelievingly at the arrow now protruding from his chest, mouthing some unheard question.

Zedd stepped out of the cave entrance back into the light, grinning freely at the sight before him. *Vintenar* Yeroth fell to his knees, arrow gripped in both hands.

"Oh, I knew there was something else – I forgot to tell you, there's a paladin on the mountainside above us with a bow, and she's quite a good shot," Zedd said light-heartedly. *Vintenar* Yeroth's eyes widened briefly as he realised Zedd's deception. Then he fell forward, driving the arrow clean through his back, and another, much larger death-pulse was felt by many on the mountainside.

Zedd turned to face *Vintenar* Yeroth's two remaining men, both were staring open mouthed at their dead commander, unable, or unwilling to accept the fact he had just been killed by an arrow.

"You," Zedd said pointing to one of the men, "levitate their bodies over there." Zedd pointed to an area outside the cave; a place where the female paladin would be unable to see from her vantage point. The man did as requested and brought the two dead bodies to where Zedd had indicated he wanted them. `He wouldn't have if he knew what their ultimate fate would be,` Zedd thought to himself.

"Bring those three over here too," Zedd commanded, pointing at the three dead agents who had been shot the last time he was up here. Again the man complied without question. Once all five bodies were together, Zedd turned to the man who had reanimated the previous agents, and instructed him to raise the five bodies. Both of the new men let out gasps of disbelief when they heard his command, but neither man questioned Zedd's orders. `Apparently, they are smart enough to realise that if I've killed a Vintenar, then their lives would mean nothing to me,` Zedd thought.

Zedd removed the two arrows from the dead men, and tossed them into the back of the cave. `That's another two fewer arrows she has now,` he thought. Adding them all up in his mind, he realised that she couldn't have that many left, and with no way to make any more, it was a simple question of what would run out first, her arrows, or his men. Smiling to himself, he entered the cave and made himself as comfortable as possible, while he waited for the man to reanimate the dead agents outside.

Ten minutes later the man entered the cave and informed Zedd he had finished reanimating the dead agents. Zedd had been thinking about his next move. He knew the girl would still be watching from above, hoping they would try to levitate over the rockslide and give her an easy target. He had no intention of giving her that opportunity. If he couldn't go over the rockslide, and he couldn't go around it – he would go through it instead.

"Order your minions to clear the rockslide away from the rock face. I want a gap making so we can pass through safely right next to the rock face," Zedd commanded, not bothering to stand up. The man nodded, and left the cave. Moments later Zedd could hear the sounds of rocks being moved around outside the cave entrance, and he smiled at the thought of *Vintenar* Yeroth being made to work for him.

Chapter Fifteen

Lying flat on his stomach, and with his aura completely hidden, Lusam watched from the edge of the path as the agents made their way towards the cave. Concern amongst Lusam's party had grown rapidly several minutes earlier, as four more Empire agents were spotted in the distance heading towards the others in the camp below. At first they were afraid that even more Empire agents would soon arrive, but it turned out to be only those four in the end, thankfully. They could no longer hope to kill all of the Empire agents here, instead the plan had become one of containment. They planned to kill as many as they could in the ambush, then wait to see if they would attempt to cross the rockslide. If they did, there would be a further chance to reduce their numbers.

Lusam watched as the agents disappeared from view. For some reason they were walking very close to the rock face, which made it impossible to see them from his vantage point. For a while Lusam wondered if they had been spotted somehow, and that was the reason why they were hugging the rock face like they were. Alexia was behind him now, and crouching down a little further back on the path. The plan was that Lusam would tell her when the agents were out in the open, then she would quickly stand up and take her shots, while he shielded them both in case the agents returned fire.

"How far?" Alexia whispered from behind.

"I don't know, I can't see them. They're staying too

close to the rock face for me to be able to see them. Do you think they could have seen us here?"

"I don't see how. I didn't come onto the path until you told me to, and the Empire agents couldn't possibly have seen me from where they were. Maybe they simply suspect a trap, and are being cautious."

"Maybe. I guess we'll soon see," Lusam whispered back. Time seemed to stand still as Lusam waited. Then suddenly an agent emerged from the cover of the rock face, then a second. He waited for more, but none came out into the open. He could see the two exposed agents checking the dead bodies for something, then he noticed something else; one of the two men had a very bright aura. He was one of the new Empire agents, and quite possibly their leader. Lusam would have preferred more available targets before giving the signal for Alexia to shoot, but killing one as powerful as him, was probably better than killing two or three regular agents anyway.

Lusam gave Alexia the signal, and she quickly stood up and released her first arrow in one fluid motion. A heartbeat later, a second arrow was on its way. The first arrow killed its target almost instantly, confirmed by the death-pulse felt by Lusam and Renn. The second arrow also found its target, thudding into the chest of the agent with the brightest aura. Lusam watched as the man's eyes widened with shock and disbelief. It also looked like he was trying to say something, his mouth working silently, as he fell to his knees. He gripped the arrow with both hands, then fell forward, driving the arrow right through him. The death-pulse was the largest Lusam had ever felt. He wasn't sure how far away a regular death-pulse could be felt, but this one had him worried. `If there were any other Empire agents in the area, they would certainly have felt that,` Lusam thought to himself, subconsciously scanning the horizon for signs of movement.

Lusam and Alexia stood like statues, waiting for any other agents to break cover and give them an opportunity to reduce their numbers further, but none did. After a few minutes Lusam detected the use of magic below, and braced himself for an imminent attack – none came. Instead he saw one of the two dead agents begin to levitate, and move towards the cover of the rock face. He understood the implications almost immediately; they intended to reanimate them.

"Alexia shoot that corpse!" Lusam said, pointing at the moving body.

"No!" Renn said sharply from behind them, startling them both. Lusam hadn't even noticed Renn's approach, and by the reaction of Alexia, neither had she.

"But they intend to reanimate them all!" Lusam said exasperated. "We can't let them ..."

"I know, but shooting a dead body would do nothing to help. They would simply remove the arrow before reanimating it, and Alexia would have one less arrow. I'm afraid we will have to deal with them later," Renn said.

"Alexia doesn't have enough arrows to deal with them all later," Lusam replied.

"Don't worry lad, they can't reanimate them all. It only works once, so they can't reanimate the ones you killed earlier again."

"So what you're saying is that we should have thrown the bodies of the ones Alexia killed first over the edge, so they couldn't reanimate them. I wish you had told me that earlier," Lusam said sarcastically.

"You're right, I should have thought about that earlier. Sorry lad," Renn replied genuinely. Lusam instantly felt guilty for blaming Renn. He knew he should have thought about the possibility too, but he hadn't.

"Don't worry Renn, it's not your fault. I guess we all should have thought about the possibility they would use those bodies against us," Lusam said apologetically.

Five minutes later they started to hear the sounds of rocks moving. At first Lusam thought there was a small rockslide nearby, but when he focused on where the sound was coming from, he suddenly realised what the Empire agents were doing below.

"Oh no!" Lusam whispered.

"What?" Neala asked stealing a glance over the edge of the path.

"They're using those undead-agents to dig through the rockslide. We have to go, right now!" Lusam said frantically. Renn came to stand by Lusam's side and looked over the edge of the path towards the cave.

"I think you're right lad, but even with those five undead-agents it's going to take them a while to dig through all of that rock. If they intended to simply levitate up the mountain after us, they wouldn't be doing what they're doing now. I'm sure they know how deadly Alexia is with that bow by now, so I doubt they'll give her any opportunities to use it, especially if they can avoid it. I also don't think they'll try another frontal attack either, and the undead are of little concern to us any longer, so long as we maintain a lookout at night. Having said all of that, I do agree with Lusam that we should move on now. There's little advantage to be gained by staying here any longer, as I doubt they'll give Alexia another chance at killing any of them," Renn said.

***

It had been two hours since they left the narrow path above the cave. Lusam had been watching carefully for any signs of movement below them, but had seen nothing so far. The path became ever steeper as it climbed the mountainside, and now, it also became enclosed on both sides, restricting their view of anything below, or above. It took Lusam a few moments to realise that the walls on either side of them were not naturally formed, but instead had been cut into the rock of the mountainside to create a long uphill corridor. He marvelled at the amount of time it would have taken to perform such a task, calculating it in years, rather than months. The path was covered with lichen here, but here and there he could clearly see the cobbles underneath, more evidence of human construction.

When they reached the crest of the hill, they all

stopped in mid-stride. Before them was the remains of a large stone archway. It was as tall as any house, and wide enough for two wagons to easily pass each other. The huge stones that used to form the top of the arch were lying on the ground, half-blocking the entrance. Two large columns remained, one either side of the path. The size of each of the stones was huge, twice the height of any man, and must have weighed more than a hundred.

"Coldmont ..." Renn gasped.

"What's Coldmont?" Neala asked, before the others were able.

"Coldmont was the legendary temple built by the Guardians when their order was first formed. It was used to train their men, and some say dragons for battle. The history books have various conflicting stories about Coldmont, but one thing they all agree on, was that it was supposed to have been completely destroyed by some natural disaster about a century after the Dragon-Mage Wars ended.

"One book I read described how Coldmont was built in a location inaccessible to Netherworld creatures. I always assumed that to be a type of magical protection, but it seems it was much simpler than that," Renn said, sounding almost overawed.

"What do you mean?" Lusam asked, checking for magical force-fields and barriers, but seeing none.

"It's simple really. The Guardians built Coldmont on the top of a mountain of solid rock. Not even a Netherworld creature can rise through solid rock, and I'm sure I don't have to tell any of you that it wouldn't be possible to reach here during a single night, even for the fleetest of Netherworld creatures," Renn replied.

"The simplest plans *are* usually the best. Or at least that's what my old guild leader used to tell me," Neala said smiling. "But, what makes you so sure this is Coldmont?"

Renn pointed to the huge keystone of the arch, now lying in the centre of the path and half-covered with moss. "That," he said simply. Lusam hadn't noticed it until Renn pointed it out, but carved into the huge stone was a picture of a dragon, with what looked like a man on its back, and several symbols below it, none of which Lusam recognised.

"I recognise that symbol from several of the history books in the High Temple's library. It depicts the Guardians main seat of power: Coldmont. I should have realised if there *was* a Guardian book in these mountains, it would *have* to be in Coldmont. But I always believed, like everyone else, that Coldmont had been destroyed centuries ago." Renn said, almost whispering his words, as if he were scared to voice them loudly, in case the fabled temple vanished before his eyes.

Neala began walking towards the arch, eager to see what lay beyond. If this had truly been the main seat of power for the Guardians, who knew what treasures would lie within? When she passed through the twin columns of what had once had been a grand archway, she once again stopped dead in her tracks. She couldn't believe what she was seeing. There, in front of her, was the largest single building she had ever seen in her life—or more accurately what was left of it. The destruction was almost complete. Several huge round stone pillars lay toppled on what once must have been the main stone stairs to the building, each gigantic pillar now nothing more than segments of its former glory. Two massive statues of dragons adorned the base of the stone stairs, each as big as a small house, and so intricately carved that they looked like they might take flight at any moment. If it hadn't been for the fact that one was split in two by some great force, and the other had part of its head sheered away, she might even have believed them to be real.

There were the remains of what looked like four huge water basins in front of the building. Each one stretched two hundred paces or more on each side, and each one with a different statue at its centre—all long since dried out. The building itself was of a different scale from anything Neala had ever seen before in her life. The blocks of stone that made up the building were truly gigantic. She was still a long way from the building, but she guessed each stone would be several times her height at least. How anyone could even move such a stone was beyond her understanding, let alone how they could construct a building with them.

The longer she looked, the more she saw. The huge remains of a beautifully decorated dome perched on top of the building, now little more than half intact. And remnants of windows so colourful that it must have been like looking through precious gemstones to the world outside. Four huge stone towers once graced the corners of the immense building; now only part of one remained standing, the rest nothing more than rubble, in what must have once been a spectacular courtyard. Statues of unimaginable size and value lay scattered in pieces everywhere she looked. The greatest destruction however, was reserved for the building itself. Three enormous cracks ran through the entire building, each one wide enough for several people to walk through at once. Various portions of the roof had collapsed, and many of the decorative carvings that had once graced the outside of the building now lay smashed on the floor below. How it was still standing, she had no idea.

Chapter Sixteen

Neala hadn't even noticed the others now standing at her side. Each one slack-jawed at the sight before them.

"Gods! How can anyone build such a thing?" Alexia whispered to herself, completely overawed by what she was seeing.

"Magic," Lusam replied, checking out the building with his mage-sight. He could clearly see how the magical protection of the building had failed all around the damaged areas. It was as if the walls themselves had contained the magical protections, but when those walls had been damaged, it had also left gaps in that protection. He had no proof, but he suspected that was why he was able to detect the existence of the Guardian book here. The shield in Helveel was still intact, that's why he couldn't detect the book there, but this one was discoverable by anyone with the ability, and will, to search for it—something that made him feel very uneasy indeed.

"It looks like that building could come crashing down any minute," Alexia said.

"No, I don't think so," Lusam replied. "It still has many parts of it protected by magic. Only the damaged areas are vulnerable—I hope."

"Well, I'm glad I'm not the one going in there," Alexia replied, shaking her head.

"You're not?" Neala asked, amazed that Alexia would pass up the opportunity to explore such a potentially rich find.

"No, I think it would be best if I stayed here with Renn. That narrow path should be easy enough to defend whilst you two go poke around in there for that book," Alexia replied. Renn looked totally devastated when he realised Alexia was right, and that he wasn't going to be joining Lusam and Neala inside Coldmont, but he didn't complain, instead, he simply nodded his acceptance.

"I knew it!" Lusam suddenly said excitedly.

"Knew what lad?" Renn asked.

"I knew I had seen this building before. Neala, do you remember that painting on the ceiling in Helveel?" Neala looked again at Coldmont, this time trying to imagine it whole again.

"Yeah, you're right Lusam, it's the same place. I remember those towers, and those large flat areas up there too," Neala said, pointing to two large platforms halfway up the building. "In the picture that's where the dragons were, and that huge dome on top of the building is the same too."

"I wish I had seen that picture myself," Renn said. "Coldmont must have been very special indeed when it was still in use."

"Well, maybe you will get the chance to see it when we visit Helveel on our way to Lamuria," Lusam said, turning away before Renn could see his grin.

"I thought we agreed it was too dangerous to enter Helveel lad, and we were going to bypass it completely," Renn said sternly.

"No ... *you* said it was too dangerous. *I* said it wasn't. I think your exact words were along the lines of: "W*e will see*." So, now we have another good reason to call in at Helveel on our way past," Lusam said, barely able to contain his humour. Renn refused to be baited, instead he just grunted, then replied.

"We'll see."

Alexia, not getting the joke, simply changed the subject. "How long do you think you two will be in there?" she asked, nodding towards the huge temple.

"I suppose that depends how long it takes us to find

the book room. Providing of course, that it's even in a room like the last one. But I suppose the sooner we start looking, the sooner we might find it," Lusam replied.

"Finding the book room is one thing, but don't forget how long you were unconscious the last time you touched one of those books. It was at least forty minutes—I was worried sick," Neala added.

"I suggest you both go now then. Those agents can't be much more than a couple of hours behind us. And that's if they didn't take a gamble, and levitate up the mountainside a little when we weren't looking," Renn said, removing his sword and shield. "Hopefully, those undead-agents will give us a little forewarning of their arrival anyway," he said gesturing to his sword, which currently wasn't showing any signs of detecting the presence of any undead.

"Okay, good luck. We'll try to be as quick as possible," Lusam said, walking in the direction of the huge temple, with Neala following at his side.

"Good luck to you too," Renn called out after them both.

The sheer size of the building played tricks with their minds as they approached it. From where they had first seen the building it looked huge, but it didn't look too far away. In reality, everything about the building was far larger than they thought it was, so when they finally reached the stone stairs, and looked back towards Renn and Alexia, they were little more than specks in the distance.

Each stone step was enormous, and far too large for any man to use. Each one was taller than Lusam, and twice as deep as he was tall. Trying to climb each step would have been almost impossible, so instead they simply walked up the steep slope at the side of the staircase. Two gigantic doors greeted them at the top, each one with a decorative inlay depicting a dragon. Lusam looked over his shoulder at the staircase behind him, and from here he could clearly see the score marks on each stone step. `Score marks made by the talons of hundreds of dragons,` he thought to himself, now beginning to understand the reasoning behind such enormous stairs and doors.

Fortunately for them, one of the huge cracks that ran through the building was located directly at the top of the staircase to the left, which was lucky, because Lusam didn't relish the thought of having to try and open those huge doors. He constantly slipped in and out of his mage-sight, testing for any potential traps. He doubted there would be any here, given the fact that this was once the headquarters of the Guardians—the most powerful magi ever to have existed—not to mention the presence of their dragons.

Lusam and Neala walked through the gigantic crack in the wall, and found themselves at the other side of the great doors in a vast chamber. The floor was littered with rubble and debris, most of which looked like it used to be either statues or ornamental decorations made of stone. It was surprisingly light inside the huge room, and when Lusam glanced up he saw why. High above them was the remains of the huge dome they could see from outside. Far from being opaque—as it appeared from outside—instead, it flooded the room with multicoloured light as the sun shone through the numerous coloured glass panels, reminding Lusam of the equally beautiful, but much smaller glass dome in Mr Daffer's shop.

The light flooding through the glass dome was certainly spectacular, but nothing in comparison to what was below it. Covering the entire ceiling was another incredibly detailed painting, similar to the one they had seen in Helveel. This time, instead of a domed temple, it showed a beautiful white marble-clad building, with a huge tower rising high above it, and all enclosed by massive circular wall. There was also something that resembled a glowing gem set in the sky, just above the massive tower. Lusam thought it might represent the sun, but given the immense detail in the rest of the picture, he couldn't understand why it should look like a gem instead of the sun. He nudged Neala, and pointed up to the masterpiece that was the ceiling above them.

"Whoa! That's amazing," Neala said breathlessly. "I

wonder where *that* building is?"

"I don't know, but it definitely looks amazing," Lusam replied, as they slowly continued to the centre of the room. Lusam borrowed one of Neala's knives and used it to locate the direction of the book. It pointed to the east section of the building, but unfortunately there was no way to determine if the book was above or below them. Lusam took a gamble, and started looking for a staircase that led downwards. It only took them a few minutes to find a wide stone staircase that led down to a basement below the main room. Lusam created a light orb and they continued down the stairs.

The stairs went down several more flights, but when they finally reached the bottom they entered a huge darkened room, not dissimilar to the one in Mr Daffer's basement. Lusam was still using his mage-sight intermittently to check for any possible traps, and immediately recognised the walls in the basement as being the same as the ones in Helveel. He formed a small weak fireball in his right hand and sent it towards the wall. As expected the fireball was absorbed by the wall, as its magical red surface rippled around the huge room.

"I guess they only had one architect for these places," Neala said sarcastically.

Lusam laughed and replied, "Well, I guess if it isn't broken..."

Lusam created another couple of light orbs towards the far end of the room, banishing the darkness, and revealing nothing but a large empty room. There were more corridors leading away from the main room here, than there had been in Helveel. `*Possibly to house a greater number of residents,*` Lusam thought to himself.

"So, any suggestions which corridor we should try first?" Lusam asked, shrugging his shoulders.

"Yeah … whichever one the knife points to," Neala replied, rolling her eyes and shaking her head a little.

"Oh yeah, good idea," Lusam said sheepishly. He cast his locator spell on the knife, and wasn't surprised at all when it pointed to the second corridor along – the same one as in

Helveel.

"See, I told you they only had one architect," Neala said with a beaming smile. Lusam really loved that smile, and he'd missed seeing it over the last few weeks whilst they had all been running for their lives. It reminded him just how much he loved her. He didn't know if it was because he was feeling a little nostalgic—being in a place so similar to Mr Daffer's basement in Helveel—or the fact this was the first time they had been alone in weeks, but he realised he hadn't told Neala he loved her in far too long.

"I love you Neala," he said smiling at her. Neala's smile widened further, as she took a step closer to him.

"I love you too Lusam," she said, kissing him gently on the lips. He wanted nothing more than to spend some time alone, here, with Neala, but he also knew his friends outside were in danger, and needed them to hurry. He gave her one last kiss on the forehead, and sighed softly.

"I suppose we better go find this book then," he said, holding out his hand for her. She took his hand, and they both headed for the second corridor.

The corridors were also longer than the ones in Helveel, confirming Lusam's theory of more sleeping cells. They passed several open doors, and the cells looked almost identical to the ones they had spent so much time in during their stay at Mr Daffer's shop. One thing that wasn't the same however, was the amount of damage they began to see the further they travelled down the long corridor. It started with a few small lumps of stone that had been dislodged from the ceiling, but soon turned into partial blockages of the entire corridor. Whatever forces had caused the destruction of Coldmont above ground, had also effected it far below ground as well.

Lusam had been speculating as to the possible causes of the destruction suffered by Coldmont ever since he first set eyes on it, and was about to ask Neala what she thought, when the floor beneath their feet began to tremble. Instinctively he erected a shield around them both, and held Neala close to him. Dust and debris fell from the ceiling all around them, coating his shield so they couldn't see. They could hear masonry falling both in the corridor, and throughout the underground chamber. Lusam had no doubt that the same would be true on the upper floors as well. A large chunk of stone fell and hit his shield, bouncing harmlessly off its domed surface, and coming to rest against the wall by their side. The sudden impact sapped a chunk of magical power from Lusam's reserves, but he maintained his shield until the tremor had passed. He remembered vividly Renn's broken and twisted leg when he had failed to maintain his shield under similar circumstances only a couple of days before. He wasn't about to make the same mistake again.

The ground stopped moving underfoot, and the sounds of falling debris began to subside. Lusam kept his shield up, and waited for the dust to settle a little before moving on. He rapidly increased the size of his shield a little, then reduced it again in quick succession. Like a dog shaking off a wet coat, he dislodged the dust clinging to the outside of his shield, allowing them both to see once more beyond the confines of his shield.

"Well, I guess that answers the question of what destroyed Coldmont," Lusam said quietly, not daring to make too much noise in case it somehow brought the entire ceiling down on them.

"Yeah, I guess it did," Neala replied, looking very nervous. "I suppose that's why there were so many rocks on the path coming up this mountain too. If the ground shakes like that, it's bound to cause lots of rock slides."

"I hadn't thought of that, but I think you're right, it would certainly dislodge a few rocks."

"Oh no … what happens if it does that while you're unconscious? I don't have a shield to protect either of us," Neala said, almost panicking. Lusam had no idea how to answer her question. He couldn't guarantee another tremor wouldn't occur, neither could he offer her any solution other than hope.

"We'll be fine Neala. That was the first time we've felt it since we entered these mountains, what's the chances of having another tremor in the next forty minutes or so?" he said smiling at her, trying his best to convince her that his logic was right. It did absolutely nothing to convince her of his prediction, when moments later another tremor shook the ground. This time it was far less aggressive, only dislodging dust from above them, rather than stonework. Neala gave him a stern look of disapproval. He simply raised his eyebrows and shrugged. Once again he shook off the dust from his shield and they continued towards the end of the corridor.

A few moments later they reached the far end of the corridor. They expected to see a stone door, with the familiar five pointed star carved into it, but instead they saw a mound of rubble and a dark void behind. Lusam tried to send his light orb above the rubble and into the dark void, but as soon as it crossed the threshold it was extinguished. He tried several times, but each time with the same results.

"Wait here, I'll take a look inside," Lusam said, carefully making his way up the mound of rubble.

"Don't go inside without me," Neala said from behind him.

"I'm not going inside. I just want to see if I can see anything from up here." The pile of rubble seemed more stable than it looked, and Lusam was soon at the top peering into the pitch black room beyond. He moved his light orb as close to the opening as possible without it actually entering the room, but still no light penetrated the darkness inside. Gritting his teeth against the possible pain, he gingerly reached his hand towards the opening, half-expecting to be jolted backward by the force-field he had felt once before. Instead of a force-field hitting him, the room seemed to sense his presence within it, and the familiar blindingly bright light came to life inside the room. Lusam shielded his eyes against the glare, gradually allowing vision to adjust to the intense white light. Once it had, he peered into the room. There before him, on a pedestal identical to the one in Helveel, sat another Guardian book.

"It's here!" he said excitedly. "Come on up." He

offered Neala his hand, pulled her to the top of the rubble pile, and then they both slid down the other side into the book room. Lusam approached the pedestal, and was about to take hold of the book when Neala spoke.

"Wait!" she said, throwing her arms around his neck, and hugging him so tight he could barely breathe. "I love you Lusam. Please be careful."

"I love you too Neala," he said kissing her lips tenderly, then he gently pushed her back to arms length. "Remember not to touch me while I'm unconscious, the force-field could send you into that rubble pile and bury you alive." Neala nodded to him, tears beginning to form in her eyes. Lusam smiled at her one last time, then stepped up onto the pedestal platform and opened the book. Neala watched helplessly as the light burst forth from within the book and Lusam froze in position, just like the first time she had witnessed him open the book in Helveel. Only this time, what she didn't see, was the small trickle of blood that came from his ear, and dripped onto his shoulder furthest from her view.

Chapter Seventeen

Renn and Alexia took their positions at the remains of the stone archway. They had watched Lusam and Neala safely enter Coldmont from a distance, and neither of them could quite believe the actual size of the place. It became truly apparent when they saw them both standing next to the huge steps, and later the gigantic doors that led into the temple beyond.

Renn had scanned the horizon for an alternative route out of there, but the area around Coldmont was so vast, it simply appeared to melt into the clouds beyond the mountain top. He estimated that it would take the best part of a day to walk the perimeter and check for alternative routes—time they didn't have. It seemed their only alternative, was to fight.

"How many arrows do you have left?" Renn asked.

"Four," Alexia replied, obviously already aware of her limited numbers. Renn nodded slowly, thinking about what strategy best to use in the coming battle. After a few minutes of silence he turned to Alexia and said,

"As far as I can tell there are ten of them, including the undead-agents. We have to assume they don't know Lusam is inside Coldmont, or the number of arrows you have left. If they did, they could simply use the undead-agents as a shield against your arrows, and march right up here, knowing that Lusam wasn't here to shield us against their attacks. I don't think that will be the case however—or at least I hope it won't."

"So, what do you think they'll do then?" Alexia asked nervously.

"I'm not sure really. Their biggest concern has to be you, and your arrows. So their main priority has to be depleting your stock of arrows. They've been taking all the arrows they can each time you've killed one of them. I think it's safe to assume, that even though they don't know how many arrows you have left, they'll know that you don't have enough left to kill them all..." Renn said, trailing off into deeper thought.

"The way I see it, it's going to be a fine balance between resources, information, and misinformation," Renn added a moment later.

"What do you mean?" Alexia asked confused.

"Well, we don't want them to know we're alone here, or how many shots you have left, right?"

"Right, but how can we achieve that? If they see us, they'll know Lusam isn't with us," Alexia replied.

"Then we don't let them see us. Well, not at first anyway. I think we should hide behind one of these pillars, stay completely hidden, and wait for them to come to us."

"That sounds dangerous to me. What if they surprise us, and we end up having to fight all ten of them at close quarters? We wouldn't stand a chance!" Alexia said, concerned at his plan.

"I doubt they *could* surprise us, we'll definitely know when they're approaching," Renn said, tapping the blade of his sword with his finger. "Let me ask you a question. If you were their commander, and you came across this stone gateway – one that you couldn't possibly see what was waiting for you on the other side – what would you do?" Alexia thought about it for a moment, then smiled at Renn.

"I would send one of my undead-agents through the gap, to see if it was a trap," she said confidently.

"Exactly! And if we're a few paces from the stone archway when we kill it, they won't know how it died, or who killed it," Renn said smiling back at her.

Alexia's eyes went wide, as she said excitedly, "Wait a

minute!" She then ran along the ridge above the path for a short distance, and peered over the edge. She expected to be able to see the path, but instead found that it was obscured by the man-made wall. The wall had been purposely built at a slight angle to overhang the path, making it impossible to attack anyone from above. `It doesn't make any sense! Why would people capable of constructing such an incredible temple overlook the simple advantage of being able to attack potential invaders from above?` Alexia thought to herself. She knew that the giant stone archway had once had some kind of gates in place, because she could see the massive corroded iron brackets still attached to the blocks of stone, where they had once been hung. The gates had long since decayed to dust, or possibly been blown over the edge of the mountain by some huge storm, but evidence remained of their past existence nonetheless.

"Is there a problem?" Renn asked from the side of her. She hadn't even noticed him approach, and that was the second time today he had managed to sneak up on her without being noticed, something not many people could do. `He's certainly light on his feet for a big man,` she thought to herself.

"Not really. It just doesn't make sense," she said out loud, mainly to herself.

"What doesn't?" Renn asked curiously. Alexia's attention seemed to snap back to the present momentarily as she glanced at Renn, but then, she seemed to drift back off into whatever thoughts she had just been having earlier. Suddenly she gasped, turning in circles, as if looking for something on the floor, but there was nothing nearby.

"Renn, lend me your sword a moment please," she said, holding out her hand, but still scanning the floor all around her feet. Renn looked at her strangely for a moment, but couldn't see any reason not to give her his sword, so he removed it from his scabbard and handed it to her. She took it without a word, then started pacing the top of the wall, all the time seemingly looking at her own feet. Renn was about to ask her what she was doing, but she spoke first.

"Is the metal of your sword toughened by magic?" she asked, still looking at her own feet.

"It is, but what do you intend to do with it?" Renn asked, starting to become concerned for the welfare of his trusty weapon. Alexia didn't answer him, instead she jabbed the tip of his sword into the centre of the flagstone she was standing on, then moved on to the next, and did it again. Clang ... Clang ... Clang ... Thud!

"I knew it!" Alexia exclaimed, dropping to her knees. She removed one of her daggers and started to dig around the flagstone that she had hit last. From where Renn stood it looked the same as all the others, but he too heard the different sound it made when his sword struck it. Less than a minute later Alexia had prised up the flagstone to reveal a murder-hole beneath. It was relativity small, maybe only two hand-widths square, but it gave her a perfect view of the path below. Renn boomed out a laugh behind her, startling her so much that she was glad she had been kneeling down, and not standing near the edge of the wall.

"Well done lass! I'd say that might have just tipped the balance in our favour. How did you know that would be there?" Renn said, offering her a hand up.

"I didn't know for sure, but nothing else would have made sense if it hadn't been there. I expect there are at least several more along this edge too," She said pointing along the line she had just been walking. "At first I thought I might be able to see the path below from the edge of that wall. It would have been a good spot to shoot from, but the wall next to the path has been built at a slight angle, so from above you can't see the path at all. I noticed earlier when we first arrived, that the stone arch used to have a substantial gate attached to it. Then I started thinking—if the stone arch and its gate was a defensive measure, why would you intentionally block any chance to attack a potential enemy below, especially if they were trying to storm your gate?

"The only thing that made sense were these murder-holes. They would have been far more effective than standing on the edge of the wall, out in the open. Imagine trying to storm that gate, with arrows, or burning oil raining down on you from above. In fact, I'm sure you remember just how steep that last section of path was? Imagine what would happen if it suddenly became slick with oil. I wouldn't be surprised if their enemies simply slid off the edge of the mountainside to their deaths, without so much as a shot being fired." Alexia said, chuckling at the imagined image of a line of Empire agents sliding down the steep path, and vanishing over the edge of the mountain at the bottom.

"You might just be right there lass," Renn agreed, clasping her shoulder and smiling. Renn began to say something else, but was suddenly interrupted by the ground shaking beneath their feet. He pulled Alexia away from the edge of the wall, just in case it collapsed beneath them. Even on the flat surface of the immense courtyard they struggled to remain standing. Renn watched as giant chunks of masonry fell from the façade of Coldmont, crashing onto the huge steps below. Dust bellowed out through the damaged half-open dome on the roof, and sections of gigantic stone pillars rolled around the courtyard like a child's toy. The tremors only lasted for a few seconds, but it felt like minutes past before the ground grew still once more beneath their feet.

"Do you think they're alright in there?" Alexia said nodding towards Coldmont.

"I hope so. I would have felt it if Lusam had died, but that doesn't mean they might not be injured, or even worse in Neala's case I'm afraid. Unfortunately we have a job to do here, we'll have to just hope and pray that they will be okay in there," Renn replied, just as a second, much less powerful tremor was felt beneath their feet.

"Maybe praying isn't such a bad idea after all," Alexia said, still looking at Coldmont in the distance.

"It rarely is lass ... *it rarely is*," Renn replied stoically.

Chapter Eighteen

Renn estimated it had been the best part of two hours since they had watched Lusam and Alexia enter Coldmont—and still they waited—with no sign of them, or the Empire agents. Alexia had started to show signs of worry after the first hour, but Renn had reassured her that all would be well, and they were probably having to search the huge building room-by-room. It seemed to pacify her for a while, but he had to admit, even *he* was beginning to get worried for Lusam and Neala's well-being now.

Renn and Alexia had discussed at length their plans for the coming battle. They had decided that they would strike fast, then fallback to Coldmont. Alexia had managed to uncover several more murder-holes, giving her an almost unrestricted view of the entire path below. One of their biggest concerns was the sheer size of Coldmont's courtyard. Even running at full speed it would take too long to cross if they were being shot at by the Empire agents. Without Lusam's magical shield, they would be relying totally on Renn's shield for protection against any incoming missiles. Against one or two agents it wouldn't have been much of a problem for Renn, but against five—and a further five undead-agents—probably meant that neither of them would likely make it across the huge courtyard alive. So the plan was, to try kill at least one of the Empire agents through the murder-holes. Then while the Empire agents were in disarray, Renn and Alexia would cross the courtyard as quickly as possible—hopefully without being seen—and re-establish a defensible position inside Coldmont itself.

Thirty minutes later Renn's sword, and Alexia's bow began to glow with a soft blue light. Renn nodded to Alexia, then took his place behind the huge stone pillar of the ruined arch. Alexia stood above the furthest murder-hole, making sure she didn't move and attract any unwanted attention from below. Then they waited. Time seemed to slow to almost a standstill. No movement could be seen below, or sound heard in the still air. Alexia realised she had no idea just how far away her blessed bow would detect the undead, and knew it was too late to ask Renn about it now. So there she stood, arrow nocked, and bow half-drawn, waiting for whichever Empire agent was unlucky enough to walk through her sights.

Moments later she had her first glimpse of an Empire agent below, and almost loosed her arrow at him. It was only through sheer luck that she noticed the blood stain in the centre of its chest, signifying it to be one of the undead-agents. Panic flooded through her, as she realised for the first time that she would be unable to tell the difference between the undead-agents, and the living ones she needed to kill. She looked towards Renn and saw that he was watching her. She signalled to Renn the approach of an undead-agent, and he nodded his understanding. Thinking fast on her feet, she realised it would be unlikely that any other Empire agent— undead, or living—would approach the arch until they knew the fate of this one first. She quickly stepped back away from the murder-hole, and ran towards Renn.

Renn noticed her sudden rapid approach, and immediately suspected she was coming to warn him of some unforeseen danger they had overlooked. He half-expected the entire Empire force to emerge from behind the ruined stone arch at any moment. But halfway to his position, he noticed Alexia holding up a hand, signalling all was still well. Confused, he waited for her to arrive and explain what was going on.

"Renn, we have a problem. I can't tell which agents are

alive and which are undead. I almost shot the one coming up the path, but luckily I saw the bloodstain on its chest just in time. What are we going to do?" Alexia said in a whisper, sounding very concerned.

"Go back to your murder-hole and watch for any more coming up the path. After I kill this one I'll come and join you there. If I tap your shoulder, you'll know to shoot the agent," Renn replied calmly. Alexia nodded her understanding, then ran back to her murder-hole, glancing through all the others as she passed them, just in case any more agents were on their way up the path—she saw nothing.

Back at her murder-hole she watched intently for any movement below. Even when she saw the flash of Renn's sword kill the undead-agent, she remained vigilant. She intentionally listened for Renn's approach, but knew that if she hadn't been expecting him, it would have been the third time that day he had managed to sneak up on her. She smiled to herself, as she realised she knew highly trained thieves with less stealth ability than the big man at her side. She made a mental note to ask him about it later, providing they both survived the next few minutes of course.

It was another five minutes before they sent the next undead-agent up the path. Renn whispered in Alexia's ear to hold her fire, and let the undead-agent come to them. They waited for another ten minutes, but there was no sign of the undead-agent. Renn had half-expected this tactic after the first undead-agent had been killed.

"I think they have instructed that undead-agent to stand still, out in the open, so they can see it die. Or more precisely *how* it dies. I was hoping they wouldn't do that," Renn whispered.

"Why? What difference does it make how it dies?" Alexia whispered back slightly confused.

"Well, they know you probably won't waste an arrow on it, and I can't go out there and kill it because they would all fire at me ..."

"Oh Gods! They're testing to see if Lusam is here with us," Alexia whispered desperately, as she realised exactly what Renn was trying to tell her. Renn was about to reply, when they both noticed three agents walk past the murder-hole. Renn could clearly see they were all undead-agents. They walked three-abreast up the path, creating a walking shield, behind which one living agent followed closely. Renn indicated silently to Alexia which one to shoot, but by the time she understood, it was too late, and they had missed their opportunity. Quickly, they raced to another murder-hole further along the path, and prepared to shoot. The Empire agent didn't stand a chance. The arrow thudded into his collar bone, shattering it, and driving deep into his heart. Renn felt the death-pulse a moment later, but was already running with Alexia towards Coldmont when he did.

***

Zedd's undead-agents had almost finished digging their way through the huge pile of rocks at the cave site, when the tremor struck. Not only did it collapse the remaining rocks and debris around it—refilling the almost complete tunnel they had just dug out—it also buried two of his undead-agents under the rubble. Zedd cursed loudly, knowing that with each passing minute the boy-mage and his party could be getting further and further away from him. In frustration he almost ordered one of his men to levitate over the rock pile, just to see if he would be shot by the waiting girl or not, but decided against it. He realised he would probably have to kill the first man that he commanded to do it as punishment for refusing his orders, and he knew he could ill afford to lose another two of his men right now.

At least two hours had past by the time the undead-agents had dug through the rocks for the second time. Zedd's mood improved slightly when they managed to dig out the two buried undead-agents, and found that they were at least still viable—all he had lost was more time. They travelled as swiftly as they could along the path, whilst checking for any signs of possible ambush. On several occasions nerves were frayed, when birds and small animals rustled nearby bushes and undergrowth as they passed by.

After following the path for a further two hours they reached a section very different from anything they had seen so far. It was far steeper, and enclosed on both sides, making it feel almost tunnel-like. There was an overhang that covered the entire width of the path, but daylight still entered between the right-hand wall and the overhang above, creating a type of long uninterrupted window to the outside world beyond. Zedd knew it wasn't a natural rock formation, and seeing the moss covered cobblestones underfoot only strengthened that assumption. Warily they followed the steep mossy path, until it crested a small hill. Zedd called a halt, and they all stood staring at the remains of a huge stone archway at the end of the path. It wasn't the stone arch that made Zedd pause, but the uncertainty of what lay beyond it. He could clearly see that the wall to their right—the one he guessed had been built to stop wagons slipping off the edge of the mountainside—disappeared at the other side of the stone arch. `It would make a perfect ambush site,` he thought. Even a moderately powerful mage could easily push his enemies off the edge of the mountainside, and either watch them die on the rocks below, or send a missile at them whilst they concentrated on levitating.

Zedd wondered if this had been the boy-mage's plan all along, to lure them to this place—whatever this place was —and send them all to their deaths far below. For all he knew, this could be Afaraon's secret training facility that was rumoured to exist by many within the Empire. `If it was, he need not even bother killing the boy-mage. The information alone would see him almost guaranteed a promotion, and then returned back home to the Empire,` Zedd thought to himself excitedly. Then just as quickly, his excitement faded again. He realised that if this was Afaraon's secret training facility, they would likely never make it back off this mountain alive. Afaraon would try to protect their secrets at all costs, and likely send every man they had after Zedd and his men.

`But something was wrong,` Zedd thought. `The boy-

mage and his party had had at least a two hour head start over him and his men. If this was Afaraon's secret training facility, surely they would have mounted an attack already.`

He knew his options were limited, but first he needed to know if the boy-mage had indeed set an ambush for them beyond the stone arch.

"Send one of you minions through the arch, and tell it to attack anyone it sees," Zedd commanded the man who had reanimated the dead agents. The man obeyed, and they all watched as the undead-agent walked up the steep path and through the remains of the stone arch. A moment after the undead-agent disappeared from view, the man who had sent it spoke up,

"Sir—the minion just died."

Zedd nodded to himself. Pleased with himself that he had outsmarted the boy-mage's attempt to ambush his party, but also unsure of what to do next. He knew the girl wouldn't have many arrows left, but even one, was one too many if it had his name on it. Zedd knew he didn't have enough men to take them by force either. The girl would simply shoot his few remaining men first, leaving the undead-agents to the paladin or boy-mage. That, of course, was if the boy-mage didn't simply just blast them all over the edge of the mountainside to begin with. His only option was to try and tempt the girl into wasting her arrows, something he doubted she would do willingly, but he had to at least try.

"Send another minion. This time have it stop just the other side of the stone arch, and command it not to attack anyone," Zedd said. The man once again obeyed, and the undead-agent took its place at the far side of the stone arch. Zedd expected the boy-mage to simply incinerate it, or at least blast it over the edge of the mountainside, but nothing happened. The undead-agent stood motionless in plain sight for almost ten minutes, and nothing happened to it.

"Maybe they've gone sir," Cole said quietly at Zedd's side.

"Or maybe that's what they want us to think," Zedd replied, deep in thought.

"Command your three remaining minions to form a walking shield. And you," Zedd said, pointing to another man," you will walk behind the minions and go see if the boy-mage's party is still there, or not. Communicate what you see through your ring." The man paled at Zedd's command, but to his credit, obeyed nonetheless.

The three undead-agents walked side by side up the cobbled path, closely followed by one of Zedd's remaining men. He only walked about thirty paces before Zedd and the others felt his death-pulse. At first Zedd was completely confused as to how his man had just died, but from where he stood he could just about see the shaft of an arrow protruding from the man's shoulder. Looking up, he noticed for the first time, a series of evenly spaced shafts along the entire length of the path. They had been cleverly created at slight angles to make them almost invisible to anyone walking on the path below. In fact, the only evidence of their existence at all, was a slightly lightened area within each of the long shafts, and even those could easily have been dismissed as reflected light.

"Recall those three minions," Zedd said to the man controlling them.

"What about the one at the far end sir?" the man asked. Zedd thought for a moment.

"No. Leave that one where it is, for now." Zedd replied, still confused as to why the boy-mage hadn't disposed of that minion yet. There were no advantages to the boy-mage—or his party—allowing the undead-agent to remain alive, and yet, there it remained, but why? Zedd tried to think of a reason why, but could only come to one possible conclusion: the boy-mage was no longer there, or maybe never was.

Chapter Nineteen

Zedd began to formulate a plan. One that would end this stalemate, once and for all. He knew he had to get to the other side of the ruined stone arch, or they may as well all turn back to Stelgad right now. Secretly, he communicated with Cole using his ring—something only higher ranking Empire agents could do—and told him to stay close to him, in case they had to jump over the edge of the mountainside when they emerged through the arch. Zedd had no feelings of loyalty towards Cole, but knew having his magical shield active while they levitated down the mountainside might mean the difference between making it down alive or not.

"Reform your minions into a walking shield again. This time, we all go," Zedd commanded. Zedd started to cast a levitation spell on the freshly killed agent's body. It was made far more difficult by the distance between himself and the corpse, but he managed to achieve his goal, and the corpse floated towards where he stood. Once the corpse was directly below the first of the openings in the ceiling, he levitated it up to block the shaft, pinning the corpse tightly over the hole. Then he signalled to move forward, towards the next opening. Once they arrived, he repositioned the corpse to block that hole instead. He repeated this process all the way along the path until they all safely reached the stone arch. Positioning himself at the back of his men—closest to the drop-off should he need to jump—and with Cole very nearby, he gave the command to move through the ruined stone arch.

Each man moved beyond the huge stone pillars of the ruined arch, crouching as best they could, behind the undead-agents they were using as a shield against the girl's arrows. All were expecting to see the boy-mage's party waiting for them, and feel the sting of death any moment, but all they saw instead, were two people in the distance, running towards a huge ruined building. Zedd brought the fresh corpse back down to the ground at his feet.

"Reanimate it," he said to the man who still controlled the other minions. The man nodded and did as instructed without question, while Zedd studied the immense building before him. The expanse of courtyard to the building was enormous, but offered little in the way of protection against the arrows of the girl. He could see two huge dragon statues, one each side of the massive staircase that led to the front of the building. `*They'll provide excellent cover—if we can reach them without being killed first,*` he thought to himself.

"I want all the minions up front forming a shield around us while we cross this courtyard. If one of them falls in front of you, levitate that corpse to reform the shield. We will head for the dragon statue on the right of the stairs," Zedd commanded—nobody argued.

***

Neala was going out of her mind with worry. She had fully expected Lusam to be unconscious for about forty minutes—like the last time he touched the book in Helveel—but it had now been at least two hours. At first, she had simply sat down and made herself comfortable for the expected wait. But after the first forty minutes had elapsed, she started to become more and more worried as each minute slowly passed. She tried to tell herself that maybe it had actually taken longer than forty minutes in Helveel, and that she had lost track of time, but after the first hour, she knew that wasn't the case.

It wasn't until she walked around the outside of the room, and saw the dried blood that had tricked from Lusam's ear earlier, that real panic set in. That had made her feel extremely anxious for Lusam's safety, but not as much as the fresh blood that was now dripping freely from his nose. Even though she knew he couldn't hear her, she still called out to him, but there was nothing she could do to help him. Long before they had found Coldmont, they both knew the moment he touched that book, he would be on his own.

A few minutes later she thought she heard the start of another tremor. Unlike the large tremor they felt earlier, this one felt much more distant, and the floor didn't shake underfoot. She could just about hear the occasional muffled impact of falling masonry, as it crashed onto the floor somewhere above her. Instinctively, she backed away from the rubble pile that blocked the doorway, half expecting it to suddenly slide into the room, but nothing moved. Neala was no expert when it came to tremors, but this one didn't seem quite right to her. There were sounds, but no movement. Tentatively, she placed her ear to the wall—a trick she had learned as a young thief in Stelgad—to amplify the sounds, and make them much easier to hear. What she heard, turned her blood cold. It wasn't a tremor at all. It was the sound of many distant explosions. Each one resonating through the very foundations of the building. Renn and Alexia must have been forced to retreat to Coldmont, and now they were under attack by the Empire agents. Neala desperately wanted to go and see if they were alright, but knew she couldn't leave Lusam here alone in case there *was* another tremor. She also knew her weapons would be ineffective against the agents' shields, and would do little to slow any undead-agents either. All she could do was wait, and pray that Lusam would awaken before it was too late.

***

Renn and Alexia braced themselves at either side of the huge crack in the wall. Outside, the Empire agents had taken shelter behind one of the massive dragon statues at the foot of the stone staircase, making it almost impossible for Alexia to shoot at them. Every time Alexia or Renn tried to look through the crack to see what the Empire agents were doing, they were met by a barrage of magical-missiles. Several of their missiles entered the building through the huge crack, impacting against the walls and ceilings inside Coldmont, and causing untold damage to the intricate artwork and masonry inside.

Renn began to use the inside of his shield as a mirror, so he could keep an eye on their movements outside. Several times his shield was almost ripped from his grip when a missile struck it, but he managed to just about keep hold of it. At first when the magical-missiles had started to strike the weakened structure of Coldmont, both Renn and Alexia became very concerned about the stability of its walls. They fully expected the imminent collapse of large sections, with the distinct possibility of them both being under it when it happened. It wasn't until Renn noticed the red shimmer of the walls as they were struck, that he realised they were actually protected by some kind of magical shield. The only other building Renn knew of with a shield was the High Temple in Lamuria. He had never seen it himself, but he had overheard one of the magi speak of a room deep within the temple with such a shield.

"So, what's the plan?" Alexia said, back braced against the wall, and arrow nocked ready to shoot.

"I'm afraid I don't have one lass. To be honest, I was hoping Lusam would be back before now. If he was, and you had the protection of his shield, you could go out there and kill them easily. I just hope whatever is protecting this building lasts long enough until Lusam gets here," Renn replied, raising his shield to take another look outside. What he saw startled him so much, that he almost dropped his shield on the floor. Staring back at him in the reflection was an Empire agent, and he was no more than an arm's-length away from him. Renn quickly jumped back away from the opening, giving himself more space to attack the agent. A heartbeat later the agent came through the opening, turning towards where he had seen Renn. It wasn't until the agent had fully entered the room that Renn noticed it was actually an undead-agent, and so, much less of a threat to him. Stepping forward, he ended the undead-agent with a single thrust of his sword to its chest, then quickly retook his place beside the huge crack, once again checking the reflection in his shield.

"I'll have to remember that I can't tell the difference between the dead and the living agents by their reflection in my shield," Renn said chuckling to himself, as his heart rate began to return to normal after the sudden shock.

"I wondered why you hesitated so long," Alexia replied, trying to hide her amusement at the shock she had seen on Renn's face. "I was about to shoot it, but I saw the bloodstain on its back where my arrow had passed through it, so I left it for you to kill."

"Thanks," Renn replied sarcastically.

"You're welcome," she replied biting her lip.

Chapter Twenty

Lusam dropped to his knees like a sack of coal when the book's force-field released him to gravity. Luckily for him, Neala was standing close enough to catch him before he hit the floor as he toppled sideways.

"Lusam!" she half-screamed, helping him to sit back up. Lusam held his head in both hands, eyes closed against the blinding white light in the room. His head pounded with pain, far worse than anything he had ever felt before, and he also felt like vomiting. Even when he had almost drained himself entirely in Helveel after healing Lucy, his head hadn't hurt like it did right now. He knew something was *very* wrong, and he knew he had to fix it before he lost consciousness to whatever was causing the excruciating pain in his head. Once he gathered himself enough to concentrate, it only took him a few moments to find the cause of the pain. He found that he had two burst blood vessels within his head, each one bleeding freely, and each one threatening his life. He immediately repaired the damage to the blood vessels, then began checking for any other problems, but found none. Although the pain lessened considerably, he still felt like he'd been kicked in the head by a dozen galloping horses. After checking one last time to make sure he hadn't missed anything, he blocked the remaining pain using his magic. When he opened his eyes he saw Neala by his side, tears rolling down her face, and a look of despair in her eyes.

"Oh—Lusam! Are you alright? I was *so* worried about you," she said, hugging him tightly.

"I'm okay," he said hugging her back. "My head is still trying to sort itself out though, but that's how it felt the last time too. It took a while for everything to start making sense before, so I guess it will be the same this time."

"We have to go Lusam ..." Neala started to say, but was interrupted by Lusam.

"Whoa! What's that?" he said pointing towards the book pedestal. Neala looked, but couldn't see anything.

"I don't see anything," she said. Lusam looked at her, then back to whatever he had seen.

"You don't see that sparkling green light leading away from the pedestal?" Lusam asked, still pointing towards the pedestal.

"No, I can't see anything, only the stone pedestal. Are you sure you're okay Lusam?" Neala asked in a concerned voice.

"Yes, I'm fine. It's right here look." He stood up and walked towards where he'd been pointing. He bent down towards the green light and pointed it out once more to Neala, but she still insisted she couldn't see anything. Lusam wondered if it was part of the door opening mechanism that had been damaged by the tremors. It seemed to be the same colour as the light he had seen in Helveel, but whereas that light had been a constant beam, this light seemed to be moving. It almost looked like it was travelling from the pedestal, through the wall. He didn't want to touch the light with his bare hand—just in case it was some kind of force-field—so instead he picked up a small piece stone from the floor and touched the green light with it. Instantly the light of the room seemed to flare incredibly brightly. Instinctively he covered his eyes from the sudden glare, and felt himself falling—it was like the falling sensation he sometimes got when he dreamt that he was falling. A moment later the light dimmed again, and the falling sensation subsided.

"Whoa, that's weird," he said, readjusting his eyes to the light. "Did you see that bright light Neala?" She didn't reply, but he did notice that the green light had now shifted its position to the opposite side of the pedestal. "I suppose we better get out of here, and rejoin the others," he said turning towards Neala, but she was gone. He stood up and spun around, expecting her to be behind him, but she was nowhere to be seen. He called out her name, smiling to himself. He thought the sudden bright light must have scared her into fleeing the room, over the rubble mound, and back into the corridor outside. His smile vanished when he turned towards the exit. Instead of seeing the rubble mound, he saw a perfectly intact door. It was at that moment he realised he was no longer in Coldmont—but where he actually was, he had no idea.

At first glance everything inside the room looked exactly the same, except the exit. It wasn't until he looked a little closer at the green light emanating from the pedestal that he noticed something strange. On the upright of the pedestal, and at the same side the light was emanating from, there was a single word. It was glowing green, just like the light itself, and it read `Absolution.` He checked all around the pedestal for any more words, but there was nothing visible, not even to his mage-sight. Then he noticed the book itself. The writing on the book cover was still written in the strange language, but now he found that he could read the words. The book also had a single word written in gold letters on the cover, and that word was `Freedom.` Had he just found a third Guardian book? He knew he couldn't attempt to read it right now, he had already been unconscious for forty minutes, and needed to get back to Coldmont and help the others as quickly as possible—if he could.

Lusam had no idea if he could return to Coldmont using the same method that had brought him here, nor did he know whether or not he could return here again in the future, even if he could. He had no idea what lay at the other side of the door, but he knew he must risk taking a look. If he was unable to return here later using the strange green light, whatever knowledge he might gain from the other side of the door now, could be crucial in finding this place again later.

He easily located the five indentations using his mage-sight, and connected all five points using his magic like he had done the first time in Helveel. The door began to open very slowly, and he waited to see what lay beyond. When the door had opened enough to peer through the gap, all he could see was complete darkness at the other side. He created a light orb, and found while doing so, that his magical reserves were extremely low. At first he was confused. He knew that when he had entered Coldmont he wasn't fully rested, but he did have a reasonable amount of reserves available, but now his magical reserves felt almost completely depleted. A moment later realisation struck him; he did in fact have the *same* amount of magical reserves left as when he'd entered Coldmont, it was just that now, it seemed to be stored in a much larger reservoir somehow. What he would have once considered as a good amount of magical power, now appeared to be almost completely empty to him. He guessed his storage capacity had at least quadrupled, and maybe even more.

Lusam sent the light orb through the door opening, and into the darkened corridor beyond. He didn't want to illuminate the area too much, just in case wherever he had found himself was still inhabited. He needn't have worried, because only a few seconds later he recognised the first of many familiar rooms and objects—he was back in Helveel. Realising the possible implications, he raced back to the book room, hoping he could get back to Coldmont, and possibly use the pedestal as an escape route for all of them. Somehow, he knew for certain that he could, as the knowledge from the second Guardian book began to come more into focus within his mind.

He reached the book room just as the door began to close, but still had plenty of time to enter the room safely. The room instantly sensed his presence and illuminated the walls and ceiling around him, banishing the darkness inside. He extinguished his light orb, then reached for the green light that was still emanating from the book pedestal. He saw the bright flash of light again, and felt the same strange sensation of falling, and once more found himself in Coldmont.

"LUSAM!" Neala shouted, diving on top of him and

almost knocking him to the ground.

"I'm fine, don't worry," he said, laughing at her over exuberance. She clung to him like a limpet to a rock, kissing him over and over. He was certainly enjoying all the attention from Neala, but he couldn't help noticing how upset she was too.

"What's the matter Neala? Has something happened while I was gone?" Lusam asked, concerned at how upset Neala was.

"Yes … no, not when you disappeared just then, but before, while you were with the book. You were unconscious for much longer than we expected. I've been hearing explosions coming from upstairs. I think Renn and Alexia might be in trouble. We need to go help them Lusam, now!" Neala said through her tears.

"How long was I out?"

"I don't know, maybe just over two hours," Neala replied halfway up the rubble mound.

"Gods! And Renn and Alexia have been trying to fight them alone for all that time? No wonder you're so upset," Lusam replied, shocked at how long he had been unconscious, and how long his friends had been left to hold off the Empire agents alone. He scrambled over the top of the rubble pile, creating a light orb as he went.

"So what happened when you vanished?" Neala asked, following him over the rubble pile.

"I'll tell you all about it later, but we better go help Renn and Alexia first," Lusam replied, sliding down the other side of the rubble pile into the corridor beyond. Neala agreed, and they both hurried towards the main chamber.

Many things were becoming clearer now in his mind from the Guardian book. None more so, than a much deeper understanding of magical power, its origins, and how to use it. He had always known that everything living contained a certain amount of magic, and even a few non-living things, but he had never fully understood how it all worked, until now. How everything was interconnected, from a blade of grass, to the air he breathed. Magic was everywhere—and now he knew how to access it.

Lusam and Neala sprinted down the rest of the corridor towards the main underground chamber. With each footstep they could hear the echoes of explosions grow louder from up above them. When they reached the huge underground chamber Lusam stopped dead in his tracks. Neala noticed him stop, and turned to berate him, but she was cut short by his voice.

"Neala, wait a second please. I've just discovered something important," Lusam said, jogging over to the wall that was protected by the red force-field. He placed his hand flat on the wall, and called forth the power from within it. Within a heartbeat his magical power reserves were full to capacity, and he felt the massive surge of energy within him. He understood now how the walls had been made, and why. Every time anyone had used magic against the wall in the past, it had stored that energy, creating an immense power source. That power had once provided heat, protection and a safe environment in which to practice magic. It was even possible that the magi of old would not simply stop practising when they ran low on magic, they may have recharged their reserves directly from the wall, just as Lusam had done—he wasn't sure of this, but he felt it was a distinct possibility.

"Okay, let's go," Lusam said, taking Neala's hand, and heading towards the stairs that led to the ground floor above. Lusam created a force-field around himself and Neala, but it felt different compared to any he had ever created before. He could feel how much more powerful it was now, and he knew that if he wanted to, he could project his force-field much further than he could ever have thought possible before. Suddenly, the few remaining Empire agents outside seemed far less of a threat to him. `I'm going to enjoy this,` he thought, grinning to himself.

Chapter Twenty-One

Tristan watched with revulsion as Lord Zelroth ordered his Darkseed Elite to torture the poor man for over two hours, before he finally fell into unconsciousness. Tristan couldn't understand why the man hadn't just told Lord Zelroth what he wanted to know, instead of enduring such incredible pain. When, eventually, Tristan and the man had been thrown into a cell together, Tristan had tried to care for his wounds as best he could. He had no bandages or medicine, or even clean water to tend his wounds, but he did what he could, with the little he had.

Twenty minutes later he heard the door to their cell unlock from the outside, and in walked one of the Darkseed Elite. It was impossible to tell if it was one of the ten that had attended Lord Zelroth earlier, but Tristan suspected it was by his actions. With outstretched hands, he began speaking the strange words again. Then a moment later the same light Tristan had seen in the large chamber started to emanate from his hands, and entered the body of the unconscious man by his side. Tristan watched in astonishment, as one after another of the man's injuries healed themselves right before his eyes. `All of this, just so he can be tortured again,` Tristan thought, as he watched through eyes filled with sheer hatred towards his captors.

"Why doesn't he just kill us and have done with it?" Tristan spat at the Darkseed Elite as he began to leave the room. His question was answered only with manic laughter, as the door to their cell was slammed shut and relocked once more.

"Because you want him to," came a gravelly voice from a neighbouring cell. "He knows what you want, and he'll do the exact opposite, just for entertainment. Then, when he gets bored of you, he'll either kill you, or leave you down here to rot like me, depending on which he thinks will cause you the most misery."

"*But*, why? Why would anyone do that?" Tristan asked, desperately not wanting to believe the stranger's words, but knowing deep down that he spoke the truth. A long period of silence stretched out, and Tristan resigned himself to the probability that the man had said all he was going to say.

Then, with no further prompting, he broke the silence and said, "I asked myself that same question when I first arrived here. And I've heard the same question asked hundreds of times since, from hundreds of different men and women during my time here. I still don't have an answer—other than, it's because he can."

"How long have you been here?" Tristan asked, dreading the answer. The man laughed loudly, but ended up in the midst of an uncontrollable coughing bout. It was several minutes before he managed to speak again.

"All of my life. Or at least it seems that way now. I was a young man when I first came here." He began coughing again, but this time he managed to control it easier. Catching his breath once more, he continued, "The Empire had killed my parents, and all I wanted was revenge. It didn't matter *who* it was, as long as they died, and the more, the better. I managed to poison six wells before they caught me. I brought death and fear to the Empire, and it felt good. I was ready to die after my success, but Lord Zelroth had other plans for me.

"Many times he tortured me until I was nearly dead—once, for each of the lives I'd taken. Then he allowed the families of my victims to inflict their revenge on me. He knew the very first time I came face to face with him, that all I wanted, was to die. But *he* made sure that never happened. Each time I thought I would finally die and find peace, that monster who was just in here came and healed my wounds, and shortly afterwards, a fresh wave of torture began once more.

"To answer your original question—I don't know how long I've been here, I have no way to record the passage of time. I *can* tell you this: the year I arrived was the year of High Priest Joshua's coronation. You're the first person I've spoken to in years—apart from the silent one in the end cell —most arrive here like your friend, and as soon as they wake up, they're off again for their next round of torture. Eventually, Lord Zelroth tires of them, and kills them," the man said, between interspersed coughs. Tristan knew that the current High Priest wasn't called Joshua, but he also knew that he had heard the name before. He thought back to his childhood, and remembered the name from that period, but it was the funeral of High Priest Joshua he remembered, not his coronation. That was almost thirty years ago, but he had no idea how old the High Priest had been at his coronation, let alone when he died. One thing however was certain, the man in the next cell had been there a very long time indeed. Tristan couldn't see any reason to enlighten the man as to the full extent of his years held there. It could do nothing to help him, but would likely make him feel much worse, so Tristan decided to keep the information to himself.

"I'm sorry, I don't know much about the High Priests. I come from a small fishing village in the south—if it doesn't float or swim, it doesn't interest me much I'm afraid," Tristan replied, trying to avoid answering the man directly. The man tried to laugh again, but once more ended up coughing instead. He seemed to understand Tristan's reluctance to answer.

"I understand son, don't worry. It'd be little comfort knowing the actual number of years I've spent rotting here anyhow. Probably best not to know … eh?"

Tristan tried to steer the conversation away from the current subject. "What did you mean earlier by *'the silent one'*?"

"Ah, there's a woman in the end cell—a pretty one, at

that—but she never speaks. Now and then they send an Inquisitor to question her, but she never tells them anything, willingly or otherwise. The few times I've seen her, she looks like she's in a trance of some kind. Even Lord Zelroth himself can't get anything out of her, but he seems unwilling to harm her for some reason," the man said. "By the way, my name's Cedrik."

"Tristan—and I'm sorry, I don't know the name of my cellmate yet."

"Probably best not to ask. I stopped introducing myself to the others here a long time ago. Like your cellmate there, they spend most of their time unconscious, then one day, they simply don't return. No point spending time getting to know someone, when you know they won't be around for long," Cedrik said matter-of-factly. Tristan glanced down at the man, and was relieved to see that he was still unconscious, and had not been aware of their conversation.

"I'm curious, what makes me any different from all the others, why bother introducing yourself to me?" Tristan asked, heart sinking, as he felt sure he knew the answer even before Cedrik replied. There was a long pause before Cedrik spoke, almost as if he were trying hard to choose his words.

"Because you're the first I've ever seen here like me. Everyone else has always been like your cellmate—defiant and uncooperative. Lord Zelroth revels in their defiance. To him, it's just a game. He could simply read their minds, or kill them and reanimate them. Either way, he would gain whatever knowledge he desired from them. But you … you offer him no challenge … as did I. For now, I expect he'll simply make you watch as he breaks your cellmate's spirit, and then eventually kills him in front of you. But, if I were you son, I'd pray that more spies are discovered before he tires of your cellmate. If they're not, his attention will likely turn towards you for his twisted entertainment.

"Besides, I thought it would be impolite not to introduce myself to my own replacement," he said laughing between coughs. "My body is getting old and tired, and no matter how good that monster is at healing, I know even he can't keep me alive much longer. So son, as you can see, it appears that you've become my unwitting successor. I know it must be difficult hearing the small amount of joy in my voice—and I *am* sorry for that—but at some point, in the far distant future, when you've spent untold years here as I have, and someone arrives to take *your* place, then you'll understand son."

As each hour passed, Tristan's utter despair seemed only to be amplified by the deathly silence of his cell. Neither he nor Cedrik had spoken again, and the unconscious man had not yet shown any signs of waking. Tristan was lost so deep in his depressive thoughts, that he barely noticed the four Darkseed Elite entering his cell. He only partially noticed the movement in his cell—that was until half a bucket of freezing cold water hit him in the face. The water had been mostly intended for the unconscious man, so now he sat bolt upright, disorientated, gasping for breath, and dripping from head to toe. He didn't get the chance to fully recover before he was unceremoniously dragged out of the cell, closely followed by Tristan—two Darkseed Elite guards to each man. The man started to kick violently at the Darkseed Elite guards, but not for long. One of the Darkseed Elite spoke a single word, and both the man's legs shattered. He screamed in agony, but the Darkseed Elite simply ignored him, dragging him along the floor, and up the stairs towards the main chamber.

Tristan and the man soon found themselves once again chained to the floor in the main throne room. They were alone, apart from two men who stood to the sides of the massive chamber. Tristan guessed they must be servants of some kind, but paid them little attention. The man had stopped whimpering a few minutes earlier, when his injuries had been healed once more by the Darkseed Elite healer.

Tristan watched impassively as the two huge doors on the east wall slowly opened. Moments later Lord Zelroth emerged through the open doors into the giant chamber, escorted by ten Darkseed Elite guards. He walked slowly towards the centre of the room, seemingly studying Tristan and the man all the way to his throne platform. He turned and slowly began to climb the three golden stairs to his throne, but stopped suddenly on the second step. His gaze seemed to be fixed on a glowing object that sat on a table at the back of the room. He quickly spun around, and addressed one of the two men standing to the either side of Tristan.

"Why was I not informed immediately when the Deceiver God's stronghold was entered?" Lord Zelroth hissed in a malevolent voice. Tristan had no idea what Lord Zelroth was talking about, but when he glanced towards the man he had just addressed, it was obvious that *he* did. His face had turned white with fear, and he trembled visibly under the gaze of his master. When Tristan turned his eyes to look at the other of the two servants, he too showed similar signs of fear. Neither man replied to Lord Zelroth's question.

Lord Zelroth thrust out his arms towards each of his servants, and a blinding crimson light shot forth from his outstretched hands. The intense crimson light struck them squarely in the chest, burning straight through them, and leaving a gaping hole the size of a large water melon in its wake. Neither man made a sound, except for the soggy thud when they hit the ground.

Lord Zelroth rushed from the giant chamber, all ten of his Darkseed Elite hurrying to keep up.

`Whatever it is, it has him rattled,` Tristan thought to himself.

***

A few minutes later Tristan was returned to his cell, alone. The other man remained chained to the floor in the throne room, where several more Empire agents resumed his torture once more. When Tristan reached the bottom of the stairs that led to his cell, he saw the cell next to his open, and an old man was being carried out by one of the guards. It was obvious that Cedrik was dead—and not by natural causes— but he still wore a smile on his face: he had finally won *his* battle against Lord Zelroth.

Chapter Twenty-Two

Lusam and Neala reached the top of the stairs and entered the main chamber of Coldmont. Relief flooded through Lusam once he saw Renn and Alexia still alive near the entrance.

"Oh, thank the Gods!" Neala said, equally relieved at seeing them both unharmed. "But, now what are we to do? We're trapped in here."

Lusam laughed, and gave her hand a little squeeze. "I don't think we need to worry about those Empire agents any more," he said grinning at her. "Just stay behind the walls when I go outside, I won't be long."

"You're going outside alone?" Neala asked in a shrill voice, fearful for his safety.

"Don't worry, I'll be fine. I learnt some interesting things from that second Guardian book," Lusam replied winking at her. Neala look at him sceptically, but held her tongue.

"About time! We've been worried about you both. Where've you been lad?" Renn said, still trying to see the agents outside Coldmont through the reflection in his shield.

"It's a long story, but first let me deal with these Empire agents," Lusam replied, as four magical-missiles struck his shield, barely registering in his mind. "Everyone stay inside please, I won't be long."

As Lusam walked towards the giant crack in the front wall, he noticed for the first time, the strong magic that ran through its construction. It seemed to share the same type of magical protection as the walls in the basement, and now, he could clearly see the pulses of energy flowing throughout it. His attention drifted to the dead Empire agent on the ground —directly in front of the opening. Something about the dead Empire agent being inside Coldmont bothered Lusam deeply. It was almost as if his presence somehow sullied the sanctity of Coldmont. He noticed the Necromatic ring on the dead agent's finger, and remembered what Renn had told him earlier about the rings: *nobody in Afaraon really knew how they worked, and most of their spies were caught and killed, all because they wore easily recognisable fake rings*. With the knowledge he'd just gained from the second Guardian book, Lusam thought he had a good idea how the rings worked. He felt confident that if he had time to study the enchantments on one of the rings, he *could* work out how they had been created. He decided to remove the ring from the dead agent's finger, and keep it for later, when he had more time to study its enchantments. He ignored the increased number of missiles striking his shield, as he removed the ring in full view of the agents outside Coldmont. Once he had the ring safely in his pocket, he levitated the dead Empire agent off the floor, and walked through the giant crack with the corpse in tow. The missiles that now struck his force-field felt like nothing more than pin-pricks, in comparison to the hammer blows that he'd felt before reading the second Guardian book.

Lusam walked casually to the top of the giant stone staircase, and looked down to the agents below. He could see four living, and four undead agents. The undead agents began moving towards him as one, but he simply encased them all in a single force-field, then levitated them into the air. He added the dead Empire agent from inside Coldmont to the others within the force-field, then contemplated what to do with them all. He remembered Renn's earlier words: `necromancy is a vile and dark magic—an affront to Aysha and all that she represents.` Having seen it for himself, he tended to agree wholeheartedly. Without a second thought, he rapidly increased the temperature within the force-field holding the five undead-agents, incinerating them instantly. A few seconds later when he released his force-field, only ash remained, and being so high up in the mountains, the strong winds had no trouble at all carrying it away.

Two of the Empire agents stopped attacking, and retreated behind one of the huge stone dragons, but the other two continued to move towards Lusam, firing at him with everything they had. Lusam knew that they no longer posed a threat to him, but they *did* do something that had always annoyed him greatly—they cast the silence spell on him. `It's the first time any of them have bothered doing that for a long time,` he thought to himself. He knew that killing the Empire agents would free him of their spell, but he suddenly realised he didn't need to do that. He now knew exactly how to counteract the spell—the book in Coldmont had given him the knowledge to break their spell.

Lusam smiled at the two agents approaching him, making them pause mid-stride. "I'm afraid that particular spell no longer works," he said, enclosing them both within another forcefield. "I hope you both know how to fly," Lusam said, tilting his head to the side, and smiling openly at the look of sheer terror on their faces. Lusam used a simple push spell on the force-field holding the agents, but instead of pushing gently, he put a huge amount of force behind his push. The force-field containing the two Empire agents shot away from Coldmont like and arrow, and once it was beyond the courtyard, he released his force-field, allowing them to fall to the valley floor below. He knew they were dead the instant his force-field moved—he didn't think anyone could survive the sudden increase in speed—the twin death-pulses he felt confirmed it.

Lusam glanced towards the two remaining agents, still cowering behind the large dragon statue. For a moment he considered killing them both, but decided against it—they had chosen to stop attacking him—he could think of no good reason to kill them, other than revenge, and that, somehow felt wrong to Lusam.

"It's over—I suggest you go home," Lusam said, loud enough for the remaining two agents to hear him, but he heard no reply. Lusam turned around, and headed back inside Coldmont. He was met by three astonished faces as he walked through the giant crack in the wall.

"What?" Lusam asked innocently.

"Are you kidding me! That was incredible!" Neala said, throwing her arms around him, and giving him a big hug.

"Yeah, none too shabby lover-boy," Alexia said grinning. Lusam waited for Renn to say something, but he remained silent, simply shaking his head. Lusam grinned at him, and was about to try and say something witty, when Renn interrupted him.

"That *was* very impressive lad, but don't you even dare think you're getting out of going to the High Temple with me to complete your training," he said in a serious voice.

"The thought never crossed my mind," Lusam lied.

"Glad to hear it," Renn said, dragging him into a bear hug, and slapping him on the back. "Well done lad. Seeing that alone was almost worth the climb up this mountain. But now, I guess we have to climb all the way back down again," Renn said laughing.

"Actually no, we don't," Lusam replied with a smug grin. Renn raised an enquiring eyebrow. "Some things that I absorbed from the book are still a bit fuzzy in my mind, but I'm pretty sure we can all get out of here much quicker and easier than we arrived," Lusam said cryptically.

"But, what about those two agents out there?" Alexia said, peering through the crack at the two remaining agents. "If we leave them alive, won't they just follow us?"

"I was just thinking the same thing. And what about the book—if they were to read it, wouldn't they become more powerful too? I know we can't take the book out of the room, but surely we should stop them from discovering it in the first place," Neala said, looking a little worried.

"They can't read it. I've no idea how I know that, but I do. If they try to read the book, it will kill them. And as for them following us—they can't do that either. I'm sorry, I can't fully explain it at the moment, but trust me, I know I'm right," Lusam said confidently. All three looked a little sceptical at

Lusam's words, but no one questioned his judgement in the matter.

"So, how do we get out of here then, lad?" Renn asked.

"It's something I discovered inside the book room, follow me, I'll show you," Lusam replied, turning, and heading back towards the basement stairs, with Renn, Neala and Alexia following close behind. Lusam created another light orb, and they all descended the dark stone stairs into the basement. As they reached the final few steps to the basement, another small tremor shook the ground beneath their feet. Lusam strengthened his shield, just in case any masonry fell from above, but the tremor stopped as suddenly as it had started.

"Maybe we should hurry," Alexia said, looking nervously up at the ceiling, and the falling dust. Lusam felt confident that most of the building would remain standing for a very long time to come, and would only succumb to the tremors once its magical enchantments failed. But he also couldn't deny the damage he'd already seen with his own eyes—most noticeably the giant crack that ran through the front wall of Coldmont—so he knew the building must be vulnerable if the tremors were strong enough.

"You're probably right," Lusam agreed, maintaining his shield around everyone. They all jogged the entire length of the corridor to the book room, stopping only when they reached the pile of rubble that blocked the doorway.

"Who's climbing over first?" Neala enquired, "I don't think it's safe for all of us to try and climb over at once."

"Wait, I might have an idea," Lusam said thoughtfully. He extended his mage-sight into the rubble pile, and searched for a route through to the other side. Although there were many large pieces of stone and debris within the rubble pile, it was far from a solid barrier. Even though some of the gaps were extremely small, he still easily found a way through it to the room beyond. He sent out a thin strand of force-field along the route he had found, and once he had reached the book room, he stopped. Encasing the whole rubble pile in another force-field so it didn't collapse, he expanded the thin strand running through its centre. It was like watching a door open, as his central force-field pushed apart the two halves of the rubble pile, to reveal the darkened room behind it.

"Show off!" Neala half-whispered jokingly, rolling her eyes and shaking her head.

"Hey! I wasn't showing off!" Lusam replied, in a fake hurt voice. "I intended to fully block the doorway before we left Coldmont, just in case anyone else stumbles across this place. I figured that if I had to move the rubble pile to cover the door, I may as well move it to let us into the room too. But if you prefer, I can close it back up again after the rest of us are inside, and let you climb over the top of it." Neala narrowed her eyes and pouted her lips at Lusam, almost daring him to try it.

Alexia laughed. "You're braver than I gave you credit for lover-boy."

"Hey, don't encourage him," Neala said, trying to hide her smile, but failing miserably.

Lusam gave a mock bow, gesturing for Neala to enter the room first, but Alexia had already beaten her to it. The bright light erupted from the ceiling and walls, illuminating the Guardian book which sat upon its pedestal. It was then that Lusam noticed the name on the book for the first time, it read: *Absolution.* It was the same word he had seen on the pedestal in Helveel, but when he looked at the pedestal here, he saw a different word, this one said: *Freedom.* And that was the name on the book in Helveel. Suddenly it all made sense to him—the pedestals had five sides, one for each of the Guardian books—the various names on the pedestals referred to whichever destination book you wished to reach. It was incredibly simple, but by its very nature had its own inbuilt safeguards.

Renn noticed Lusam's sudden distraction. "Is there something wrong lad?" he asked, trying to see what Lusam was staring at.

Renn's voice brought Lusam back from his wandering

thoughts. "No, not really. I've just discovered something interesting about the Guardian books, that's all," Lusam replied. He couldn't help noticing that Renn's curiosity suddenly piqued at his words. Smiling at Renn, he added, "Don't worry, I'll explain later." Renn nodded, then glanced back at the Guardian book and pedestal, just in case he'd missed something important, but saw nothing.

"I don't understand. There's no other way out of this room. I thought you said you had a way out of here for us?" Alexia said, looking around the small circular room with a confused look on her face.

Lusam chuckled. "Don't worry, I'll explain," he said walking towards the book pedestal. "I know you all can't see it, but there's a green beam of light emanating from this pedestal. It was only after I finished reading this Guardian book, that I was able to see it myself for the first time. I thought at first the light was caused by the damage to the building, but when I touched the light, it did something incredible. First I saw a bright flash, then I felt a distinct falling sensation, and then, Neala disappeared—or at least I thought she had. I soon realised that it wasn't Neala who had disappeared, it was me. I was in an identical room to this one, except the door was still intact. After I opened the door, I soon recognised that I was somehow back in Helveel. As the information from the book settled into my mind, I realised that I can use the pedestal light to instantly transport us all to Helveel."

Lusam positioned himself next to the green beam of light that emanated from the pedestal, ready to make contact with it, and take them all instantly to Helveel.

"I think we all need to join hands for this to work. Actually, I'm pretty sure any physical contact would do, but holding hands seems the easiest solution," Lusam said, taking hold of Neala's hand. He waited until they were all in physical contact with one another, then reached towards the green light.

Before his hand even touched the beam of light, a bright flash erupted within the room. Lusam turned his head towards where the light had flashed, and was astonished to see a group of men in black robes standing before him. He immediately felt the silence spell envelop him, quickly followed by a restraining spell. It was similar to the one used by the Empire agent in Helveel when Neala had been kidnapped, but this one was many times more powerful. Lusam was about to try and free himself from the restraining spell, when a man in a bright red robe stepped out from behind the others. Suddenly, it felt like his mind was on fire. Lusam had never felt pain like it before, and judging by the screams of his friends, neither had they. Lusam could barely think through the intense agony, but eventually he managed to open his eyes and look at his assailant. He detected an almost imperceptibly thin line of power emanating from the man's head, reaching out towards him and his friends.

Lusam reached for the thin strand of power, and found it within his own mind, at the source of his own pain. He followed the thin strand of power back to its origin, making a two-way connection between himself and the man in the red robes. Once Lusam's conduit was open, he sent forth a huge pulse of magic along the connection. The man's eyes widened in shock, as his brain liquefied within his skull, and he fell to the floor, dead. The agony Lusam and his party had been feeling ceased immediately, but the sheer force of the death-pulse he felt rocked him. `Whoever the man in red robes had been, he'd certainly been a very powerful mage,` Lusam thought, trying to regain his composure.

Lusam felt the grip of the restraining force-field suddenly intensify, so much so, that it even restricted his breathing. He could see the magic flowing freely between the men standing before him. They were combining their power, amplifying their strength many times over. Lusam pushed back with his own force-field, just enough to breathe, but no more. He was unable to turn his head to see the others, but he still held Neala's hand tightly—he just hoped the others hadn't released their grip on each other. One man stepped forward, his crimson aura burned like a sun to Lusam's mage-sight. Never had he seen such a powerful aura in anyone before. He wore a black robe like the others, but his was edged with gold and silver around the hem, sleeves and hood. Lusam could feel him trying to get into his mind. Probing and prodding for weaknesses in his defences.

Lusam reached deep within his magical reserves, and prepared to channel a huge amount of power into his own force-field. He would try to push the restraining force-field off himself, and his friends. All he needed to do was reach the green light, then they would all be safely away from Coldmont, and out of the reach of these men. Taking a steadying breath, he violently released the energy into his own force-field, expanding it as fast as he could. The instant Lusam's power spiked, all the men seemed to become aware, and visibly braced themselves. Lusam sent out a massive blast of energy into their restraining force-field, collapsing it instantly, and slamming most of them against the far wall of the room. He reached forward, touching the green light, and the world grew blindingly bright as they all felt the strange falling sensation. A moment later, they were all in the book room in Helveel—or at least three of them were—Renn had not made it through.

Lusam released Neala's hand, and dived towards the green light emanating from the pedestal, increasing the strength of his force-field as he did so. When he appeared in Coldmont, several of the men were still either getting to their feet, or were still dazed on the floor. One was about to attack Renn, but when he saw Lusam suddenly appear in front of him, he switched targets instead. Lusam absorbed the attack on his shield, noting how much more powerful the blast was compared to the Empire agents outside. He grabbed Renn's arm, and again, dived for the green light emanating from the pedestal. After a brief period of blinding light, and the now familiar falling sensation, Lusam and Renn found themselves reunited with Neala and Alexia in Helveel.

Chapter Twenty-Three

Zedd knew he'd lost the battle the moment he saw the boy-mage appear through the crack in the wall. He had only ever seen one other person with an aura as powerful in his entire life, and that was Lord Zelroth himself. The boy-mage had been very powerful even before he had arrived here, but now, his power had grown immeasurably. Whatever he had found, or done, within the walls of this gigantic building, had made him into and incredibly powerful mage.

Zedd secretly ordered Cole to withdraw behind the huge dragon statue with him, and then sent all the remaining agents to attack the boy-mage. Zedd didn't really believe that he could withstand a direct hit from the boy-mage, not even with Cole's extra magic at his disposal. His plan had been to use the sacrifice of his men as a distraction against the boy-mage, and hopefully gain enough time to escape around the edge of the building. He only needed a few seconds to cross the open space between the dragon statue and the wall of the gigantic building. Once he was safely to the wall of the building, and shielded from any direct line of sight attack from the boy-mage, he could choose to either levitate up to the roof, or keep running—but he never got the opportunity.

Zedd watched in awe, as the undead minions were incinerated before his eyes, and his two remaining agents were effortlessly tossed aside like rag dolls. He fully expected to die at any moment, and by the look on Cole's face, so did he. Instead, he heard the boy-mage call out something in the northern tongue, something he didn't understand, but judging by the reaction of Cole, he did.

"What did he say?" Zedd asked Cole.

"He said: *It's over, and we should go home.*" Cole replied, hoping Zedd would take the boy-mage's advice, but instinctively knowing he wouldn't.

Zedd watched as the boy-mage disappeared back inside the gigantic building. `Killing or capturing the boy was now completely out of the question, but gaining access to whatever had made him so powerful... now that was a prize worth a thousand trips up this mountain,` Zedd thought, smiling to himself.

Cole knew his fate lay in Zedd's hands. He'd known ever since they first entered the forest outside Helveel in search of the boy-mage. He also knew that Zedd would never allow him to go free; he knew far too much. Even *if* they ever made it out of these mountain alive, he felt sure Zedd would dispose of him long before they ever reached civilization again. Cole had witnessed Zedd breaking so many of their laws, from failing to report their—and the boy-mage's—position in Stelgad, to commandeering over a dozen men without permission. He'd witnessed him not only threaten, but actually execute his own men, then have them reanimated—as if they were nothing more than northern dogs—to do his bidding. He'd even bore witness to Zedd leading *Vintenar* Yeroth into a deadly trap, knowing full well that he'd be killed. And now, he had just seen him send the remainder of his men to their certain deaths, for nothing more, than to gain a few precious seconds to save his own skin. Any one of his many transgressions would earn him severe punishment, or even death within the Empire. Cole was the only one alive who knew what had happened. Without him, Zedd could simply walk out of these mountains without anyone knowing what had transpired, and return to his life without consequence. There was no way he would allow Cole to live, and they both knew it.

"Go take a look, see if they're still there," Zedd said casually, as if he were merely asking someone to go outside and check what the weather was like, or to see if the bread in the oven had finished baking yet.

Cole didn't argue—`what difference did it make how he died now?` he thought to himself. He scrambled up the giant slope at the side of the stone staircase, expecting at any moment to feel the sting of death, but it never came. When he finally reached the top, he placed his back to the wall and shuffled towards the giant crack in the wall. It was then that he felt yet another tremor beneath his feet. He already had his magical shield up, and was about to try and strengthen it, when the tremor suddenly ceased again. He listened intently for a moment, but couldn't hear anything over the blustery wind outside, as it whistled around the building and statues. Taking a steadying breath, he poked his head around the corner, hoping he wasn't about to be impaled on one of the girls arrows, or blasted by the boy-mage—but there was nobody there. He signalled to Zedd that the coast was clear, and breathed a sigh of relief.

A few moments later Zedd joined Cole, and they both entered the building through the giant crack in the front wall. It looked even bigger on the inside, than it did on the outside. Zedd had only ever seen one room as large and grand as this before, and that was inside Azmarin, back in the Empire of Thule. Azmarin was the seat of power for Lord Zelroth, and had been for countless centuries. It didn't appear to be as large from the outside, because most of it resided within Mount Nuxvar.

Legend has it, that the God Erebi sought refuge within Mount Nuxvar whilst trying to evade the wrath of Aamon during the first days of the Gods' war. Erebi's location was soon discovered by Aamon, and during the ensuing battle, a large section of the mountain was destroyed, leaving a gaping hole within its side. Later—after the Deceiver Goddess Aysha and her brother Driden, had trapped Aamon within the Netherworld—Mount Nuxvar first became a place of pilgrimage for the people of Thule, then, a century later, Lord Zelroth claimed it as his own, and built the mighty Azmarin there.

Fortunately for Zedd and Cole, the floor of the huge

chamber held countless centuries of dust and dirt, making it easy to trace the footsteps of the boy-mage and his party. They followed the clear trail to the rear of the huge chamber, and then into the almost total darkness of a descending stone staircase. They could hear muffled voices somewhere in the distant darkness, but they could see no lights or movement from where they were. Zedd created a small light source, and they both slowly descended the stone staircase into the blackness below. As they reached the bottom of the stone staircase, they saw a bright flash in the distance—but no sound followed it. The muffled voices suddenly stopped, but were quickly replaced by loud screams of pain. Zedd froze to the spot, listening intently for any clues as to who, or what could be down here with them in the darkness. Whatever it was, it was capable of causing the boy-mage and his party great pain, and that certainly deserved Zedd's attention.

A moment later, Zedd felt the largest death-pulse he had ever felt in his entire life. It was so powerful that it momentarily disorientated him, and he was forced to steady himself against the side wall. Cole wasn't so lucky, and found himself on his knees by Zedd's side.

"Do you think that was the boy-mage's death-pulse?" Cole whispered next to Zedd's ear a moment later.

"I don't know—but it was far too powerful to have come from one of the paladins," Zedd replied, mostly to himself.

Zedd could now see a light at the end of one of the corridors. He extinguished his own light source, and slowly started walking towards the light, Cole followed close behind. There was a brief sound of movement, quickly followed by another flash of bright light, and then a cry of anger. Almost immediately, another bright flash—more voices—and yet another bright flash. `Something strange was going on in that room,` Zedd thought to himself.

"Cole, go see if you can see what's happening down there," Zedd said in a hushed voice. Cole paused, contemplating refusal, but a moment later his fatalism took over once more, and he did as commanded without question.

Slowly and carefully, he approached the lit room at the far end of the corridor. When he was within twenty paces of the room, he could hear voices; Empire voices.

In an instant, Cole's spirits were lifted by the mere sounds of their voices. `Whoever they were, they had to be very powerful to have killed the boy-mage, and now Zedd could no longer kill him—well, not in front of an agent so powerful anyway,` Cole thought, smiling to himself. Cole stepped into the brightly lit room, and his world instantly came crashing back down around him. What he saw staggered him. On the floor, wearing the red robe of his station, was a dead Inquisitor. Inquisitors were considered to be the most powerful of all magi, and all but invincible. They could render almost any mage powerless through their special mind magic, and were used to interrogate anyone who managed to resist the mind reading abilities of lesser magi: almost nobody could hide information from an Inquisitor.

It was then that Cole noticed the ten Darkseed Elite guards that towered over the body of the Inquisitor. `Darkseed Elite guards, here? But that would mean...` Cole thought numbly. Then he saw him—Lord Zelroth stepped out from behind the ten Darkseed Elite guards. Cole fell to his knees, prostrating himself in front of his Lord.

As Cole's knees hit the floor, Zedd appeared in the doorway behind him. Just like Cole, it took his mind a while to comprehend what he was seeing before him. Zedd's face lost all its colour, as the magnitude of his situation began to sink in. In moments his mind would be read by Lord Zelroth, and he would be killed. His family would be stripped of all their wealth, and either killed, or forced to become beggars on the streets of the capital, Azmarin—he wasn't sure which fate was worse.

"Who are you, and what are you doing here?" Lord Zelroth asked, glowering at them both.

"Sire, My name is Zedd, and this is Cole," Zedd replied, trying to think of a plausible story as to why they were here. "Sire, we were searching for the boy-mage in the base of the mountains near Stelgad, when we stumbled across his tracks. I sent word back to Stelgad that we intended to follow his trail, and for them to send reinforcements, but none came. We had no food or water, or provisions of any kind for such a journey, but I felt we must follow him, no matter what the risk to ourselves. We followed the boy-mage and his party for over two weeks in these mountains. It was my suspicion that he was heading for their secret training facility, and I knew how important it was for the Empire to discover its location, so we continued alone," Zedd said, realising that everything he had told Lord Zelroth would soon be found out to be a lie after he read his mind. `If he read his mind,` Zedd thought. `Maybe he should embellish his story more, just in case he neglected to read his mind.`

"Sire, I'm sorry to report that we lost several men during our pursuit, but we did kill some of the boy-mage's party, and badly injured the paladin who travels with him. However, I think the boy-mage possesses healing abilities, because when we last saw the paladin, he seemed to be moving around quite freely," Zedd said, hoping Lord Zelroth didn't know the true number of travelling companions the boy-mage started out with.

"And you... Cole wasn't it?" Lord Zelroth said, moving to stand directly in front of Cole.

"Yes sire."

"Do you agree, that your commander's story is accurate?" Lord Zelroth asked. "I suggest you consider your answer carefully."

Cole paused, knowing, that the instant he began to deny Zedd's story, he would kill him. However, if he collaborated with Zedd, and Lord Zelroth read their minds, they would both die anyway.` At least he had no family, and therefore the punishment would end here for him, unlike Zedd,` Cole thought to himself, gaining a little bit of twisted self-satisfaction from the situation.

"Yes sire, it's all true," Cole replied calmly. Zedd showed no outward signs of surprise at his words, but inside he breathed a sigh of relief. Lord Zelroth paced back and forth in silence for what seemed like an age. Neither Zedd nor Cole moved, both keeping their heads bowed, and both waiting for the inevitable feeling of their minds being read.

"So—you killed some of the boy-mage's party, did you? And how *exactly* did you manage that?" Lord Zelroth asked sarcastically, with more than a hint of menace behind his words. Zedd thought quickly, knowing the trap Lord Zelroth was trying to set for him: if the boy-mage had just managed to escape ten Darkseed Elite, an Inquisitor, and Lord Zelroth himself, how could Zedd ever have killed his companions?

"Sire, I devised a plan to deplete the boy-mage's magical reserves, then take advantage of that fact. I first created a situation where either the boy-mage or the paladin had to always be on lookout duty during the night, reducing his ability to regenerate his magical reserves. We attacked his shield during the day, and recharged the magic we had used by night. I repeated this process for twelve days and nights, then I caused a large rockslide, severely injuring the paladin, and killing several of the boy-mage's travelling companions when his shield failed against the falling rocks. After that I reanimated the dead corpses, and sent them against the boy-mage's party, thus further depleting his magical reserves, and denying them all any rest. Unfortunately my plan failed to deliver the boy-mage to you sire, for that, I beg your forgiveness. I just wish I'd had more men at my disposal, and I'm sure things would have turned out very differently," Zedd said, with as much sincerity in his voice as he could muster.

Lord Zelroth remained silent for a long time. Zedd desperately wanted to look up and see his face, but dare not raise his bowed head. He was waiting for the inevitable feeling of his mind being read, and the no-doubt, the painful death that would follow.

"You have impressed me Zedd, and *that* is not something that happens very often. Your ability to take such a disadvantage in both numbers and power, and turn it to your own advantage, through careful planning, is commendable. I only wish I had more like you within our forces. I see the strength of your aura puts you towards the upper end of your current rank. But I also see that your understanding of battlefield tactics far outweighs your rank.

"It seems that the boy-mage has managed to evade my grasp once more. I believe he has travelled to the Deceivers temple in Lamuria, but he can not be allowed to assist the temple in strengthening their defences. Not after I have spent so long depleting them. Time is no longer on our side. I have already set in motion the plans for attacking the Deceiver's temple, but now, I fear that we must speed thing up greatly if we are to succeed in capturing the temple. I need someone to take command of our forces attacking Lamuria. Someone who can see the opportunities others can not—and take full advantage of those opportunities. And that *someone,* is you Zedd. I intend to promote you to the rank of *Baliaeter.* You will then travel to Lamuria and take control of our forces there. Use whatever tactics you feel will be most effective to take control of the Deceiver's temple," Lord Zelroth said turning away from Zedd and Cole.

Zedd's heart raced at Lord Zelroth's words. Finally he had achieved what he set out to do: climb the almost impossible ladder of power within the Empire. Becoming a *Baliaeter* was not a simple promotion in rank, it was one of the highest ranks within the entire Empire: only the Inquisitors and Darkseed Elite were higher.

"Thank you sire" Zedd said breathlessly, "I am humbled beyond words that you would choose me for this task."

"Of course you are," Lord Zelroth replied smoothly, turning back towards Zedd with a menacing grin on his face— only just visible from deep within the shadows of his hood. "But first, let us confirm the validity of your story shall we..."

Chapter Twenty-Four

"Are you alright lad?" Renn asked by Lusam's side. Neala also raced over to him.

"Did they hurt you Lusam?" Neala asked sounding very concerned, and taking hold of his hand.

"No—no I'm fine. But I don't think travelling through the pedestals more than once in quick succession is a good idea," Lusam replied, fighting the strong feelings of nausea. "Give me a minute, I'll be fine."

"Err—shouldn't we be going now? What happens if they just follow us here through the pedestals?" Alexia asked, looking nervously around the book room, obviously expecting them to appear at any moment.

"I think we're safe here," Lusam replied sitting up, and putting his back against the wall.

"I hope you're right lad," Renn said, looking equally concerned. "I'm pretty sure that was Lord Zelroth himself back there. The men with him were Darkseed Elite guards, and the one in the red robes—the one you somehow managed to kill—was an Inquisitor."

Lusam remained silent, running through the recent events in his mind. Many things were becoming much clearer now. His understanding of the book's contents, and how things worked were neatly slotting into place within his mind. He should have been shocked to discover that it was Lord Zelroth in Coldmont, but somehow, he wasn't. He now had a much better understanding of how the books worked, and how they were linked with each other. Lord Zelroth appearing in Coldmont as he did, could only mean one thing: he had read the book in Coldmont before, and had access to at least one other book.

Lusam's thoughts were interrupted by Neala's voice, "What's an Inquisitor?"

"An Inquisitor is an incredibly powerful mage who uses a secret, and highly specialized type of mind magic. It's said that they can gain access to anyone's mind, no matter how powerful they are, and control them through pain, fear or direct mind control. They are by far the most feared of all the Empire forces. They are supposed to be all but invincible, and to my knowledge nobody has ever defeated one—well ... not until today, anyway," Renn replied, still looking at Lusam.

"If they're so invincible, how did Lusam kill that one?" Alexia asked, still scanning the room for any signs of Lord Zelroth and his Darkseed Elite guards.

"That's a good question, and one that I'd like to know the answer to myself," Renn replied. Lusam looked up from his sitting position to find all three of them looking at him expectantly, all waiting for an explanation as to how he had managed to kill the `invincible` Inquisitor. Lusam sighed and stood up, his nausea now thankfully beginning to subside.

"It really wasn't so difficult. When I managed to look at him, I could see the link he had made to each of our minds. There were several long strands of dark energy that came from his mind, and each strand connected to one of our minds. All I did was follow my strand back to him, creating a conduit of my own within his dark energy stream. Then I sent a powerful pulse back down it and into his brain, killing him," Lusam said, shrugging his shoulders a little.

"You know Lusam, you *really* are special. It's no wonder Aysha favours you so," Renn said, smiling and shaking his head slightly. "And thank you for coming back to rescue me like that, I appreciate it lad."

"No problem," Lusam replied. "If I'm honest, I did consider leaving you there so I wouldn't have to go to the High Temple with you. But I figured they'd only send someone else to fetch me, and they might not be as much fun to tease as you are," Lusam said, disappearing through the door and into the corridor beyond, trying hard not to burst out laughing at the look on Renn's face. Neala saw Renn close his eyes and look up, then he seemed to whisper something under his breath. She thought she read his lip movement as *"give me strength,"* but she wasn't completely sure.

Lusam waited in the corridor for the rest of them to catch up. Alexia was the last one to leave the book room, and as she stepped out, the bright light inside was extinguished, and the door started slowly closing behind her. Everyone stopped mid-stride, and at first Lusam thought they had seen, or heard something behind him. He spun round to look down the corridor towards the main chamber, but he couldn't see any movement there. Then he began to listen intently, but again, he could hear nothing. Looking back to the others, he noticed that they were still standing very still, as if they were waiting for something.

"What are you waiting for?" Lusam whispered, just in case he had missed something important.

Neala's voice echoed loud and clear in the stone corridor. "What kind of stupid question is that? We're waiting for you to create some light, so we can see where we're going," she said, sounding a little annoyed. Lusam hadn't even realised the corridor was now in total darkness. His mind had somehow activated one of his new spells by itself, enabling him to see in the dark. It seemed to be an extension of his mage-sight, one that allowed him to see in perfect detail, even though there was no light whatsoever.

"Oh—sorry, I didn't realise. Apparently I can now see in complete darkness. It must be one of the new abilities from Coldmont's book I guess," Lusam said apologetically.

"That's great lover-boy, but none of *us* can see in the dark. Would you mind?" Alexia said sarcastically. Lusam created one of his light orbs, almost blinding everyone standing before him with its sudden brightness.

"Thanks," Alexia said rubbing her eyes.

"No problem," Lusam replied grinning.

"You should get your things and we should leave as

soon as possible," Renn said.

"Leave? But why? We're safe here. We've been running for weeks. None of us has had much sleep lately, and we could all do with a good meal inside us," Neala said.

"Not to mention a bath and some clean clothes," Alexia said. "I've had these clothes on since before I was taken prisoner by the Hawks' guild. If I don't get out of them soon, I'm pretty sure they will be stuck to me forever."

"I have to agree with Neala and Alexia. Besides, it will be dark in a couple of hours anyway, so why not spend the night here in relative comfort and safety. We also have plenty of gold coins here, so we can buy whatever provisions we'll need for our onward journey from within Helveel," Lusam said.

Renn didn't reply immediately, instead, he chose his words carefully. "You said that you thought we were safe here, and that Lord Zelroth and his men couldn't follow us— tell me why you think that lad?"

"It's because of the way the books work. You can only travel to a book that you have already read," Lusam replied confidently.

"So, what you're telling me is that Lord Zelroth hasn't read this book, because if he had, he could come here just like we did?"

"Yes, exactly."

"And because there are no guards here keeping this book safe, we have to assume that Lord Zelroth—and probably everyone else in the world apart from us—doesn't even know that this place exists."

"Yeah, you're probably right, so why not stay here a night or two and take advantage of that?" Lusam asked slightly confused.

"Well ... Lord Zelroth now knows what you look like. And we also have to assume that there are still Empire agents within Helveel. If he distributes a description of you—or any of us for that matter—and we're spotted here in Helveel, not only will he know where *we* are, he'll also know there is another Guardian book somewhere here in Helveel. He would tear this city apart until he found it, and there would be nothing we could do about it," Renn replied. Lusam nodded slowly, taking what Renn had said seriously, but applying his own logic to Renn's argument.

"I agree with what you say, but, if you were in Lord Zelroth's shoes, and had the same information as he had about me, what would be your conclusion as to where I gained access to my first book? He knows that I've read at least two books, and he knows one was Coldmont's book. He also suspected that I lived in Helveel for a long time, just as you did."

Renn's face showed that he fully understood Lusam's implication. He hadn't seen how obvious it was. Helveel was now doomed to fall, and Lord Zelroth would become even more powerful than he already was. Lusam waited for Renn to reply, but when he didn't, he decided to continue anyway.

"From what you've told me, Lord Zelroth wants something important from the High Temple in Lamuria. I'm guessing there's another Guardian book there," Lusam said, but was interrupted by Renn.

"No, there is no Guardian book in the High Temple. If there was, I would know about it," Renn said with conviction.

"Okay, so not a Guardian book, then maybe something else he covets greatly. Something he is willing to spend decades, possibly even centuries to obtain," Lusam replied.

"Possibly, but what that might be, I do not know," Renn said.

"How can he, or anyone else have been doing anything for centuries?" Alexia asked confused.

"He's incredibly old. Some say he even lived during the time of The Dragon-Mage Wars. Others, that he was born shortly afterwards, but all agree he is extremely old indeed. Nobody knows for sure how he extends his life, but many scholars believe it's linked to his twisted use of necromancy. And it's not only restricted to Lord Zelroth, his Darkseed Elite, and his Inquisitors are said to be almost as old as he is. Most likely the one you just killed was many centuries old himself," Renn replied.

"Well ... there must be something in the High Temple that he wants badly. You already told me that his forces were sporadically attacking the High Temple even before you left to come and find me. And we know they've stepped up their attacks massively from what Hershel told us, when we were at The Sanctum of Light in Stelgad. Whether or not Lord Zelroth believes there is a book within Helveel or not, I doubt he will change his plans for attacking the High Temple. He has far too much time invested in it, and far too many of his forces committed to it," Lusam said.

"So what are you suggesting lad?"

"If I had to guess where Lord Zelroth came from when he appeared in Coldmont's book room, I would have to say somewhere within the Empire. If I'm right, that would mean he only had two options available to him. The first would be to walk all the way to Lamuria—which I think you'll agree is slightly absurd. The second option would be to return to the Empire. Either way, it would take him and his Darkseed Elite guards a long time to reach the High Temple, that's even if he wished to make the journey himself.

"So that leaves only his regular forces attacking the High Temple right now. If we can reach the High Temple before he sends further reinforcements, I believe that I might be able to inflict heavy losses on his forces."

Renn laughed loudly, then slapped Lusam on the back. "Having seen how you easily dealt with those Empire agents outside Coldmont, I dare say you could at that, lad."

"Then we're agreed. We will stay here tonight, and possibly tomorrow night to rest. We'll buy horses and provisions for our journey here in Helveel, and that way we will arrive much sooner at the High Temple than if we set off right now on foot—without rest or provisions. Not to mention the fact that we should arrive there in much better shape to fight," Lusam said, turning away and walking out into the main chamber.

Renn looked at Neala, his jaw slightly slack, and she simply shrugged her shoulders at him.

"I know ... I know ..." was all she said, turning and

following in Lusam's wake. Alexia chuckled to herself, and followed close behind, leaving only Renn in the darkened corridor, to contemplate how and where, he actually lost the argument.

Chapter Twenty-Five

Lusam walked directly to the enchanted wall within the large chamber. He placed his hand flat on its surface, and refilled his own magical reserves to maximum capacity. It felt good. It was like a cool drink of water after a long run, or a dip in the river on a hot summer's day. As he drew the magical power from the wall, it sparkled red all around the room.

"What was that?" Alexia asked from behind him.

"It's something I discovered by accident when we first arrived here. I think this chamber was used by the monks who lived here to practice their magic. Watch this," Lusam said, creating a small fireball in his right hand, and then sending it at the wall. Just as before, when the fireball struck the wall, it radiated a red pulse outwards from the impact, dissipating all around the room.

"Whoa!" Alexia whispered.

"There's one just like it in Coldmont. After I read the book there I began to understand more about how it worked. The wall absorbs any magic used against it, strengthening itself in the process. Over the centuries it must have absorbed huge amounts of magic from the monks who used to live here. I don't know how, or where the magic is stored, but I do know it's used to heat, cool and strengthen the building automatically.

"Once the knowledge from the book in Coldmont began to establish itself in my mind, I discovered that I was able to draw magical power directly from the wall, and fully recharge my own reserves with it. I don't know if that function was intentional, or if it's simply due to my better understanding of how magical power works after reading the second Guardian book," Lusam said.

Renn knew that the High Temple in Lamuria possessed several walls very similar in nature to this one. Although they were considered to be secret, it was common knowledge amongst the paladins who had trained there. Occasionally, during particularly energetic training sessions, a wall may be accidentally struck by a weapon, creating a very similar effect to the one he had just witnessed—only not as pronounced. Renn guessed that it must have been commonplace to enchant walls like this in the past—when there were many more magi around to train within their confines—but now, the knowledge of how to create them had no doubt been lost to time.

Lusam had noticed the strange writing on the wall when he had first arrived there, but now, he realised that he could actually read it. He stood looking at the words, trying to figure out what their true meaning was, but, it seemed to be some kind of riddle.

"Is there something wrong lad?" Renn asked, wondering why Lusam was staring at the wall for so long. Lusam looked over his shoulder at Renn, and shook his head.

"Can you see those words on the wall Renn?" he asked.

"All I can see are some strange glowing symbols. I do recognise a few of them, however. I think it's written in an ancient language that's used by a select few within the High Temple. I believe they use it to communicate secretly between one another. Can you read it lad?"

"Yes, it says: *The final five created five—the five creates one—and one you must possess to seek the five, and then become one.*" Lusam said.

"Hmm, well I would say the first part is obvious: `*The final five created five,*` more than likely refers to the final five Guardians who created the five books. The rest, I'm not sure about. It could mean many different things," Renn said, still pondering over the words in his mind.

"I guess you're right," Lusam said, remembering something else Renn had said earlier. "Didn't you say you wanted to see the painting on the ceiling here?"

"Yes, I did. I'd love to see it in fact," Renn replied enthusiastically.

"It's over here," Lusam said, walking over to the spot directly under where the incredible work of art was painted high above on the ceiling. Lusam created a second light orb and sent it up towards the ceiling, illuminating the intricately detailed picture.

"Gods! that's amazing," Alexia half-whispered looking up at the painting.

"Well lad ... I thought Coldmont looked impressive when we first saw it in its current state, but after seeing that picture, apparently it used to look a *whole* lot more impressive with all its dragons, fountains and ponds. And just look at that glass dome on top of the roof—it's a work of art," Renn said, sounding overawed at the image.

"Coldmont," Lusam said, chuckling to himself slightly, then he repeated the word again. "Coldmont."

"Yes, I think we've established it's Coldmont," Alexia said jokingly. Lusam looked at her, as if he had only half-heard her words. Then realising he was the butt of her joke he replied,

"No ... I mean yes ... of course it's Coldmont, but it actually says the word `Coldmont` up there on the ceiling. I just couldn't read it before," Lusam said excitedly.

"I don't see why that's so important any more. We already know about the book in Coldmont now. So how can reading about it now excite you so much?" Neala said, confused at Lusam's reactions.

"Don't you remember the other picture in Coldmont?" Lusam asked Neala.

"Sure, what about it?"

"Maybe that has a name on it too. Maybe I could ..."

"Oh, no you don't," Neala said, cutting him off mid-sentence. "There's no way you're gong back there just to check if some long dead artist decided to write a city name on the ceiling or not. For all we know, Lord Zelroth could still be there waiting for you, or he may have set a trap for you. Not to mention the fact the whole building could collapse at any moment. I don't suppose you've even given it any thought as to why Lord Zelroth and his men turned up just as we got there? I somehow doubt it was just a coincidence."

Lusam flushed at Neala's words. He knew she was right: Lord Zelroth must have had some way of knowing they were there. He knew the Empire agents outside Coldmont couldn't possibly have communicated over such a long distance. It was obvious they couldn't even communicate as far as Stelgad, or the whole mountain would have been full of Empire agents. But, if Lord Zelroth *had* known they were there, why did he take so long to arrive? Lusam had been unconscious for over two hours when he read the book. That would have been more than enough time to gather his forces and arrive in Coldmont. It was then he noticed the scowl on Neala's face: she obviously expected an answer—and it better be the right one.

"I know … I know, I was just thinking aloud, that's all," Lusam said defensively. Neala stared at him intently for a moment, trying to detect any signs of deception, but relented when she became convinced he was telling the truth—much to Lusam's relief.

"I guess we better announce our return to Mr Daffer and Lucy," Neala said, starting to walk towards the main stairs that led to the shop above.

"Wait!" Lusam called out after her. "We can't simply walk into their shop and announce that we're back."

"Why not?" Neala asked, shrugging her shoulders. "They already know about your magic, and they did say we were welcome back at anytime."

"Yes, I know, but—look at us! If we walk into the shop from their basement looking like this, and they were dealing with important customers there …" Lusam began to say, then he realised there was a much more important reason not to simply walk in on Mr and Mrs Daffer. "Besides, the last thing we want to do right now is create any gossip within Helveel. If anyone saw us emerge from their basement dressed like we are, and then witnessed Mr and Mrs Daffer's reactions to our sudden appearance, well ... let's just say we might as well hang a sign above their door for Lord Zelroth—"*Guardian book this way*." Not to mention the potential danger we would be putting them both in."

Renn grunted. "He's right. Which is exactly why I suggested we shouldn't stay here in the first place. The longer we're here, the more chance we have of being spotted. Don't forget one thing: the Empire agents can read peoples' minds. Once a description of us has been circulated, they don't even need to see us themselves. They can simply take the information straight out of the minds of people in the streets. Anyone who had seen us coming or going, could unintentionally betray us to the Empire agents."

Everyone remained silent for what felt like a long time. All knew that Renn's words were true, and nobody doubted the effectiveness of the Empire agents to gather information. They would have to tread very carefully while they remained within Helveel.

"May I say something?" Alexia said, breaking the extended silence.

"Sure Alexia," Neala replied, with both Renn and Lusam also nodding.

"I'm sure Lord Zelroth and his men never saw my face. After Lusam asked us all to join hands, I turned my head away towards the wall. I guess I was a little nervous about what would happen to us when Lusam touched the pedestal. A moment later we were all frozen in place, and then the pain started. I never saw any of them. So if I were the one who went to buy our supplies and horses, nobody could possibly link me to the rest of you," Alexia said.

"Are you sure none of them saw you?" Renn asked.

"Yes, completely sure."

"Okay, that's one problem solved. What about our impromptu arrival here in Helveel. How are we going to announce our arrival, without creating any unwanted attention?" Renn said.

"I think I might have an idea," Lusam replied, still deep in thought. He had been thinking about the problem even before Renn had brought it up: how they could make sure nobody was in the shop before they entered it. Lusam thought he had discovered an answer amongst the new skills he had acquired from Coldmont's Guardian book. He realised that it wasn't only his shield he could now extend much further, but his mage-sight too. He walked over to one of the huge stone pillars that ran down the centre of the main chamber, and hid behind it, blocking his view of the others. Then he activated his mage-sight. At first, the only difference he noticed was the expected appearance of various glowing symbols and words on the walls and ceiling. But when he concentrated on pushing through the stone pillar with his mage-sight, he found he could clearly see his three friends on the other side, almost as clearly as if the stone pillar wasn't even there.

"Err … what are you doing Lusam?" Neala asked, beginning to wonder if the Guardian book in Coldmont hadn't scrambled his brains more than they thought. Lusam smiled to himself, realising how strange what he was doing must look to the others.

"I was just checking to see if I could see you all through this stone pillar," Lusam replied, trying hard not to let the humour enter his voice.

Alexia burst out laughing. "I think lover-boy has finally lost the plot," she said jokingly. Neala gave her a stern look, obviously concerned for Lusam's sanity herself.

"Are you feeling alright Lusam?" Neala asked, starting to walk towards him.

"I'm fine thanks. Stay there, and hold up a few fingers. I'll show you that I can see through this pillar."

"What?" Neala said.

"Please, just do as I ask, and you'll see."

Neala sighed, and held up four fingers towards the stone pillar. Lusam was tempted to give her the wrong number on purpose, but decided against prolonging her worry about his sanity any further.

"Four," he said. She changed the number to five. "Five ... two ... three ... six," he called out as she changed the number of fingers she held up.

"How can you do that?" Renn asked. Lusam stepped out from behind the pillar and walked back towards the others.

"It's an extension to my mage-sight. Something I gained from the book in Coldmont. It's difficult to describe, but I can project my sight through solid objects. I'm not sure what the maximum range is yet. I'll have to experiment with it later, but it's certainly enough to see through most walls," Lusam said.

"Gods! Can you imagine how much money you could make as a thief with that skill? The ability to see through solid walls. You could find the loot even before you entered the building. You could even see if anyone was guarding the place," Alexia said excitedly.

Neala frowned at Alexia's words, then she turned and started walking towards the corridor where they used to sleep. She walked past the first and second cells, then stopped by the doorway to the third.

"Lusam, try looking through the walls, see if you can see me in this room," she said.

Lusam watched as she disappeared into the third sleeping cell. He moved close to the wall, then sent out his mage-sight. He could just about still see her, so he called out to her.

"Yes, I can still see you."

Neala exited the sleeping cell and moved on to the next.

"What about now?" she shouted. Lusam tried to stretch his mage-sight further, but no matter how hard he tried, he couldn't see through the next wall along.

"No, I can't see that far," he shouted back. Neala emerged from the cell smiling, and rejoined the others in the main chamber.

"It seems we managed to find the limit of your new ability to see through walls," Neala said.

"Yeah, but he can still see through three walls—that's amazing!" Alexia said in awe.

Neala turned to face Lusam, but spoke to Alexia, "Yes, it's *too* amazing, that's why you'll be sleeping at least four cells away from him." Lusam's face flushed brightly as the meaning of Neala's words sank in. Both Alexia and Renn burst out laughing, and even Neala couldn't quite hide her smile as she headed towards the main stairs, leaving Lusam behind to protest his innocence.

Chapter Twenty-Six

Using his newly enhanced mage-sight, Lusam watched patiently from behind the basement door for over an hour, before giving the all-clear to enter the shop. Lucy had been wrapping parcels at the counter, and Mr Daffer had been scurrying around helping various customers during that time. Only when Lusam was certain that they had both finally left the shop area, did he open the basement door. He then quickly ushered Neala, Alexia and Renn through, before closing the door quietly behind himself. They swiftly made their way to the main shop entrance, trying hard not to make a sound as they went. With a quick glance over his shoulder—to make sure nobody had seen them cross the shop area—Lusam opened the main shop door. The bell rang out from the rear of the premises, and a few seconds later, he closed it again—firmly—and waited.

A few moments later, Lucy appeared from the back of the shop carrying a pile of several books in her arms. She could barely see over the top of the books, and called out from behind the pile.

"Sorry for the delay. I'll be right with you in a moment, as soon as I …" Lucy started to say, but once she saw Lusam and Neala, she froze mid-stride. She unceremoniously dumped the pile of books onto the floor, and ran the length of the shop to embrace them both.

"Where have you been? We've been so worried about you both," Lucy said, turning towards the back of the shop and shouting, "Tom … Tom … come quickly." A moment later

Mr Daffer came racing into the shop brandishing a strange looking piece of wood. From the concerned look on his face, it was apparent that he had mistaken Lucy's calls, as a call for help. When he noticed Lucy embracing Lusam and Neala he visibly relaxed, lowering the improvised weapon, and placing it on the counter as he approached them.

"We're sorry for having to leave as we did, but you have to trust me when I say, there was no way to let you know. We didn't even know we were leaving ourselves," Lusam said apologetically.

"Likely story," Mr Daffer said, frowning slightly, then looking at Renn and Alexia.

"Tom!" Lucy chastised. "If Lusam says he couldn't let us know—then he couldn't let us know."

"What the lad says is true sir. I can vouch for him. In fact, it was due to my insistence that he left so hastily," Renn said, stepping out from behind Lusam and Neala.

"Is that so? And who ... " Mr Daffer started to say, but suddenly stopped mid-sentence. Renn had surreptitiously opened his tunic to reveal his sigil of Aysha, and when Mr Daffer caught sight of it, his eyes opened wide, as did his mouth.

"I ... I ... I meant no disrespect holy one. Please forgive my words, they were spoken only in jest. I can assure you, we owe Lusam and Neala a debt that could never be repaid, and if he says he couldn't let us know they were leaving—well that's good enough for me," Mr Daffer said, with his head bowed.

Lusam was shocked by the reactions of Mr Daffer, and even Lucy stood with her head bowed to Renn. He knew that the paladins of Aysha were held in high esteem throughout all of Afaraon, but he had no idea they were revered this much. It made him feel slightly guilty remembering his first encounter with Renn. He hadn't bowed his head, or even shown him much courtesy at all—in fact, he had blasted him with his magic. It was strange, but Lusam got the distinct impression—by the way Renn was now fidgeting—that he would probably prefer being blasted by magic, than being bowed to like this.

The silence stretched on and on. Lusam knew Mr Daffer and Lucy were waiting for a response from Renn, but he also knew that Renn wouldn't want to extend any further reverence towards himself either. He decided to end the silence, and introduce Renn and Alexia himself.

"Mr Daffer, Lucy, may I introduce to you Renn and Alexia. Renn, as I'm sure you're already aware, is a paladin of Aysha, and Alexia is an old friend of Neala's."

"We're both very honoured to meet you Renn—and you too Alexia," Mr Daffer said, offering his hand to them both.

"Mr Daffer, do you remember when I asked you to keep my ... abilities secret?" Lusam said quietly.

"Yes, of course Lusam, and we have ... I swear," Mr Daffer said, looking a little worried.

"I don't doubt you have, but, I must also ask another similar request," Lusam replied.

"Of course. What is it you need us to do?" Lucy said smiling.

"Would it be okay if we locked the shop door for a few minutes, while we discuss it?" Neala asked hopefully. Mr Daffer nodded to her request, so she quickly turned the sign over to read "Closed" and locked the door.

"Maybe we should discuss the matter in the dining room, where we will all be out of sight, and I'm sure, much more comfortable," Mr Daffer suggested.

"Under the circumstances, that sounds sensible," Renn said nodding.

A few moments later they were all in the dining room and seated at the large table. Lucy offered them some refreshments, which they all accepted gratefully, and then sat down to hear Lusam's request. After a few moments silence Lusam cleared his throat.

"I'm not really sure where to start, or what I can safely tell you both. Please understand, I'd trust you both with any amount of information, but the enemy we're facing, could simply read the information directly from your minds. It's for your own well being, as well as ours, that I must withhold certain information from you right now. I hope you both understand," Lusam said apologetically. Both Mr Daffer and Lucy nodded, but remained silent.

"Firstly, I apologise for us disappearing suddenly like we did. It's a long story, but it involved Neala being abducted and taken to Stelgad against her will. After the carnival we were attacked. I was stabbed in the stomach, and Neala was drugged, abducted, and taken to Stelgad." Lucy took a sharp intake of breath at the news, covering her mouth with her hands.

"Oh, you poor things!" she said looking shocked. "Are you both okay now?"

"Yes, we're fine now thank you," Lusam replied smiling, trying his best to allay her fears, so he could move on with his story swiftly.

"I healed my own wounds with magic, and was about to confront Neala's attacker, when I was attacked once more," Lusam said, pausing. He wasn't sure if revealing the existence of the Empire agents would be a good thing or not. Renn caught his eye, and nodded that he should continue his story.

"It was an Empire agent who attacked me."

"An Empire agent? Why would an Empire agent attack you?" Mr Daffer asked—obviously aware of their existence. Lusam wasn't sure if Lucy understood the significance or not, but he decided she could ask Mr Daffer about it later if she chose to do so.

"That's where I come in," Renn said from the end of the table. "I understand that you're already aware of Lusam's magical ability. The High Temple in Lamuria is also aware of it, and they sent me to find and protect him, then return him to Lamuria to complete his training. Unfortunately, the Empire has also discovered Lusam's abilities, and now they hunt him day and night. They will stop at nothing to find and kill him. When Neala was abducted, the man who took her travelled by road to Stelgad, but because of all the Empire agents looking for Lusam, we were unable to use the roads. We were forced to travel through The Dark Forest to Stelgad, but even then, we were pursued by Empire agents. That's why you must try keep this meeting a secret. If word got out that you had a paladin of Aysha here in your shop—even to people you trust—it's only a matter of time before that information is intercepted by an Empire agent.

"The betrayal may not even be intentional. The Empire agents possess magic capable of reading people's minds, and only people trained to resist it can avoid divulging their secrets inadvertently. At the moment, the Empire doesn't know for sure where we are. We hope to keep it that way for as long as possible," Renn said.

Mr Daffer and Lucy sat silently for a long time, absorbing the information they had just been given.

"Obviously your passage through The Dark Forest, and subsequent rescue of Neala went well, but there's one thing I don't understand," Mr Daffer said looking confused. "If you were already in Stelgad, why would you come back to Helveel if you needed to go south to Lamuria?"

"For their money," Lucy said out loud, whilst deep in thought. Then she suddenly realised what she had said. "Oh, I'm so sorry. Your money is perfectly safe, we haven't touched it. We weren't snooping or anything. It's just ... when you left, we were very worried about you both. We went into the basement looking for you—thinking that maybe you were ill, or had been injured down there somehow. When we looked inside one of your sleeping cells, we saw an open box full of gold coins. I know it's none of our business, but it confused us greatly. We couldn't understand why you would want to work so hard for a few silver coins, when you had such wealth already."

"I can see why that would look strange," Lusam said laughing, "but, to be honest, when we first started here, we didn't have any money at all." Once again Lusam became conscious of just how much he could safely tell Mr Daffer and Lucy. If he revealed exactly how he had gained the knowledge to mine gold from the river, it could place them both in great danger. He decided that omitting some of the truth would be better than outright lies.

"I'm quite new to my own magic abilities. Often I don't realise what I am capable of doing until I actually try—like when I healed you, Lucy. Neala and I would often walk along the riverbank on Seventh-day, and it was during one of those excursions that I discovered something interesting. If I concentrated hard enough, I found I was able to sense very small particles of gold on the riverbed. I worked out a way to collect the gold, and over several weeks turned it into the coins you discovered. And yes … the coins were one of the reasons we returned to Helveel, but not the only one. Unfortunately, the main reason we returned to Helveel is one of those things I can't discuss. I'm sorry," Lusam said.

"So, you still intend to travel to Lamuria?" Mr Daffer asked. Lusam looked to Renn for guidance, but was only greeted by a raised eyebrow: he seemed to be prepared to let Lusam decide, whether or not to answer that particular question. He decided to err on the side of caution with his reply.

"We're not sure yet," Lusam said, still looking at Renn.

"I see," replied Mr Daffer.

"Tom … the rumours may, or may not be true, but if there is a chance they will be heading that way, they should know," Lucy said quietly.

"Rumours?" Renn enquired. Mr Daffer's attention snapped back to the paladin at the end of the table, almost as if he'd forgotten he was sitting there.

"It's probably nothing … I conduct a small amount of business with several large noble families within Lamuria, and I have not received any payments for my latest shipments. I could understand one late payment, but all of them not paying seemed strange to me. I spoke with several other traders around Helveel, and it seems I'm not alone. Many have not received expected deliveries of goods from Lamuria, or payments that were due."

"Tell them the rest Tom," Lucy said. Mr Daffer looked at Lucy sternly, then after a moment he seemed to soften his glare, eventually sighing loudly.

"Very well," he said taking a deep breath. "Over the last several days I have spoken with just about every trader and businessman in Helveel regarding trade with Lamuria, and all told pretty much the same story: no one had seen or heard anything from Lamuria in over a month. No one that is, except old Greg the cobbler. His brother Earl takes his shipments to Lamuria, and brings back any materials they need from there. He's renowned for spending more time in the taverns between here and Lamuria, than he does travelling the roads themselves. He claims that he was unable to reach Lamuria with his shipment, but the story he gave—well, it seems more to do with the amount of time he spent in the taverns, than reality, if you ask me."

"What story?" Renn asked leaning forward.

"He claims the city was under attack, and when he tried to take a closer look, he himself was attacked. It sounded almost believable, until, that is, he described his attacker," Mr Daffer said shaking his head.

"Who did he say attacked him?" Renn asked impatiently.

"He said his attacker was already a corpse. He said he was attacked by a dead man. I told you—he's a crazy old drunk," Mr Daffer said chuckling to himself.

"Aysha be blessed!" Renn half-whispered. "A drunk he may be—but crazy, I think not. It looks like the Empire has finally chosen its time to attack Lamuria. If Lamuria falls, all of Afaraon will follow. We have to get to Lamuria as fast as we can before it's too late—that's if it's not already too late.

"Then we stick to our original plan. We buy horses and supplies today, and leave at first light tomorrow," Lusam said, then quickly added, "That is, providing Mr Daffer and Lucy don't mind us spending the night in their basement."

"Of course not. You're all welcome to stay as long as you like. But you don't have to stay in the basement. We have plenty of spare rooms in the house you could use," Lucy replied.

"Thank you Lucy, but given the circumstances, I think the basement would be the safest option. The fewer people who see us here, the better for all of us. Besides, it kind of feels like home down there," Lusam said smiling.

"Okay, but if you change your minds, just let me know. I can get Lillian to prepare the rooms for you in no time at all."

"Thanks Lucy, but we'll be fine in the basement," Neala said.

"Thank you for your hospitality Mr and Mrs Daffer. I'm sorry we couldn't have met under better circumstances," Renn said, standing up and offering his hand to Mr Daffer.

"Any friends of Lusam and Neala would always be welcome here—but having a Paladin of Aysha under our roof, well, that is an honour indeed sir," Mr Daffer said, shaking Renn's hand vigorously.

"It's a pleasure to meet you too Lucy," Renn said, offering her his hand.

"And you too," Lucy replied, "but I was hoping that you would all join us for the evening meal. I'm sure a good meal, followed by some sleep would stand you all in good stead for your onward journey to Lamuria."

Lusam's eyes lit up at the thought of food—as did the others—but it was Lusam's stomach that clinched the deal, with a mighty rumble reminiscent of the recent tremors in Coldmont.

"I guess there's your answer Lucy," Neala said rolling her eyes, and laughing along with the rest of them.

Chapter Twenty-Seven

Zedd braced himself for the forthcoming mind read, and his impending death. Lord Zelroth's ability to read the minds of his subjects was legendary. Zedd held out no hope of being able to hide any details of what had *actually* happened from Lord Zelroth. He contemplated changing his story, but knew it was already too late. He would be killed no mater what he did now.

Zedd felt the tendrils of power reach into his mind and begin searching for the relevant information. Due to nothing more than his natural instincts of survival, Zedd instinctively began offering up false images, and blocking access to his real thoughts. He had scored highly in mind control exercises during his many years of training in the Empire, but he held no illusions of being able to hold out against the immense power of Lord Zelroth.

The force within his mind pushed, and he pushed back. He challenged each incursion into his memories, by providing false ones to take their place.

`Something is very wrong,` Zedd thought to himself, confused at the inability of Lord Zelroth to easily read his mind. Zedd raised his eyes slightly, making sure to keep his head bowed. What he saw stunned him—so much so, that he almost lost control of his mind defences. Just at the edge of his vision, he could clearly see the golden edged hem of Lord Zelroth's robe: the man stood before him attempting to read his mind, was not Lord Zelroth. Zedd almost felt giddy with renewed hope. It all suddenly made perfect sense to him: the boy had killed the Inquisitor, and so Lord Zelroth was allowing one of his Darkseed Elite to conduct the interrogation.

The Darkseed Elite specialised in a single disciplines of magic—usually either attack or defensive magic—making them incredibly powerful in that particular discipline. Some even specialised in healing, but generally only because it allowed them to keep their torture victims alive for longer. None of them, however, specialised in mind control magic. That was a speciality reserved solely for Inquisitors—and the Inquisitor here, was dead.

The power of the Darkseed Elite was vast, but it was also blunt and undisciplined. Zedd saw each move, and countered it seamlessly, leading the Darkseed Elite through a vast array of false memories. Each memory he offered up, fell perfectly into place, validating his earlier story, and taking him one step closer to his redemption.

Several minutes later the mind read ceased abruptly, and the Darkseed Elite stepped away towards Lord Zelroth. Zedd couldn't help himself, he glanced up just in time to see the acknowledging nod of the Darkseed Elite to Lord Zelroth: he had done it.

"Well, it seems your story was true after all Zedd," Lord Zelroth said, walking over to where he still knelt with his head bowed. "Stand!" he commanded. Zedd obeyed.

"Give me your skull pendent," Lord Zelroth said holding out his hand. Zedd quickly removed his silver skull pendent and handed it to him. Lord Zelroth closed his hand around the pendent, and began to quietly chant a spell. A moment later he opened his hand to reveal a fully reshaped pendent. Now, instead of a single skull, it was a skull with two faces, and it had the symbol of the *Baliaeter* clearly visible upon it. Lord Zelroth handed back the pendent, and gestured towards Zedd's ring. Zedd offered up his ring, and Lord Zelroth touched it with his own ring. As the two rings touched, Lord Zelroth spoke a single word, and Zedd felt the power change within his own ring. Although it didn't actually increase Zedd's own power, he knew that he now had the ability to command almost anyone within the Empire. He could draw magical power from almost anyone, and he could kill almost anyone for disobeying his orders—and that made him feel incredibly powerful.

"Thank you sire," Zedd said, bowing his head in gratitude.

"I give you nothing," Lord Zelroth replied with a cruel laugh. "The *Baliaeter* currently in charge of my army will not relinquish power to you easily, or willingly. He is a capable commander, but he lacks your ... vision. The boy-mage's power has grown significantly since his discovery here in Coldmont. He can not be allowed time to strengthen the defences of Lamuria. The city must fall—and quickly. Our forces are already engaged outside Lamuria, and more reinforcements will shortly make landfall to swell their numbers. Use whatever tactics you deem necessary to gain the swiftest victory."

"Sire, please forgive me, but ... if your current *Baliaeter* will not relinquish command to me, how will I take command of your army from him?"

Lord Zelroth let out a manic laugh that chilled Zedd to his very bones. "That, my dear Zedd, is for you to work out for yourself. You have already triumphed over the boy-mage's power, what kind of challenge can a single *Baliaeter* hold for you?" he said turning away from Zedd to face Cole. "But, know this—if you fail me Zedd, your family will pay a high price for it. Of course, you wouldn't care, you'd already be dead."

"I won't fail you, sire," Zedd replied, knowing he would find a way to defeat the *Baliaeter,* one way or another.

"Oh, I know you won't Zedd. I've already seen how you use your subordinates—sending them into potential danger first, with no regard for their safety. Just like you did with Cole here," Lord Zelroth said staring down at Cole still kneeling before him. "I wonder ... do you trust Zedd's judgement enough to follow him into battle of your own free will, or do you just blindly following his orders, under punishment of death?"

Nothing would have pleased Cole more, than to say

what he actually thought of Zedd. Instead he knew he had to lie—a lie that could quite easily cost him his life.

"Yes sire, I would follow him freely," Cole replied, trying to sound as genuine as he could.

"Why?" Lord Zelroth asked bluntly, tilting his head a little, as he looked back towards Zedd. Cole's mind raced at the simple question. He knew—given a choice—he wanted to be as far away from Zedd as possible. But, he was also smart enough to realise, that the only possible way he would ever leave this place, was *with* Zedd. If he openly questioned Zedd's ability to command, either Lord Zelroth would kill him now, or Zedd would later.

"Sire, I have served under Zedd for only a few weeks, but during that time, he has proved himself a most competent commander. He sees opportunities others do not —and takes full advantage of those opportunities," Cole replied truthfully, hoping that Lord Zelroth didn't discover exactly what those *opportunities* were, that Zedd had taken full advantage of.

Lord Zelroth laughed loudly. "Such loyalty—and in such a short amount of time. It seems I have to conclude, that either Zedd is one of the most brilliant commanders ever to have served me, or, for some other hidden reason, you speak falsely of his deeds to me."

"I speak only the truth, sire, I swear," Cole said nervously.

"We shall see," Lord Zelroth replied, turning and nodding to his Darkseed Elite.

Zedd watched in horror as the Darkseed Elite approached Cole and began to read his mind. Cole was weak. There was no way that he could withstand the scrutiny of the Darkseed Elite's mind reading abilities. He contemplated killing Cole, but knew he would die moments later if he did. The strength in his legs almost failed him, and he took a small involuntary step forward, before steadying himself once more. He had been so close to his goals, and now ... now it was all ruined because of this weak fool kneeling before him. `I should have killed him much sooner,` Zedd thought to himself bitterly, `now I'm going to die, and my family will be made to pay the price of my failure.`

It probably took less than a minute, but it felt like an hour to Zedd as he watched the Darkseed Elite complete his simple task. When the Darkseed Elite finished, he turned to Lord Zelroth and began to report his findings. `This is it—this is the end,` Zedd thought to himself. He wasn't really listening to the Darkseed Elite's words, instead his mind was numb with defeat.

Lord Zelroth walked slowly towards Zedd, face hidden within the deep shadows of his hood. He stopped directly in front of Zedd, and raised his hand. Zedd cringed, expecting this moment to be his last. Instead Lord Zelroth pointed towards the book pedestal.

"Do you know what that is?" he asked Zedd, then turned his head to include Cole in his question. Zedd just shook his head, not knowing, or trusting himself to speak yet.

"What about you Cole. Do you know what that is?"

Cole nodded. "Yes sire, I think so. From what I have read about this place in our history books, and the effect it seemed to have on the boy-mage, I would guess it's a Guardian book, sire," Cole replied.

"Excellent, Cole," Lord Zelroth said, sounding genuinely pleased at his answer. "I can assume then, that you also know the consequences of trying to read such a book?"

"Yes, sire."

"Good—then you know that if either of you tried to read this book, it would kill you." Cole nodded, whilst looking nervously towards the book, and hoping Lord Zelroth wasn't about to suggest that he *did* try to read it.

"The existence of the Guardian books is well known and documented. What is not well known, are their locations. I myself, have been aware of this particular one for many centuries, as well as the location of certain others. The location of Coldmont, and this book, is known only to a handful of people, most of whom are in this room right now. I have certain ... safeguards in place, to ensure that no one ever enters this room without my knowledge. So, should you ever try and revisit this place, or even utter a hint of its location to anyone … well, let's just say it would seriously spoil your outlook on life," Lord Zelroth said, leaving absolutely no doubt about his implied threat, or his willingness to act upon it.

"Yes sire, I understand," Cole replied. When Lord Zelroth's gaze fell upon Zedd, he simply nodded mutely.

"Good! Then we have an understanding gentlemen," Lord Zelroth said, almost jovially. "I've always liked gambling, especially when the odds are in my favour. And I'm willing to bet, that you couldn't have achieved what you have without the help of Cole here—or am I wrong, Zedd?"

Zedd looked at Lord Zelroth warily. He still suspected a trap in his every word. His mind raced with unanswered questions, not least of which, was how Cole had just managed to withstand a mind read from a Darkseed Elite. One thing, however, was true: if he did survive this encounter with Lord Zelroth, he couldn't have done it without Cole's help.

"Yes, sire. You are correct," Zedd admitted. Although the words were true, speaking them out loud still seemed to leave a bitter after-taste in his mouth.

"Then it seems only fair, that Cole should receive a promotion too. Don't you agree, Zedd?"

"I do, sire," Zedd replied. He wasn't really bothered if Cole received a promotion, or not. All he wanted, was for all this to be over. He wanted to be as far away from Lord Zelroth and his Darkseed Elite guards as possible. He couldn't help feeling that Lord Zelroth was simply playing with them both: like a cat plays with a mouse, just before it kills it.

Zedd watched impassively as Lord Zelroth first touched Cole's ring with his own, then turned to one of his Darkseed Elite guards and asked for his silver chain and pendent. At Cole's current rank, agents didn't wear a silver chain, only a gold one—usually with the sigil of Aamon attached to it. It seemed perfectly reasonable to Zedd, that Lord Zelroth would create a new silver skull pendent for Cole, using the donated silver chain and pendent from the Darkseed Elite guard. He watched as Lord Zelroth placed the Darkseed Elite pendent in his hand, and quietly chanted a short spell.

Keeping hold of the newly formed pendant, Lord Zelroth placed the chain over Cole's still bowed head.

"Thank you, sire," Cole said, with genuine feeling.

"Rise," Lord Zelroth commanded, and Cole obeyed, revealing his new silver pendent to all in the room. Zedd's eyes widened, and his jaw hung loose at the sight of Cole's new silver pendent: it was the pendent of a *Baliaeter*. Lord Zelroth had made Cole an equal with him. He could no longer command him to do anything, nor could he kill him using his own ring. `How could Lord Zelroth promote this weak man to the rank of Baliaeter?` Zedd thought angrily. But then realised, he himself, was far weaker than any normal *Baliaeter* should ever be.

"I'll expect a report as soon as you both arrive at Lamuria, and regular updates of your progress. Do not fail me gentlemen. Now get out … and, I suggest that you forget you ever saw this place," Lord Zelroth said, pointing towards the recently cleared doorway behind Zedd and Cole. They both bowed their heads, turned towards the door, and exited the brightly lit room into the darkened corridor beyond.

"And make sure you hide the entrance to this room," Lord Zelroth called after them, "we wouldn't want anyone else stumbling across it now, would we?"

Before they could answer, a bright flash came from the room, and it then fell into complete darkness. Zedd created a light source which illuminated the dark corridor, then went to confirm what he already knew: Lord Zelroth and his Darkseed Elite had already gone. Remembering Lord Zelroth's words of warning, he decided against re-entering the room. Instead he made his way back to where Cole was waiting.

Cole remained still—as if waiting for Zedd's next move. Zedd could of course still kill him through sheer force, but should he? Somehow, he had withstood the scrutiny of a Darkseed Elite—one that Zedd himself had felt the power of. All of Zedd's concerns regarding Cole, had stemmed from the possibility of him either purposely, or inadvertently revealing what had occurred since leaving Helveel. If Cole had ever intended reporting Zedd for his transgressions, he could have done it easily in that room. And if he could hold out mentally against the power of a Darkseed Elite, no one short of an Inquisitor, or Lord Zelroth himself, would be able to take the information from him forcefully. If they ever did find themselves in that situation, Zedd knew that even he wouldn't be able to hide anything—so now, it made little sense remaining concerned over Cole's future ability to hide information. Cole began to look a little uncomfortable under Zedd's intense gaze, and began to shuffle a little.

"How? How did you do that?" Zedd asked, nodding towards the now darkened room. Cole simply placed a finger to his lips, signalling to Zedd to be quiet. At first Zedd's anger began to flare at the flippant dismissal of his question, but before he could reply, Cole said,

"Remember what Lord Zelroth said about having certain *"safeguards"* in place to monitor that room—maybe he can also hear what is said."

`He has a good point,` Zedd thought to himself.

"Let's block the entrance like he asked. We can talk about it later," Cole suggested. It seemed Cole's new rank had given him more confidence to voice his opinions—and as long as they were beneficial, Zedd wouldn't hold it against him, not right now anyway.

Zedd ended up doing most of the magical work to block the entrance of the book room. Not because Cole refused to help, but because he was incapable of wielding the magic required to move that amount of rubble.

Zedd hadn't spoken since leaving the basement of Coldmont. He was still trying to understand, how this incredibly weak mage had defeated a mind read from a Darkseed Elite. As they emerged from Coldmont into the daylight, Zedd decided he couldn't take it any more.

"Okay, so how did you do it?" he asked bluntly. Cole actually smiled at his question before answering.

"I have tier eight mind control," Cole replied, his smile

broadening further.

"Impossible!" Zedd spat back. "Inquisitors only have to achieve tier seven. You can't possibly be tier eight."

"I can—and I am. I know what you're thinking: that I am weak, so I can't be tier eight. I hoped to be an Inquisitor once, but my base magic scores were not high enough to make the grade, so I was assigned my low rank instead."

"If that were true, you would be able to read my mind easily. So do it now. Tell me what I am thinking right now," Zedd said, preparing his mental defences. Cole willingly accepted the challenge. If for nothing else, only to prove that he was better at something than Zedd was. He delved into Zedd's mind, easily finding the information he tried desperately to hide, and told him exactly what it was.

"Again!" Zedd half-screamed in frustration.

Three more times Zedd made Cole read his mind, each time Zedd employed more and more complex defences against him, but nothing could keep him out. Next Zedd attempted to read Cole's mind, but he blocked absolutely everything from him. After twenty minutes, Zedd had a new found respect for Cole's abilities. He wasn't powerful magically like Zedd was, but mentally, he was a giant amongst men. With his level of mind control, he could force almost anyone, to do whatever he wanted. With enough pressure exerted on someone's mind, he could control them almost like a puppet—even if it were only for short periods of time. `I may just have discovered a way to defeat the Baliaeter who is now in control of the army outside Lamuria,` Zedd thought, grinning to himself. For once, he was glad he hadn't killed Cole.

Chapter Twenty-Eight

After several heated discussions, they finally decided amongst themselves who would do what in their preparations to leave Helveel. It had been decided, that Neala and Alexia would go together to buy the horses and travel supplies for their journey. Although Lusam hadn't wanted Neala out on the streets of Helveel without him, eventually he had been forced to agree with their argument to be the ones to go. Alexia was completely unknown in Helveel, and hopefully unrecognisable by any Empire agents—even if their descriptions had already been circulated. Neala on the other hand, knew Helveel's streets and shops very well. She had already proven her ability to lose a pursuing Empire agent when Lusam and she had been spotted at the carnival. That made her the perfect choice to quickly acquire the resources they would need for their onward journey.

Renn had spoken of a temple within Helveel, one that neither Lusam nor Neala had ever seen, or even heard of before. He insisted it existed, and told Lusam it had been the only means of communication between his grandmother and the High Temple in Lamuria. The location of the temple was only known to a select few, including Hermingild and paladins. Its primary function was to keep track of any Empire movements in the far north, and report its findings back to the High Temple. Renn said it was possible that they may know something more of the attack in Lamuria, and if not, it was his duty to inform them of the information he now had regarding it.

The plan was for Neala and Alexia to acquire the horses and supplies, then make their way towards the eastern gate. They would exit the city, making their way to the small forest where Lusam and Neala had spent so much time together. Then they would secure the horses and supplies in a secluded spot, before returning to Helveel, and rejoining the others in the basement of *The Old Ink Well*.

At first light they would all leave Helveel, but not together. Renn had a plan for Neala and him to leave via the north part of the city, Lusam and Alexia via the east gate. Lusam and Alexia would reclaim the horses and supplies, then meet up with the others further along the eastern road. If all went well, no one would mark their departure as a group of four people matching the description the Empire now had of them.

So it was, that Lusam found himself alone in the basement. At first he'd felt like a caged animal—pacing back and forth in his sleeping cell, worried about the others, especially Neala. Eventually, he convinced himself that they could take care of themselves, and that it was unlikely that anyone would even be on the lookout for people matching their descriptions yet. He didn't know if Lord Zelroth knew where they had gone, or not. What he did know, however, was that Lord Zelroth hadn't been able follow them here.

`Obviously he was unaware of the Guardian book in Helveel—and hopefully it would remain that way,` Lusam thought.

It had been an incredibly arduous few weeks since the last time he had been in his cosy sleeping cell. He, like the others, was bone-tired. He would have liked nothing more than to close his eyes and sleep, but he couldn't—not until the others were safely back. He spent a while lying down on his bed, going over things in his mind—things that had happened, and things that he had seen and done. It seemed incredible to him that only a few short months ago, he was nothing more than a lonely street kid here in Helveel—and now, he was possibly the greatest hope Afaraon had of defeating the Empire. Or at least that was what Renn and the others believed—even if he didn't. Surely someone other than him deserved the attention of Aysha more. After all, he wasn't even a particularly religious person, so why choose him?

As he lay there on his bed thinking about the implications of it all, his heart began to race more and more. Before long, he found himself almost panting as the sheer panic rose within him. His heart felt like it was about to burst from his chest, as he finally realised, there was nothing he could do to change his fate. But it wasn't just his fate—it was quite possibly the fate of the entire world he held in his hands. If Lord Zelroth managed to re-open The Great Rift, and released the creatures of the Netherworld again, everything would be lost—this time, there would be no Guardians to save the world.

Lusam sat bolt-upright on his bed, panting, and on the verge of a panic attack. He had to occupy his mind with something else ... anything else. He found himself walking towards the main chamber. Halfway there, he decided to run. He knew it was crazy, but running seemed to make him feel better—like he could distance himself from his dark thoughts somehow. Thankfully it didn't take him long to regain control of his thoughts, and he began to study the walls and ceiling in the vast chamber. He thought he might discover something new, something he had missed earlier—but he didn't. All he saw was the riddle, and it still made little or no sense to him.

He found himself absent-mindedly heading for the book room, and was surprised to see it in almost exactly the same state as when they had finished cataloguing the books. He never thought he would be happy to see all these books again, but they held fond memories for him. If it weren't for these books, he would never have had the chance to become so close to Neala.

There were hundreds of piles of books, but one in particular caught his eye. It was the pile of uncatalogued books. The ones written in a foreign language. It wasn't a large pile compared to the others—maybe only twenty or so books. But now, he could clearly read the cover of the top book in the pile: it was written in the same language as the Guardian books. He knelt by the side of the books, and began to look through the pile. Most were still written in various languages that Lusam couldn't understand—but three were not.

Lusam collected the three large leather-bound books, and took them over to the writing desk where he had done all of his earlier writing. He strengthened his light orb so he could read the words clearly, and opened the first book. It appeared to be some kind of ledger. Some of the items it listed were unfamiliar to Lusam, but many he recognised as trade goods still used today. He placed the ledger to one side, and opened the second book. To his great disappointment, this too contained nothing but facts and figures, all relating to the various trade deals of some long dead merchant.

The third and final book looked different from the other two. It was larger in all of its dimensions, and the binding was of much higher quality. Lusam placed the book before him, and opened it to the first page:

Judd II – Second cycle – Seventh-day – One

Since the Empire's retreat back to Thule, we have been making slow progress in the fight against the foul creatures of the Netherworld. Although we all mourn the passing of the mighty Guardians and their dragons, we still hold strong to our faith in Aysha.

The King has finally approved the funds to build a new outpost south of The Great Rift, and its construction has already begun in earnest. It is to be called The Sanctum of Light, and Aysha herself has ordained that a new breed of holy knights be created to man the new outpost. Rumours abound, that the King's long term refusal to fund such a bold and expensive venture, came to an abrupt end with the sudden appearance of several Netherworld creatures in the capital itself. One can not help wonder if it was pure coincidence, or if some higher power had a hand in their sudden and inexplicable appearance, but I know, it is not for us to question such things.

Judd II – Second cycle – Third-day – Two

Myself and several other monks from our order have been called before the High Priest of Aysha in Lamuria. We have been instructed to maintain absolute secrecy regarding our visit to the capital, and even instructed not to wear our sacred robes for the journey south. We will travel at dawn, disguised as simple merchants. It has been many years since I have left these walls, and I feel no small amount of apprehension at the thought of doing so again. May Aysha bless our journey.

Judd II – Fourth cycle – Sixth-day – Four

It has been over two months since I wrote in this journal. I was forced to leave it behind in Ula'ree when we travelled to the High Temple. We were sworn to secrecy regarding the true nature of our visit to Lamuria, but I feel it is my sacred duty to the future monks of this order to know the truth. We are to begin construction of a new room within our temple. Complex spells were taught to our delegation during our visit to the High Temple. Spells to be used in the construction of a strange new room within Ula'ree. We were also told to expect a visit from one of the five surviving Guardians, and he would instruct us further. On a more personal note, I was pleased to lay eyes once more on my old childhood friend, Isidro, whom I have not seen since he left to join his order at Lohlaen many years ago. He was leaving the High Temple as we first arrived, but unfortunately he did not seem to recognise me after so many years. At least he still appeared in good health for his years, far better than myself, I fear. Maybe it can be attributed to the clear air on The Pearl Isle, but *whatever...*

Lusam was suddenly startled from his reading by Renn's voice.

"Are you alright lad?" Renn asked, sounding a little concerned.

"Yes, of course. Why wouldn't I be?" Lusam replied, slightly confused.

"I've been calling to you for a while. I thought you'd

gone out alone somewhere, then I noticed your light in here," Renn said, noticing the book Lusam was reading. "What's that you're reading lad?"

"I'm pretty sure it's someone's private journal. I think it was written by one of the monks who used to live here. It seems to have been written just after The Great Rift was closed, and it even refers to the construction of The Sanctum of Light, and the creation of the paladins," Lusam said excitedly.

"May I see it?" Renn asked, eagerly stepping towards the book.

"You can, but I doubt you'll be able to read any of it. It's written in the same language as the Guardian books." Renn visibly sagged at the news. He was obviously very anxious to learn about the creation of his holy order of paladins.

"Would you like me to read you the passage?" Lusam asked, grinning at the look of disappointment on Renn's face. Renn nodded eagerly, and Lusam obliged by reading the passage to him.

After he had finished reading Renn the first three entries, he paused. He very much wanted to continue reading the journal, but wondered if it would be better if he read it alone first. There was no telling what information may be contained within this book. And although he trusted Renn completely, he still felt an overwhelming and inexplicable desire to keep the contents to himself—at least for now.

Lusam closed the journal, and seeing the look of disappointment on Renn's face, actually felt guilty for not continuing to read.

"Don't worry, I'll read some more of it later. If there's anything else of interest, I'll let you know," Lusam said.

"Okay, lad," Renn replied, nodding slightly. "There was something else, but you said you would explain later." Lusam looked a little confused, as he tried to think of what Renn could be referring to, then he suddenly remembered.

"Oh, yes. It was about the Guardian books and the pedestals."

"Yes, you said you'd discovered something about them," Renn replied patiently.

"That's right, I have. As you know, since reading the Guardian book in Coldmont, I've been able to read the ancient language they are written in. When I first touched the —actually I don't know what to call it—green light, emanating from the pedestal in Coldmont, and I found myself back here in Helveel. I noticed that I could read the name on the Guardian book for the first time, and it read: *Freedom*. Then I also noticed a name on the pedestal here, and that read: *Absolution*.

"At first it didn't mean anything to me, but after I returned to Coldmont, it all became clear. The Guardian book in Coldmont was called: *Absolution*. And the name on the pedestal was: *Freedom*."

"I'm not sure I follow you lad," Renn said looking puzzled.

"Well, at first I thought I'd somehow missed seeing the writing on the pedestal in Helveel when I first read the book here. But the more I thought about it, the more certain I became—it just wasn't here before. I believe, that for each book read, a new name relating to that book appears on the pedestal. More importantly, the pedestal then allows you to travel to any given book you have already read. You simply choose where you want to go, by touching the green light emanating from the name of whichever book you wish to visit. Put simply: if you have read the book, you can travel to its location using the pedestal," Lusam said.

"So, Lord Zelroth couldn't follow us here … " Renn started to say, but was interrupted when Lusam finished his sentence for him.

"Because he's never read the book here in Helveel. It's quite possible that he doesn't even know it's here. Or at least I hope he doesn't."

Renn remained silent for a few moments, thinking about Lusam's words carefully. "If Lord Zelroth and his Darkseed Elite travelled to Coldmont using the pedestals, that would mean he had already previously read the Guardian book in Coldmont."

"Actually, it would mean he had read at least two Guardian books, *including* the one in Coldmont. He obviously travelled from another pedestal to get to Coldmont," Lusam replied.

"No wonder he's so powerful," Renn half-whispered to himself. "If he doesn't know about the book here, then that means he knows the location of at least one other Guardian book—one that we don't."

"I'm certain of it. And I'm pretty sure I know the general location of the other one," Lusam said confidently.

"Really?"

"Think about it. It has to be somewhere in Thule, otherwise Lord Zelroth wouldn't have arrived in Coldmont so quickly."

"No, it can't be in Thule, lad. The Guardians would never have have hidden a book there. The book would have been far too exposed after the withdrawal from Irragin ..." Renn took a sharp intake of breath. "Oh, no ... I don't believe it. It's been right in front of our eyes the whole time, and no one has ever realised—until now."

"What has?" Lusam asked. Renn didn't reply to his question straight away, instead, he paced back and forth around the room with his hands clasped above his head, occasionally contorting his face in strange ways. Eventually, he came to a stop at the opposite side of the desk where Lusam was sitting, and leant against it. He then pulled a chair over to the desk and sat down opposite Lusam.

"Lad, it all makes perfect sense now," Renn said, still resting his hands on top of his head. Lusam was about to ask, what exactly Renn was talking about, when he began to explain.

"No one ever understood how Lord Zelroth had gained so much power. Many theories have been put forward over the centuries, but none have been proven—or even agreed upon—but now, I think you have just uncovered his secret."

"I'm sorry, I don't quite follow you. I thought you just said that the Guardians would never have left a book in

Thule, so Lord Zelroth couldn't possibly have one there."

"I did—but I was wrong lad. Let me try to explain. After The Great Rift was finally closed, Afaraon quickly destroyed the Thulian forces stationed here. Our armies crushed the Thulian soldiers, forcing them to flee back to Thule, or die here. The King, however, wasn't content with simply letting the enemy retreat back to Thule. Instead, he pursued them remorselessly, right to the very heart of Thule, killing and destroying everything as he went. Their government soon collapsed, and their country fell into anarchy. Local warlords sprung up overnight, taking control of small pockets of land, and they fought amongst themselves for the scraps left behind by our forces.

"The King ordered an outpost to be built in Thule, and the location chosen was Mount Nuxvar. Thousands of Thulian slaves were used to build the outpost, and once it was completed, its barracks contained over twenty thousand troops. At first it was used to put down any potential uprisings, or overly ambitious warlords that might raise their heads a little too high. After a while, it was also used by the church. The High Priest of the time, had somehow got it into his head, that it would be a good idea to try and convert the people of Thule to worship Aysha, instead of Aamon. His plan met with little success.

"Thule remained in chaotic upheaval for over a century. People starved by the thousands, and plagues ravaged their population. Unfortunately, the plagues didn't discriminate between peoples, and little more than a century after its construction Irragin was abandoned. Its occupants were wiped out by one of the many infections, and our leaders declared it a lost cause. Thule was no longer considered a threat to Afaraon, and the church's attempt to convert its populace was viewed as a complete failure. The cost of maintaining an outpost so far away was deemed unnecessary, and at the time, potentially deadly, as the previous occupants found out to their cost. Also at that time, Afaraon faced another potential threat from a land to the far north. So the attention of the King, the council, and even the

High Temple were firmly focused north, and not south towards a broken continent.

"Irragin was forgotten, but not for long. One of those warlords took control of Irragin, and renamed it Azmarin. That warlord, was Lord Zelroth. His rise to power was incredible. Within five years he had killed all of the rival warlords. Within ten, he had established his control over the entire continent, and formed the beginnings of The Thule Empire we know today. His movements were watched carefully by our spies, but none of them ever discovered the source of his power. He also seemed to be more focussed on rebuilding the society of Thule, rather than being any particular threat to Afaraon. With the new threat looming from the north, it was decided that we couldn't start a war on two fronts, so Lord Zelroth was left to do as he willed.

"Looking back now, it seems like a lost opportunity to rid the world of a tyrant, but you have to understand, Afaraon was a mighty nation back then. One man was no threat against the thousands of magi we had. Once The Great Rift had been sealed, and the Netherworld creatures contained or destroyed, we had easily crushed the forces of Thule.

"What no one knew of course, was the fact they had just given him access to one of the Guardian books. It seems that by keeping the locations of the books *such* a secret, it actually worked against us in the end. If we had only known Irragin contained a Guardian book, it would never have been abandoned. But, I guess the same could be said about this place, or even Coldmont for that matter."

Lusam tried to imagine a time when Afaraon was so powerful. A time when magic was commonplace, and the constant threat from the Empire didn't exist yet. He remembered what Renn had told him, about how the Empire had secretly been killing newborn magi in Afaraon for at least two centuries, and probably much longer than that. How the *Hermingild* had been formed to protect newborn magi and their mothers. And how his grandmother had in fact been his mother's *Hermingild*, and not his actual grandmother at all. Then another thought struck him.

"Renn, were the magi in Afaraon powerful back then?" Lusam asked.

"I suppose they varied in power, just like they do today. Why do you ask?"

"Well, when I say powerful ... I mean, were they as powerful as I am now?"

Renn laughed loudly. "I'm not sure, but I doubt it lad. I've never read about anyone doing some of the things you can do. The battles that are documented were fought using magic as you would imagine, but only in the normal sense. They would hurl magical-missiles at each other until one side ran out of power, and their shields failed. Sometimes several magi would concentrate their fire-power on a single mage, overwhelming them with brute force."

Lusam nodded, but didn't seem convinced by Renn's words.

"Let me ask you something lad. If you were on a battlefield, and there were paladins fighting against you, how would you defeat them? How would you bypass their shields and weapons?"

Lusam thought about it for a moment, and easily came up with several methods to quickly dispatch a paladin.

"That's easy, I ..." Lusam began to say, but was cut short by Renn's laughter booming out once more.

"You see lad. A paladin wouldn't pose much of a problem for you, but to an Empire agent, we're a real threat. I saw how easily you dealt with those agents outside Coldmont, and I can say this—no mage I have ever read about in the history books ever made such light work of killing another mage, let alone several at once," Renn said, still chuckling to himself.

"If you're right, then that possibly answers another question we might have," Lusam replied.

"Oh?"

"Well, before I read the book in Coldmont, I wasn't much more powerful than some of the Empire agents. I might have won a battle against a single agent, or possibly two, but I certainly couldn't have done what I did outside Coldmont."

"And?" Renn prompted.

"Isn't it obvious? ... Lord Zelroth wasn't powerful enough to challenge Afaraon until after he had read the book in Coldmont. I suspect it was just after reading Coldmont's book that he first started killing newborn magi in Afaraon. If that's true, it would mean he discovered the book over two hundred years ago," Lusam said excitedly.

"I'm not following you lad. How does that information help us now?"

"Don't you see? Lord Zelroth hasn't changed his tactics for the last two hundred years. Nothing has changed. He's continued to try and exterminate our newborn magi, simply trying to make us weaker and weaker."

Renn shot to his feet, knocking over the chair as he did so. "Aysha be blessed! You're right lad. That must mean he hasn't found a third book yet. If he had, he would have become even more powerful and stepped up his attacks a long time ago," Renn said, sounding even more excited than Lusam had.

"Exactly!" Lusam said grinning widely.

"So, if we could find a third book, potentially you could be even more powerful than Lord Zelroth is."

"Possibly—but he's had centuries to practise. I, on the other hand, barely know what I'm capable of yet. Not to mention the fact, he's also had centuries to look for the other books, and still not found them."

"True, but we have one thing that he doesn't," Renn said grinning.

"What's that?" Lusam asked confused.

Renn leant over the desk and tapped on the book in front of Lusam. "The journal, of course. Who knows what secrets it might reveal?"

Neala and Alexia returned to *The Old Ink Well* just before nightfall. Even though they had left the horses and supplies behind in the eastern forest, they still carried several bundles with them. As they entered the basement, they noticed that Mr Daffer had brought down two more mattresses for their sleeping cells, along with a fresh supply of lamp oil. There were already a few lanterns lit within the large chamber, but an even brighter light spilled out from inside the book room. As they got closer, Neala could clearly hear both Lusam and Renn's voices coming from within the room. Strangely, they seemed to be discussing ancient history, both in Afaraon and the Empire—something Neala knew little about, nor did she wish to learn about it.

"It sounds like you're both having fun in here," Neala said entering the room, closely followed by Alexia. Lusam stood up from behind the desk and quickly went to greet Neala with a big hug. He'd been worried since she and Alexia had left earlier that day, but now she was back safely, he began to relax again.

"Don't I get a hug too lover-boy? I did do half the work you know," Alexia teased.

"No, you don't," replied Neala, wearing a fake scowl, and making everyone laugh.

"What you got there?" Renn asked, nodding towards the bundles Neala and Alexia had been carrying when they entered the room.

"We thought it best if we bought some fresh clothes for us all. We don't have time to wash and repair the ones we're wearing, and let's face it—we all stink," Alexia said wrinkling her nose, as if to demonstrate her point.

"She might be right," Renn said, surreptitiously sniffing his own armpit, "we do smell a little—ripe."

"Speak for yourself," Lusam replied laughing.

"There's also another reason we bought new clothes. If the Empire has already circulated our descriptions, you can bet it also includes what clothes we were wearing," Neala said.

"Good thinking. It certainly can't hurt, anyway," Renn agreed.

"There's a small wash room upstairs that Neala and I used the last time we were here. I'm sure Mr Daffer and Lucy wouldn't mind us all using it before we eat dinner. In fact, I'm fairly certain they'll insist on it," Lusam said chuckling to himself. "Talking of dinner, I hope it's ready soon, I'm starving."

"Nothing new there then," Neala said rolling her eyes. "To be honest, I'm more looking forward to a good night's sleep for once. I can't remember the last time I was able to close my eyes, and not have to worry whether we were about to be attacked, or not."

"Talking of sleep. It looks like Mr Daffer has brought another two mattresses down for us. I noticed them at the bottom of the stairs when we got back," Alexia said.

"Maybe we should take them to the sleeping cells, while we wait for dinner to be ready," Renn suggested. They all agreed and headed back out into the large chamber to where the mattresses leant against the wall. Renn and Lusam grabbed each end of one mattress and lifted it off the ground.

"Where should we put it?" Renn asked, nodding towards the mattress.

"At least four cells down that corridor," Neala replied, glancing sideways at Alexia, who burst out laughing as she remembered their earlier conversation. Lusam's face flushed as he too understood Neala's meaning, but he remained silent. Renn also wore a wide grin, as he and Lusam set off down the long corridor towards one of the cells at the far end. When they returned—slightly out of breath—Neala and Alexia were still standing in the exact same spot, and the second mattress remained leaning against the wall untouched. Renn didn't seem to notice that the girls hadn't even attempted to move the mattress, and instead, simply picked up one end and waited for Lusam to grab the other.

"Where do you want this one?" Renn asked.

"Oh, there is just fine thanks, Renn. We'll only be needing three mattresses tonight," Neala said winking at Lusam, who instantly turned a bright scarlet colour. Everyone burst out laughing at the look on Lusam's face, and he was immensely grateful when the door at the top of the basement stairs opened, and Mr Daffer called down to them that dinner was ready.

Chapter Twenty-Nine

Rebekah squinted at the horizon, checking for any signs of the returning ship, whilst her younger brother Kayden played with his wooden spinning top on the dockside. The Good Ship Tuthna was due to return with its precious cargo any time now, and when it did, there would be a large celebration in Prystone, just like the last one she remembered three months earlier. Except, this time it would be even better. It wasn't just one birth they would be celebrating, but two. Two expectant mothers had gone aboard The Good Ship Tuthna to give birth, and Deas willing, two would return with their new precious babies.

Kayden spoke the words over and over, as his wooden top spun faster and faster. He had discovered that he could make the wooden toy spin using words only three days before, and since then, his favourite toy had barely stopped moving. He was barely five-years-old, but he excelled at annoying his older sister—or at least she would have most people think so. In reality she loved her younger brother, and although Rebekah herself was only ten-years-old, she was more like a mother to him than an older sister. She was the one who cared for him whilst her mother worked the fields each day. Her father was the captain of The Good Ship Tuthna, and as such his days spent at sea, sometimes outnumbered the ones he spent on land.

When her father did make it home, he often brought Rebekah and Kayden gifts: gifts that were no doubt given to him by the families of the newborns he had helped to bring into the world. Every time he spent a night at home, Rebekah would pester him to tell them the story of the *Rebirth* again. She knew the story well, and often told it to her younger brother when they were alone, but she still loved to hear it from her father's lips.

The story tells that before the *Rebirth*, most children would die shortly after being born, and often their parents too. At first, some believed the village of Prystone to be cursed, and they moved to neighbouring villages, only to find the same fate awaited their newborns there too. It wasn't until her father's great grandfather took his pregnant wife aboard The Good Ship Tuthna, and sailed out to sea, that things changed. When they returned to Prystone with a new child, rumours began to circulate within the village. It was said that The Good Ship Tuthna must be blessed by Deas himself.

At first it took time to gain credence within the village, with only close friends and family taking to the sea aboard the Tuthna to give birth. But soon people began to realise, that each time a pregnant woman went to sea aboard The Good Ship Tuthna, she would return with a healthy baby in her arms. Soon, everyone in Prystone booked passage aboard the Tuthna to give birth at sea, and a new-found religion was born. One that worshipped the God Deas—creator of all things in the sea, and now upon it.

It wasn't long before the neighbouring villages took notice of the swelling numbers within Prystone, and soon after, The Good Ship Tuthna began taking even more women out to sea to give birth. Now, there wasn't a single person in Prystone, or its neighbouring villages, who hadn't been born aboard The Good Ship Tuthna.

Rebekah had first taken on the job of watching for the return of her father's ship when she was about Kayden's age. She would sit there for hours waiting for the mast to appear on the horizon, then go running to her mother in the fields when she finally spotted it, shouting out all the way there. She could spot the ship before anyone else—something she was very proud of. During her long hours staring at the horizon, she had discovered a way to enhance her own vision using only a few words, something no one else was able to do in her village. It was true that almost everyone in the village had a special gift, sometimes even more than one. Hers was the ability to see further, and it seemed her younger brother's was to make his wooden toy spin. `Hopefully he would find a better use for his skill later,` she thought to herself.

Rebekah had been taught that each gift you were born with came from Deas, and it was important never to use that gift against anyone else. In fact, the exact opposite was true: if you could use your gift to help others, you should. That was the reason why Rebekah stood watch on the dockside, come rain or shine.

Rebekah squealed in pain as her younger brother's wooden spinning top crashed into her bare ankle, burning away a small patch of skin as it spun.

"Sorry Bekah," he said, quickly moving out of his big sister's range, as she hopped on one foot. He had always called his sister "Bekah," ever since he could first talk. He could never quite say her full name when he was younger, and had always shortened it to "Bekah" instead.

"Kay!" she said through gritted teeth. He knew she was angry with him. She only ever called him "Kay" when she was angry.

"I'm sorry Bekah. It was an accident. I didn't mean to do it," Kayden said, trying his best to sound sincere, but secretly finding it incredibly amusing watching his big sister hop around the dockside.

***

The magical pulse was felt by everyone aboard ship. Either a birth, or the death of a weak mage had just occurred somewhere close by. The trouble was they were still at sea—several hours from land—with no way to determine the direction the pulse had come from. Usually it took several Empire agents on land to determine the precise location of any pulse generated. As they intercepted the pulse at slightly different times, an accurate direction could be calculated by three or more agents working together using their Necromatic rings to communicate with each other. At sea, with only one point of reference it would be impossible to know which direction it came from. That was until the shout came from high above in the rigging.

"Ship ahoy!"

Praetor Dante was in command of the reinforcements aboard ship on their way to Lamuria to bolster the Empire's forces there. They had been instructed to land north of Lamuria and cause as much death and destruction as possible on their way to the Afaraon capital. His orders were simple: to destroy the food supplies and kill any civilians they encountered. He would then reanimate the dead and create his own army to use against the High Temple in Lamuria. Any non-viable corpses likely to slow their progress would be left to roam the countryside and cause as much havoc as possible.

Although each ship carried around a hundred men—each one a capable mage—it would be the overall size of each Praetors undead army when they arrived at Lamuria that would be most likely to assure them of personal success on the battlefield. Praetor Dante was more than happy to start his undead army, even before making landfall.

"Intercept that ship, captain," he said, pointing to the sails on the horizon.

"Aye sir," the captain replied, shouting instruction to the ship's crew and setting an intercept course for the distant vessel.

***

The cheers went up as the midwife emerged from the main cabin holding the newborn. Songs of celebration and praise to Deas began in earnest. Not one, but two successful births on a single trip called for nothing less. There would be feasting and drinking a-plenty tonight in Prystone.

The crew of The Good Ship Tuthna were well practised in these birthing trips. The distance from shore would never be less than twenty miles, and most of the time exceed thirty in fair weather. After the successful birth—or births in this case—they would immediately set sail back to Prystone, where Captain James' daughter Rebekah would be watching for their return. They would hoist their white flag for a successful trip so she could announce to the villagers that they could start their preparations for the forthcoming celebrations. Occasionally, a black flag would have to be flown, but thankfully that didn't happen often. Any child who didn't survive, was offered back to Deas and buried at sea before returning to land. Local superstitions believed that the bad luck should remain out at sea, and not be returned to the land with the grieving family.

The white flag had already been raised, and The Good Ship Tuthna was almost underway when the shouts came from above.

"Captain … enemy vessel astern!"

Captain James took out his spyglass and scanned the horizon, expecting to see a pirate vessel, which occasionally ventured this far north from the main trade routes to Lamuria. What he saw turned his blood to ice: the unmistakable flag of the Empire.

"Weigh anchor!" shouted the captain. A moment later came the reply.

"Anchor's aweigh captain."

"Raise the mainsail. Best speed to port." Captain James watched his well trained crew go to work as they set sail for home-port. The Good Ship Tuthna was no warship, nor was it considered fast by any stretch of the imagination. It would be a miracle if they outrun the Empire war ship back to port in time to warn the other villagers to flee. Never had twenty miles seemed so far before. He estimated the Empire war ship to be at most seven miles behind them—and closing fast.

***

Rebekah spotted her father's ship the moment it appeared on the horizon flying its white flag. Excitedly she turned to Kayden and asked him to fetch their mother from the fields, while she informed the rest of the village of their return. `It will be a grand celebration tonight,` she thought to herself, imagining all the sweet pastries and other delicious treats that usually accompanied such an event. She watched as Kayden picked up his wooden spinning top and ran off to fetch their mother. Rebekah then skipped down the road towards the centre of the village, where she knew she would find most of the people going about their daily business. She had no intention of going house to house and informing every single resident of the Tuthna's return, and possibly missing her father coming ashore—bearing whatever gifts he may have for her and Kayden from his trip. Instead, she would tell anyone she encountered on the streets, and let the news spread by itself, as it always seemed to do anyway. Then she would return to the docks and wait for her father to arrive.

When Rebekah returned to the docks she found both her mother and brother waiting for her. Kayden was still playing with his wooden spinning top, but his mother was looking out to sea in the direction of the Tuthna with a strange look on her face. Rebekah followed her gaze to see what she was looking at, and was surprised to see her father's ship closely followed by another ship. Then she saw it. The Tuthna was no longer flying its white flag. It was now flying a red one, and red meant only one thing—danger. Her stomach filled with butterflies at the sight of the red flag. She had always been told that if the Tuthna—or any other ship—was flying the red flag, she should find her mother and flee the village or hide as fast as possible.

"Mother, they have a red flag up," Rebekah said, not sure if her mother would be able to see it as clearly as *she* could with her ability. Her mother took a sharp intake of breath.

"Deas watch over us," She whispered. By this time a few of the villagers had joined them on the docks to await the return of the Tuthna, and assure themselves of a good position in the welcome party. It seemed to take long time for her mother to react to Rebekah's news, but suddenly she did, turning to the growing crowd and shouting, "The Tuthna flies the red flag!"

People ran in all directions, some calling out to family members to flee or hide, others calling the men to arms, to defend against whatever was coming. Rebekah's mother simply stood still, staring out to sea towards her husband's ship, and the enemy ship that was now almost on top of them. She watched silently as dozens of fireballs suddenly came from the enemy ship and engulfed the Tuthna. She screamed out loud as the ship literally exploded out of the water, broke in half, then sunk below the waves right before her eyes.

Less than a minute later, and all she could see now was debris and bodies floating in the water, where only moments before her husband's ship had been. Then something even stranger started to happen. Bodies started to rise up out of the water and float through the air towards the enemy ship. Some were unceremoniously dumped back overboard, but most remained on the deck of the enemy ship. It reminded her of a fishing vessel, deciding which fish to keep, and which to throw back overboard.

"Mother," Rebekah said, desperately tugging at her mother's hand to regain her attention. Her mother slowly turned her head towards her, eyes filled with tears, and looked at her with a strange expression on her face—as if not recognising who she was for a moment. It took her several seconds to regain some composure, by which time many of the villagers were massing themselves near the docks ready to defend their homes and families. Most had not seen the almost instant destruction of her husband's ship, and were frantically speculating where the Tuthna had gone.

"Mother, what should we do?" Rebekah asked, tugging at her hand again. The ship was almost to the docks now, but her mother still didn't move. Rebekah let go of her hand and ran over to her little brother, who was still playing with his wooden spinning top. She picked it up, and hauled him to his feet.

"Hey! Leave that alone Bekah, it's not yours," he said, annoyed at her taking his toy from him.

"Come on Kayden, we have to go and hide like father taught us," she said dragging him away by his hand. She had no idea if her father was actually still alive or not, but she knew if anyone could survive the sinking of a ship, he could, and for now that would have to be enough. She was just happy that Kayden had not witnessed the attack on the ship himself. She headed straight for the large barn where she usually hid whenever she and Kayden played hide and seek, but Kayden pulled her back.

"No. Not in there Bekah. It's too easy to find us. I *always* find you in there. I know a better hiding place," he said dragging his sister in the opposite direction. Rebekah caught just a glimpse of the enemy landing on the docks before Kayden pulled her behind the small temple building.

"Where are we going Kayden?" Rebekah asked in a whisper, scared that the men on the dock might hear her somehow.

"In here Bekah. They'll never find us in here," he said, freezing in mid-stride. "Bekah ... who are we playing hide and seek with?"

"I'll tell you later, quick, show me where to hide before they find us," she said, looking over her shoulder nervously. Kayden's face lit up with a huge grin, obviously pleased he knew something his big sister didn't—even if it was only his secret hiding place. `I'll have to find a new secret hiding place that Bekah doesn't know about later if I'm to win our next game of hide and seek. But at least I'll win this one first,` he thought to himself, as he bent down to remove the grate cover below the temple window.

"Quick climb in Bekah," he said, waving his arms frantically at the open grate. Rebekah would never climb into such a dark foreboding place usually, but given her choices she didn't complain, and quickly climbed inside. Kayden swiftly followed her in and pulled the grate back over their heads. At first Rebekah thought it was some kind of drainage system, but it wasn't. It was actually a storage room for firewood. The grate cover didn't seal the room as she feared it might, instead it was raised a few inches around its base to stop water entering the room when it rained, and had air gaps all the way around the edge to encourage the wood to dry. Once her eyes had adjusted to the darkness, she found there was still just enough light entering the underground room to make out its contents; piles of stacked firewood.

Kayden had obviously been here on a regular basis, because he had built himself a perfect height platform to stand on so he could see through the multitude of air gaps around the grate. `No doubt he'd spent many times laughing at her from inside here while she desperately tried to find his secret hiding spot in the past,` she thought to herself. She saw him slide a catch at each side of the grate into place, locking it to the outside world. `Even if she had found his secret hiding place, she still wouldn't have been able to find him,` she thought to herself, also finding a new respect for her little brother's ingenuity. She wondered why the grate would be lockable from the inside, but it didn't take her long to spot a doorway at the back of the room in the heavy shadows. She surmised it would lead up into the temple above somehow.

"So, who we hiding from Bekah?" Kayden asked peering out of the tiny air vents to the world beyond. She was about to answer him when the screams started. She could hear explosions coming from the direction of the docks, and voices raised in terror. She climbed up next to Kayden and put her eye next to one of the air vent holes, just in time to see a poor soul stumble into their alley blazing like a human torch, only to fall face first into the dirt and not move again. Kayden gasped at the sight.

"Get down ... now!" Rebekah said sternly to her small brother, helping him off the pile of wood to the floor below, not wanting him to see the horrible things happening outside in the streets above. Kayden started to cry, calling for his mother between sobs. Rebekah climbed down and went to comfort him, putting her arm around him and hugging him tight. "Shush ... It's going to be alright, I promise."

"What's happening Bekah?" he asked, sobbing into her dress.

"I don't know, Kayden. But we *have* to stay quiet and hide here until mother or father comes for us, do you understand Kay?" He nodded his head, but didn't look up.

"It's not really a game is it Bekah?" he asked in a whisper.

"No. No, it's not a game Kayden," Rebekah replied, kissing his head and hugging him close to her.

Chapter Thirty

Lusam woke to find Neala's smiling face very close to his own. She kissed him gently on the forehead, then said in a sultry voice, "Good morning sleepy-head." Memories of the previous night—fresh in Lusam's memory—surfaced once more, and he began to smile back at her.

"Good morning to you, too," he said in a whisper, then kissed her gently on her soft lips. Her smile widened even further, as she propped herself up on one elbow facing him, seemingly studying his face in minute detail. Lusam felt more than a little self-conscious at the close scrutiny his face was suddenly receiving from Neala, and was about to ask exactly what she was looking at, when she broke the silence.

"I think we better get up. I don't know what time it is, but I've already heard the others moving around for quite some time now."

"You sure we can't just stay here all day?" Lusam asked playfully, raising his eyebrows. Neala gave him a gentle nudge on his arm, and then faked outrage at his suggestive mannerisms, before climbing out of bed and getting dressed in full view of him. Once she had finished dressing, she turned to find Lusam staring at her, and his face flushed brightly as their eyes met. She smiled at him, knowing full well what he had just been thinking.

"Come on. Get out of bed then, we're going to be late," Neala said, standing next to the door and looking back towards Lusam. But he didn't move. Neala raised one eyebrow at Lusam and smiled, knowing full well he wasn't going to get out of bed while she was still in the room watching him. Smiling to herself, she opened the door and left him in private to get dressed alone, much to Lusam's relief, she guessed.

Renn and Alexia were both in the main chamber, fully packed and ready to leave when Neala met up with them.

"Finally, you're out of bed. We thought we might have to break down your door and dowse you both with cold water," Alexia said, grinning at Neala and making her blush. "Where *is* lover-boy, anyway? I hope you haven't tired him out too much, we have a long way to travel today." Neala scowled at Alexia, and was trying to come up with a witty reply, when Lusam arrived.

"Sorry I'm late. I was … " Lusam started to say, but Alexia interrupted him.

"Yes—we know," she said winking at him, then turned and walked towards the stairs that led to the shop above without another word. Lusam's face turned bright red as he stood there with his mouth open, wondering exactly what had been said in the short time he'd been absent. Renn and Neala both burst out laughing at the expression on Lusam's face, and quickly followed Alexia to the stairs, leaving Lusam behind to his own thoughts.

Lusam soon caught up with the others, and together they entered the darkened shop and headed for the door. They had all said their goodbyes to Mr Daffer and Lucy the night before at dinner, and had decided to leave the bookshop before first light, hopefully avoiding any potential customers, as well as the crowds out in the streets of Helveel. Neala *had* pointed out however, that if there *were* any Empire agents already on the lookout for them in the city, it would be far easier to spot them with fewer people out and about on the streets. But they all agreed, the benefits outweighed the risks in favour of setting off before first light.

Lusam took the key from the hook on the wall and unlocked the door. He quietly opened the door and peered out, scanning not only the streets, but also the rooftops for any signs of auras—but saw none. They all exited into the street outside and Lusam relocked the door, hiding the key within a large hanging basket, as he had agreed to do the previous night with Mr Daffer.

"OK lad, we'll meet you both a couple of miles down the north road, once you've recovered our horses and supplies. Safe travels," Renn whispered. Lusam and Alexia both nodded their heads.

"Are you sure I can't go with Lusam," Neala whispered anxiously.

"We've already discussed this. The Empire agents already know your description Neala. If you were spotted with Lusam in Helveel again, we might end up having to run for our lives all the way to Fairport. And *I*, for one, don't relish the thought of doing that again," Renn whispered.

"Don't worry Neala, I'll take care of Alexia," Lusam whispered, trying to ease her worries.

"It's *not* Alexia I'm worried about," Neala replied, giving her friend an accusatory look. Alexia grinned at Neala, knowing exactly what she meant.

"Don't worry Neala, I'll take good care of him for you," Alexia teased her.

"Yes ... that's what I *am* worried about," Neala whispered through clenched teeth. Then she turned and started walking towards the north gate with Renn, glancing back over her shoulder only once before they disappeared around the corner.

Lusam was curious as to what Neala had been referring. No doubt something from their past, he guessed. He made a mental note to ask Alexia or Neala about it later, after they were safely away from Helveel.

"Come on, let's go before we're seen by someone. Stay in the shadows, and follow me," Alexia whispered. She and Neala had scouted the best route to the east gate the evening before, making sure Alexia was familiar with the street layout. Alexia was fully aware that Lusam knew the city very well himself, but he wasn't used to sneaking around in the shadows like Alexia. Whereas Lusam would undoubtedly have taken the most direct route to the east gate, Alexia on the other hand, had looked for a route that would give them the greatest amount of shadows to hide within, and as few overlooking windows as possible.

As expected, when they approached the eastern gate they noticed two city guards on duty outside—one at each side. They had all discussed this potential problem the previous evening, but Lusam had been confident he could deal with them easily enough—even though he hadn't explained exactly how he would do it. Renn and Neala however, were planning to exit the city through an underground passage that led from Renn's *secret* temple in the northern part of town.

Alexia and Lusam crept as close to the gate as they could, without leaving the dark shadows of the looming buildings overhead. Lusam could just about make out Alexia's face in the dark, and saw her silently mouth the words, *"Now what?"*

Lusam held up his hand, indicating for her to remain where she was, and she nodded her understanding. His plan had been to use the same draining spell he had used on Shiva's men in Stelgad—to quickly render them unconscious —but he'd been hoping to find only one guard on duty, or if there were two guards, for them to be at least standing closer together. Instead they were both sitting on a wooden stool, one at each side of the gate: a gate that was wide enough to allow two horse-drawn carts to pass each other with ease, and probably foot traffic all at the same time. There was no way he could reach both guards at the same time. Then he suddenly realised, he didn't need to. What he had learned from the second Guardian book sprang back into his mind. *Everything was connected by* magic. That meant both the guards, and Lusam were already in contact with each other, he just needed to reach for them. The earth connected them, even the air connected them. For no other reason than preferring to make contact with something solid, Lusam chose to bend down and touch the earth by his feet. Using his mage-sight to guide him, he sent out small tendrils of magic through the earth in the direction of the guards. He couldn't believe how much life there was in the dirt under his feet. Each minute living creature acting as a tiny conduit for his magic. At first he thought he wouldn't be able to reach the guards from where he was. It seemed the further away he probed, the harder it was to maintain the connection through all of the various living, and non living matter between him and his intended targets. It took him a great deal longer than he had anticipated to locate the larger reservoirs of magic held by the two city guards. But when he finally did, he drained all but a small amount of that magic in the blink of an eye, and the two guards slumped in their chairs, unconscious.

Silently, Alexia appeared by his side, startling him a little as she did so.

"Did you kill them both?" Alexia whispered, sounding a little more concerned than Lusam would have expected her to be, as she scanned all around them for possible witnesses, or other potential threats.

"No, I didn't," Lusam whispered back. "But they're both going to wake up with a serious headache in a few hour's time," he added, smiling. "We had better go, just in case anyone detected my use of magic. They shouldn't have, but it's better to be safe than sorry."

"OK. We need to cross that bridge and get to the treeline as quickly as possible. Follow me, I'll try to keep us hidden as best I can," Alexia whispered, then turned and briskly exited the gate without waiting for a reply. Lusam followed close behind her.

Alexia followed the bank of the river in the direction of the forest, keeping them both from creating any kind of silhouette that might be seen from within Helveel. Lusam knew this area well, having walked it many times with Neala while they collected gold from its sediment a few months earlier. He knew there was a huge fallen tree not far ahead of them, between the river and the forest beyond. He and Neala had used the tree to sit on and eat their picnics several times in the past, but he had a different use in mind for it today. Lusam caught up with Alexia and pointed in the direction of the fallen tree. It was just about visible; a slightly darker shadow in the darkness ahead. Neala nodded, and changed direction slightly towards the fallen tree, moving away from the river bank and towards the forest beyond.

When they reached the fallen tree they both stopped running and crouched down behind it for cover.

"Alexia, stay hidden behind the tree for now please. I'm going to check and see if anyone saw us leaving Helveel. I'll hide my aura so they won't see me looking," Lusam whispered.

"No problem," Alexia replied, making herself as comfortable as possible next to the fallen tree. Lusam completely shuttered his aura, then slowly moved to a vantage point where he could clearly see most of Helveel. He scanned all the rooftops, and the ground between them and the city, but he saw nothing. He could see the—still unconscious—guards at the gate, but nothing else with an aura moved within the city that he could see.

"I think we're in the clear," he said, relieved that they weren't likely to be chased again anytime soon.

"That's good news. Let's hope Renn and Neala had the same kind of luck," Alexia replied.

"Talking of Neala ... what was that all about between you two outside the book shop?" Lusam asked, guessing now was as good a time as any to discover what was going on between those two.

"Oh, it's a long story. Something that happened a long time ago in Stelgad. Something Neala doesn't seem to have forgiven, or forgotten about, by the sounds of it," Alexia replied quietly, chuckling to herself.

"I'm guessing Neala doesn't find it quite as amusing as you do," Lusam whispered, imagining all kinds of possibilities. Alexia debated with herself whether she should tell Lusam the full story or not, and finally decided she would, as she was sure Neala would tell him her version of events later anyway.

"It was about two years ago when it happened. The guild we were part of—the Crows` guild—merged with a smaller guild from Stelgad. We gained their lands and properties, and most of their members as part of the deal. It was one of those new members that caused the issue between us. His name was Swift. He was a good looking guy, and he knew it. All the girls were clamouring after him, including Neala and me. He had shown an interest in Neala during the first few days, so I backed off and left them to it.

"A few days later it was my turn on the rotor for lookout duty, so I went to the roof like always, and found Swift already there. Unfortunately, *he* too was on lookout that night. We got talking—as you do—and he made it out that he wasn't really interested in Neala, and told me he had only spoken to her so he could be near me. Even though I was young, I wasn't stupid enough to fall for his lies ... except I did. Or more precisely, I did momentarily, but that was enough. He leant in to kiss me, and for a heartbeat I kissed him back. The only problem was, Neala chose that exact moment to come visit me on lookout duty. I pushed him away, but it was too late, she had already seen us. I was devastated. All he did was laugh about it.

"I couldn't even leave my station to go after Neala and explain. If I had, and been discovered, I would have faced severe punishment for abandoning my lookout duties. So there I stayed until morning, wondering what was going through my best friend's mind downstairs, while I spent the night on the roof with her new man. Needless to say, she didn't speak to me for weeks afterwards, but it took Swift less than a day to find his next love interest within the guild, ignoring both Neala and me as if we had never mattered. He was just scum as far as I was concerned."

"Oh, I see," Lusam said, feeling strangely jealous of a guy he had never met, and likely never would, as he was probably killed along with all the other Crows` guild members the night they were attacked.

"Yes, so now you know. That's why she never wants to leave me alone with you, she thinks I might try to steal you away from her," Alexia said with a sad smile.

"I'll talk with her about it later, if you like," Lusam offered.

"Thanks, but it's all in the past as far as I'm concerned. We've already spoken about it, and we both agreed to move on and put it behind us, a long time ago. I know she's only brought it up again because she cares so much about you, and I understand that, so there's no harm done, honestly," Alexia replied grinning at him. "Besides, it's far too much fun teasing her about it to get upset."

Lusam shook his head to himself in the darkness. "Talking of `moving on`, maybe we should get going, before Neala comes looking for *us*."

"That's probably a good idea," Alexia replied standing up. "Let's go then, lover-boy. We wouldn't want to keep you two apart for any longer than necessary, would we?"

"Hey, behave. Or I might have to tell her you tried to kiss me," Lusam replied jokingly.

"You wouldn't dare," Alexia gasped.

"No. You're right, I wouldn't," Lusam replied chuckling quietly to himself.

***

Renn led Neala to a very inconspicuous looking building in the northern part of Helveel, situated between what looked like a cobbler's shop and a dress shop. He walked up to the door and Neala fully expected him to knock, but instead he pushed aside a small plaque hanging next to the door revealing a small rope. He took hold of the rope and tugged on it three times, before replacing the plaque. Neala thought she had heard a distant bell ring inside the building when he tugged the rope, but she wasn't sure. Several minutes later, and still, no one had answered the door.

"I don't think anyone is home," Neala whispered.

"Don't worry, they know we're here lass," Renn replied quietly. After another couple of minutes a small spyhole slid open in the door.

"Who goes there?" a voice enquired from behind the door. Renn didn't reply, he simply removed his sigil of Aysha and presented it to the spyhole. The spyhole snapped shut, and several locks and bolts could be heard being unfastened at the other side of the door. The door swung inwards to reveal an elderly tall skinny man dressed in his nightshirt, holding a lantern—not what Neala had been expecting at all. Renn stepped inside, and Neala followed him in, the large heavy door closing behind them with a dull thud. The man refastened all the locks and bolts on the door quickly, then checked through the spyhole one last time.

"About time Renn!" the tall man said, turning and walking away down the hall, completely ignoring Neala.

"It's good to see you again, too, Arturo," Renn said sarcastically.

"Bah!" he spat, flailing his arm as he said it.

"Don't worry, he's always like that. That's why he got assigned this post—because of his wonderful social skills," Renn whispered, grinning at Neala.

"I heard that! And I *actually* requested this assignment ya big oaf! I thought I'd get some peace and quite here, seeing as very few people were supposed to know about this place. But it seems some of the local paladins never leave me alone." Arturo griped.

"Twice in the last two years is hardly pestering you," Renn said defensively.

"It is when both visits are in the last twenty four hours!" Arturo spat back at him.

"I'll try leaving a few more years between visits next time, I guess," Renn replied, shaking his head and looking apologetically towards Neala.

"You do that! But for now, you can see yourselves to the tunnels, I'm off back to bed." And without even glancing back, he was gone.

"Pleasant chap," Neala said under her breath.

"Hmm, he seems to get worse with age. Come on lass, let's get moving. I've been told the tunnels are fairly tight, so the going is slow in places. It surfaces about a half-mile from Helveel in a copse of trees, just off the northern road. Arturo said the tunnel might be partially flooded in parts, due to the heavy rain they've had recently. I guess we'll have to keep our fingers crossed it's not too bad," Renn said.

"Oh, wonderful, I finally get to wear some clean clothes, and now we're going to be crawling through a mud filled tunnel," she said, shaking her head. Renn chuckled, and they both headed for the basement where Renn had been shown the tunnel entrance the previous day.

Arturo had left several candles burning in the basement for them, together with two oil filled lanterns. Renn lit both lanterns using one of the candles, then opened the hatch in the floor to reveal a very tight looking opening to the tunnel. He handed both of the lanterns to Neala, then said, "I'll climb down the ladder first, then you can pass me both lanterns down before you come down."

Neala nodded and took the two lit lanterns from him, then watched as he squeezed through the tight opening and disappeared into the dark tunnel below. She moved to the edge of the opening and lowered one of the lanterns into the hole. She could see Renn had reached the bottom of the ladder several feet below, and lowered the first lantern down to him. After passing him the second lantern, she climbed down the ladder, closing the hatch behind her.

Thankfully, the tunnel was larger inside than the opening had suggested. Although they still had to walk in single file, at least Neala didn't have to hunch over to walk, unlike Renn. The tunnel seemed to stretch on for a very long way, and although it smelt of damp, luckily there were little more than muddy patches here and there on their route through. When they finally reached the far end of the tunnel, they came to another ladder leading up.

"Wait here, I'll go check above for any signs of people. Turn off the lanterns and leave them at the bottom of the ladder before you come up please. Arturo said he would collect them later," Renn said, handing his lantern to Neala and starting to climb the ladder.

"No problem," Neala replied, extinguishing one of the lanterns and placing it on the ground. Renn reached the top of the ladder and listened for any movement or voices above. He didn't expect to hear any, as he had been assured the exit of the tunnel was well away from the road, and well secluded from the view of any passers-by. He listened intently for a couple of minutes, before pushing open the hatch to reveal a small clearing surrounded by dense trees. He climbed out of the hole, and remained in a crouching position, while peering between the tree trunks for any signs of movement, but saw nothing. He signalled for Neala to come up the ladder, and began to orientate himself as to which direction the road lay. The sun was just cresting the horizon to the east, and he guessed the road would be found somewhere to the south of where they were.

"Well at least we didn't have to go swimming to get through the tunnel," Neala said, brushing off what little dirt her clothing had acquired during their subterranean travels. Renn chuckled and followed her example, patting down his clothing and clearing his hair of all the cobwebs he'd encountered leading them through the tunnel. Renn pulled the cover back over the tunnel entrance, and replaced the camouflage he had disturbed, once more rendering the tunnel entrance all but invisible to anyone who might happen to pass by.

"I think the road should be that way," Renn said, indicating to the south with a nod of his head. "I think we should find the road first, then stay hidden within the trees until we see Lusam and Alexia approaching."

"Sounds good to me. Hopefully they won't be too far behind us," Neala replied, trying to rid her mind of all the unwanted thoughts she'd been having ever since leaving Helveel, about Lusam and Alexia.

***

Alexia guided Lusam to where she and Neala had left their supplies and picketed the horses the previous day. Thankfully all was untouched, and the horses still had plenty of grass left to eat. They quickly saddled the horses and collected their supplies, then headed back towards the river. There was a bridge that spanned the river about a mile downstream, which they planned to use to get back over the other side. Then they would head directly north until they intercepted the northern road. It was only referred to as the northern road because it exited Helveel via the north gate, but the road soon swung around to the east, and followed that direction all the way to the coast. They stayed well within the treeline until Helveel disappeared from view, before moving out into the more open space of the riverbank, making the travelling much easier, as they could now ride the horses, instead of just leading them.

It was less than an hour before they came across the bridge that spanned the river. The sun was beginning to rise over the hills to the east, lighting up a clear sky that promised a comfortable dry day ahead for them. Lusam hadn't mentioned it to anyone, but secretly he was excited to be going to Fairport. He had never even seen the ocean, let alone travelled aboard a ship before.

After crossing the bridge they headed due north until they intercepted the road. They had discussed their travel plans in details the previous evening, and knew that Renn and Neala would be waiting for them about a half-mile back towards Helveel. It had been suggested that Renn and Neala met them nearer the bridge, but there was no cover to hide there while they waited for Lusam and Alexia to arrive. Also, they all felt it would be unlikely to arouse suspicions if Lusam and Alexia *were* seen heading towards Helveel from the east, so the current plan was agreed by all.

Lusam and Alexia didn't even travel half the expected distance before they saw Renn and Neala emerge from the treeline up ahead and wave in their direction. Lusam's heart leapt at the sight of Neala, and he couldn't help himself when a huge grin spread across his face. It wasn't long before he could make out Neala's equally wide grin, and soon they were hugging each other tightly, as if they had been separated for months.

"Eww, put him down, will you …" Alexia said smiling, with fake disgust in her voice.

Neala had felt guilty about not trusting her best friend

the way she had. She knew it was only the fact that she loved Lusam so much, and couldn't bear to lose him that had made her even think that way. What had happened in Stelgad had been put behind them both a long time ago, and after Alexia had explained what had happened, Neala had forgiven her completely. So to bring it back up now was unfair of Neala, and she knew it. She looked over Lusam's shoulder at her friend sitting on her horse, and silently mouthed the word, *"Sorry."* Alexia winked back at her, then smiled broadly.

"I suggest we put some distance between us and Helveel as quickly as we can. The sun is just about up, and the road is bound to get a lot busier soon," Renn said, scanning the road towards Helveel for any traffic.

"How many days do you think it will take for us to reach Fairport?" Lusam asked, finally releasing Neala and mounting his horse again.

"Normally it would take nine or ten days lad, but I'm hoping we can do it in less than a week. We'll no doubt need to exchange our horses a couple of times on the way, due to the pace we'll be setting. So, I hope when you said you had plenty of gold, you weren't exaggerating too much," Renn replied.

"Don't worry, we'll have plenty of money, I'm sure," Lusam said. "I forgot to ask, did you gain any news from the temple last night?"

"No. Nothing we didn't already know I'm afraid, lad. Arturo, the temple priest said he was waiting for several letters that hadn't arrived yet, but he isn't exactly a chatty man," Renn replied dryly.

"No kidding," Neala laughed.

"There are simply far too many rumours and stories circulating for there not to be something wrong in the capital. I feel it's imperative that we reach Lamuria as fast as possible. Our entire country's survival might very well depend on it, and ultimately, on *you* lad." Lusam didn't respond, but he felt confident he could deal with almost any situation since reading the second Guardian book, he only hoped his confidence wasn't misplaced.

Chapter Thirty-One

The weather remained fair for the next six days, and as Renn had predicted, they had been forced to swap their horses twice already for fresher animals in the villages they had passed through. Only one night were they forced to sleep outside under the stars, and even then they had managed to buy fresh food from a village they had passed through earlier that day. The Inns they had stayed at were simple abodes, with only basic food and ale available to the weary travellers, and a pallet to sleep on come nightfall.

At each successive Inn—as they grew closer to Fairport—the stories regarding the imminent fall of Lamuria grew more prevalent, and more gruesome. Some of the patrons told wild stories of undead creatures wandering the countryside, killing whole families in their sleep, and laying waste to any livestock they encountered. Others told of huge armies amassing outside the capital, ready to crush Lamuria and seize the High Temple for the Empire. Most disturbing of all however, were the stories relating to the complete destruction of Lamuria that had already occurred. It was simply impossible to know which, if any, of the stories were actually true, or not. The only way they would know for sure, was to travel to Lamuria themselves, and find out how bad the situation really was there.

According to Renn, they were now only about ten miles away from Fairport, so they decided to leave the Inn a couple of hours before daybreak to continue their journey. If they could arrive in Fairport early enough, maybe they could book passage on a ship leaving that day, instead of wasting another day in port.

The weather wasn't as kind to them on the final day, and those last ten miles felt more like fifty. The rain was more ice than water, and with the easterly wind, it drove it hard into their faces for most of the way there. Lusam was very tempted to create a shield around them, to keep them warm and dry, but doing so would have been foolish under the circumstances, so he endured the unpleasant weather without complaint.

The first glimpse they got of Fairport, was from the top of the hill overlooking the bay. It was a reasonably sized town, with many large warehouses situated near the docks, and numerous houses nestled towards the base of the cliffs. It was apparent by the many people moving around on the dockside below, that an early start to the working day was not uncommon here. Lusam counted five large ships being loaded and unloaded at the dockside, as well as three more at anchor a little further offshore. The road that led to the town below took a long meandering route down the hillside, making the journey up, or down the road as easy as possible for anyone hauling goods in or out of the harbour area. What amazed Lusam the most however, was the sheer size or the ocean. It stretched as far as he could see to the horizon, both to the north and south. He wondered just how big it actually was, but he didn't want to ask, in case it made him look stupid in front of Neala, or the others.

Renn continued down the gently sloping road towards the docks without pause, and the others followed close behind. Once they reached the bottom they dismounted from their horses, and tied them to a sturdy looking fence.

"Best you three wait here and watch our stuff, while I go see if I can find Byron, the harbour master. Fairport is well know for having more than its fair share of vagabonds and thieves. They wouldn't think twice about helping themselves to any of our unattended items. Hopefully we can book passage south on one of these ships," Renn said, nodding towards the docked vessels. Lusam had noticed several scruffy looking men hanging around the warehouses, but they seemed more interested with the contents of the buildings, than their arrival in Fairport—for the moment at least.

"No problem, we'll watch our supplies," Lusam replied, watching as one of the scruffy looking men was chased away from a warehouse opposite them by a guard of some kind. Renn nodded, then set off walking towards one of the many buildings lining the dockside. He knew exactly where he might find Byron, and was proved right moments later when he knocked at the harbour master's office door, and was met with Byron's voice from the other side.

"Come in," he yelled from within the office. Renn opened the door and stepped inside to find Byron sitting behind his desk, looking intently at what appeared to be some ship manifest papers. Renn closed the door behind himself, then moved further into the room.

"What, no hello for an old friend?" Renn said jokingly, as Byron finally looked up from his stack of paperwork.

"Renn, you old dog ... how are you? It's been a while," Byron said standing up and vigorously clasping arms with Renn.

"That it has, old friend," Renn replied smiling back at him.

"Finally given up the search and heading back to Lamuria, I guess," Byron said, returning to his seat and gesturing for Renn to take the seat opposite him.

"On the contrary, I found him, Byron," Renn replied, beaming a smile at his old friend.

"That's great news, Renn! But I fear it may already be too late for the lad's training to count for much, any more. It seems the Empire may have already made their move against us. We lost three ships just yesterday to Empire forces east of Lamuria, and several more are still overdue," Byron said with regret in his voice.

"That's indeed bad news, old friend. We heard various rumours on the way here at the villages we passed through, but to have it confirmed by you ... well, it just means our arrival at Lamuria is even more urgent now," Renn replied sadly.

"Please Renn, don't take this the wrong way, but how can one paladin and an untrained boy possibly change the outcome at Lamuria? You would just both be killed. I'm sorry, but you'll just have to face it—it's too late now."

Renn gave his friend a huge smile, shaking his head slowly. "Oh, Byron. The boy, Lusam, is *far* more powerful than the High Temple could possibly have imagined. I have seen him do things I once thought impossible. He *is*, without doubt, the most powerful mage we have, and the best chance of turning the tide of this war in our favour. If we can get him to Lamuria before it's truly too late, we stand a real chance of changing the outcome of this war."

Byron paused for a moment, considering Renn's words carefully, then replied, "If what you say is true, and I have no reason to doubt you old friend, then that is heartening news indeed. Unfortunately, we have no way to get you to Lamuria right now. Most of the Captains are choosing not to sail at all, but the few who are, refuse to travel further south than The Serpent Isles."

"Maybe we could convince one of the Captains to take us further south than The Serpent Isles. We have plenty of gold to buy passage with them, and I'm sure even the Empire's recent activities hasn't changed their appetite for gold," Renn replied.

Byron looked out of the window towards the docks, a thoughtful expression on his face, trying to work out which Captain was most likely to accept the risks involved. He wasn't sure any of them would risk their lives and ship for a purse of gold right now, but he thought he knew of one Captain who might be convinced, depending on the weight of that purse, of course.

"I think your best hope is probably Captain Waylon of the Pelorus. I hear his luck at the card table hasn't been so good of late. He's apparently run up quite a sizeable gambling debt with the local money lenders, and they're becoming eager to collect from what I hear. Word has it that they intend to take his ship if payment isn't forthcoming by the end of the month. I'd say he would have little to lose by taking you up on your offer right now, and, according to his ship's manifest papers I read before you arrived, it looks like he's heading to The Serpent Isles anyway," Byron said.

"Do you think we could arrange a meeting with this Captain Waylon? He sounds like a promising candidate to me," Renn asked hopefully.

"Yes, that shouldn't be a problem. He's scheduled to leave in about an hour at high tide, and he can't leave without his paperwork from me anyway. But, before I introduce you to Captain Waylon, maybe you should introduce me to this remarkable young lad of yours, what did you call him … Lusam?" Byron replied, motioning towards the door behind Renn.

"Of course," Renn replied, feeling a swelling sense of pride in Lusam—one that was usually reserved for the relationship between fathers and sons he guessed, smiling and gently shaking his head to himself.

Outside Renn and Byron approached the others still watching over their horses and supplies. Byron caught Renn's eye and looked questioningly towards Neala and Alexia, but said nothing.

Renn Chuckled and said, "It's a long story, but needless to say we will need passage for four people and our horses."

"People are one thing, but the horses won't be travelling on the Pelorus, even if Captain Waylon agrees to your offer. There's just nowhere to keep the horses on the ship. Unfortunately, the ship's hold is designed for grain storage, not livestock. I'm afraid you will have to dispose of your horses here, then procure new ones later on. There's a horse merchant in the north west corner of town, maybe he'll buy the animals from you," Byron said.

A moment later they met up with Lusam, Neala and Alexia, all of whom had been watching their approach silently.

"Everyone, this is Byron, the harbour master, and an old friend of mine. This is Lusam, Neala and Alexia," Renn said introducing each in turn to Byron.

Byron shook all their hands in greeting, then turned to Lusam and said, "I've been waiting a long time to meet you Lusam."

Lusam looked confused, and turned to Renn for any clarity he might be able to offer. Renn chuckled at the look on Lusam's face, then said, "Byron was sent here by the High Temple not long after you were born. He was our northern contact for passing on the updates between your *Hermingild* ... sorry, your grandmother, and the High Temple in Lamuria. When you vanished after Asima's death, Byron was the one who relayed any information about your suspected whereabouts to myself, and the High Temple. We needed someone we could trust with the reports, and once a year he made the journey himself to Lamuria—under the guise of visiting family members there—to deliver the reports to the High Temple. He was the one who first reported the potential activity of Empire agents in Helveel to the High Temple. The priest of the small temple in Helveel had inadvertently discovered the presence of an Empire agent, and reported it to Byron through one of his missives. Unfortunately, that was the last we ever heard from that priest, he just vanished, and that led to the appointment of the current charming fellow in residence there now. If Byron hadn't been here, it's highly unlikely any of us would be here today," Renn said, patting his old friend on the back.

"So, are you also a paladin?" Neala asked.

Byron looked at Renn, obviously concerned as to what information he could safely divulge in front of them. Renn nodded his head, indicating he could speak freely here.

"No Neala, I'm not a paladin. I work for the High Temple though. I suppose you could call me a sleeper agent. There are many of us in Afaraon in key positions around the country. Wherever the High Temple needs information or influence you will usually find us," Byron replied quietly enough for only them to hear.

"So, you've been stuck here all these years because of me?" Lusam said, feeling a little guilty that his simple existence could impact someone else's life so much. Byron laughed loudly.

"No, Lusam. I could have requested a different post at any time, but believe it or not, I actually like it here. In fact, unless I'm recalled to the High Temple, I intend to stay here as long as possible," he said, still chuckling to himself.

"That's good to know," Lusam replied, feeling a lot less guilty now.

"Renn, Maybe you and I should go and speak with Captain Waylon now. Time isn't on our side I'm afraid, and as the saying goes: *the tide waits for no man.* I'm sure he'll be wanting to leave dock in less than an hour, before the tide gets too low. If he agrees to your proposal you'll need time to sell your horses before boarding too." Renn nodded, but made no effort to leave.

"Lusam, I'm sorry to ask this lad, but just how much gold do you have? I'm afraid we might need a large amount of it to convince Captain Waylon to travel far enough south past The Serpent Isles to suit our purposes. Apparently, there's a lot of Empire ship activity in the area, and they've been losing ships at an alarming rate. I was hoping we'd only need to pay a reasonable price for passage, but it appears we will probably have to make him a vastly inflated offer to get him to agree to our destination," Renn said apologetically.

"I have about ninety gold coins left, I think," Lusam said, hoping it would now be enough.

"I have about the same, too," Neala offered.

"You do? Where in Aysha's name did you get *that* much money from?" Alexia gasped.

"Lusam makes it," Neala replied, laughing at her own insanely sounding statement.

"He what?" Alexia asked, her mouth hanging open at Neala's reply.

"I said, he makes it. He pulls the gold out of the river, and turns it into coins. It's really amazing to watch," Neala said, trying very hard not to burst out laughing at the look on Alexia's face, or Byron's for that matter.

Renn turned to Byron with a wide grin on his face, and

simply said, "Told you." Then nodded his head towards the docks, indicating they should go and talk with the Captain now. Byron alternated between looking at Lusam and Renn, then silently followed his friend towards the docks, leaving the two girls and Lusam to chat amongst themselves.

"Was that true?" Byron whispered as they walked away from the others.

"I've never seen him actually do that, but I'm certain it's well within his abilities to do it," Renn replied.

"Remind me when this is all over to plan my next fishing trip with him," Byron said chuckling to himself.

The two men soon arrived at the gangplank of the Pelorus. Men were frantically scurrying back and forth, loading and unloading cargo, and generally making ready for their next trip to sea. The Quartermaster was standing at the ship's rail, watching the progress of his men carefully. He noticed Byron and Renn approach the gangplank, and called down to them below, "If you're looking for the Captain, he just went to your office for the paperwork." Byron nodded to the man, and turned on his heels to head back to his office.

"That's probably a blessing," Byron said to himself, but Renn overheard him anyway.

"Why's that?" Renn asked curiously.

Byron looked at him a moment, then replied, "It's probably better discussing the prospect of travelling further south than The Serpent Isles away from the crew. If they're not aware of it until after you leave The Serpent Isles, there's far less chance of the crew becoming restless on the journey, and doing something foolish."

"You think they could mutiny over it?" Renn asked in surprise.

"It's certainly not beyond the realms of possibility. Generally speaking, the crews of ships are a suspicious lot at the best of times. Add in the current wild tales that are circulating amongst them, and who knows what they could do. I know one thing though—if I were the Captain, I'd sleep a lot better if the crew didn't know that I was going to be responsible for putting their lives in danger later in the voyage," Byron replied quietly.

"I see your point. If we do manage to come to an agreement with Captain Waylon, I think it's best we keep our true destination a secret from the crew for as long as possible," Renn said.

"I agree," Byron replied.

As they reached the harbour master's office building they met Captain Waylon on his way back out. He was a large muscular man in his middle years. His bald head was almost completely covered with tattoos, and his skin the colour of tanned hide. He was wearing a pair of calf-high black boots, leather trousers and a leather waistcoat. In fact, the only thing he was wearing that wasn't leather, was a shirt that at one time had probably been white, Renn thought.

"Good day Captain Waylon," Byron greeted him.

"Aye, it might be if I had my paperwork to leave 'ere," he replied coolly. Byron ignored his comment, and continued as if nothing had been said.

"This is my friend Renn. He has a business proposition he'd like to discuss with you, but I suggest we take the matter inside my office," Byron said, gesturing with his hand towards his office door. Captain Waylon sent an appraising look towards Renn but said nothing, instead he followed the two men back inside Byron's office. Byron took a seat behind his desk and sorted through the paperwork in front of him. After a moment he pulled several pieces of paper out of the pile and placed them in front of himself.

"According to this you're heading to The Serpent Isles Captain," Byron stated, then raised his eyes to meet Captain Waylon's.

"Aye, that's the plan, but if I don't weigh anchor soon, I won't be going anywhere today," he replied.

"Well, it just so happens my friend here wants to book passage south for himself and three travelling companions, and I thought, seeing as you're heading that way anyway, a slight extension to your journey might be mutually beneficial to both parties."

"That depends on what `slight extension` means, exactly," Captain Waylon said sounding a little dubious.

"I will make it plain Captain. Renn and his companions need to reach Lamuria ..." Byron began to say, but was cut short by the booming laughter of the Captain.

"You're crazy if you think I'm about to turn my ship into a ferry service and risk the waters south of The Serpent Isles," Captain Waylon said scowling at Byron.

"Tell me Captain, how many days does it take for the round trip to The Serpent Isles?" Byron asked.

"You know full well it's a ten day round trip including loading and unloading, so why bother asking?"

Byron smiled at the Captain, but said nothing for a few seconds, as if contemplating the best way to approach the man, then said, "Because Captain, from what I hear you have only until the end of the month to pay off your gambling debts, at which point, if you can't, the Pelorus will no longer be *your* ship. You know as well as I that you won't make it back in time to make your payment deadline, not to mention, looking at this manifest, I highly doubt the trip will cover what you owe anyway after paying your crew. What Renn is offering here, is a way to keep your ship, at least until you decide to play your next card game. It would, of course, be up to you when to tell your crew of the slight detour, but I'm sure a skilled Captain such as yourself could handle his crew adequately."

Captain Waylon remained silent after Byron had finished speaking, which Renn took as a good sign. `At least he hadn't reject the offer out of hand,` he thought to himself. After a long awkward silence the Captain finally spoke.

"One hundred gold, fifty now and the rest when we arrive," he said without preamble.

"Fifty gold," Byron countered. Another long silence ensued.

"I see you've done your homework harbour master, seen as you know my debt is fifty gold. Unfortunately, I'll also need to convince my crew that it's a good idea, and that my friend, will cost more gold."

"I understand Captain. My final offer is seventy gold pieces. Take it or leave it, the choice is yours. I'm sure one of the other Captains would consider the journey for such a sum if you don't want to take it," Byron said convincingly, but he knew it was highly unlikely any other Captain would consider the journey for any amount of gold right now. After yet more stony silence, Captain Waylon finally spoke.

"Half before we sail, the rest when we arrive at your destination. You sleep on the aft deck, provide your own food, and no fires whilst you're aboard. And under no circumstances must my crew learn of your intended destination until we leave The Serpent Isles, at which point I will address them regarding the matter myself. If any of my crew asks, you're travelling to The Serpent Isles, and only *after* we reached The Serpent Isles did you decide you wanted to travel further. Do you understand my terms?" Captain Waylon asked looking directly at Renn.

"I agree to your terms Captain. I will make my travelling companions aware of your terms also. And thank you Captain. You have no idea how important this trip is to all of us," Renn said, holding out his hand to Captain Waylon.

"I care little for your reasons for wanting to reach Lamuria, but I *will* see the colour of your gold before we depart, if you don't mind," Captain Waylon said taking Renn's hand.

"Of course Captain, but in the meantime I must speak with my travelling companions, and arrange sale of our horses and tack. I believe you are scheduled to depart just after the hour mark. If that's correct, I'll make sure we're aboard in plenty of time to avoid delaying you," Renn said.

"You do that," the Captain said, turning his attention to Byron once more. "Now, may I please have my documents so I can prepare my ship for departure?"

"Certainly, everything seems to be in order Captain," Byron said, handing the paperwork to Captain Waylon with a smile. Captain Waylon took the papers and placed them inside his leather waistcoat, nodded to Byron and Renn, then turned and left the office without another word. Byron waited until the Captain's footsteps faded into the distance before speaking.

"Well, that went better than I thought it might do," he said, breathing a sigh of relief.

"Yes, thanks for that. I've never been good at dealing with men like that. I tend to end up hitting them for some reason, and that rarely achieves the desired outcome I was hoping for," Renn said grinning at Byron.

"I bet it doesn't," Byron replied, chuckling to himself.

"Anyway, I'd better be off. We need to sell those horses and board the ship before Captain Waylon sets sail without us. It was good seeing you again, old friend," Renn said, slapping Byron on the shoulder as he stood up from behind his desk.

"You take care of yourself out there, Renn. Don't be playing the hero and getting yourself killed, that won't achieve anything. Besides, I need you to bring Lusam back safe next summer for that fishing trip, remember?" Byron said winking at Renn.

Renn winked back at Byron, and replied, "I'll try to bear that in mind."

"What ... the part about not getting yourself killed, or the fishing trip?" he asked, but Renn simply raised his hand in a goodbye gesture as he vanished through the doorway, shaking his head slightly to himself as he left.

Chapter Thirty-Two

It did not take them long to find the horse trader in Fairport. It took them even less time however, to realise they were never going to sell their horses for a fair price there. The man bordered on rude whilst inspecting their horses, suggesting he had never seen such a sorry bunch of animals, and that his own mother would be able to haul heavier payloads than they could. Renn suspected the man's attitude was a combination of two things: knowing they *needed* to sell the horses—because why else would anyone ride to a sea port and try to sell the animals?—and that probably, he only had a ready market for much heavier horses, to be used for haulage purposes in and around the general area of Fairport. Given their time restraints and lack of choice, Renn reluctantly accepted the man's offer of six gold pieces for the four horses, and they were soon on their way back towards the docks.

Renn had already brought the others up to date with their current departure plans, costs, and that they should not mention travelling further south than The Serpent Isles to any of the crew, or even discuss it amongst themselves whilst aboard ship. They all understood the risks of a rebellious crew, and what impact it could have on their journey, or even their lives. They had done a quick inventory of their supplies before selling their horses, and found that they should have enough food to last them the five-day sea journey. This was something Renn was thankful for, as it would have been unlikely that they would have had enough time to procure more supplies before boarding the Pelorus anyway.

It was obvious when they reached the dockside that the Pelorus was only waiting for them to board before setting sail. One of the crew was standing impatiently at the bottom of the gangplank, ready to quickly usher them onto the ship. Renn climbed the gangplank first—noting how much steeper it was now, compared with only an hour ago when the tide wasn't full yet—closely followed by Lusam, Neala and at the rear, Alexia.

"Welcome aboard the Pelorus," another crewman said as they reached the deck of the ship. "Please take your bags to the aft of the ship, and remain there. The main deck will be busy for a while, best if you stay out of the way, at least until we hit open water. Captain Waylon said he'll come talk with you once we're underway. Now, if you don't need anything else, I'll be getting back to my regular duties." He nodded towards the aft deck, then turned and headed the other way, leaving Renn and the others to find their own way. There was a narrow wooden staircase that led to the aft deck, and each took their turn to climb up it, and onto the bare deck above.

`At least the high ship's rail would offer some protection against the wind and sea spray,` Renn thought, knowing full well how uncomfortable an open sea passage could be if you were too exposed to the elements, especially if the weather turned bad.

"So, I guess this is home for the next five days," Alexia said, walking the width of the deck area in a few short strides.

"Well, I for one plan to catch up on some sleep," Lusam said, finding himself a corner to sit in, and making it as comfortable as possible.

"Not even *you* could sleep for five days," Neala said, teasing him.

"Maybe not. But I can try," Lusam replied, grinning at her. Neala rolled her eyes at him, then went to join Renn, who was leaning over the rail watching the men below prepare the ship for departure.

"Have you travelled on a ship before Renn?" Neala

asked curiously, still watching the men below.

"Yes, many times. Actually, I originally came to Helveel by ship. To this very port, as it happens. How about you?"

"Once. But it was a long time ago, and the ship was smaller as I remember," Neala replied, but didn't elaborate further.

After the anchor had been lifted, and the ropes cast off the dock, the men raised the jib sail, and the ship began to move slowly forward. The front of the ship slowly turned starboard towards the open sea, and more sails were unfurled, making the ship lurch forward with a slight jolt. Moments later the mainsail was set, and their speed increased noticeably, and so did the movement of the ship.

"Is it normally this bad?" asked Alexia looking slightly concerned, holding tight to the ship's rail, as the ship bucked over some waves, and crashed through others.

"No. It can get much worse than this in open water," Renn replied laughing. "Don't worry, you'll get used to it after a while."

"How in Aysha's name can you ever get used to the ground beneath your feet disappearing whenever it feels like it?" Alexia squealed, attempting to walk back to where she'd left her possessions, and failing miserably. Instead, she ended up crawling on her hands an knees across the deck, while everyone   else   found   it   most   amusing.

It was much longer than they had anticipated before Captain Waylon finally paid them a visit. The sun had almost reached its highest point in the sky, and the sea had calmed down a lot since the early morning, much to Alexia's relief. Lusam, thankfully, had the good sense to separate two lots of thirty-five gold pieces from his purse before boarding the ship, so when the Captain came to claim his initial payment, he didn't have to count it out in front of the crew. Captain Waylon showed them where the clean drinking water keg was kept, and where the ship's facilities were to be found, if you could even call them that. He also provided them with a large piece of old canvas and some rope. It looked like the remains of a larger torn sail that had been modified, with metal eyelets running along all four sides. The Captain assured them it would fit snugly over the aft deck should the weather take a turn for the worse, and if not, it would at least give them something more comfortable to sit on than the hard deck. But the best thing he gave them, was the news that the wind was currently very favourable to their trip, and they could shave as much as a whole day off their journey time if it continued the way it was. Renn silently thanked Aysha for their current good luck.

By the second day aboard ship they were all thoroughly bored. Even Lusam had reached his limits for dozing away the day. Their supplies and equipment had been well-packed away before boarding the ship, and it was well into the second day that Lusam remembered the monk's journal he had discovered in Mr Daffer's basement. It wasn't until he was searching through one of the packed bundles of equipment, he realised Renn had also packed away his blessed sword and shield. Lusam didn't expect any trouble on the ship—not until they had announced their true intended destination to the crew, anyway—but it seemed strange to think of Renn without them by his side.

Lusam saw Renn's face light up as he realised what Lusam was digging out of the bundle. He had been more than a little curious as to what more the journal contained when Lusam had read three of the entries to him back at *The Old Inkwell*.

"Don't worry, I'll let you know if I find anything interesting," Lusam promised Renn, smiling at the disappointed look on his face. Feeling slightly guilty, Lusam tried to change the subject.

"How come you packed your `things` away?" he asked, nodding towards the bundle that contained Renn's blessed sword and shield.

Renn seemed to check that none of the crew were in earshot, before moving closer to Lusam and answering quietly, "You'll find that sailors are a superstitious lot lad, if you spent enough time around them. Most worship Deas, due to the fact their lives and livelihoods are so entwined with the sea. I doubt any would openly object to my presence here, not until something went wrong during the trip, of course, and then the superstitious whisperings would no doubt be aimed my way."

"Sounds like your speaking from experience," Lusam replied quietly.

"Aye, lad, I am. And it's not something I'd wish to repeat anytime soon. If it hadn't been for the Captain's intervention on my behalf, I'm sure I'd have had a very long swim back to shore that day," Renn said in a serious voice. Lusam knew he was deadly serious about what he had just said, but he found it difficult keeping a straight face at the thought of Renn being tossed overboard, and forced to swim back to shore.

"I'll be at the front of the ship if you need me for anything," Lusam informed the others. He had discovered a small secluded spot at the bow of the ship the previous day. It was sheltered from the sea spray and wind, but it also allowed the sun to warm him there, unlike the aft deck, which was perpetually in shade from the ship's sails. Nobody had objected to him being there the previous day, so he decided it would make the most comfortable place to read some more of the journal. No one gave him more than a cursory glance as he made his way forward towards the bow of the ship. Once there, he settled down and began to search for any other interesting entries in the journal.

Judd II – Sixth Cycle – Second-day – Two

It has taken us several weeks to construct the room within Ula'ree to the exact specifications required by the High Temple. The excavation work went swiftly, but the room's interior took a great deal of magic to complete, draining many of our monks to near exhaustion in the process. The intricate spells we were taught at the High Temple have been woven into the walls, floor and ceiling of the room, creating what would be a powerful shield indeed, if we but had a power source capable of maintaining such a shield.

Judd II – Sixth Cycle – Fourth-day – Two

Our stonemasons completed the massive door to the room yesterday, and the magical locking mechanism was finished today. It has been designed to look like nothing more than a regular wall from the outside. For what reason, nobody truly knows. No one here speaks openly about their speculation as to what may ultimately be hidden within the room, but one thing is certain: whatever was placed inside, would become invisible to the entire world beyond should the spells be activated.

Judd II – Seventh Cycle – First-day – One

Today was indeed a joyous occasion for all of our brethren at Ula'ree, for the mighty Guardian Lucius has blessed us with his presence this day. Although the delegation who recently travelled to the High Temple, myself included, were made aware of a future Guardian visit, no one, however, expected one to arrive unannounced, and in the manner he did. Apparently Guardian Lucius has journeyed alone from Coldmont, disguised as a mere travelling merchant, and sleeping on the ground outside each night. One must only assume the importance of his mission dictates such a degrading method of travel for one so revered by everyone in Afaraon.

Judd II – Seventh Cycle – Second-day – One

The reason behind the great secrecy and the Guardian's visit has finally been revealed to all at Ula'ree. It has been ordained by Aysha herself, that our brethren at Ula'ree will become the keepers of one of five books created by the Guardians themselves. Each of the five remaining Guardians has constructed a book of great power, each with its own portion of the Guardian's immense knowledge contained within. Aysha has decreed that the Guardian line will end with the final five who still remain. Such power was never meant to be in the hands of mere mortals, and was only brought to pass by Aysha in direct response to the actions of her brother, The Dark God Aamon. Since Aamon is trapped in the Netherworld and no longer a threat to the world, Aysha is now duty-bound by an agreement with her brother Driden to *end the Guardian line. The immense knowledge of the Guardians will remain however, hidden, and in the form of these five books, in case the world ever has need of it again. We pray to Aysha that such a scenario will never come to pass.*

Our leader, and all future leaders of Ula'ree are to gain the knowledge of our new book, but not before they undertake an extended period of preparation and meditation, which is to be set out by the Guardian himself. By doing so, we will create a leader capable of defending the book against any mortal mage intent on stealing the book from Ula'ree, should it ever be discovered. We have been assured that anyone trying to read one of the Guardian's books without such preparation would surely die, and even with it in some cases. The Guardian has told us that only the strongest of mages have the capacity to absorb all the knowledge within a Guardian book, and we should therefore choose our future leaders very carefully. It is a great honour indeed, that Ula'ree has been chosen as one of the keepers of a Guardian book. One that all of our brethren feels a deep sense of pride over. I can not help wondering, if my old friend Isidro has found himself in a similar situation, and that was also the reason for his visit to the High Temple. It would be wonderful to share the news with my old friend, but alas, we have all been sworn to utter secrecy until we part this world.

Lusam sat bolt upright. The implications of what he had just read almost overwhelmed him. Had he just discovered the potential location of another one of the Guardian books? Or was this just the ramblings of an old man missing a childhood friend? Quickly, he thumbed back through the journal until he came to the entry where he had read the name of the location mentioned. *"Lohlaen, on The Pearl Island"* He said out loud to himself.

"Long ways from 'ere that is, boy," a voice said in a thick accent, making him jump. Lusam hadn't even noticed anyone approach whilst he read the book, but now found that there were three men on the foredeck with him, coiling ropes and stowing equipment. The man who had spoken was quite possibly the oldest man Lusam had ever seen. How he was still working aboard a ship, Lusam had no idea. His unruly white hair and silver stubble stood out in stark contrast to his dark wind-beaten skin, and his ice-blue eyes seemed almost ancient as he looked at Lusam. After his initial shock, Lusam began to realise what the old man had just said.

"Do you know where The Pearl Isle is, sir?" Lusam asked the old man.

"No, boy. But I knows where Lohlaen is, I do. And that be on Monmeriath Isle, boy."

"Could you tell me where that is please?" Lusam asked, excited that the old man might actually know its location. The man paused, turning his head slightly, as if he had heard something that caught his attention. Then after a moment he turned his vacant gaze back to Lusam.

"Yes," he said simply. Lusam waited for him to start, but he turned away and started coiling the ropes again, as if forgetting Lusam was even there. The other two men laughed loudly, startling Lusam again.

"Don't put paid to anything old Lamar tells you boy, he's a few sails short of a full set o' rigging, that one," one of the men said loudly, making his colleague burst into laughter again. Lamar didn't seem to notice, or care that he was the butt of their jokes, and just kept coiling the rope onto the deck.

"Cap'ain only keeps him aboard as a good luck charm, he does. Says the twice he left him behind on shore for not pulling his weight, terrible luck they 'ad all trip. Won't take the chance 'nay more. So 'ere he is, as old as the sea 'erself, and as useless as a two-pound anchor," the second man said, nodding towards Lamar, and eliciting even more laughter from the first man.

Lusam smiled at the men—even though he didn't find the treatment of their fellow crewman amusing at all—then pretended to go back to reading his journal. He kept glancing at the old man, hoping the spark might return to his old eyes and they could continue their conversation, but he seemed different now somehow; as if part of his mind had shut down, and only left him with enough capacity to perform his basic tasks. It wasn't long before the two younger men finished what they were doing and left the foredeck, leaving Lusam and the old man alone at the front of the ship.

Lusam tried rousing his attention by speaking aloud the place names again, but this time there was no reaction from the old man. Lusam wondered if the old man was simply crazy, or if he was suffering from some kind of age-related problem. `He must have been a capable sailor at some point in his life, or why else would he be aboard a ship?` Lusam thought to himself. He wondered if he could search the mind of the old man for the information himself, then immediately felt guilty about even thinking about it. But, surely if the old man truly knew the location of where one of the Guardian books were possibly hidden, it would be an acceptable thing to do. He doubted the old man would even realise, given his current condition. Lusam decided to at least try, but soon realised that he had no idea how to go about it. When the Inquisitor had tried to gain access to his mind in Coldmont, he had done so along an almost hair-like strand of power he had created. Lusam had no knowledge of how to create that hair-like strand of power between himself and the old man. He had been able to send a pulse of magic along the connection, killing the Inquisitor, but he simply couldn't create a link of his own.

Lusam thought about it for a while, and eventually came to the conclusion that it was quite possible, that the ability to read minds was something Lord Zelroth had discovered by reading his own Guardian book at Irragin in Mount Nuxvar, and since, had taught the spell to his fellow agents. But whatever the reason was, Lusam knew that he could not do it himself, and that frustrated him no end. The only way that Lusam could enter the old man's mind, was to be in physical contact with him, and that would look very strange to the rest of the crew if he was seen doing it for any length of time. Eventually, Lusam decided he would approach the old man under the guise of offering to help him coil his ropes. That way if anyone was near enough to pay him any attention, it shouldn't look too strange—he hoped.

Lusam stood up from where he had been reading the journal, and approached the old man. Once he was close enough he placed his hand on the old man's shoulder, then asked, "Would you like any help with that, sir?" He didn't expect an answer, and he didn't get one either. The old man continued his slow methodical coiling of his rope, paying no attention to Lusam whatsoever. Lusam quickly delved into the old man's mind, but what he found left him in no doubt about his true mental state. His mind was a disjointed jumble of all his lifelong experiences. Lusam was unable to locate a single coherent thought within his mind. It was no wonder the old man was so confused and paid no attention to his fellow crew members' jibes. Disappointed that his potential discovery of another Guardian book had only been wishful thinking, he made his way back towards the others at the rear of the ship.

When Lusam reached the aft deck he found Renn and Alexia playing some kind of board game. Apparently one of the ship's crew had taken a liking to Alexia, and offered to lend her his game board and pieces. Neala was sitting quietly at the opposite end of the deck, watching them play, but obviously had something else on her mind, as she never even noticed Lusam's return. Lusam crossed the aft deck towards her, and was almost by her side before she noticed his approach.

"Oh, hi. Sorry, I didn't see you come back," Neala apologised.

"That's fine," Lusam replied smiling at her. "What's on your mind?" he asked sitting down next to her.

"How do you know there's something on my mind?" Neala asked a little defensively.

"Because you're sitting over here all alone, staring blankly at Renn and Alexia's board game with no real interest," Lusam replied. Neala didn't reply straight away, but she did take hold of Lusam's hand and gave it a small squeeze, which was nice, but it somehow made him feel nervous that she was about to tell him something he didn't want to hear.

After what felt like an awfully long time to Lusam, Neala turned to face him and blurted out, "I just feel useless!"

"What?" Lusam asked, confused. "What do you mean?"

"Do you remember when we were on the road to Coldmont, and we were attacked by those undead-agents?"

"I wish I didn't, but yes, I do. Why, what about it?" Lusam asked.

"Well, I was completely useless to you all back there. You have your magic, Renn has his blessed sword and shield, and even Alexia has her blessed bow now, but me ..." she said, trailing off her sentence. "I couldn't even defend myself against those things, let alone help defend you and the others against them. And the same thing applied to the Empire agents for that matter. I'm scared Lusam. I'm scared that I am going to get you killed, or one of the others. I'm just a liability to you all now, just someone extra for you or Renn to protect with your shields. And who knows what we will be up against when we reach Lamuria?" Neala said, sounding more and more upset with each word.

Lusam squeezed her hand gently, looked into her eyes and replied, "We're a team, remember? You will never be useless, or a liability to me Neala. Besides, I've already given some thought as to how I can magically upgrade your knives and make them more effective against those creatures."

"You have?" Neala replied, sitting up a little straighter and eagerly awaiting his reply.

"Yes. In fact, I'm quite sure they will be very effective against any reanimated undead creature once I'm done with them. However, there will be two slight limitations with them, ones that I can not do anything about I'm afraid."

"What do you mean by, *limitations?*"

"Well, here's what I came up with, so you can judge for yourself. After reading the book in Coldmont, I now have a much better understanding of how magical power is transmitted between objects, both animate and inanimate.

I've known for a long time that all things living hold a certain amount of magic within them, and even some inanimate objects do to a certain degree. When a person or creature dies, its magic is released back into the world, and if a mage dies, that release can be large enough to be felt many miles away by other magic users. So when an Empire agent reanimates a corpse, he or she has to imbue that corpse with a small amount of their own magic to give it life again. The amount of magic required is very small, which is why a single mage can reanimate multiple corpses without suffering any ill effects themselves.

"I still have no idea how the Empire agents control their minions from a distance, but I believe that should have no bearing on my plan to upgrade your knives. All I have to do is give your knives the ability to quickly absorb magic upon contact. That way, when you strike any undead creature, it should kill it almost instantly. Now, here come limitations. Firstly, because your knives are only made of steel, they will only be able to absorb a certain amount of magic before they become saturated, at which point they will become ineffective once more. I can easily drain the magic back out of them if you're close enough to me, but you'll just have to bear that in mind, and not get yourself cut off from me during a battle. The second limitation is that they won't be effective at all against any Empire agents. The amount of magic that the knives will be able to hold is relatively small, and if you even touch one of their shields, it will become saturated instantly without doing any damage at all to the Empire agent."

"How many undead could I kill before each knife becomes saturated?" Neala asked, sounding a lot more upbeat than she had only a few moments ago.

"I'm not sure. I would guess ten or twelve, but there is no way to know for sure until we test them in battle," Lusam replied.

"Well, that's a damn sight better than what I can do right now," Neala replied grinning at Lusam. Then she began to frown a little. "I do have one question, though."

"What's that?" Lusam asked.

"You just said all living creatures have magic within them, so what happens if I touch them?"

"Hmm, good point. I hadn't thought of that. But the answer is, you would saturate them with your own magical power reserves. They wouldn't be able to take enough from you to kill you, but you would render your own knives useless. Fortunately, the charms I've already placed on your knives keep them sharp and free from corrosion, so I guess you'll just have to avoid the temptation to take them out and play with them from now on," Lusam said smiling at her.

"Very funny ... but seriously, how can I even hold them without making them useless?" she asked looking a little confused.

"Oh, that's not a problem, I will only enchant the blade, not the whole knife. And as long as they don't make direct contact with your skin, they will be fine. Just remember, they need to penetrate the undead's clothing to be effective too," Lusam replied.

"Great! How long will it take you to do?" Neala asked enthusiastically.

"I can do it right now if you pass me them," Lusam replied, nodding towards her knives. Neala unbuckled her knife belt and handed it to Lusam, who took each knife out in turn, and placed them on the deck in front of him. He picked up the first knife and concentrated hard on the enchantment he wished to imbue the knife with. First he would have to rearrange the centre of the blade to act as a small storage device for the magical power, then imbue the actual blade with a magical power draining spell. He tried several variations—testing each one on himself—before finding the best combination of enchantments. He repeated the enchantments on the remaining knives, but not before Alexia noticed what he was doing, and came over to investigate.

Lusam found himself repeating much of the conversation he had just had with Neala, and unsurprisingly, discovered that he suddenly had a request to enchant a second pair of knives for Alexia. He didn't mind really, and when he thought about it, it made a lot of sense to also enchant Alexia's weapons. After all, bows were great for long range combat, but of little use at all in a close quarter hand-to-hand battle. Alexia thanked Lusam for her knives, then returned quietly to her game with Renn, leaving Lusam and Neala alone once more. Lusam was grateful for this, because Neala seemed a lot happier now, and snuggled into him as they sat in the corner of the deck together, holding hands, and whispering sweet nothings to each other.

Chapter Thirty-Three

It had been five days since the strange men in black robes had descended on Rebekah and Kayden's village. They, themselves hadn't stayed long, but the terror and devastation they had left behind was terrible. They had killed everyone they found that first day, and Rebekah and Kayden were forced to listen to their screams and pleas from within their hiding place, powerless to do anything about it.

Rebekah could not understand what the men were saying, even when they had been close enough to hear them clearly. They spoke in a strange language Rebekah had never heard before, and their laughter at her own villagers' suffering was almost more than she could bear. She witnessed the killing of dozens of her friends and kin through the small openings in the grate, unable, or unwilling to look away from their suffering as they died horrible deaths. The strange men left them all where they fell for what seemed like a very long time to Rebekah, some still burning, and others horribly mutilated from what they had done to them.

She witnessed incredible balls of flame appearing in the hands of the strange men, before they threw them with inhuman force towards her fellow villagers. From others came what looked like bolts of lightning, or some simply raised their arms, and Rebekah watched as people she knew began to sail through the sky, only to return to earth with a sickening crunch moments later. They rained down the same balls of fire upon many of the buildings in her village, and many were completely destroyed by the flames. If it had not been for the fact that they'd had a heavy rainstorm shortly after the men left her village, Rebekah felt sure that the village would have been completely destroyed by the spreading fire.

By far the strangest thing that Rebekah witnessed that first day, was the men in black robes making the dead people come back to life again—except, they were no longer alive somehow. The people she had once known, now dead in the streets, were twisted and burned beyond all recognition. But it didn't seem to matter to the strange men, they chanted some strange words over and over, and made them move again. Some had legs and arms so badly damaged that they could barely move, others were so burned that they no longer even looked like people.

After the strange men brought them back to life, they all went to the centre of the village and just stood there, not moving, like horribly twisted and burned statues. As time went by, more and more joined them, until it looked like her whole village had gathered in the same spot. Desperately, she scanned the forms for any sign of her mother, but it was almost impossible to recognise anyone amongst the crowd. She could not be sure, but she didn't think her mother was among them, and that gave her a small amount of hope that she had somehow escaped the men before the killing had begun.

It seemed that once the men had finished with their grisly task of making the dead bodies live again, they too gathered in the centre of the village. There was some kind of order given by one of the men, and soon after, they all began to leave the village in single file. At first, none of the villagers followed, but once the last man had joined the back of the line, the first of the villagers also set off in single file after them. Rebekah watched, praying to Deas that they would *all* leave, so she and Kayden could emerge from their hiding place and find their mother. But moments later, her hopes were dashed. All of the badly injured villagers were left behind, and after several more minutes, they began to

257

wander aimlessly up and down the streets, as if searching for something. That was two days ago.

The sun had gone down over an hour ago, and it was beginning to get cold again inside the room where Rebekah and Kayden were still hiding. During the day the sun warmed the room to a comfortable temperature, but by night the grate cover acted like a chimney, evacuating all the heat from within the small room quite rapidly through all of the holes. Rebekah knew that she desperately needed to leave the small wood-drying room to find food and water, but there had always been at least one of the undead villagers nearby most of the time. She tried to open the door they had found inside the room, but it was firmly bolted from the other side, so she watched the streets from her firewood platform, waiting for an opportunity to exit the grate unseen.

"I'm hungry and thirsty, Bekah," Kayden said weakly from the shadows. Neither of them had eaten anything much in the last two days, and now they were both very hungry indeed. Luckily, Rebekah had saved the remains of their lunch in her dress pocket from the first day on the docks, which they had managed to ration out over the last two days, but now they were completely out of food. It had also rained quite heavily during the first two days, and Rebekah had managed to peel off a length of bark from a piece of firewood and used it to collect water for them both. She had pushed the length of bark through one of the holes in the grate, and as the rain fell, it collected in the curved bark and ran back towards them, supplying them with an almost constant trickle of clean drinking water. Unfortunately, there had been no way to store the water, and now that the rain had stopped, they were also beginning to dehydrate too.

"I know you are Kayden, I'm sorry," Rebekah replied quietly, still watching for an opportunity to leave their hiding place unseen. "Kay, I need you to listen to me carefully. Do you understand?" Rebekah said in her most serious big sister voice. Kayden had already stood up and moved to where his big sister was peering down at him from her platform. She could just about make him out, as the moonlight trickled in through the multitude of gaps around the grate. He nodded his head, and waited for her to continue.

"I have to go outside..." she began to say, but was cut short by her little brother's whine of a reply.

"No Bekah! I don't want you to go. Those ... things will get you. Please don't go. Please," he pleaded with her, tears rolling down his cheeks.

"I have to Kay. We need food and water. We'll get sick if I don't go fetch us something soon," she replied, climbing down from the platform to hug her little brother.

"No Bekah, please don't go out there ... please. I won't say I'm hungry again, I promise," he said, sobbing between breaths. Rebekah hugged him tightly as he cried and sobbed into her dress.

"Kayden, listen to me," Rebekah said, kneeling down to his level and brushing away his tears with her thumbs. "I promise I'll be alright. I've been watching those things out there for a long time now, and they don't seem to move very fast. I saw one of farmer Tarquin's pigs loose in the street today, down by the village well. A few of those things tried to catch it, but it was way too fast for them. Their legs don't seem to work like they should. Maybe that's why those men left them behind, and only took the ones that weren't damaged."

"But, I'm scared Bekah. I don't want to be here all alone in the dark. I want to come with you," Kayden sobbed, grabbing hold of his big sister in a bear hug and not letting go.

"No, Kay, you can't come with me. But, I do need you to do a *very* important job for me here while I'm gone. Do you think you could do that for me?" Rebekah said, disengaging herself from the bear hug, and pushing Kayden out to arms length so she could look into his teary eyes. He nodded mutely at his big sister, and continued to sob quietly while she explained what she needed him to do.

"When I go outside, I need you to lock the grate behind me, then I need you to stay up there on the wood pile and watch for me coming back. When you see me coming, I need you to unlock the grate quickly so I can get back inside, before any of those things out there see me. Do you understand Kay?"

Kayden nodded at his big sister, as he wiped his nose with his sleeve, leaving what his big sister had always called `a slug trail` behind. Normally she would have berated him for it, but here, now, it seemed such a trivial a thing to do.

"You see, I knew you could be a big boy and help me do this," Rebekah said, kissing her little brother on the top of his head, and causing him to smile at her words of praise. Rebekah returned to the platform of firewood and resumed her lookout, waiting for an opportunity to present itself for her to leave the grate unseen. It took a while, but eventually she spotted an opening. As long as the undead villager at the end of the street didn't turn back in her direction, she felt sure she could make it to the cover of the barn on the opposite side of the street without being seen.

"Kayden, get ready. I'll be back soon. Make sure you watch for me, you hear?" Rebekah whispered loudly.

"Okay, Bekah," Kayden replied, getting ready to take his sister's place on the firewood platform. Rebekah quietly slid the bolts open on the grate lid and gently lifted off the cover, being careful not to clang it on the rim as she did so. She then quickly climbed out of the hole and onto the street above, replacing the grate cover with great care, so as not to make a sound. She was about to remind Kayden to relock the cover, but she heard the bolts slide into place before she had to. With one last check up and down the street, she lifted her dress and ran for the safety of the large barn opposite.

By the time she had reached the barn a short distance away, her heart was beating so hard and fast that she feared the creatures outside would hear it for sure. Leaning with her back against the wall she tried to steady her breathing, while at the same time taking in the once familiar surrounding of the large barn. What she saw made her first gasp out loud, then gag, as she tried hard not to throw up at the grisly sight before her. Where there were once pens full of healthy animals, now there were only the mutilated remains of disembowelled carcasses, crawling with maggots and flies. The smell was overpowering, and it took all of her self control not to vomit at the sight or smell of what was in front of her.

It took Rebekah a few moments to steel herself against the grisly sight and smell, and then she reminded herself why she had chosen to come here in the first place. She knew there was no way she could approach the village well down the street without being seen, let alone use it to draw any water. The only other source of water that she knew about was inside this barn, and often when she had frequented the barn in the past, she had also seen many types of root vegetables being stored there, ready to feed the animals. She only hoped that there were still some here now. It was difficult to see inside the barn, as the only light was from the moonlight outside which filtered in through the loose fitting wall boards of the structure—creating a strange striped pattern on the barn floor.

Fortunately, Rebekah knew where most things were stored inside the barn, and quickly located two wooden buckets hanging from hooks on the wall. As she took them down from their hooks, she heard a shuffling sound coming from the other side of the barn wall. Carefully she approached the wall of the barn and peered through one of the gaps between the boards. The badly burned, inhuman form at the other side of the wall startled her so much, that she dropped her bucket with a loud clattering sound on the floor, seemingly amplified further by the barn's cavernous structure. The shadow beyond the barn wall instantly looked in her direction, turning her blood to ice, as she stood there frozen with terror. Suddenly the shadow began to move, shuffling towards the entrance of the barn. Instinctively, Rebekah ran for her preferred hiding spot; one that she had used many times while playing hide and seek with her smaller brother and other friends, but also one they had always seemed to find far too easily for her liking. She dived head first into the pile of hay, and quickly buried herself under it, leaving only a small gap so she could see the floor of the barn. She watched as the shadow approached the barn entrance, and involuntarily held her breath as the creature appeared in the doorway, casting a long moonlit shadow far into the barn.

The creature shuffled into the barn doorway, then stopped, as if listening for any movement within. Rebekah could barely breathe past her terror. After a few moments the creature shuffled further inside the barn, and headed straight for where she was hiding. She wanted to flee, but her legs had turned to stone and she couldn't move. Suddenly, the creature kicked over the same bucket she had dropped earlier, and it froze in its tracks, looking down at the upended bucket on the floor. It seemed to be slowly studying the bucket for some reason. Then it did something even stranger. It bent down, picked up the bucket, and returned it to the exact hook Rebekah had removed it from a few moments earlier. It was at that instant she knew exactly who this creature had once been: farmer Tarquin. She suddenly felt a new wave of revulsion at what he had become, and prayed her mother or father had not met a similar fate. After returning the bucket to its rightful hook, the creature took one last look around—lingering longest on what were once his prized animals—then began shuffling slowly back towards the barn entrance.

It wasn't until the shadow had long since disappeared from outside the barn that Rebekah dared to breathe freely once more, let alone move again. When she tried to stand up, her legs almost buckled under her, and she had to steady herself on the rails of the animal pen for a moment. Her eyes had adjusted more to the darkened barn now, and she could clearly see the outline of the storage barrel which normally contained the vegetables for the animals. Warily, she made her way over to the corner of the barn, never taking her eyes off the walls for more than a few seconds at a time, watching for any more shadowy movements outside.

When she reached the large barrel in the corner, she lifted the lid and felt inside. To her great relief, she found there were still plenty of vegetables inside the barrel. For a moment she wondered what had happened to the second bucket, then realised, in her haste to hide she had taken it with her into the pile of hay. Not wanting to be in the barn any longer than she had to be, she ignored that bucket, and took down two more from the hooks on the wall instead. She quickly filled one of the buckets with vegetables, then used the other to collect water from the animal watering trough. It was far too dark to see, but she just hoped there were no discarded animal parts in the watering trough as she scooped up a bucketload of water. The bucket was very heavy for her to lift, and although she knew she could have managed to carry it under normal circumstances, running with it—as well as a second bucket full of vegetables—was not an option right now. Reluctantly, she quietly emptied half the bucket of water onto the barn floor, always watching and listening for any sign of movement outside the barn. She retrieved the bucket of vegetables, and crept slowly towards the entrance of the barn.

The moonlight outside seemed much brighter to her eyes now, since she had become used to the much darker interior of the barn. She knew it would make spotting the creatures much easier for her, but unfortunately, she also knew that they could spot her easily too, especially in the light blue dress she was wearing. There simply was nowhere to hide between the barn and the relative safety of the grate. She needed something to cover her dress with. Something dark. She thought about smearing herself with mud or manure to camouflage herself, but then remembered she had often seen a horse blanket hanging on the back wall of the barn. Placing the two buckets down quietly, she peered carefully around the barn doorway and onto the street outside. The street was clear, apart from the creature that used to be farmer Tarquin, which was still slowly shuffling along in the distance—thankfully now heading away from her.

Rebekah turned and headed directly for where she had last seen the blanket, stopping in her tracks almost immediately, as she realised she would have to walk through the main animal pen full of disembowelled animal carcasses. Taking a deep breath—through her mouth so she didn't retch from the stench—she opened the pen, and picked her way through the carnage as best she could. She made her way to the far rear corner of the barn, hidden in the deepest shadows, and found what she was looking for. It was a thick coarse blanket made from heavy weave, and smelled of the rotting carcases all around her. But at least it was dark brown, and hopefully that would help conceal her out in the open, so she gratefully took it and headed back towards the barn entrance. She cloaked herself in the blanket and retrieved the two buckets, before once again carefully checking the street outside for any signs of the creatures. She was relieved to see that nothing had changed, and the only movement was in the distance, as the remains of poor farmer Tarquin continued to shuffle further down the street. She took a deep breath, then ran for the refuge of the grate, hoping Kayden was paying attention and watching for her return.

It was so much more difficult to run whilst carrying the two heavy buckets, and on two occasions she almost tripped and fell, spilling part of the buckets' contents on the floor as she did so. By the time she reached the grate, she was panting hard for breath. She heard two faint clicks when Kayden released the bolts on the other side of the cover as she crouched down next to it, trying to make her form as small as possible. It was at that point she realised she might have a problem: the buckets were heavy for her to lift, but there was no way Kayden would be able to carry them if she handed them down to him. `She would just have to do the best she could,` she thought to herself, checking the street for any creatures again.

She lifted the grate cover carefully, and placed it on the ground close to the opening, then peered into the dark hole, just about making out her little brother in the darkness below. The platform below was too far to reach with the buckets, and she would risk falling in head first if she tried to lower them onto it. Instead, she moved the buckets as close as she could to the opening, and climbed inside, onto the platform below. Once her footing was secure, she reached out for the first of the two buckets, and found it was almost impossible to lift it from where she was. Eventually, she managed to ease the bucket over the lip of the grate and get a hand underneath it, spilling a little of the water as it sloshed around inside the bucket. Kayden offered to take the bucket of water from his big sister, but she dared not risk spilling more of its precious cargo, so she carefully climbed down and placed it on the floor herself.

Returning to the firewood platform, she reached out for the second bucket, then froze with fear. Another of the creatures had entered the street from the direction of the docks, and was heading their way. Panic gripped her, as she pulled frantically at the bucket of vegetables, desperate to pull it inside and close the grate before the creature spotted her. As she pulled hard on the bucket, its bottom snagged on the lip of the grate, tipping the bucket towards her, and emptying its contents into the room below with a multitude of small thuds, as the vegetables struck the stacked wood beneath her. Very slowly, she lowered the—now almost empty—bucket towards Kayden without taking her eyes off the creature in the street. It took a moment, but he seemed to to understand what his big sister wanted, and took the bucket from her hand. Rebekah barely dared to breathe. Her heart was thundering so hard in her chest, she feared it would burst free at any moment. The creature was far too close to attempt replacing the grate lid, she would be discovered for sure. The moon had shifted its position, and the grate was now in the shadow of the temple building, but she had no idea if that would be enough to conceal their location until the creature passed them by.

Very slowly, Rebekah climbed down from the firewood platform, being especially careful not to make any sound. Kayden watched with terror in his eyes, too scared to move or say anything. Rebekah put a finger to her lips, indicating that he should remain silent, then crept towards him. She bent down so she was close to his ear.

"Be very quiet. There's one right outside," She whispered to him. He immediately started to hug his big sister, and she prayed he wouldn't start to cry and draw attention to them. After a moment she pushed away from him a little and whispered in his ear, "I might need to go back outside and lure it away from here Kayden. I think it would follow anything that moved, just like that pig earlier."

Kayden shook his head furiously and grabbed at his big sister again, hugging her tightly. Rebekah tried to free herself, but was surprised at the strength of her little brother's grip on her.

"Kay, don't fight me, please," she whispered pleadingly. Kayden surprised her by releasing her almost immediately, but still stood there, with his hand held out towards her. It took her a moment to realise he was holding something in his hand. It was his wooden spinning top. He made a throwing motion with his hand, then a spinning motion with his finger above the wooden spinning top. Rebekah grasped what he wanted to do, but wasn't sure she could throw it far enough away from the grate to make much difference, and even if she could, there was no guarantee the creature would see or hear it so far away.

"It's a good idea Kayden, but I don't think I can throw it far enough away from here, and the creature might not even see it anyway, it's so small," she whispered, placing a hand on his shoulder. He shook his head again, then beckoned for her to come close so that he could whisper something to her.

"No Bekah, throw it close to the monster, I can make it spin away down the street."

"I thought you could only make it spin in one spot. How long have you been able to move it as well?" she asked in a whisper.

"Ages and ages," he replied in a whisper, grinning with pride. Rebekah shook her head to herself and narrowed her eyes at him.

"So, when you skinned my ankle the other day on the dockside, you were controlling it?" His eyes widened as he realised his big sister was on to him.

"Sorry Bekah," he whispered, looking down at his own feet, with a guilty look on his face. Rebekah shook her head again, but didn't say anything more about the subject.

"How far can you make it go?"

"Oh, a long way Bekah. I was chasing the seagulls with it. I got one too when it wasn't looking, and..." he whispered, but seemed to stop what he was saying abruptly, half expecting his sister to berate him for his behaviour. He watched his sister for any signs of a reaction, then continued when she didn't say anything more. "When I know it's going too far away, I make it spin faster, and push it hard, so it goes much further by itself," he added in a whisper.

"Okay, let's try. But make sure your words are very quiet when you make it spin," she whispered, holding out her hand for the wooden spinning top. He nodded and handed her his prize possession. Slowly she crept towards the opening and looked up through the hole, half expecting to see a monstrous face peering back at her, but all she saw were stars in the sky high above. Carefully, she climbed back onto the platform, and gingerly peered through the holes on the lip of the grate. Her blood turned to ice when she saw not one, but two of the creatures outside in the street. Both were less than twenty paces away from their hiding spot, and both shuffling slowly towards them. She quickly offered Kayden a hand, so he could climb up beside her. Whereas she had to crouch to stay hidden, Kayden had to stand on his tiptoes to see through the gaps. There was no time to spare, either they did this now, or not at all. Any closer, and the creatures would no doubt see her throw the spinning top from the hole.

"Ready?" she whispered. Kayden nodded, and waited for his sister to throw his spinning top. Rebekah took one last look through the gaps to judge the distance and direction of her throw, then let it fly. She held her breath as she watched it sail through the night air—barely visible in the darkness— then heard a dull thud, as it hit the packed earth of the street outside. It had landed only a few paces away from the closest creature, and it had stopped dead in its tracks to see what the sound was. The second creature had failed to notice it, and was continuing its slow shuffling towards them. Kayden had already begun his whispered chant to make the wooden spinning top move, and within a couple of heartbeats, it began to spin. The first creature attempted to pick it up, but Kayden moved the spinning top away from its grasp long before it had a chance to grab it. As soon as the wooden spinning top started moving towards the second creature, it changed its direction of travel to intercept it. It wasn't long before Kayden had the two creatures walking in circles, much to his great delight, judging by the look on his face. It had been several days since Rebekah had seen him smile, and although she was reluctant to end his fun, she knew she had to.

"Kay, that's enough now. Send them away from here before any more come, please," she pleaded quietly into his ear. She knew he couldn't answer her while he was controlling the spinning top, but also knew he had done as she asked when she saw the toy slowly moving away from them, with both creatures following close behind it. After one final check that there were no more creatures close by, Rebekah quickly located the grate cover and secured it into position, locking the bolts in place with an audible sigh of relief. Her legs finally gave out beneath her, and she found herself sitting down, hugging Kayden around his waist, and crying into his shirt.

"It's okay Bekah, we did it," he said, smoothing his hand over his big sister's hair. All she could do was nod her head, as the tears fell freely at the utter relief she felt.

It wasn't long before Rebekah regained control of herself, and resumed the role of big sister again. She noticed Kayden shivering with the cold, and quickly wrapped him in the heavy horse blanket to keep him warm, while she collected all the spilled vegetables back into the bucket. They had made themselves two sleeping platforms out of stacked firewood the first night they had spent there, and by the time Rebekah had finished collecting all the food from the floor in the dark, she noticed that Kayden was now lying down on his. She didn't want him to go to sleep without eating something first, so she collected a couple of vegetables and went to sit with him.

"Kayden, eat some of this before you go to sleep, and have a drink too," she said, sitting on the edge of his sleeping platform.

"I'm not hungry Bekah," he said quietly, but didn't sit up, or even turn in her direction. Rebekah began to worry he was unwell, and almost at the same instant he let out a chesty cough, as if to confirm her fears. She turned him over to face her and felt his forehead—it was hot and clammy.

"Oh, no, not now ... please," she said, out loud to herself. The last thing they needed right now was for Kayden to become ill and start coughing, attracting the attention of the creatures outside. She forced him to sit up and drink some water, then made him eat something, before finally letting him go to sleep.

Chapter Thirty-Four

Early on the fifth day they finally came within sight of The Serpent Isles. The weather had been fair and the wind favourable, but the boredom aboard ship had been almost unbearable for Neala and Alexia. Lusam had read a large portion of the journal he had discovered in Helveel, and Renn had whiled away the hours in quiet meditation and prayer. Lusam also shared the information he'd found earlier in the journal with Renn, as well as all of the new information he had discovered that he thought would be of interest to him. Most of what Lusam had read in the journal after the entry regarding the arrival of the Guardian, had been far less interesting to him. It was mostly dealing with the day-to-day running of the monastery, with only one other brief entry regarding the writer's old friend Isidro in Lohlaen, but nothing that suggested a possible location for it. Lusam had asked Renn if he had heard of Lohlaen, or even Pearl Isle where it was supposed to be situated, but disappointingly for Lusam, he said he had never heard of either place before. He suggested that Lusam might want to speak with one of the many historians at the High Temple, or search for information in the High Temple library once they arrived in Lamuria. That was, of course, if there was still a High Temple there by the time they arrived. Lusam promised himself that he would take Renn's advice, but secretly hoped he would find the information he needed himself later in the journal.

Captain Waylon had surreptitiously spoken to Renn the day before, suggesting that he asked one of his crew for a meeting with him about an hour before they docked at The Serpent Isles. This would hopefully lend credence to his story, that Renn and his party were only now requesting passage further south than The Serpent Isles, and had *not* already agreed it with the Captain before leaving Fairport, without the crew's knowledge or acceptance.

Renn knew that Captain Waylon's ruse stood a better chance of succeeding if more people noticed him entering the Captain's cabin, and he knew just how to achieve that. First he loosened his shirt, exposing his sigil of Aysha for all to see. Then he located the large bundle with his sword and shield, and started rummaging through it. Lusam guessed what he was looking for in the bundle, even before he pulled them out, but had no idea why he would suddenly need his weapons. Neala and Alexia must have felt exactly the same way, because they both stopped what they were doing and began to look for potential danger. Renn noticed the sudden tension he had caused in the others, and made a hand signal to indicate there was no problem at present. Then he motioned with his head for Lusam to join him at the bundle of equipment. Lusam casually approached and knelt by his side, as if also looking for something in the large bundle.

"Problem?" Lusam asked quietly.

"No lad. Not yet, anyway. I'm going to ask to see the Captain as he suggested. I figured the more of the crew that noticed me enter his cabin, the more credible his story will be later on. Or at least that's what I hope. Sorry to ask you for it, but I need the rest of that gold too. Just in case Captain Waylon has to flash it around a little, to get the crew onboard with our little planned detour," Renn said quietly.

"Of course," Lusam replied, handing over a small coin pouch with the remaining thirty-five gold coins in it. Renn fastened the coin pouch to his belt, then strapped his shield across his back, before finally securing his sword at his waist.

"Thanks lad," Renn said, placing a hand on Lusam's shoulder. "I need you all to wait here and act normally, as if nothing has changed. As far as you're all concerned, I'm simply going for a chat with the Captain about a business proposition if anyone asks, the details of which you're not privy to. I'll no doubt be with the captain for while, but when I do re-emerge, be ready for any trouble that may arise, especially if the Captain chooses that moment to make his announcement to the crew."

"Okay," Lusam replied quietly. "I'll let Neala and Alexia know what to expect. Good luck."

"Thanks, I'm sure we'll need it lad," Renn replied, giving Lusam one last pat on the shoulder before standing up in full view of the crew. Lusam walked over to Neala and Alexia and leant back against the ship's rail, close enough to talk privately with them, but also with a good view of the main deck below. He watched as Renn descended the wooden stairs onto the main deck below.

"Excuse me," Renn said to a crew member swabbing the deck. The man turned towards Renn's voice, and his eyes went wide as he took in Renn's new appearance.

"Er ... yes sir?" he stuttered, standing up a little straighter.

"I would like to request a meeting with Captain Waylon about a possible business proposal. Would you please inform him right away," Renn said, pretending not to notice the reaction he had just evoked in the man.

"Yes ... of course sir, right away sir," the man replied dropping his mop and hurrying towards the Captain's cabin, but glancing back over his shoulder several times on the way there. At first nobody else seemed to notice an armed paladin of Aysha among them, but that quickly changed, as one after another of the crew spotted him walking slowly to the port side of the ship. He casually stood there, looking out to sea, as if he were merely sight seeing. Lusam smiled to himself, as he witnessed men nudging their fellow crew members and pointing towards Renn at the ship's rail. It was only a matter of seconds before every man on the ship had stopped what he was doing, and focused his attention on Renn.

A few moments later the man Renn had sent to speak with the Captain returned.

"Sir, the Cap'ain said he would see you in his cabin

right away," the man said, gesturing in the direction of Captain Waylon's cabin.

"Thank you," Renn replied, inclining his head slightly to the man. He crossed the deck with far more purpose towards Captain Waylon's cabin, knocked once on the door, and entered at the Captain's request. As soon as the door closed behind him, the crewmen outside went back to work, but not without far more chatter than usual between them. No doubt they were all curious as to what a paladin of Aysha was doing aboard their ship, and what he now wanted from their Captain. That theory was proven right a short time later, when the man who Renn had sent to speak with the Captain, suddenly became a very popular figure amongst the other crew members.

Captain Waylon was sitting behind his desk studying a sea chart when Renn entered his cabin. It was far more luxurious on the inside than Renn would have expected for a ship of that type. The dark wood furniture was expertly crafted with decorative inlays made from exotic woods, and the small chandelier that hung from the ceiling was probably worth a month's wages of any man aboard. He had several ornate cut glass decanters on his desk, as well as various quality wall hangings decorating the walls of the small cabin. Looking around, Renn suspected that Captain Waylon and the Pelorus had seen far more profitable times in the past than they were doing of late. `Something that was no doubt attributed to the Captain's current gambling problem,` Renn thought to himself.

"Good afternoon, Captain," Renn said in greeting.

"I guess we'll soon see," the Captain replied coolly, taking in Renn's new appearance, but not commenting on it. "Did you bring the balance of payment, as agreed?"

"I did," Renn replied, placing the small bag of coins on the desk in front of him. Captain Waylon took the bag and emptied the coins onto the desk in front of him, counting them out in to two piles. Fifteen coins he took for himself to add to the original thirty-five—enough to clear his current gambling debts—the rest he returned to the coin pouch.

"May I ask what you plan on telling your men?" Renn enquired.

"I'm not planning on telling them anything, yet. After we dock at The Serpent Isles I will collect payment for our shipment. I will add the profits of that to what's in this bag, and hopefully that will be enough to convince them to risk their necks for you," Captain Waylon replied, hefting the now much lighter coin pouch in his right hand.

"And if it's not?" Renn asked.

"Then I would say we both have a big problem," Captain Waylon replied flatly. Renn didn't respond to the Captain's remarks, he simply stared at him, letting him know that his answer was not going to be enough. Captain Waylon seemed to get the message loud and clear, licking his lips he added, "I know you are aware of my gambling debts, and unfortunately, so are most of my crew. They hear the rumours in the taverns too, you know. And they also know this may be our last voyage together. I doubt any of them have failed to notice the disappearance of many of the fleet who have ventured further south than here, but neither will they have failed to notice the lack of business opportunities available now that those routes are closed to us. It has already started a price war within the fleet. Each Captain undercutting the next for the fewer and fewer jobs that become available. Crews' pay has been cut badly of late, on all ships, including the Pelorus. They know that soon there won't be enough business to go around, and when that happens, Captains will go out of business, and their men lose their livelihoods.

"What little coin this pouch contains, added to the profits from this run, adds up to more than these men would earn in the next three months. Possibly even longer if the situation gets any worse. I'm hoping that will be enough. But like I said, if it isn't, we *both* have a problem. You with your travel plans, and me with my ship and crew."

Renn nodded at the Captain's assessment of the situation, and couldn't help gaining a little more respect for the man, hearing the concern for his crew's welfare in his voice.

"Alright Captain, I will leave the details and timing of the announcement in your capable hands," Renn said, nodding his farewell to Captain Waylon, and heading for the door. As he exited the Captain's cabin he almost fell over the same man he had sent earlier to see Captain Waylon. He had obviously been trying to eavesdrop on their conversation.

"Beggin' your pardon, sir," he said bobbing his head and moving out of the way. Renn ignored the man and headed back to meet up with the others on the aft deck, hoping that the man hadn't overheard any of his discussion with Captain Waylon.

"How did it go?" Lusam asked as Renn reached the top of the stairs and stepped onto the deck.

"The meeting went fine, but we might have another problem now," Renn replied, looking at the man swabbing the deck below.

"Oh, don't worry about him. When I saw him moving closer to Captain Waylon's cabin door I guessed what he was up to, so I erected a magical soundproof barrier in front of his door. I can assure you, he never heard a word," Lusam said grinning at Renn. Renn burst out laughing, and slapped Lusam on the back.

"Good thinking. Well done lad, " Renn replied still smiling. After a moment he added, "If you can do the same thing up here, I can tell you all what was said in Captain Waylon's cabin."

"It's already done," Lusam replied grinning. Renn chuckled once more, then began to recount in detail the conversation he'd just had with Captain Waylon to them all.

Just over an hour later the Pelorus sailed into The Serpent Isles' harbour. It was a natural harbour that had been created by the sea over countless centuries as it had eroded away the softer rocks, leaving only the much harder granite behind in a horseshoe shape. The floating wooden docks were build directly from shore, and stretched well out into the deeper water of the harbour. Lusam was fascinated watching the skill of the men as they expertly manoeuvred the ship into position alongside the floating dock. As soon as the Pelorus was secure, they started unloading their cargo onto the dockside. Several men with carts were already waiting patiently on the dockside for the cargo to be unloaded, and as soon as all the goods were unloaded and checked, they stacked them onto their carts and hauled them away. Captain Waylon was also on the dockside conducting some kind of business with one of the men. Lusam guessed it was for the payment of goods he had just delivered, but had no way of knowing for sure.

It wasn't long before the Pelorus' crew were back on board and making ready to leave harbour once more. There had been several curious glances in their direction over the past half an hour, as the men were no doubt wondering why they hadn't already disembarked the ship.

"Best be ready now. The Captain can't possibly hold off telling his crew for much longer," Renn said quietly to the group, just as Captain Waylon climbed the gangplank back onto his ship.

"Quartermaster!" Captain Waylon shouted.

"Yes Captain," he replied from bow of the ship, making his way quickly over to his Captain.

"Gather the men. I have an announcement to make."

"Yes, sir," he replied to the Captain, then he addressed the crew. "You heard the Captain, drop what you're doing and gather 'round, right now!" he bellowed. All the men quickly gathered on the main deck in front of the quartermaster, while Captain Waylon climbed up to the aft deck so he could address his men from above. Lusam guessed he had also chosen that particular location to be near the protection of a paladin, should his announcement not go down too well with his crew.

Captain Waylon waited until his crew fell silent, then began.

"Gentlemen, most of you have sailed with me for many a year now. Through good times, and bad. And I think you will agree with me when I say, we have had few, if any, bad times worse than it is right now," Captain Waylon said, bringing forth a loud rumbling of assent from his men.

"I'm sure you all knew that this was likely our last run together on the Pelorus. Not something I'm proud of, I can assure you. But given the lack of business opportunities available to anyone right now, I doubt my own indiscretions have made much difference to the inevitable outcome anyway," he said, pausing a long time for effect, while the men muttered to each other, contemplating their new status without jobs. It was expertly done. The crew visibly sagged at the news. Their faces turned from hope to desperation in the space of a few short heartbeats. Then the Captain spoke again.

"But don't despair just yet, men," he called out above the raucous voices below, silencing all to a man, as they stood there transfixed on his every word. "I have some *good* news to share. Our paladin friend here has offered us a unique business opportunity. One that will see us both keep possession of the Pelorus, and earn every man here three months' pay to boot." The crew cheered loudly, hope blossoming on all of their faces as they took in the good news. Captain Waylon held up his hand to quieten down his men, then continued. "After we have successfully completed our new contract, we will return to Fairport, where we will bid for any new work that's still available to the fleet. The extra money we all earn on this trip will see us in a far better position to wait out these bad times than many others within the fleet.

"Before everyone gets too excited about the news, I must tell you that the contract does not come without risk, as you would imagine for that amount of coin. We are to sail south, to..." The Captains words were drowned out by the sudden angry and concerned cries of his men below. He held up his hand again to try and silence them, but it took the quartermaster's bellowing orders to silence the men once more. The Captain decided to change tactics slightly, and instead of ordering the crew to undertake the journey, he offered them a choice instead.

"I know how you feel gentlemen, because I feel the same way too. That's why I will not order any man aboard this ship to make the journey with me. Anyone who wishes to remain here on The Serpent Isles is welcome to do so, along with any monies owed to that man. You can gain passage back to Fairport, or try for new employment here if you prefer. For anyone wishing to stay, the surplus money will be divided up equally amongst you. Each man must make his own decision, and I expect that man to stand by that decision come what may.

"I intend to sail the Pelorus swiftly, and unhindered by cargo. We would be skirting close to the shoreline, and avoiding open water wherever possible. I estimate two days each way at most. That's four days' work, for three months' pay. But more than that, gentlemen. It's four days' work, for a possible future!

"Each man has one hour to decide what he will do. At which point you will either be on, or off the Pelorus. The quartermaster will dispense any monies owed to any man wishing to leave. That's all. Dismissed!" The Captain turned away from the ship's rail and walked to the stern of his ship, away from the gaze of his men below.

"That was a bold move Captain. I have to say, I wasn't expecting that. And by the look on your men's faces, neither were they," Renn said, joining Captain Waylon at the ship's rail.

"To be honest, neither was I. Of course, I expected *some* dissent amongst the men once I told them of our planned route, but not on the scale we just witnessed. If I had tried to order them to sail south, I'm sure we would have had a full-blown mutiny to contend with," Captain Waylon replied.

"I think you're right Captain, but what happens to your ship if they all decide to leave?" The captain gave a mirthless chuckle to Renn's question, then turned to face him.

"I have a lot of good men aboard the Pelorus, Renn. Many I would consider as close to a friend, as any Captain could with a crew member under his command. It would cut me deeply to lose any of them, but without your coin, I would lose all of them regardless. If we end up without a crew … well, I have no doubt that we could find enough desperate men here at The Serpent Isles to sail south with us. I would get to keep my ship, you would get to your destination, and my men … my friends, would be tossed overboard as if they were nothing more than garbage. And that Renn, sticks in my throat, and I can't do a damn thing about it! I swear to Deas himself, if I make it through this, I shall never gamble again, ever!" Renn could tell he meant every word he'd just spoken, and felt very sympathetic towards the Captain's current situation, even if it *had* been mainly brought about by his own hand.

"Let's just wait and see what happens in an hour, Captain," Renn said, giving Captain Waylon a supportive pat on the shoulder. Captain Waylon bobbed his head, obviously too emotional to respond, then solemnly headed for the sanctuary of his own cabin.

"What do you think will happen in an hour?" Neala asked. Renn hadn't noticed her approach as he stared over the Ship's rail at the water below.

"I'm not sure lass. But one thing *is* certain: one man has learned a valuable lesson this day."

Chapter Thirty-Five

Captain Waylon stayed in his cabin for the next hour, contemplating where he had gone so wrong in his life lately. He knew, of course, it all boiled down to his recent gambling habits; something he had sworn never to do again, and he intended full well to keep that promise, come what may. He was dreading going back out on deck to see how many of his men remained—if any. He knew he could not blame any of them for leaving, especially the ones with families back home in Fairport. He alone, was responsible for backing them all into this corner, and he alone would have to deal with the consequences—even if those consequences meant losing life long friends amongst his crew.

A knock at Captain Waylon's cabin door startled him from his pondering.

"Enter," he said loudly. The door opened a fraction, and the quartermaster poked his head inside the cabin.

"We're ready Captain," he reported.

"Thank you. I'll be right out," Captain Waylon replied. The quartermaster nodded to the Captain, then swiftly disappeared again, as he closed the door behind himself, leaving the Captain alone once more to his hopes and fears. Captain Waylon stood up from behind his desk, took a deep breath to steady his nerves, and after straightening his jacket, headed for the cabin door, and whatever lay beyond.

Captain Waylon opened the cabin door and stepped onto the deck outside. His heart sank as he took in the sight before him. Only two men stood before him: the quartermaster, and old Lamar.

"Captain," the quartermaster reported, "all the men willing to sail south are aboard ship."

Captain Waylon found it hard to speak, but he managed a nod to his faithful quartermaster, and to say, "Thank you." The quartermaster nodded in return, but his eyes went beyond the Captain to the foredeck above him when he did so. In unison the sound of rapid footsteps on wood echoed throughout the Pelorus, as men streamed down both wooden staircases—one each side of the ship— from the upper foredeck and onto the main deck below. Within seconds the whole Pelorus' crew were standing to attention in front of their Captain.

"All crew present and accounted for, Captain," the quartermaster reported, wearing a huge grin and bristling with pride. Captain Waylon met the eyes of every one of his crew as his gaze slowly passed over them, seeing for the first time the true loyalty each man shared for both the Pelorus and their Captain; something he vowed never to take for granted, ever again. He struggled to regain control of his emotions, but when he did, he took a deep breath, puffed out his chest, and addressed his men.

"Thank you, quartermaster," Captain Waylon said with a slight nod, then turned back to his crew. "And, thank you too, gentlemen. Thank you for giving me another chance. I promise that I won't let you down again. You have my word on that."

"Na, it wasn't anything to do with that Captain. The men just didn't want old Lamar here taking all their money, that's all," the quartermaster said jokingly, causing the gathered men to laugh loudly, and Lamar to give him a strange look. Captain Waylon briefly joined in with the laughter, thankful for the lifted tension, then addressed his quartermaster once more.

"Prepare the ship for departure, quartermaster," he commanded.

"Yes sir," replied the quartermaster, and followed it

with orders of his own to the men on deck. The men quickly dispersed and attended to their individual duties, as the ship was made ready for leaving port. Captain Waylon simply turned and re-entered his cabin. His relief was evident as he collapsed into his chair with a loud sigh, and poured himself a large glass of brandy.

Lusam noticed that the mood aboard ship was different since they had left The Serpent Isles. The men went about their tasks quietly and efficiently, but always with an eye on the horizon for potential danger. Captain Waylon had ordered two men to remain in the rigging as lookouts, both for enemy vessels, and underwater hazards. Lusam had become accustomed to life aboard ship over the last six days, and even Alexia had found her sea legs by the second day aboard the Pelorus, but now that they were skirting the shoreline, the ship seemed to take on a whole new persona. The waves and swell were much larger being so close to shore, and they often found themselves stumbling around the deck if they tried to walk anywhere. On more than one occasion, Lusam and Neala had both found themselves sliding across the deck on their backs, as the ship pitched violently from one side to the other.

Renn had explained to them, that the Pelorus was a shallow bottomed vessel, used for carrying heavy cargo, and ill suited for large waves and swell, especially unloaded as she was right now. Renn, however, seemed to handle the movement of the ship almost as well as the crew, and if Lusam hadn't have known better, he would have sworn they were all using some kind of magic to keep their feet attached to the deck. Alexia, on the other hand, wasn't coping very well at all with the ship's constant pitching from side to side, and front to back. In fact, she looked terrible. Less than thirty minutes into their journey she had lost her breakfast over the side of the ship's rail, and in between repeat visits, she spent all of her time lying down on the deck, huddled in a ball. Lusam had felt sorry for her and tried to alleviate her suffering with his magic, but nothing he tried seemed to help.

All they could do was make sure she drank plenty of water, and assure her that the trip would soon be over—none of which seemed to help much.

By the end of the first day even Lusam and Neala were feeling a little seasick, and were relieved when Captain Waylon came to inform them that he intended to stop for the night in a sheltered bay a little further down the coast. During their trip to The Serpent Isles they had sailed straight through the night, but running so close to the shoreline as they were now, meant that was no longer an option.

They arrived at the small bay just before dusk, and the men set about securing the ship for the coming night. It was well sheltered from the wind and waves, and gave a welcome respite to the swell and waves outside the bay. Any enemy ships sailing to the south of the bay would not be able to see the Pelorus behind the high cliffs, but even so, the Captain posted an overnight lookout in the rigging, just to be safe.

Alexia was still sleeping when the ship's activities started to calm down. Most of the men had retreated below decks, no doubt to eat and relax after a hard day at sea. Only the lookout in the rigging high above, and a couple of men on the foredeck coiling ropes were still to be seen above decks. It suddenly struck Lusam that he had never considered the crew's position in all this. When they had first boarded the Pelorus in Fairport, he had given little thought about the men aboard, they were simply the crew of the ship that was going to take them where they were going. He realised that it wasn't until they reached The Serpent Isles, and Captain Waylon had tried to convince his crew to remain with him, that he had actually started to see them as men. Men with families, and loved ones waiting for them back home, no doubt. Lusam felt sure that he could defend the ship against any hostile Empire ships they might encounter, but what would happen to these men once he and the others had left the ship, and they were alone, without his protection on their trip home? It made him feel uncomfortable, knowing that a few gold coins could cause someone to risk their lives in such a way, and that he was partially responsible for that.

"Are you alright?" Neala asked, as she came to sit beside him.

"Yes, I'm fine thanks. I was just thinking about the crew, and how they'll be completely defenceless once we've left the ship for their journey home," he replied as she snuggled up close to him.

Neala thought for a while, obviously not wanting to belittle his concerns, then replied, "I know they mainly chose to do it for the money, but if they actually knew who you were, or what you could do to help Afaraon, I'm sure they would have chosen to help willingly."

"Maybe, but they were never given that choice. And what do *we* gain by risking all *their* lives? ... making it to Lamuria a few days sooner," he replied glumly.

"That's right, lad," Renn said, startling them both as he sat down by the side of them, "if we can make it to Lamuria a few days sooner, you may very well be able to save countless lives there, not to mention the whole continent of Afaraon. There's nothing to say the Pelorus won't make it home completely unscathed once we leave, anyway. There again, she could be attacked and sunk with all hands as soon as she sets sail for home. We are at war lad, and in war there are always casualties, on both sides. If you want to blame someone, blame the Empire, not yourself. Those men understood the risk to themselves and their ship, and each one chose to take on that risk. They believe they are doing it for the coin and a possible future, and that is enough for them. When we arrive, maybe we should enlighten them as to the real reason they risked their lives. That way, if they do happen to meet their end during their trip home, they can at least die knowing they have dealt a massive blow to the Empire by delivering you swiftly to Lamuria." Lusam knew he was right, but it still felt wrong somehow, so he simply nodded and left it at that.

Alexia awoke not long after, and propped herself up against the ship's rail. She certainly looked better than she had during the voyage, but she was still very pale.

"How are you feeling?" Neala asked.

"I've been better," Alexia replied, stretching out her back. "Where are we?"

"Captain Waylon found us a nice sheltered cove to spend the night in," Lusam replied.

"Thank Aysha for that," Alexia half-whispered to herself, rubbing her eyes and attempting to stand. She almost ended up back on the floor in a heap, but managed to steady herself in time. "It feels like the damn ship is still moving around under my feet, even though it's not."

Renn laughed. "Yes, your mind gets used to the movement of the ship, and when it stops, it takes a while to adjust again. You'll notice it even when we're on solid ground I'm afraid."

"Oh Gods. I never want to travel by ship ever again," Alexia stated flatly, making the others chuckle at her words.

"I know you probably don't feel like it, but you really should eat something Alexia," Renn said. Alexia responded by putting her hand over her mouth and shaking her head, whilst turning a lighter shade of grey. Neala handed her a waterskin so she could at least have a drink of water, then went back to their supply bag to find the rest of them some food. She soon discovered that all they had left was a small piece of dried travel bread, and some smoked sausage— nowhere near enough for the four of them to share as a meal.

"Hmm, I think we have a small problem," Neala said over her shoulder.

"What's that?" Lusam replied.

"We don't seem to have enough food left for our trip," she said, holding out the two remaining morsels of food for the others to see.

"That's not good, I'm starving," Lusam said, standing up rubbing his stomach.

"You're always starving, so there's nothing new there," Neala replied rolling her eyes at him.

"I'm sorry, I should have remembered to get us some more supplies when we reached The Serpent Isles. With everything that was happening aboard ship I completely forgot," Renn said.

"It's not your fault, Renn. We all knew we had only five days' worth of food when we left Fairport, so we all should have remembered to restock," Neala replied.

"We'll be fine, I can catch us some fish," Lusam offered.

"How are you going to attract the fish without any bait?" Neala asked, curious if he could attract the fish like he had the other animals in the forest near Helveel.

"Oh, that's easy," Lusam replied grinning, "we just give Alexia that bread and sausage to eat, and I'm sure we'll have plenty of bait a few seconds later."

Alexia tried to respond, but couldn't because of her dry retching.

"Oh! You're really going to pay for that one later," Neala said, stifling a laugh of her own.

Chapter Thirty-Six

The entire crew were up well before first light preparing the Pelorus for her onward journey, and by the time the sun began to rise, they were already underway. Lusam had managed to catch several good sized fish the previous evening and cook them using his magic—and, without any of the crew even noticing. After eating nothing but travel rations for most of the previous week, the freshly cooked fish had tasted truly delicious. And after recovering her appetite, even Alexia had asked for a second helping. Lusam was, however, far less enthusiastic about the prospect of having to eat it for breakfast the following day, and did little more than pick at it. Alexia refused it altogether, most likely knowing she would be seeing it again very soon if she did eat any. Fortunately, the sea was much calmer than it had been the previous day, and the wind had also eased somewhat. The sun felt warmer on their skin today, and they dozed away the early part of the morning together on the aft deck.

Lusam and the others were rudely awoken by loud shouts coming from the rigging high above, and what sounded like a large wave breaking over a rock close to the ship. Renn was the first up to see what all the commotion was about, closely followed by Neala. He expected to see the ship had strayed too close to the rocks, but what he saw instead, was far worse. In the distance, directly off the port side, was an Empire ship. The noise they had heard wasn't waves breaking over rocks, but instead, huge fireballs missing their intended target, and hitting the sea close to their ship.

"Lusam! Get up lad!" Renn shouted, removing his shield and trying to intercept one of the magical-missiles, but failing. It exploded through the upper deck close to where they were now standing, and out through the side of the ship, ending its flight in the sea with a loud splash and hissing sound. The ship rocked violently, and shards of wood showered the upper and lower decks. Lusam immediately erected a force-field around the side of the ship facing the enemy vessel, but not before another fireball found its target, thankfully only damaging the forward starboard rail. Men soon appeared with buckets of water to dowse the flames caused by the two impacts and assess the damage.

Captain Waylon had appeared on deck as soon as the first calls went up, ordering his men to set more sails and increase their speed to maximum. The Empire ship was coming at them directly from the east, trapping the Pelorus between it, and the cliffs to their west. The only direction his ship could turn was to the east—away from the cliffs—but that would put them on a direct intercept course with the Empire vessel. His only option was to try and outrun them south, and he knew that was never going to happen. This time he had gambled with his, and his crew's lives—and lost again.

"Renn, we need to get the captain to turn the ship towards them. There's no point me wasting my energy shielding the whole length of the ship, when I can protect us just as effectively by shielding only the front. And, it will give them a much smaller target to hit once they're within range to hit us with any kind of accuracy," Lusam said, watching the enemy ship as it came ever closer. So far the Empire ship had been sending magical-missiles their way without any real accuracy, most landing harmlessly in the sea around their ship, But Lusam knew it wouldn't take them long to come within range for a much more focused attack. All the Captain was doing right now, was delaying the inevitable by trying to outrun them.

"I suggest we both go speak with him lad. He's not likely to listen to me, especially if you're not there to *convince* him otherwise," Renn replied. Lusam nodded, and within seconds they were on the main deck approaching the Captain.

"Captain," Renn shouted. The Captain glanced his way, but ignored his call, continuing to issue orders to his men.

"Captain Waylon," Renn repeated.

"I'm a little busy right now. If you haven't noticed we're under attack!" Captain Waylon said angrily.

"You need to turn the ship towards them," Renn said, ignoring his tone.

"Are you crazy? This isn't a war ship, you know! We don't even have any weapons onboard to fight with. Not that we would get close enough to use them, even if we did," Captain Waylon spat at Renn.

"Actually, yes, we do have a weapon onboard. And it's quite possibly the most powerful weapon in Afaraon, Captain," Renn replied with a smug grin.

The Captain laughed mirthlessly. "I've heard about your blessed weapons before paladin, but what use is a sword going to be against a ship full of magi?"

"I wasn't referring to *my* weapon, Captain," Renn replied, putting his hand on Lusam's shoulder. "This is *our* weapon, right here. And the very reason we are travelling to Lamuria in the first place. He may very well turn the tide of this war for us, Captain."

"A boy! What can he possibly do against that?" Captain Waylon said pointing towards the Empire ship. Lusam raised his right hand in front of himself, and created a fireball in the palm of his hand the size of a man's head. The Captain's eyes went wide at the sight, and he took an involuntary step back in shock.

"Turn the ship Captain, and I'll show you what I can do about that," Lusam said nodding towards the enemy ship, which had now started to turn towards a parallel course, so it could fire more accurately at the Pelorus. The Captain seemed to be too shocked to move, and it wasn't until Lusam had extinguished his fireball that he seemed to fully come back to himself.

He looked at Lusam for a moment, before shouting his new orders to his crew. "Helmsman, hard to port. Set an intercept course," he bellowed.

"Captain?" came back a questioning call from his helmsman.

"Just do it. That's an order!" Captain Waylon yelled.

"Aye, Captain. Hard to port," came the helmsman's reply.

"I hope you're right," Captain Waylon said to Renn, but remained staring at Lusam. Renn just smiled at the captain and nodded.

Lusam quickly made his way to the bow of the ship, with Neala, Alexia and Renn following close behind. The two ships were still about a mile apart, and the Pelorus was now heading straight for the Empire ship. Lusam slipped into his mage-sight and was shocked by what he saw. There were at least a hundred magi aboard the enemy vessel. Their collective aura burned like a crimson flame across the full width of the enemy vessel's deck. He could easily pick out the most powerful mage aboard, and from what Renn had already told him about Empire hierarchy, deduced that he would most likely be their leader. He could clearly see the enemy lined up on the deck ready to fire at the Pelorus, waiting until they thought they could swifty destroy it.

"Renn, there must be at least a hundred men on board that ship," Lusam said quietly.

Renn whistled. "That's a lot of fire-power lad, are you sure you can handle it?" he asked, noticing the number of auras himself, and sounding slightly concerned. Then the assault began. Lusam raised his shield to protect the Pelorus, but didn't return fire. Lusam staggered slightly as over a thirty missiles impacted on his shield.

"Why don't you fire back?" Neala asked, also sounding a little worried.

"There's over a hundred men on board that ship," Lusam repeated, as if that was an answer to any of their questions. He knew he could easily destroy the ship. But it wasn't *just* a ship, it was a ship with over a hundred men aboard, and he didn't know if he could kill all those men and live with his conscience afterwards. There was a slight pause in the assault after their initial volley. No doubt the Empire magi were trying to figure out why their missiles had been blocked, when there was apparently no mage aboard to stop them. That gave Lusam an idea. Maybe he could convince them to leave by revealing his true strength to them.

Lusam sent a single missile directly at the man he judged to be their leader. He didn't intend for it to kill the man, only to shock him by its strength. He had judged how much power to put into the missile by the strength of the man's aura—he hoped he hadn't overestimated the man's magical ability. At the same time Lusam loosed his missile, another volley erupted from the enemy vessel, this time all heading directly towards him. They had obviously seen him create his own missile, and now knew exactly who was responsible for shielding the ship. It actually made it easier for Lusam to defend against, as he could reduce the overall size of his shield due to the concentrated fire. Lusam took the impacts again, staggering at the increased power the magi had put behind them this time.

"Lusam, what are you doing lad?" Renn asked frantically.

"I can't just kill all those men—I just can't," Lusam replied, regaining his footing. Lusam watched as his missile found its target. Then he felt the unmistakable death-pulse of three magi, as did Renn standing by his side. At first Lusam thought he had overestimated the power he had put into his magical-missile and killed the man outright, as well as two others that must have been close by when his shield had failed. But when he looked again, their leader was getting back to his feet, as were a dozen more men scattered across the deck. It all started to make sense when he remembered what Renn had told him, of how the Empire agents shared their magical power through their Necromatic rings. The sudden massive strike on their leader's shield, must have completely drained two of his underlings, killing them instantly.

Lusam thought his plan had worked, as no more missiles came from the enemy vessel for more than a minute after he had struck their leader. Then they suddenly started again. This time with even more power behind them. `What's wrong with these people?` Lusam thought to himself, as he braced himself for the incoming missiles. Again he staggered as they impacted heavily on his shield.

"What's wrong with you lad? Finish them!" Renn half-shouted at Lusam.

Lusam ignored him, and instead fully lowered the shutter around his aura. His aura was so bright, Renn had to shield his own eyes, and even the attacks from the Empire ship ceased, as they stood on their deck open-mouthed at the sight before them.

"Listen to me, Lad. I understand what you're trying to do here. I really do. But making them run away will not help anyone in the long term. Either they will call for more support, or simply wait until the Pelorus is on her homeward journey before destroying her. And even if that didn't happen, where do you suppose they were heading before they spotted us? Lamuria of course. If you don't finish them off now, you'll only allow them to kill more innocent people later, whether it's the crew of this ship, another ship, or even innocent women and children as they carve their way to Lamuria," Renn said passionately. Lusam knew he was right, but how could it ever be right to kill so many people. He knew for certain that the men aboard that ship would kill everyone they came across if he didn't stop them, and so he also knew at that moment he *had* to stop them, no matter what it cost him personally. Lusam turned to face Renn, and with misty eyes, nodded that he understood what he must do.

Even though Lusam knew these men were his enemy, and worshipped Aamon not Aysha, he still said a silent prayer for their souls as he prepared to do what must be done; something he would have considered unthinkable only a few short minutes earlier. He shuttered his aura once more, and summoned a powerful ball of flame in his right hand, before letting it fly in the direction of the same man he had hit earlier, quickly followed by two others. The two ships were much closer to each other now, and it left little chance for the man to dodge his fate. The first one struck cleanly, killing at least fifteen of his underlings, as he drew magic from them into his own shield to survive. He managed to dodge the second one, but it still took down three of his men who were unfortunate enough to be standing in the line of fire. The third and final missile also found its target, sealing the fate of every man aboard the enemy vessel, including their leader.

The only men who remained, were the crew of the ship, who were now frantically trying to retreat. Lusam was numbed by feeling so many death-pulses. Never before had he felt death so intensely. He knew he couldn't allow the ship to remain afloat and retreat back to the Empire, only to bring more of its evil to the shores of Afaraon. He had no desire to kill the men aboard however, as they posed little threat to anyone, even if they did manage to swim back to shore. The two ships were now less than a hundred paces apart, and the helmsman aboard the Pelorus had already adjusted their course so they didn't collide with the enemy ship. Lusam reached for the sea between the two ships with his mind, and isolated a narrow column of water. He encased the water within a force-field and instantly froze its contents, creating a long blade-like structure twice as high as the enemy ship, and twice as long as the ship was wide. The newly formed ice-blade desperately wanted to escape his grasp and shoot to the surface by itself, but Lusam still gave it a strong push of his own to help it on its way. The giant shard of ice broke through the surface of the sea, cutting the enemy ship cleanly in half, scattering men, bodies and timber from the enemy ship over a large area. The two halves of the ship quickly sank, leaving only the flotsam of what once was. The giant ice-blade was the only refuge for the few men who had survived, but even that began to melt rapidly in the relatively warm waters.

Neala could tell what it had just cost Lusam to kill all those men, and she knew there was nothing she could say that would make him feel any different, so she simply hugged him tightly, and reminded him that she *still* loved him. Renn only gave his shoulder a squeeze, but remained silent, and even Alexia chose not to try and lighten the mood with any of her jokes or jibes. The absolute stillness aboard ship was palpable. Not a soul moved on deck, not a sound made, or an order issued. It was as if they were suddenly afloat a ghost ship.

Lusam eventually broke their embrace, realising himself there was something amiss with the crew. He reached for Neala's hand, intending to return to the aft deck to seek out some much needed solitude, but when he turned around, he found every member of the crew frozen to the spot with a complete look of awe on their faces. Then as one, a huge cheer went up, and men started scurrying like ants towards him to congratulate him for his destruction of the enemy ship. They surrounded him in seconds, lifting him off the deck onto their shoulders, and forcing him to release Neala's hand. At first Lusam tried to resist the praise and attention of the men, but their overwhelming jubilant mood was infectious, even to him, and he found himself smiling at their obvious relieved joy. The celebrations continued for several more minutes, until Captain Waylon joined them on the fore deck, at which point the men quietened a little, and returned Lusam back to his feet in front of the Captain. The Captain smiled and held out his hand to Lusam, who took it in return.

"Thank you," The Captain said, shaking his hand firmly. Lusam nodded to the captain, not sure he was ready for words just yet, and the men cheered loudly again, but thankfully left him on his own two feet this time. Lusam couldn't help thinking about how many men, just like these, must have lost their lives, and how many ships had been destroyed lately by the Empire ships in this area. He wasn't sure he wanted to know the precise numbers, but he knew from what he had heard that it must be in the hundreds, if not thousands.

He suddenly realised that he no longer had the right to risk the lives of these men—and certainly not to simply reach Lamuria a few days sooner than they might otherwise. If he had not been here to protect the Pelorus, it would have been destroyed for sure, and everyone aboard killed. He found that he could no longer morally justify asking the Captain and his men to travel any further south, not when he knew full well they would have to retrace the same route home *without* his protection. Every extra mile they travelled further south, made it less likely these men would ever make it home alive, and that *was* something Lusam could change.

"Captain, may I have a word, in private please?" Lusam asked, as the Captain started heading for the main deck.

"Of course," he replied, gesturing that Lusam should follow him.

"I think you should all come too. What I have to say affects all of us," Lusam said to Renn, Neala and Alexia, who all exchanged curious glances, but remained silent and followed Lusam to the Captain's cabin.

They all entered the Captain's cabin, closing the door firmly behind them just as the quartermaster began issuing orders for the men to return back to work. Captain Waylon took to his chair behind his dark wooden desk, waiting expectantly for Lusam to speak.

"Captain, I would like you to drop us off at the next available port we come to," Lusam said bluntly, and without preamble.

"But, we had a deal," The Captain replied defensively, sitting up straighter in his chair, ready for an argument. Lusam held up his hand to the Captain, indicating he should listen.

"Yes, we did," Renn agreed from Lusam's side, looking at him curiously.

"Yes, I know we did. And we *still* do. I am not suggesting we renegotiate the payment terms, Captain, only the destination. Captain Waylon, let me ask you this: what would have happened to you, your ship, and its crew if I had not been here today? I'll tell you, Captain—exactly the same thing that would happen to you on your return journey, when I'm *not* here to protect you. I can not ask you, or your men to risk their lives any further than you already have for us. Every minute we sail further south, is one extra minute you must travel back north, alone, and unprotected. I *have* to live with my conscience whenever I kill our enemies, but I can choose *not* to live with your deaths on my conscience too. And so, I ask again, Captain. Please drop us at the next available port, and take your men and ship home, safely," Lusam said, almost pleading with the man.

Captain Waylon looked to Renn for direction, as it was with him he had made the deal, and wanted to make sure he was in agreement with Lusam before setting out any new plans. Renn nodded mutely to the Captain, then returned his gaze back to Lusam. `*How he's grown, in such a short space of time,*` Renn thought to himself, no longer recognising Lusam as the innocent boy he had first met only a short time ago. It reminded him of something his old friend and tutor, Hershel had once told him: `*Sometimes the prize is not worth the eventual cost, and often, men discover that too late to be of any use to them.*` Renn felt a great sense of pride in Lusam, that he had seen what he himself had not. And an equal sense of shame for himself, because he had been so blinded by his own mission to reach Lamuria, at *any* cost, even at the expense of these innocent men's lives.

"Lusam is right Captain, we can not risk your lives any further on this trip," Renn agreed, placing a hand on Lusam's shoulder and giving it a small squeeze.

"Very well," Captain Waylon said, leaning over to a map rack and retrieving one of them. He unrolled it on his desk, weighting each corner with a brass weight, and began to study the coastline. "Here's the closest port to our current position. In fact, we should be almost there," he said pointing to an area on the map. Renn looked closely and read the name: *Prystone*.

"Prystone it is then, Captain," Renn said. "I guess we should gather our things together if we're already so close. Well, Captain, it's been a pleasure doing business with you."

"Likewise," the Captain replied, standing up and offering each of them in turn his hand. When it came to Lusam's turn, he said, "And thank *you*, young man. We all owe you a debt of gratitude. One which I hope I can repay someday."

"Knowing that you and your men are safely on your way home is enough for me, Captain," Lusam replied shaking his hand. Captain Waylon smiled and nodded.

The quartermaster was on the main deck when they all stepped out, and the Captain gave him his new orders to pass on to the helmsman: they were to dock at Prystone, then return home to their families in Fairport.

"Yes sir," the quartermaster said enthusiastically, obviously relieved that their trip was being cut short.

It didn't take long for the good news to spread throughout the ship, as was evident by the men's lifted spirits. Many of the crew sung old seafaring songs, and there was a noticeable spring in the step of almost every man aboard ship.

Neala was busy packing her things away on the lower deck, and Alexia had gone to return the board game she had borrowed earlier from one of the crew, leaving Lusam and Renn to themselves on the aft deck of the ship. Lusam noticed Renn watching him, as he watched the crew go about their own work on the deck below. He was smiling at Lusam in strange sort of way, which surprised Lusam quite a bit, considering he had just scuppered Renn's plans to reach Lamuria as fast as they might have, if they had gone further south before making landfall. He was about to ask Renn what was up, but he spoke first, breaking the silence between them.

"You know, I'm really proud of you, lad," Renn said beaming a smile at Lusam.

"Proud of me... for what?" Lusam asked, slightly confused.

"For seeing what I couldn't, or at least, what I chose not to see. For putting the lives of others before your own goals. And for using your own morality to guide your actions. I saw how hard you struggled with yourself, when you were faced with ending the lives of those Empire men, and for that I thank Aysha. Not because it caused you great pain to have to kill those men, but because you paused long enough to think about it, before you did. There's no doubt that you wield great power now Lusam, but with that power, comes even greater responsibility. And having witnessed that responsibility in you today, is what makes me so proud of you, lad."

Lusam had been thinking of little else since he had destroyed the enemy ship and its crew. Each man aboard probably had a family of their own back home in the Empire. One they would never see again. He knew Renn had seen his fair share of combat, and wondered how he dealt with it.

"Renn … how do you do it? How do you live with yourself after you've killed someone? I know that I killed those Empire agents outside Coldmont, but that felt different somehow, especially at the time. They had been trying to kill us for days, and it seemed almost *reasonable* to kill them for what they had done to us. But those men on the ship … they were just following orders. I know they would likely have killed innocent people if I had let them live, but what gives *me* the right to choose who lives and dies?" Lusam asked in a quiet voice, looking to Renn for guidance. Renn remained silent for quite a while, trying to think of how best to answer such an important question.

"That's a very difficult question to answer lad, but I will say this: killing is *never* easy. Nor should it ever become so. But it *is* sometimes necessary. Always remember, in war there are no such thing as innocent soldiers, they have either killed already, or *will* kill eventually, given the opportunity. That is true, of course, on both sides of any war. But, it is not the war that will eventually decide who is right or wrong, it is whoever is left standing at the end of that war. I have always put my faith in Aysha, that she will guide my hand to do what is *necessary*, and grant me the wisdom to see when it is not. I also truly believe, that Aysha would not have granted you these powers, if she did not intend for you to use them justly, in defence of our people and lands.

"I will also say this, Lusam: the day you stop feeling bad about killing, is the day you are truly lost. Up until that day, you must choose your actions according to your own judgements, and pray that day never comes," Renn replied stoically. Lusam nodded at Renn's words of wisdom.

"Thank you Renn. I think I understand better now," Lusam replied, feeling a little better about it than he had a few minutes earlier.

It wasn't long before Neala had finished her packing, and Alexia had returned from her own chores and joined the others again. Both Lusam and Renn had already packed their things away earlier that day, and all they were waiting for now, was to dock at Prystone.

When the small port came into view about ten minutes later, it didn't take them long to realise that it had already suffered its fate at the hands of the Empire. Many of the buildings were completely, or partially burned to the ground. The dock had also suffered minor damage by the look of it, but it still appeared to be usable.

"What do you suppose happened?" Neala asked, knowing the answer was quite obvious looking at the damage strewn village.

"If I were to guess, I would say at least one of those Empire ships decided to dock here too," Renn replied.

"I don't see any people moving around," Alexia said, scanning the streets and houses she could see.

"The Empire don't tend to leave many people alive after they pass through a place. Many of the sea ports on our southern shores have been destroyed over the past few years. The only reported survivors were the ones that were either smart enough to run at the first sight of trouble, or the ones who were lucky enough to be out of the towns or villages when they were attacked in the first place. In each case, the Empire destroyed the village or town completely. They didn't steal anything, they simply destroyed it: buildings, people, animals and crops alike," Renn said.

"Maybe they got interrupted here," Lusam suggested, nodding towards a few remaining buildings that were left standing.

"Possibly, but it's more likely they were simply in a

hurry when they passed through here. On their way to Lamuria, no doubt," Renn replied. "Alexia, keep your bow handy, you might need it soon."

"Oh?" Alexia enquired.

"Like I said, the Empire don't tend to leave *much* behind them, but one thing they often *do* leave behind, are their reanimated minions. They use them to kill or dissuade any returnees of the villages or towns. I suspect it's quite effective seeing a dead loved one, or neighbour walking around and trying to kill people," Renn said sarcastically.

"I bet," Neala agreed grimacing.

They were now only a short distance from the dockside, and as if on cue, both Renn's sword and Alexia's bow started to glow blue with the presence of the undead nearby. Renn simply tilted his head to the others, as if to say, `I told you so.`

"Okay, get ready. There may be an entire village here to deal with. You better stay close to one of us Neala," Renn suggested.

"No need. Lusam enchanted my knives so I can kill them now," Neala replied grinning.

"Ah, so that's what Lusam was doing with them the other day. I forgot to ask you about it with everything that has been going on. And yours too Alexia, I take it?" Renn asked. Alexia nodded, performing a fancy twirl with a knife in each hand as she did so.

"You'd think she actually knew how to use those things, wouldn't you," Neala said, teasing her friend. Alexia inclined her head, smiled, and returned the two spinning blades back to their sheaths in one fluid motion, without even looking.

"Show off," Neala said, rolling her eyes.

"You're only jealous because when you try it, your knives usually end up in lover-boy's foot," Alexia replied, trying very hard not to laugh.

"Hey! I told you, that was an accident. *And* you promised not to tell anyone that I told you about that," Neala said, scowling at her friend.

"Oops... sorry," Alexia replied, finally laughing at her friends pouting face.

Renn looked inquisitively at Lusam, then at his foot. Lusam sighed, and said, "It's a long story. I'll tell you about it later." Renn simply nodded, picked up his things, and headed to the starboard side of the ship, where they would soon be disembarking. Lusam followed his example, as did Neala and Alexia, but not without jostling each other all the way there first.

Renn wished he'd had enough time and foresight to warn the crew about the possible danger, but it was too late by the time the ship was approaching the dock. Men were shouting commands to each other, and things were generally noisy aboard the Pelorus. `More than loud enough to attract some unwanted attention from within the village,` Renn thought to himself. And even before the ship made contact with the dock, the first of the undead villagers appeared at the far end of the street, quickly followed by several more.

"It's okay, I've got these," Alexia said, removing her bow and nocking an arrow in one fluid motion. Her aim was true, and each of her five remaining arrows found their targets with a dull thud, dropping the undead minions where they stood. Just before the ship made contact with the dock, two crewmen jumped across the narrow gap onto the wooden platform and began to fasten thick ropes to the dock moorings, both nervously looking towards the direction of the undead creatures. A moment later the ship made gentle contact with the dockside, and Renn, Alexia and Neala all jumped down onto the wooden platform of the dock. Fortunately the tide was low, and the wooden dock was only a couple of feet below the side of the ship.

Lusam was just about to jump down and join the others, when he was knocked off his feet by a huge explosion further along the dock. Broken timbers, ropes and sea water rained down on the ship as he struggled frantically to regain his feet. His immediate concern was for Neala and the others, but when he finally managed to stand up again, he noticed they were already further away from the dockside, engaging with the undead minions. Instinctively, he raised a shield around the Pelorus, then ran to the other side of the ship to see where the enemy was firing from. The Pelorus' crew were all now aware of the enemy vessel closing in on their location, and the two men who had been securing the ship to the dockside had removed the ropes again, freeing the Pelorus from the restraints of the dock. There were many calls in Lusam's direction, all trying to make sure that he was aware of the enemy ship, and that he was also prepared to defend them against it.

The Empire ship had appeared around the headland to the south, giving them little warning of its approach. It didn't seem likely that they could have seen the Pelorus approaching Prystone, so either they were intending to dock here anyway, or more likely Lusam thought, they had been summoned by someone aboard the ship they had destroyed earlier. Lusam knew the Empire agents had the ability to communicate with each other using their Necromatic rings, and guessed that was the most likely reason for the sudden appearance of this second vessel.

Although Lusam had already erected a force-field to protect the side of the ship facing the enemy vessel, nothing had yet made contact with it. At first he thought the aim of the men aboard the Empire ship was bad, but then he suddenly realised with horror, they were not actually firing at the Pelorus, they were trying to hit Renn and the others on the shore instead. They had obviously mistaken Renn's brighter aura for his own. There was no way Lusam could protect them from so far away, and the incoming missiles were too high above the ship, arcing through the air, and intentionally avoiding the Pelorus. Lusam watched as Renn intercepted two massive fireballs on his blessed shield, both winking out of existence as they made contact, but not before sending him crashing to the ground each time with the force of their impact. Neala and Alexia were busy fighting their own group of undead minions, but thankfully, Alexia spotted the danger to Renn, and took down two of them that were about to attack him while he was still flat on his back.

Lusam thought he heard Alexia shout something to Renn, but he couldn't make out what she said over the noise of the crew and the explosions coming from onshore.

Renn got back to his feet just in time to see three more huge fireballs heading directly for him. He didn't even try to block any of them this time, instead he dived to the side out of their path, and they exploded at the precise spot where he had been only a heartbeat before, incinerating the two dead minions, and unfortunately both of Alexia's precious blessed arrows. Lusam knew he had to quickly draw the fire of the enemy ship off Renn and the others, and onto himself. He lowered his mental shutter, revealing the true strength of his aura to the men aboard the Empire ship, then sent a powerful fireball of his own towards the bow of the enemy vessel. It struck the front of the ship, exploding a huge section of the forward deck, sending debris and bodies high into the air. It was hard to tell the exact number of men who died, but Lusam thought he had felt at least twenty death-pulses, maybe more.

There was a long pause in the Empire ship's attack, as the men aboard gathered themselves once more for another assault. Lusam planned to swiftly end the ship and the crew the same way he had the first, and began searching the enemy vessel for the telltale signs of their leader's brighter aura. It took him only a moment to realise that there was no obvious leader aboard their ship. Then he realised, any commander would most likely have been on the bow of their ship as it sailed towards its intended quarry, so he could see his enemy targets, and command his men to attack them accordingly. The men aboard the Empire ship had not been expecting any attack to come from the Pelorus, and had put all their efforts into the power of their attacks on Renn, instead of shielding themselves. Lusam's missile had hit them whilst they were unprepared, and had killed their leader outright, as well as all the other men in the line of fire behind him. He knew he could no longer drain the remaining Empire agents using the same method as he had used with the first ship, because only higher ranking agents could draw magical power from their subordinates, therefore his previous tactic would now be useless against the regular agents who remained aboard.

It wasn't long before the assault resumed from the Empire vessel. Lusam had expected the focus to shift to him and the Pelorus, but instead—possibly due to the lack of command aboard the Empire ship—they decided to split their efforts between the Pelorus and Renn. The Pelorus was now slowly moving away from the dockside, but not nearly fast enough for Lusam's liking. His shield had already taken over forty direct hits, and he was beginning to feel the effects of every one. The faster the Pelorus turned towards the enemy vessel the better. That way he would only need to shield the front of the ship again, instead of its whole length. He needed a way to speed things up and swing the bow out towards the Empire ship much faster than it was moving right now. Lusam glanced back to shore to see how the others were doing, but could only see Renn. Many of the buildings near Renn were burning or completely destroyed, and the air was thick with smoke and debris. Lusam guessed by Renn's actions that he was intentionally drawing fire to himself, and therefore splitting the attack of the Empire ship between himself and the Pelorus. Lusam was grateful for his help, but hoped that it wouldn't end badly for Renn.

Lusam heard Captain Waylon's voice before he saw him, shouting orders to his crew. After their last encounter, Captain Waylon also seemed to know that the best course of action was to steer the ship directly towards the enemy vessel, and gave those orders loud and clear. Lusam had an idea how to help the ship turn more swiftly towards that goal, and shouted to the Captain.

"Captain!" he yelled. The Captain turned towards Lusam's call and raised his chin in query.

"Tell your crew to brace themselves, I'm about to give us a push off from the docks. I don't want anyone falling overboard, or out of the rigging," Lusam yelled to the Captain.

"Understood," The Captain replied, and relayed the

information to his crew. Once Lusam was sure the order had been received by his men, he formed another force-field between the Pelorus and the docks, then rapidly expanded it to force the bow of the ship towards the approaching Empire ship. As soon as the huge pressure was applied against the dock, it shattered and splintered loudly, as it tore free from its foundations, completely destroying that section of dock.

"Oops," Lusam said to himself cringing, as the Captain raced to the ship's rail to see if it was his ship that had just been torn apart, or only the dock. His relieved look suggested only the latter, much to Lusam's own relief. He shifted his shield to the bow of the ship, and immediately felt the benefit of only having to shield a much smaller section of the ship, even though the frequency and ferocity of the attacks remained unchanged. Lusam had already contemplated destroying the enemy ship whilst they were still at the dockside, but that would have simply allowed many of the surviving men to swim to shore, and wreak havoc on anyone they came across later. He knew the destruction of the enemy vessel and its crew had to be absolute.

Captain Waylon had ordered full speed ahead, and they were now rapidly closing in on the Empire ship. More and more of the fire-power aboard the enemy ship became targeted against Lusam on the Pelorus, as the distance between the two ships rapidly reduced. Lusam's magical reserves were beginning to run low, and he acutely felt the impact of every missile his shield now absorbed. He doubted he had enough reserves left to kill each man aboard the Empire ship individually, not while having to maintain the shield around the Pelorus at the same time. A shield which he would soon have to expand to cover the entire length of the ship again, as they approached the enemy ship on a parallel intercept course. As they drew side by side with the enemy vessel, both ships dropped their sails to avoid sailing past each other, leaving both ships only about fifty paces apart, and parallel to each other.

Lusam watched nervously as the eighty or so Empire agents spread out along the entire length of the deck opposite him, preparing to fire. He couldn't simply assume they would all target him, and not the Pelorus. If he did, and tried to only shield himself, the Pelorus and her crew may be lost, so he *had* to shield the entire ship. A moment later the assault started. Lusam's shield absorbed the massive impact of over seventy missiles, dropping him to his knees with the sudden spike of magic required to maintain his shield. Instinctively, he sent two missiles of his own, neither of which were particularly powerful, but they still tore through their shields, killing at least fifteen of their numbers. Lusam was quickly back to his feet, and could see clearly the disarray he had caused aboard the enemy vessel. It seemed many of them were now having second thoughts about having a direct confrontation with such a powerful mage, and with no one in command, their ranks were beginning to quickly fall apart. Two of the Empire agents willingly dived overboard into the sea, obviously calculating their chances of surviving the swim to shore, as better than a direct confrontation with Lusam.

Lusam knew the Empire agents who were swimming to shore would soon become a problem for his friends if he didn't stop them, but he couldn't afford to concentrate his attention on only two men, not when there were still over sixty men aboard the enemy ship. He needed to end this now, before they regrouped and once more started a co-ordinated attack against him. It was actually the men jumping overboard that gave him an idea, or at least, the necessity to stop more of them jumping overboard. For a brief moment he thought about erecting a second force-field around the enemy vessel, to stop any more Empire agents trying to swim to shore. He soon realised that he neither had the magical reserves, or the need to do such a thing. He only needed to erect a single shield around the enemy vessel, not both ships. That way it would prevent any more of them escaping into the sea, and prevent their missiles from reaching the Pelorus.

Lusam quickly replaced the Pelorus' shield with one around the Empire ship, making sure to completely encase the vessel. The Empire ship was smaller than the Pelorus, but it still took a lot more energy to surround the whole vessel.

He noticed one of the Empire agents create another fireball and attempt to launch it towards the Pelorus. Lusam felt the impact as it exploded on the inside of his force-field, but what he didn't expect to see, was the Empire agent half-incinerated by his own fireball, when it exploded against his shield only a short distance from his hand. Three other Empire agents who were standing nearby also suffered burns from the explosion, and were now screaming in pain as their fellow magi tried to extinguish their burning clothes.

At that precise moment Lusam knew he had won the battle. The Empire agents could no longer fire any missiles without causing injuries or deaths amongst their own men, or at the very least, badly damaging their ship in the process. Lusam took full advantage of the confusion aboard the enemy vessel, and started to shrink his force-field with devastating results. At first the Empire ship started to groan loudly under the immense pressure. Then one after another the main timbers gave way with a loud snapping noise, sending both the bow and stern crashing together as the ship folded in half in a mass of broken timbers, crushing every man aboard in the process. Lusam's force-field was now no bigger than a tenth of its original size, and contained no life within. He released its broken contents into the sea with a loud splash, then turned his attention to the two Empire agents who were still trying to reach the shore. He located the two men easily, and encased both inside a force-field, letting each one fill with water until there was no air left inside either of them. Then he rapidly froze both, killing the men instantly.

Lusam collapsed to his knees once more, partly through exertion, and partly through his own revulsion at what he had once again been forced to do. He prayed to Aysha for the souls of the men he had just been forced to kill, and asked for the strength to complete whatever she had ordained would be his destiny.

Lusam remained motionless on his knees for a long time before Captain Waylon approached him, his vision blurred, and his head thundering with pain.

"Are you alright?" he asked, with an air of concern in his voice. Lusam wasn't sure if it was actually concern for *his* welfare, or his own, after witnessing what Lusam had just done to the other ship and its crew. Lusam gave a stifled manic laugh to the Captain's question.

"As alright as I'm ever likely to be again," Lusam replied quietly, mostly to himself. He tried to stand, but his legs buckled under him, forcing Captain Waylon to catch him before he hit the deck.

"Steady there, son" the Captain said, helping him back to his feet. "You better take it easy for a while. You look completely exhausted. You're welcome to take my bunk for a while until you regain some of your strength ..."

"No. no, thank you Captain. I need to go help the others, right away. They're all in danger, and I must help them," Lusam interrupted.

"I don't think you're in any fit state to help anyone right now. Is there anything I can do to help?" Captain Waylon asked. Lusam thought about it for a moment, knowing the Captain was absolutely right about his current ability to fight. But if they waited here too long and another Empire ship turned up, they would all perish. The Pelorus needed to be underway as soon as possible to give them the best chance of making it back to Fairport alive.

"Captain, I do know one way that you and your crew could help me," Lusam said reluctantly, knowing what he was about to suggest would sound bizarre to anyone, let alone a group of superstitions sailors.

"Anything, just name it," Captain Waylon offered, far too freely for Lusam's liking.

"Well, if you would allow me, I have the ability to take a small amount of magic from each of your crew to replenish my own reserves a little. I can assure you, it's completely painless, and won't affect any of you in the slightest. And whatever I take will be restored naturally over the next day or so anyway," Lusam said, keeping his voice low so the crew wouldn't hear.

"What do you have to do to take the magic?" Captain

Waylon asked, also keeping his voice low.

"Nothing much, just touch the person," Lusam replied, grimacing at the pain in his head.

"Anywhere in particular?"

"No, it doesn't matter, as long as it's skin to skin contact," Lusam replied. The Captain nodded, then offered Lusam his hand.

"Show me," Captain Waylon said. Lusam nodded, took his hand, and immediately located his magical reserves, syphoning off a small amount of that power and adding it to his own, all in the time it took for a brief handshake.

"That's it?" Captain Waylon asked, shocked at the brief contact. Lusam nodded. "I didn't feel a thing."

"I said you wouldn't feel anything," Lusam replied grinning, his throbbing head easing a little.

"Then I don't see why anyone else needs to know about it. Don't get me wrong, I know we all owe you a great deal more than this, but sailors are a superstitions lot when it comes to things they don't understand, and I don't want them blaming this on every minor thing that goes wrong during our journey home. In fact, they'd probably use it as an excuse for the next few months," Captain Waylon said laughing.

"So I've heard," Lusam agreed, smiling back at the Captain.

"Just leave it to me," Captain Waylon said winking at him. Within five minutes every man aboard ship was lined up against the starboard rail waiting to shake Lusam's hand, and thank him for defending them twice against the Empire ships. The magic Lusam was able to take was nothing compared to what he had just used, but it did ease his throbbing head and steady his legs somewhat. He was under no illusion that he would lose a battle against another ship full of Empire agents, but at least for the time being, he did now have enough reserves to defend himself and his friends against lesser foes.

"I guess we should take you back to shore now, eh?" Captain Waylon said after Lusam had finished shaking everyone's hand.

"No need, thank you, Captain. It's pointless you wasting precious time taking me to shore when I can get there easily enough by myself. But before I go, let me check the area for any other Empire ships first," Lusam replied, levitating himself high into the air. The look on the face of the man nestled in the rigging was hilarious as Lusam levitated past him; he almost fell from his perch with shock. Lusam levitated himself higher than he had ever done before. So high that the ship looked like nothing more than a shoe-sized object floating on the water far below. He was able to see for many miles in all directions, and was relieved to note that they were the only ship afloat for as far as he could see. He quickly descended to the deck of the Pelorus and gave the good news to the Captain.

"Doesn't that use up magic too?" Captain Waylon asked, pointing upwards with his thumb.

"It does, but only a very small amount. Besides, it was worth it to know you will all be safe on your journey home. Good luck Captain, I hope we meet again," Lusam said, shaking his hand one last time.

"Good luck to you too," Captain Waylon replied, as he watched Lusam levitate from the deck of his ship, and head towards what was left of Prystone dock.

Chapter Thirty-Seven

Renn, Alexia and Neala were the first to jump down onto the wooden dock a few feet below the ship's rail. Alexia had already destroyed five of the undead minions with her bow, but more were now heading their way from further down the street. As soon as their feet touched the wooden dockside they all started to run towards the new undead minions. The intention was to keep them well away from the Pelorus while it left the dock again, and could head for the safety of deeper water. Neala glanced back over her shoulder to check where Lusam was, but was suddenly blown off her feet by an explosion further along the dockside. Shards of broken wood, ropes and sea waters came raining down on top of her as she quickly regained her feet. Both Alexia and Renn had managed to stay on their feet despite the explosion, and after retrieving her five arrows, Alexia caught back up with Renn at the far end of the street.

Neala kept her head down as she ran towards the others, who were now engaged in battle with the undead minions at the far end of the docks. Concerned for Lusam's well-being, she kept looking back towards the Pelorus, and was very relieved to see him stand up a moment later—seemingly unharmed. She scanned the horizon, and noticed an Empire ship that had just rounded the headland to the south of them. Cursing their bad luck, she focused her attention back on the undead minions ahead of her, and hoped that Lusam was capable of defeating the Empire ship alone, like he had the last one. Removing two of her enchanted knives, she engaged the first group of undead minions, dropping two of them instantly, as her enchanted blades made contact with their skin, completely draining their small amount of magical power.

Renn noticed a large group of undead minions heading their way from another direction, and went to intercept them before they could join up with the first group that Alexia and Neala were still fighting. He knew how dangerously strong the undead minions were, but as long as they weren't allowed to surround them in large numbers, they should be relatively easy to kill with their blessed and enchanted weapons. A far more pressing issue for him right then, however, was the rapidly increasing number of fireballs that seemed to be targeting him from the newly arrived enemy ship. As he moved towards the approaching undead minions, the incoming missiles also seemed to track him down the street, and several of them came close to hitting him. Thankfully, it didn't take him long to dispatch the new group of undead, and he was able to swiftly turn his attention back to the much greater threat now coming from the Empire ship. And not a moment too soon, as he was forced to take a massive fireball dead centre of his blessed shield. The fireball was instantly dissipated by his shield, but the force behind it was not. Renn was knocked clean off his feet, and landed hard on his back in the centre of the street. He barely made it to his feet again, before a second fireball struck his shield, and sent him crashing onto his back once more, knocking the wind right out of him. Dazed, he didn't even notice the two undead minions until their shadows crossed his vision.

"Renn ... look out!" Alexia shouted from somewhere to his left, quickly followed by two loud thuds, as her blessed arrows struck and killed both of the undead minions about to attack him. Renn rolled to his feet, shield at the ready, and scanned the sky for any more missiles. Not seeing any, he turned to Alexia and shouted his thanks.

"You're welcome, don't forget my arrows though," Alexia shouted back, and watched open-mouthed as three huge fireballs arced through the sky towards Renn. Fortunately, Renn spotted them in time, and dived to his right, narrowly avoiding being completely incinerated by them. Unfortunately, however, her blessed arrows were not so lucky. "Damn," she said, under her breath. Now she only had three left.

'I'm getting too old for this,' Renn thought to himself, as he got back to his feet for the third time in less than a minute. As he scanned the sky for yet more missiles heading his way, he noticed a bright aura appear on board the Pelorus. He immediately knew it was Lusam's, simply by its intensity. At first Renn feared that Lusam was trying to scare the enemy ship away again—by revealing his aura to them—but a moment later, he saw Lusam's attack. The whole front of the enemy ship exploded, showering the surrounding water with debris and bodies, and Renn felt the distinct death-pulses of at least twenty magi. Renn was thankful for the sudden lack of fireballs heading his way, but soon realised why they had targeted him in the first place. They must have mistaken his aura, for that of a weaker mage's. Even though Renn was not capable of performing any complex magic himself, his aura would have still appeared to be the brightest around, making him the natural target to everyone on board the enemy vessel.

Renn knew that Lusam had revealed his presence aboard the Pelorus intentionally, to draw the fire off of him. But he hoped he hadn't tipped his hand too soon by doing so. The Pelorus was barely away from the dock yet, and still broadside to the enemy ship. Renn felt sure that Lusam had already used a lot of his magical reserves fighting the first Empire ship, and now that he had revealed his presence on board the Pelorus, he was about to take another pounding. He just hoped Lusam had enough reserves left to defeat the enemy ship quickly, and not let his conscience get in the way of what must be done this time. Renn said a silent prayer to Aysha, asking her to grant Lusam her infinite wisdom, and the strength to do what he must. A moment later, the attack resumed. Renn had fully expected the Empire agents to concentrate their fire-power exclusively on the Pelorus, since Lusam had revealed his presence there, but to Renn's bewilderment, they split their attack between the Pelorus and him. Why any commanding officer would issue such an order, he had no idea, but he was more than happy to see the missiles heading his way, instead of pounding at Lusam's shield. *'If it would buy Lusam some extra time to get into position for an attack, he was more than happy to remain a target for the Empire ship, albeit a quick moving one,'* Renn thought to himself wryly.

***

Neala had already been forced to use a second pair of her knives. Her first pair had quickly become saturated from the magic absorbed by killing the undead minions. She hadn't counted the exact number each knife had managed to kill before being rendered useless, but she guessed it was no more than six or seven each. At first, Neala and Alexia had fought side by side, both expecting a much tougher fight, given the number of them that emerged from within the buildings once the explosions started. But somehow these were different from the ones they had faced in the Elveen Mountains. Although she would never have described those as fleet-footed or agile, compared with these, they were positively graceful. Some of them here could barely walk, and many had limbs that hung uselessly by their sides, or were burned to such an extent they could barely move. *'Killing them is as much a mercy, as it is a necessity,'* Neala thought to herself, ending another poor creature's suffering.

Neala noticed that Alexia's knives had also been rendered useless a few minutes earlier, and unfortunately, she only had two daggers. Now Neala watched as she resorted to killing the undead minions by casually poking them with one of her blessed arrows. Under different circumstances it might have been almost comical seeing her do little more than touch the creatures with the tip of her arrow, then watch as they collapsed in a heap on the floor in front of her. But Neala was under no illusions at all as to what these poor villagers must have suffered at the hands of the

Empire agents who had passed through here. It was sickening to think that these—*things*—were once just ordinary people, with lives of their own. People with families and friends, dreams and aspirations. And now they were nothing more than undead puppets, created by the sick Empire agents for their own twisted amusement, and then abandoned here, to cause even more death and heartache for anyone who chose to return home to their village later.

Around the docks most of the buildings had either been completely, or partially burned to the ground, but the further away from the docks that Neala looked, the more buildings remained standing. Neala could see what looked like the rooftop of a large barn in the next street, and from what she could tell, it looked untouched by the fires. It was much taller than the buildings in front of it, and she guessed it would be their best chance of finding food, or if they were really lucky, even horses for their onward journey

"Alexia, I'm going to take a look down that next street, and see if I can find any horses or supplies. It looks like there's a big barn down there at the bottom," Neala shouted across the street to Alexia.

"Okay, but if you don't mind, I'm going to stay here and watch Renn's back, at least until that ship out there stops playing target practice with him. Be careful though, I don't want lover-boy blaming me if you get hurt," Alexia shouted back, grinning at her friend. Neala nodded, but didn't reply to her jibe. Neala knew she was only joking around, but the mere thought of Lusam and the danger he was currently in made her stomach clench wildly. She knew she couldn't do anything about it, even if she had been with him on the ship, but that didn't stop her feeling sick at the thought of him being injured, or even worse. She had never needed anyone in her whole life, for anything, but she had no idea what she would do now if she lost him. Shaking the dark thoughts from her head, she turned and headed for the junction of the next street.

Neala approached what looked like the main village well, complete with bucket and winch handle. `At least we'll *have plenty of fresh water for our onward journey,`* she thought to herself, glancing over the edge, and into the darkness of the deep well below. When she rounded the corner of the street where she'd seen the barn, she froze mid-stride. She had indeed found a large barn, seemingly untouched by the Empire agents, but opposite the barn, was a large group of undead minions, all clambering around something on the floor. It was then she heard the chilling screams of what sounded like a young girl.

"Oh, Gods!" Neala cursed, imagining the undead minions tearing the young girl apart in her mind. She expected the screams to abruptly end, but instead, they became more desperate. Neala rushed forward, keeping to the centre of the street, and well away from any doorways that might be harbouring any undead surprise for her. As she got closer, she began to understand what was happening. They didn't actually have hold of the little girl—not yet, anyway. They were all trying to force their way into what looked like a sewer grate, where she was obviously taking refuge.

Neala burst into a sprint, removing two of her enchanted knives from her belt, and headed straight towards the mass of undead minions. There were at least twenty of the hideous creatures, all groping towards the sounds of the little girl's screams, and trying to rip the sewer cover free, so they could get to her inside. Neala struck fast and without warning. Five undead minions collapsed on her first pass— like sacks of coal being dropped off the back of a cart. The rest of them seemed to sense her presence, and as one, turned in her direction. The first two to come within range of Neala's knives, quickly joined their friends on the floor, dead —but the next, didn't.

Neala struck it cleanly in the chest, but nothing happened: another set of her knives were saturated with magic, and therefore useless against the undead. Removing her final two knives, she set about killing the remaining undead minions. One after another they slumped to the ground, until only four remained. That was when her final set of knives reached saturation point, and also became useless. The four that remained seemed to work as one, spreading out to corner her. Forcing her to back up towards the building behind her. She tried to run around them, but they expertly cut off her escape route, and forced her to retreat once more. She was running out of space fast, and knew if she didn't try and make a break for it soon, she would be done for. She briefly thought about shouting for help, but doubted Alexia or Renn would hear her from so far away, and the last thing she needed right now, was to attract the attention of any more undead minions that might be lurking around the area.

When her back finally made contact with the barn wall, she knew she had run out of options. Either she tried to run through them, or die here. She noticed the one on the right had a damaged arm. It seemed to hang uselessly by its side, and figured that was her best chance of escape. Trying to unbalance the creature, she threw one of her knives at its head, and ran. The knife thudded into its forehead, but had absolutely no effect whatsoever on it. Neala tried to slip past, between it and the wall she was trapped against, but as she tried to dodge the grasp of the creature, it somehow managed to catch hold of her tunic.

It was a strange sensation feeling her torso suddenly stop moving forward, and her legs carry on running under her. She found herself face to face, dangling from the grip of the one-armed creature, as the others slowly closed in around her. Frantically, she kicked at its stomach, and plunged her knife repeatedly into its good arm, but it had no effect on its grip. Changing tactics, she began to kick viciously at its knees, and was quickly rewarded with a loud snapping noise as its joint shattered under her assault, sending both of them crashing to the floor, and knocking the wind out of Neala as the undead minion landed heavily on top of her. She tried in vain to push herself out from underneath it using her feet, but she couldn't gain enough grip on the dusty street with the heels of her boots.

The other three were almost on top of her now, and would soon tear her limb-from-limb if she didn't break free from the grip of the one pinning her down. Taking her knife, she cut away the part of her tunic that the undead creature had hold of, intending to scuttle backwards a few feet out of its reach. But once again it grabbed hold of her, only this time, it managed to grab her by the wrist. She screamed in pain, as it shattered her wrist bone with its inhuman strength. She knew her life was about to end, but all she could think about, was how she had let Lusam down. And what would *he* do without her? Would he end up with her best friend Alexia? She laughed out loud at the craziness of her final thoughts, realising that even now she was suspicious of her best friend's motives, even though she had never done anything to deserve such treatment.

"Sorry," she said out loud, thinking of both Lusam and Alexia as she said it. Then she closed her eyes as the hand of the first undead minion reached out for her.

Thud! ... Thud! ... Thud!

Neala opened her eyes to see three undead minions collapsing by the sides of her, each one with an arrow protruding from its back.

"Alexia!" Neala whispered, hope rekindling within her, that she might still survive the day. The one on top of her tightened its grip on her wrist, causing her to gasp in pain. It was using its one good arm to lever itself further up her body, causing her tremendous pain as it did so. She knew it intended to kill her. Once it was high enough, it would let go of her wrist and snap her neck. Desperately, she looked past the creature, hoping to see Alexia or Renn close by, but they were still at the far end of the street, too far away to help her in time. Then she saw it; the arrow sticking out of the dead minion's back next to her. She stretched out her good arm to get the arrow, but it was just out of reach. Her fingertips brushed the arrow shaft, but she couldn't close her hand around it. Sucking in three or four rapid breaths to prepare herself for the pain, she bucked her body under the creature, and slowly moved a little closer to the arrow. Her vision darkened at the edges with the pain, but she managed to stay conscious long enough to grab the arrow and tear it free from the dead minion's body. She plunged it into the side of the creature on top of her, but nothing happened. Despair threatened to to take her under as she realised, the blessed arrow would only work for a paladin of Aysha. All she could do was grip the arrow and use it to push against, to try and slow the advance of the creature.

Neala had never been a particularly religious person, but she found herself at that moment thanking Aysha for her life, and asking her to watch over Lusam and the others after she was gone. A calm sense or serenity flowed through her as she finally accepted her own fate. She let go of the arrow, unable to hold back the creature any longer, but not before it emitted a delicate flash of blue light, and the creature slumped forward. Dead.

Neala had no idea why the blessed arrow had finally killed the creature, but she knew deep down that it had to have been the work of Aysha herself, and for that, she was incredibly grateful. She closed her eyes, and thanked Aysha for sparing her life once more, then shed a small tear of relief when she heard Lusam's voice in the distance desperately calling out her name. She tried to call back to him, but the dead weight of the body on top of her stopped her from taking a full breath. She tried to move, but pain erupted from her wrist once more. The creature's hand was still clamped tightly around it; even in death it didn't want to release her.

Renn was the first to reach her, sword drawn, and ready to run the undead minion through, but he noticed the lack of blue glow on his blade, indicating the creature was already dead.

"Are you alright, lass?" he asked, between panting breaths.

"Yeah, I guess so," she replied weakly. "No wait—AARGH!" she cried out, as Renn tried to roll the body off the top of her, twisting her broken wrist in the process. Panting through the pain, she managed to say, "My wrist is broken … and it still has tight hold of it."

"Oh, sorry lass" Renn apologised, cringing when he saw the awkward angle of her wrist, still in the grip of the dead minion's hand.

"Oh, Gods!" Alexia cursed, coming to a halt and also seeing her twisted wrist. "That looks painful."

"No kidding," Neala half-squealed, as Renn began to pry off the fingers clamping her wrist. Unbelievably, the pain actually increased after the creature's hand was removed from her wrist. Her wrist throbbed violently with every beat of her heart, now that her circulation had been restored to the area.

"Neala!" Lusam called, as he skidded to a halt next to her, then fell to his knees beside her. "Are you hurt?" he asked frantically, noticing her pale complexion and sweaty face. She was so relieved to see him alive and unharmed, that she grabbed his tunic and pulled him down on top of her, and into a tight one-armed embrace. Although her damaged wrist was well away from him, the jolt sent a fresh wave of pain through her. She gritted her teeth against it, and once it had settled back down again, she kissed Lusam so passionately, that she forgot all about her pain, at least for a little while.

It was the quiet sobbing sounds that Neala barely heard emanating from the sewer grate which ended their joyous reunion, as Neala suddenly remembered the earlier screams of the little girl. Neala pushed Lusam away from her a little, so she could tell the others about the little girl, but as she did so, Lusam saw her wrist for the first time.

"Neala ... your wrist!" he said, with a great deal of concern in his voice, and an equal amount of concern etched on his face. He didn't even wait for a reply, he immediately placed his hand on hers and magically blocked her pain. Neala visibly relaxed as the pain suddenly ceased in her wrist, but felt a fresh wave of nausea, as she heard the bones snap back into place within her wrist. Less than a minute later, and Lusam had repaired her wrist completely, but not before his head had begun to throb again through his lack of magical power reserves.

"You know, I always suspected it, but now I *know* she will do anything to hold his hand," Alexia said jokingly to Renn, whilst grinning at her friend still on the floor.

"Ha, ha, very funny," Neala replied sarcastically, as she rotated her wrist, checking for any residual effects. "By the way, there's a little girl hiding inside that grate over there," Neala said, pointing at the grate cover halfway down the street. Two of the dead minions were slumped across the top of the grate, almost hiding its existence from the others, but Neala knew exactly where it was.

"How do you know?" Alexia asked, looking for a grate in the direction Neala was pointing.

"When I first entered the street, I heard her screams. At first, I thought they already had hold of her, but when I realised they didn't, I rushed in to try and stop them. That's why I took on so many of these things alone. They were all trying to get to her inside that grate. I was going to call you for some help, but I didn't think you'd hear me from so far away, and I didn't want to attract any more of these things," Neala replied, nodding towards the numerous bodies scattered across the street.

"Well, I guess that explains why you were here, but what I don't understand, is why you waited until that one was literally on top of you, before killing it with your knives," Alexia asked a little confused, pointing to the body of the one that had broken her wrist.

"No, I couldn't kill it with my knives. They had already stopped working, that's why these four were able to corner me so easily. I don't know how, or why it worked, but I used one of your arrows to kill it. I pulled it from a corpse you'd shot, and stabbed it into its side. It didn't do anything at first, and I thought I was going to die for sure, so I prayed to Aysha, and a moment later it glowed blue and the thing died," Neala replied.

Renn chuckled. "Never underestimate the power of faith, Neala. It's truly the mightiest ally we have in this life, and without faith, we are no more than grains of sand scattered to the four winds," he said, smiling at her.

"I'm not sure I understand," Neala replied.

"That's the beauty of faith, lass—you don't have to understand it, you just need to possess it. It seems likely to me, that at the moment of your imminent demise you fully opened your heart to Aysha, and she rewarded you for it. More than that, I cannot explain why you were able to use her blessed weapon. I guess you're just going to have to take it on faith," Renn said, grinning at her confused expression. Neala nodded at Renn, unable to deny the logic of his explanation, but still not fully understanding it.

"Maybe we should go rescue that poor little girl, while these two stop slobbering over each other," Alexia suggested jovially to Renn, as she watched Neala and Lusam resume their kissing and cuddling on the ground.

"Before you go, let me clean your knives of magic please," Lusam said, breaking off a particularly passionate kiss with Neala. "Yours too Neala," he added. `It wouldn't be a lot of magic, but it might go some way to stopping this throbbing headache,` he thought to himself. It only took a quick touch of each blade to drain it of its tiny amount of magical power, but it was such a small amount of magic, it did little to ease his head. `At least the weapons would be effective again,` he consoled himself, then turned his attention back to his favourite activity—Neala.

Alexia rolled her eyes at them both, then nodded towards the grate where the little girl was supposed to be trapped. Renn chuckled quietly, and followed her lead, as the two lovebirds continued to kiss and cuddle where they had left them.

As they approached the grate, the sobbing grew louder and louder. `Whoever was inside the grate, was extremely upset by the sounds of it` Alexia thought to herself. Renn quickly dragged the bodies off the top of the grate cover, and was greeted by a fresh scream from inside the grate. The little girl had obviously mistaken the sudden movement of the corpses as them coming back to life again, and Alexia quickly tried to calm her down.

"It's okay. You're safe now. We're here to help you," Alexia said in a calming voice, trying to lift the grate cover off, but finding it was somehow locked into position. Guessing it must be locked from the inside, she gave up trying to remove it, and instead knelt down by the side of the grate. She noticed lots of small holes all the way around the lip of the grate, and tried to see if she could make out who was inside, but all she could see was the darkness beyond. She was certain that whoever was inside would be able to see her clearly, and so, she hoped by showing them her face, she could convince them that she was a friend.

"My name's Alexia, what's yours?" she said towards the grate. At first there was no reply from within the darkness, and Alexia thought whoever was inside had decided not to speak with her. Then she heard a series of weak rasping coughs from deeper inside the grate. She heard the little girl say something quietly, but couldn't quite make out her words. Alexia was about to call Lusam, and see if he could break the lid off somehow magically, but a moment later the little girl spoke.

"Rebekah … my name's Rebekah," she said quietly from inside the grate.

"Hello Rebekah, it's nice to meet you. Can you open the grate from the inside?" Alexia asked in a calming voice.

"No … no … the monsters will get us," Rebekah replied, sheer terror evident in her voice.

"No, they won't. You're safe now, I promise. We killed all the monsters outside, take a look for yourself," Alexia reassured her.

"No … more will come. They always do. When they hear Kayden coughing, they always come," she said crying and sobbing.

"Is Kayden your friend Rebekah?" Alexia asked, trying to keep the little girl talking.

"No, he's my little brother," she replied between sobs.

"He doesn't sound very well Rebekah. If you open the grate we can help him get better, I promise," Alexia said.

"Have you seen our mother and father? They were supposed to come and find us, but they didn't come yet," Rebekah asked, still sobbing.

"No, I'm afraid I haven't seen them Rebekah. But I tell

you what, open the grate for me, and we can go look for them together, as soon as we sort out your little brother. How does that sound?" Alexia offered, knowing full well that her parents would most likely be amongst the victims of the Empire agents. Rebekah didn't reply, and the silence stretched on for a long time before Alexia heard the unmistakable sound of a bolt being slid back, quickly followed by a second. Renn lifted the cover off the opening, and revealed a young blonde girl of about ten or eleven-years-old. She glanced around with wild eyes, then launched herself at Alexia, who was still on her knees beside the grate. She threw her arms around Alexia's neck, and buried her face into her shoulder, crying loudly next to her ear. Alexia rubbed her back, and fought back tears of her own, stunned at how much Rebekah reminded her of her own little sister Molly. The resemblance was uncanny, and it brought back a flood of both good and painful memories for Alexia.

Alexia had been born in a village called Dunlow, just south of Oakedge, and grew up there with her family. Her father had chosen various dubious career paths over the years, but her mother had worked on the local dairy farm each morning for many years, milking the cows and churning the butter. One day—not long after Alexia's tenth birthday—a group of soldiers had arrived to arrest her father. They said he was wanted for crimes committed against a noble family in Oakedge, and that his trial would be carried out in Oakedge the following day. That was the last time she ever saw her father, and no matter how many times she had asked what had happened to him, her mother refused to even talk about it with her.

Her sister Molly had been two years younger than Alexia, and full of life. They had often played together in the fields around their house, or down by the stream while their mother worked her long hours at the dairy farm. But no matter how hard their mother worked, it never seemed to be enough to pay for everything. Soon they were forced to move out of their comfortable home, and into a much smaller and dirtier house on the outskirts of the village. But gradually, even there, life had returned to normal, as they got used to their new humbler abode and surroundings. Even the sound of their mother's laughter had returned on occasion, and things seemed to finally be getting back to normal for them all. That was until the following spring, when almost the whole village had been affected by a deadly fever. For a long time their remote location on the outskirts of the village had been a blessing, but their mother still had to work, and two weeks later the inevitable happened. It started as a small cough, but rapidly escalated into the deadly fever. She watched helplessly as first her mother, then her little sister succumbed to it. One day they were fine, the next they were gone. Her whole world collapsed around her, and she prayed the fever would take her too, but of course, it didn't. Shortly afterwards she had gone to live on the streets of Oakedge as a street kid, then later joined a band of brigands in the nearby forest to the north.

"Alexia, are you alright?" She heard Neala ask, dragging her thoughts back to the present. Alexia hadn't realised, but she too had been crying at the painful memories brought back to her by seeing Rebekah's face. Alexia looked up at Neala, smiled and nodded, but didn't let go of Rebekah.

"Could you go take a look at her little brother, he sounds very sick. Maybe Lusam can do something to help him," Alexia said quietly over Rebekah's shoulder. Alexia tried to stand up, but Rebekah wouldn't relinquish her tight hold around her neck, so she found herself carrying Rebekah, with her legs wrapped tightly around her middle. As she glanced into the dark hole, she realised it wasn't a sewer at all, but some kind of storage room, probably belonging to the stone building behind it. She made her way to the stone steps of the building, and sat down with Rebekah still clinging tightly to her.

Lusam climbed down into the dark hole, closely followed by Neala. There was a wooden platform near the entrance which made it much easier to get in and out of the room below. It seemed the room's sole purpose was to dry firewood, as there was nothing else there apart from a few discarded vegetables, which he guessed the children had been eating to stay alive. The moment he thought about food, he realised just how hungry he actually was. It had been a long time since he had used as much of his magic reserves as he had today, and it seemed that reading the second Guardian book had made him no less dependent on food after doing so. As if to punctuate the thought, his stomach let out a huge growling sound, amplified by the stone room they were in.

"Don't even say it. I know ... I know," Neala said, shaking her head. Lusam smiled to himself, and created a small light orb to illuminate the room without even turning to face her. In the corner, lying on a wooden platform, was a young boy of about five or six-years-old. He looked very pale and sweaty, and his lips were dry and cracked from lack of moisture. Lusam tried to rouse him, but he was unable to.

"Can you heal him?" Neala asked quietly by his side.

"Maybe, but he looks very weak. Healing his illness is one thing, but it looks like he's been without food or water for quite a while. He will need time to regain his strength afterwards on his own, I think," Lusam replied, placing his hand on the boy's forehead. He could sense the boy's body fighting against the infection, and gave it a helping hand using his magic. The boy's main problem had been that his body hadn't had the fuel to burn to heal itself, giving the infection the upper hand. Now that Lusam had transferred some energy into the parts of his body that were fighting the infection, it was now just a matter of time before his body's defences began to win out over the infection. How long that would take, he didn't know. But he did know, that if they could manage to get him to eat and drink, that time period would be much less.

"He should be okay for now, but he needs food and water so his body can heal itself," Lusam said, turning to face Neala.

"Water shouldn't be a problem, there is a well at the end of this street, but food might be more difficult," Neala replied.

"I doubt it. It doesn't look like most of the villagers had much time to pack up and leave before the attack, so providing we can find some houses that haven't been burned to the ground, I'm sure we'll find something to eat there."

"Yeah, I guess you're right. We should go tell the others about the boy's condition, and arrange a search party for supplies," Neala said, heading for the opening without waiting for a reply. Lusam followed her back out into the sunlight above, squinting against the bright light until his eyes adjusted to it once more. Alexia was still holding the little girl whilst sitting on the steps of a nearby building, but Renn was nowhere to be seen.

"How is he?" Alexia asked over the shoulder of the little girl.

"He should be fine now, but we need to get some food and water into him soon," Lusam replied, glancing around for Renn. "Where did Renn go?"

"I'm not sure, he headed off down that way a few minutes ago, said he wouldn't be long," Alexia replied nodding towards the well at the end of the street.

"Any idea what this building is?" Neala asked, looking at the stout door behind Alexia.

"It's the temple," Rebekah said quietly without lifting her head.

"Thank you, err ..." Neala began to say.

"Her name is Rebekah, and she told me her brother is called Kayden. Rebekah, these are my friends, Neala and Lusam, and the big one who was here earlier is called Renn," Alexia said.

"Hello Rebekah, it's nice to meet you," Neala said, sitting on the step next to her and Alexia.

"Hello," Rebekah said shyly, glancing in Neala's direction momentarily, before burying her head once more into Alexia's shoulder. Neala raised her eyebrows at Alexia, but she just smiled back, obviously not bothered at all by the young girl's affections. Neala stood up and tried to open the heavy door of the temple, but it was securely locked. Without hesitation she removed a small pouch from her tunic that contained her lock-picks, and set to work on the door lock. She allowed herself a wry smile as she remembered the last time she had used them in the basement of Mr Daffer's shop, to unlock the cell doors, and check for any *treasure* left behind by the previous inhabitants. The lock clicked, and the door swung open on its well oiled hinges to reveal a large open room, with lines of wooden benches facing an altar on a raised platform at the far end. On the stone walls were various paintings and tapestries, all depicting the ocean in one form or another. The floor was a simple flagstone affair, with long narrow carpets running along the walkways, and up onto the raised platform where the altar was. `All in all, nothing special,` Neala thought to herself, as Lusam came to join her.

"There's a stack of bench cushions over there," Lusam said, pointing towards the back corner of the room, "if we spread some out on the floor at the front, we can bring Kayden up here and make him more comfortable, while we go find some food and water. I'm sure Alexia will watch over him while we're gone." Overhearing their conversation inside the temple, Alexia came to join them with Rebekah. She had somehow managed to convince Rebekah to let go of her neck, and now she stood by Alexia's side, holding her hand instead.

"I'm sure we can make a nice bed for your little brother, can't we Rebekah?" Alexia asked, crouching down next to her, and pushing a strand of blonde hair away from her eyes. Rebekah nodded mutely, seemingly a little less distressed than she had been earlier.

"Thank you Rebekah. I'm sure Kayden will like that very much," Neala replied smiling at her. Lusam had noticed some writing carved into the walls around the room, and was curious to see if it was magical in nature like the writing in Helveel and Coldmont. He slipped into his mage-sight and examined the text, but it remained nothing more than a simple stone carving. Disappointed, he turned back towards the others, and was stunned by what he saw. Rebekah had an aura much brighter than an average person. In fact, he was sure—given the correct training—she would not only be capable of sensing magic in others, but performing it as well. He clearly remembered the strength of his grandmother's aura, and Rebekah's was slightly brighter he judged. And so it stood to reason, that if his grandmother could perform magic, so could Rebekah.

At that moment Renn returned, carrying a large cooking pot, several wooden bowls, and a bag full of what Lusam guessed were vegetables. Alexia and Rebekah were already busy carrying cushions to the front of the room, and arranging them on the floor to create a bed for Kayden.

"Renn, can I speak with you a moment please," Lusam said, indicating with his head towards the far corner of the room.

"I guess *I'll* go get Kayden, then," Neala said sarcastically shaking her head, and heading for the door, leaving Lusam to have his chat with Renn.

"Sorry Neala," Lusam called after her, but she just raised her hand, and continued out of the door to fetch Kayden.

"What's up lad?" Renn asked quietly.

"Take a look at Rebekah's aura," Lusam replied, nodding towards the little girl. Renn's eyes widened, as he too noticed the little girl's aura for the first time.

"Interesting," he said, studying the little girl and his surroundings in more detail.

"That's it ... just *interesting?* I thought you'd be a lot more excited about discovering her potential than that," Lusam said disappointedly.

"No, I mean yes, I am ..." Renn replied, just as Neala returned carrying Kayden, "but, *that* makes it even more interesting, I'd say," Renn added, nodding towards the boy in Neala's arms. Lusam glanced towards the boy, and couldn't believe his eyes; he too had an equally bright aura.

"What's going on here Renn? I thought you said the Empire killed all the newborn magi in Afaraon, and the ones that the Hermingild managed to save were always sent to the High Temple in Lamuria to be trained. How can two children like these be missed by both the Empire, and the High Temple?"

"I'm not sure lad, but I think I might have half an answer to your question. Do you see that symbol up there?" Renn said, pointing at a carved symbol high above the altar platform. Lusam looked, but he didn't recognise the symbol.

"Yeah, what about it?" he replied.

"That's the sign for the God Deas. These people, like many seafarers worship Deas, not Aysha," Renn replied, as if that should explain everything to Lusam.

"I don't understand. What does that have to do with surviving the Empire's culling?" Lusam asked confused.

"The Empire's culling ... nothing. But it does explain why they weren't taken to the High Temple for training. You see lad, in Afaraon it's become a long tradition to visit a temple of Aysha as soon as a woman discovers she is pregnant. The priest is expected to bless her pregnancy, which he or she does, but they also examine her magically for the telltale signs of an unborn mage. These days the tradition is kept up because it's considered unlucky not to visit the temple for a blessing, and it's extremely uncommon for a priest to discover a potential unborn mage amongst the general population. But two centuries ago, when we first discovered that the Thule Empire was trying to eradicate magic from Afaraon, the visit to the local temple was the difference between life and death for many a mother and her child.

"All the priests were taught the necessary spells to detect such a child, and it was, at first, a decree of the King that every expectant mother should attend their local temple at least once during their pregnancy. Of course, the real reasons behind the decree were kept a secret from the general population, so as not to instil panic, and many ignored it completely, at least at first. But it didn't take long for people to realise that many of the mothers who didn't attend their local temples often turned up dead soon afterwards, along with their newborns. Various superstitious nonsense was blamed for their deaths, but regardless, it soon became the norm for all mothers-to-be to visit their local temples at least once during their pregnancies. And even to this day, the tradition is still upheld by most people in Afaraon. But the people of this village worship Deas, not Aysha. Therefore, the children here would not have been discovered by the High Temple, but as to why they were not discovered by the Thule Empire, I have no idea," Renn said. Lusam nodded at Renn's words, realising how little he knew about the history of Afaraon and its people. In fact, he also realised he knew very little about the Afaraon of today—something he would have to try and rectify before they reached Lamuria he expected.

"How's the boy?" Renn asked looking in his direction.

"I'm sure he'll be fine as soon as we get some food into him. I gave his body the energy it needed to fight off the infection, but he'll still need to eat and drink to speed things up. Sorry, but it looks like we're not going anywhere until tomorrow now," Lusam replied, knowing how badly Renn wanted to reach Lamuria.

"Don't worry lad, I doubt it's changed our plans much anyway," Renn replied.

"What do you mean?"

"Well, by the looks of those undead-minions out there, I'm guessing the Empire agents took the cream of the crop with them, and left the slow and damaged ones here for us to find. You can bet they'll do exactly the same thing in every village and town between here and Lamuria too," Renn said.

"I don't understand. Why should that change our original plans? It's not as if we can't kill them easy enough," Lusam replied.

"Sure we can kill them lad, but only if we can see them coming. Do you have any idea how far the next town or village is away from here?"

"No?" Lusam enquired, thinking Renn was about to tell him.

"Neither do I, lad. And, I would suggest the last thing we want to be doing right now, is sleeping outside under the stars. Especially when we have no idea how many of those things are out there. You'll almost always find that villages and towns are traversable from one another within a single day's travel. It's the simple rules of commerce that dictate that, lad. But if we set off now, without knowing how far it is to the next village or town, we might not make it before nightfall. I'd also imagine that after today's events, *you* could use some rest too, before we move on. For all we know, the Empire agents could be holed up in the next village or town waiting for us, and if we arrive unprepared, well ... I'm sure you can see my point lad," Renn said.

"Yeah, right now it would certainly be a very short, one-sided fight, that's for sure," Lusam agreed, chuckling.

"My thoughts exactly, lad. So I think we should use the time we have here wisely, to stock up on whatever supplies we can find, and recover some of your strength before we even think about moving on. Hopefully, by the morning the boy will be well enough to travel, if not, we'll have to reassess our options then. For right now though, I suggest we cook some food, and maybe get to know our two young friends a little better. I'm sure the girl knows this village better than we do, and if we're lucky, she might know how far, and how big, the next village or town is."

"Sounds good to me," Lusam agreed, as his stomach let a out another loud growl at the mere mention of food.

Chapter Thirty-Eight

It had been Lusam's original plan to build a small fire outside the temple to cook their food, but instead, Neala had discovered a doorway that led into a small room hidden behind a curtain, at the front of the temple. It looked like it had been used as an office or small study of some kind. There were book cases with various types of books, and cabinets containing everything from parchment and ink to the odd bottle of brandy and rum. But by far the best thing in the room—from their perspective—was the large stone fireplace, complete with a stone shelf for cooking on. Renn had fetched the water from the village well, while the others had prepared the vegetables, and it wasn't long before they had a large pot of bubbling broth cooking next to a roaring fire. Lusam also dug out the small amount of fish they had left from that day's uneaten breakfast, and added it to the bubbling pot, creating a delicious smelling aroma that filled the entire room.

Kayden had begun to stir a little from his deep sleep, and Alexia had even managed to coax him to drink a little water. His fever had broken, and even some colour had returned to his cheeks by the time the food was ready to eat. He didn't eat much, but it was enough for his body to start healing itself, Lusam judged.

After they had all eaten their fill, Rebekah seemed to become far more relaxed and talkative within the group, especially after Alexia had gone to close the main temple door, having realised that Rebekah had been reluctant to stop looking in that direction for too long; obviously worried that one of the creatures would somehow find its way inside.

Renn had told Rebekah an amusing story about a horse and a cat, then expertly brought the conversation around to: *had she ever seen a horse in real life, and if she had, had she ever ridden one?* Rebekah proudly revealed that she had often visited the horses in farmer Jack's paddock on the way to see her mother in the fields, but had never had the opportunity to ride one yet, even though she would like to very much. A few minutes later Renn had not only found out where the paddock was located, but also where the orchard was where Rebekah usually got her apples from to feed the horses.

"Fancy a walk, lad?" Renn asked, nodding towards the door.

"Sure," Lusam said, standing up and glancing in Neala's direction, curious to see if she wanted to join them. She shook her head slightly, smiled at him, and returned her attention back to the story Rebekah was now telling her and Alexia. Lusam guessed that Renn wanted to go and see if any of the horses had survived the initial Empire attack, or the subsequent undead that had been freely roaming around the area ever since.

Once they were outside and away from the temple entrance, Renn turned to Lusam and said, "Stay alert lad, we don't want to be caught off guard out here."

"Can't we just keep an eye on your sword's glow?" Lusam asked, wondering why Renn hadn't already thought of it.

"Yes lad, for any of the undead we can, but I'm more concerned about the living right now. I'd be very surprised if Rebekah and Kayden were the only ones to survive the initial attack. There could be people hiding out inside any of these buildings, and if they mistake us for the enemy, we might suddenly find the need to defend ourselves. I suggest we stay towards the centre of the street, well away from the doorways and windows, just in case," Renn said, checking the shadows as he walked. Lusam slipped into his mage-sight, remembering he could now see through the walls with it, and scanned the nearby buildings; no one was inside any of them.

"I don't think we have to worry too much, there's no one inside any of these," Lusam said, gesturing to the nearby buildings. There was a momentary look of confusion on Renn's face, then he too seemed to remember Lusam's new ability.

"Alright lad, just stay alert," he said, still watching the shadows for himself.

The paddock wasn't as easy to find as Rebekah had suggested it would be. They had tried three dead-end streets before they found the correct one that led out of the village to the northern fields. The street ended abruptly, and only a narrow well-travelled dirt path continued into the treeline beyond. If he hadn't been told what to look for, Renn would have probably discounted it altogether, but as promised, once they emerged at the far side of the trees, the rolling fields opened up before them.

The paddock was located on the far side of the first large field they came to, but before they reached it, Renn's sword began to emit its eerie blue glow.

"Looks like the Empire agents might have found this place after all," Lusam said, disappointed at the prospect of having to walk all the way to Lamuria, or at least the next town or village.

"Hmm, maybe, but not necessarily, lad," Renn replied scanning the area for any undead. "There are several well documented cases of the undead returning to locations they frequented whilst they were still alive. It seems they have the ability to retain some of the memories from their previous life. It's one of the things that make them such an effective tool-of-terror for the Empire, the others being how hard they are to kill, and their enhanced strength of course."

"Over there," Lusam said pointing towards the fenced off paddock. Inside there was a single undead minion slowly shuffling towards the far end of the large field, towards a group of grazing horses. At the speed it was moving, Lusam judged it would take it several minutes at least to reach the horses. More than enough time to intercept it before it could do any harm.

"If we hurry, we should catch up with it well before it reaches the horses," Lusam suggested.

"I'm sure you're right lad, but I doubt that will be necessary," Renn replied pointing to something else in the field to their left. "It looks like that *thing* has been in the field for at least a few days." When Lusam saw what Renn was pointing at, he almost lost control of his stomach. What he had taken to be a fly-ridden pile of manure, was in fact, a mutilated corpse of a horse—the stench of which now began to drift his way on the gentle breeze, making him dry retch once more.

"If I were to guess, I would say that *thing* used to be the farmer here. Farmer Jack, I believe Rebekah called him. No doubt this poor animal believed the same thing, and paid for it with its life," Renn said, nodding towards the rancid pile of horse flesh. I doubt having seen what it did to this horse, the others will let it get anywhere near them. It's probably been walking round in circles for days after those poor animals. I bet they're exhausted, poor things. Wait here, I'll deal with this," Renn said, climbing over the fence and heading towards the shuffling undead farmer. The horses saw Renn heading in their direction, and immediately began to move towards the far end of the paddock away from him.

`They seem to have lost all trust in humans, and who could blame them after what they must have been through,` Lusam thought to himself. Renn ended the creature swiftly, and Lusam was glad to see the glow on his sword wink out, indicating that there were no more undead in the immediate vicinity.

"I don't think any of the other horses are injured, but it's difficult to tell from so far away," Renn called out to Lusam as he approached the fence. "Hopefully they'll settle down now, and get some rest. It's likely the poor animals haven't slept in days with that thing chasing them around the field. I know you're tired too, lad, but is there any chance you could dispose of that?" he said, nodding towards the mutilated corpse. "I think it would go a long way towards helping them settle down again."

"Sure, no problem," Lusam replied, encasing it in a force-field and instantly incinerating it. He was more than happy to be rid of the sight and smell of it, but he had no desire to be covered in its ashes, so he manoeuvred his force-field further downwind before releasing its contents to the gentle afternoon breeze. Then he repeated the process with the farmer's corpse, hoping the horses might forget about their traumatic experience more readily, if the body was no longer there to remind them of it.

"Thanks lad," Renn said. Lusam nodded and climbed back over the fence, taking in the sights around him for the first time. Apart from the small farmhouse, there were also two large barns, and several smaller outbuildings scattered around the farmstead.

"Maybe we should go check out those buildings. They look like they haven't been touched from here," Lusam said.

"I was just about to suggest the same thing, lad. I suspect we'll find the saddles for the horses in one of those barns too," Renn replied, nodding towards the two large buildings next to the paddock. "Keep your eyes open for any rope too. It will make rounding up the horses tomorrow much easier, especially if they're still as skittish as they are right now."

"Okay, but I can help you with the horses if they become a problem," Lusam offered.

"Thanks lad, but if there's one thing I know how to handle, it's a horse. My father used to keep and train them on his farm when I was a boy. He always used to say: `there's no such thing as an unruly horse, you just need to have patience, and show them who's boss.` And if you follow those two simple rules, you can control any horse, even if it takes a little while," Renn replied confidently.

"Somehow I can't picture you working on a farm," Lusam said, chuckling at the images in his mind of Renn sitting on a small stool milking a cow, or mucking out a stable. Renn just grunted, and set off towards the first of the two large barns without saying another word, leaving Lusam to conjure up a few other amusing jobs Renn might have done on the farm when he was younger.

"I'll go check out the other buildings," Lusam called out after Renn, trying hard to keep the amusement out of his voice. Renn raised his hand to acknowledge he had heard Lusam, but didn't slow his pace towards the large barn.

The first two buildings Lusam checked only contained ploughs and other farm equipment; nothing they could use. He was heading for the main farmhouse next, when he spotted a small wooden structure off to his right. At first he thought it might be a large outhouse used for all the farmhands, but once he was close enough to see through its walls, he almost jumped for joy. It wasn't an outhouse at all, it was a smokehouse—and, a fully stocked one at that. It contained everything, from smoked fish, to smoked pork, and even some cheese. Even though he had eaten the broth less than an hour before, his stomach still gave a loud rumble at the sight of so much tasty food before him. There was far more food here than they would need to reach Lamuria, so at least they wouldn't go hungry on the trip now. It smelled and looked so good, that he couldn't resist sampling a good sized portion of it before collecting some for the others' supper. With a good amount of food in his arms, he set off back to let Renn know the good news.

As Lusam approached the two large barns, he saw Renn appear from inside one of them carrying a large bale of hay. He tossed it over the fence and into the paddock, where it joined at least three or four other bales he had thrown in earlier.

"Look what I found," Lusam called out as soon as he was close enough for Renn to hear. Renn turned in his direction, and waited for him to approach. "I found a fully stocked smokehouse back there, so we don't have to worry about food anymore."

"That's great news, lad," Renn said smiling. "I've found the saddles and some rope too. So I guess after a good night's sleep, we'll be ready to leave come first light tomorrow, providing our young friend has sufficiently recovered, of course."

"Yeah, that's good ..." Lusam replied, trailing off his sentence, as the concerns regarding his lack of knowledge about Lamuria, and Afaraon in general, resurfaced once more.

"Is there a problem lad?" Renn asked, sounding a little concerned by his sudden downturned mood.

"It's nothing, sorry," Lusam replied.

"It doesn't sound like nothing lad. Come on, spit it out. There's only the two of us here," Renn said, taking a step closer. After a moment, Lusam looked up at him, and realised he was standing there patiently, waiting for him to speak again. He hadn't wanted to bring it up in front of Neala or Alexia, because he didn't want them to think he was naïve, or uneducated. He wasn't sure how much Neala or Alexia knew about Afaraon, or even its capital Lamuria, but he was certain it would be far more than he did. His grandmother had done a fine job of teaching him how to read and write, and how to add up his numbers, but never once had she mentioned anything about the history of Afaraon, or its present day politics. In fact, until Lusam had stumbled upon Helveel, he had no real idea of what lay outside the area of his childhood in The Elveen Mountains.

Although he had learnt a fair bit about Helveel—mostly through necessity—he knew nothing at all about Lamuria, or the rest of Afaraon for that matter. He knew from what Renn had already told him, that it had always been the plan to send him to the High Temple to complete his education and training once he was old enough. So looking back, he guessed his grandmother would have taught him all he needed to know before taking him there, if she had lived long enough to do so. After several more minutes of thinking it over in his mind, he noticed Renn was still waiting patiently for him to respond.

"Renn, I think I need your help," Lusam said quietly, knowing that Renn was the only person he could turn to regarding this matter. Renn nodded and waited for him to continue. "You all keep saying I'm the best hope we have to protect Afaraon against the Empire, but I don't even know anything about the place I'm supposed to be saving. If you asked me a question about Afaraon, Lamuria, the High Temple, or anywhere other than Helveel or The Elveen Mountains, I wouldn't have a clue how to answer it. How can I be a saviour of a land that I know nothing about? I only know we're ruled by a Queen because her head is stamped on the back of our coins," Lusam said. Renn winced at Lusam's statement, realising how right he was.

"Oh, lad ... we actually have a King right now. Queen Marie died more than three years ago, and her son, Prince Theodore became King. And, the Royal Family doesn't rule Afaraon. They haven't done so, for over three hundred years. They're little more than figureheads for our nation nowadays. The real seat of power in Afaraon lies within the church, with the High Temple in Lamuria being at its core," Renn replied sympathetically.

"See what I mean!" Lusam replied, exasperatedly.

"Unfortunately, yes, I do. I think maybe we should have a long chat when we get back, lad. See if we can't fill in some of those gaps before we reach Lamuria."

"Thanks Renn, I'd really appreciate that. But, can we do it away from the others please. I don't want them thinking I'm ... well, you know," Lusam replied, slightly embarrassed.

"I understand, lad. Don't worry, I'll be discreet," Renn replied, placing his hand on Lusam's shoulder and giving it a small squeeze. Lusam nodded his thanks, and they were soon heading back to the temple, to share their good news and food with the others.

When Lusam and Renn arrived back at the temple, they discovered Kayden's condition had thankfully improved somewhat. He was now sitting upright next to his big sister, listening to a story being told by Alexia. When he first noticed Lusam and Renn enter the temple, he looked a little frightened by their sudden appearance, but Rebekah soon had him relaxed again, and he quickly returned his attention back to the story.

Neala came to greet them before they even made it halfway across the room. She gave Lusam a quick hug, then quietly said, "I think you might want to hear the story Rebekah told us while you were gone. I think you'll find it very interesting. Come, let's see if she will tell it again for you." Lusam and Renn looked at each other, then followed Neala to where Alexia and the children were sitting.

"Kayden, these are our friends, Lusam and Renn," Neala said, introducing them both.

"Hello Kayden, it's nice to meet you," Renn said, with Lusam following his example.

"Hello," Kayden replied meekly.

"Renn and Lusam just told me that they would like to hear your *Rebirth* story very much Rebekah, do you think you could tell it again, just for them?" Neala asked.

"Yes, please Bekah, please. I want to hear it again, please," Kayden pleaded, just like Neala had hoped he would, after seeing his enthusiasm the first time she told the story. Apparently it was her favourite story, because her father would tell it to her each time he came ashore, and she in turn would then tell it to her little brother, Kayden.

"Okay, but only if you tell me the horse and cat story again Renn," she offered.

"Deal," Renn replied smiling at her. So she set about telling the story of *Rebirth* once more for Renn and Lusam. She told of how most children used to die before her great grandfather had taken his pregnant wife aboard The Good Ship Tuthna to give birth, and how that had quickly turned into a tradition, not only for the inhabitants of Prystone, but for all the local towns and villages up and down the coast. She told them that the tradition had continued for several generations, until everyone locally had been born on board the Good Ship Tuthna.

By the time Rebekah had finished telling her story, Renn was completely stunned. It was obvious to him now, why the Empire had failed to detect the births of so many magically talented people in Prystone. Their tradition of giving birth out at sea, had undoubtedly saved them all. The implications of what she had just told him were immense for Afaraon. For the past two centuries Afaraon had struggled to find enough magi to serve the High Temple, and for at least half of that time, there had been countless potential magi and priests hiding in plain sight amongst the people of this village, and its neighbouring towns and villages. Who knew how many had been born, lived their lives, and died again without ever being noticed by either the Empire, or Afaraon? The lost potential was staggering. Renn just hoped that the other villages and towns nearby had been spared the fate of Prystone. They neither had the time or the resources to search for survivors right now, but he promised himself, if Afaraon prevailed once they reached Lamuria, he would personally lead the search himself.

"Okay, it's your turn Renn," Rebekah said excitedly, breaking off his train of thought.

"I suppose it is," Renn chuckled, and settled down to tell two very excited children the story about the horse and cat; several times over.

The food that Lusam and Renn brought back with them had been very well received by the others, and after eating more than their fill, Renn and Lusam made their excuses and retired to the small office to begin Lusam's education of Afaraon's affairs. Which left Neala and Alexia exchanging a multitude of stories with the children in the main room outside. Rebekah seemed to have become quite fond of Alexia, and shadowed her every move, much to the amusement of Neala, who was beginning to foster a similar relationship with Kayden, now that he was fully awake.

Renn pulled two comfy looking chairs towards the fireplace, and they both made themselves comfortable in front of the low burning fire.

"Alright lad, what would you like to know?" Renn asked.

"I'm not really sure. I guess I need to know the general history of Afaraon, and anything I'm likely need to know once we arrive at Lamuria," Lusam replied. Renn whistled and raised his eyebrows at Lusam's request.

"That's a lot of information lad. I'm not sure where to begin if I'm honest," Renn replied, then after thinking for a moment he suggested, "Can you think of anything you would like to know, and maybe we can take it from there?"

"Why don't you continue from where you left off earlier? You explained about mothers-to-be visiting their local temples, and the priests testing their unborn babies for any magical potential. But you never said what happened to them if they did find any signs of magical ability," Lusam said.

"Hmm ... well, what used to happen two hundred years ago, is very different from what would happen now, lad. But I think for it to make any sense, I should explain the entire history to you. One thing you already know, is that magic used to be far more commonplace in Afaraon before the Empire started its eradication program. No one knows for certain—because records were never kept—but it's estimated that well over half the population of Afaraon were capable of using magic to one degree or another, before the Empire started killing our people. The vast majority of people were untrained in the use of magic, and usually only knew a few spells that were passed down from their parents or grandparents. In fact, that very knowledge was often used as a bargaining tool when it came to forming marriages. Soon after the end of The Dragon-Mage Wars, families started forming marital alliances more in line with their magical abilities, than they did with their wealth. Simply because, with the right combination of magical abilities, the wealth was easier to achieve anyway. This practice did, however, have unforeseen consequences, ones we are still suffering from to this day. Because magic is hereditary, meaning that the most powerful magi usually come from a union of two powerful parents, the magical distribution within Afaraon became dangerously skewed. Instead of magical ability being distributed evenly among the population of Afaraon, often only the most powerful families had access to the most powerful magi.

"Of course, magic still occurred in the rest of the population, but because it was often a union between a lesser magi and non-magi, their subsequent offspring became weaker and more diluted over time. The larger, and more powerful families bickered and quarrelled amongst themselves for centuries, each vying for greater power over the others. It is from one of those families that our current monarchy is descended. They became the most powerful family in all of Afaraon, with both financial and magical dominance over the rest. The High Temple became little more than a relic left over from The Dragon-Mage Wars, and was forced to relinquish its power to the new monarchy. The High Temple chose to search out their new priests from within the general population, not wanting to take on any of the corrupt, self serving aristocracy into their ranks. That was when the spell was first created to discover the telltale signs of an unborn mage. Little did the priests know at the time, how important that spell would become later, for a very different reason.

"By the time the Empire decided to try and eradicate magic from Afaraon, the ruling classes had made it so much easier for them to achieve. The magical ability of Afaraon was now so concentrated within the aristocracy, it took less than a generation to wipe them out. At first they believed the deaths of their newborns were due to the abandonment of Aysha and her Temples, and threw themselves back into their religious practices of old, with little effect. One after another the families of the aristocracy fell, leaving only the ruling monarch and his family within the walls of Lamuria.

"When the High Temple discovered the reason behind all the infant magi deaths, they began petitioning the king to issue a royal decree, that all expectant mothers should visit their local temples at least once during their pregnancies. As you can imagine, the King was not held in very high regard by the general population at that time, and that is why many chose to initially ignore the decree. Even two hundred years ago, the High Temple knew an all-out attack on Lamuria was inevitable. It was only a question of when. In the past, the

High Temple's defences had been replenished by the magical donations from the large number of pilgrims that visited each year, but now, most of those same pilgrims were no longer capable of using magic, and therefore the Temple's crystal began to lose its power. The High Priest of the time, informed the king of the situation, and a bold new plan was put in action to try and save the land of Afaraon. Priests searched out anyone with magical abilities, and relocated them and their families to within the safety of Lamuria. At first no one minded the new arrivals, but later, as the city swelled with their numbers, riots broke out amongst the indigenous population. The living conditions became intolerable for many, and a mass exodus of both indigenous and newcomers took place.

"For a decade or two, the remaining number of magi who resided within Lamuria's walls were enough to maintain the High Temple's power source, but due to the dilution of magical blood, both outside, and inside the walls of Lamuria, its power soon started to dwindle once more. Fearing they would repeat the same mistake that the earlier ruling aristocracy had made, by concentrating the distribution of magic within Afaraon, the High Temple ceased their policy of relocating people to Lamuria. It was a huge gamble for the High Temple to do this, but their logic was sound. If the Empire believed that *all* of Afaraon's magi were within the walls of Lamuria, not only would they know our true strength —or lack of—they would also undoubtedly launch an all-out attack on the capital, one which they were not in any way prepared for. On the other hand, if the Empire believed there was still plenty of magic in the general population, they would continue with their eradication plans, at least for the immediate future. That was when the *Hermingild* were created. They were to work hand in hand with the priests throughout Afaraon. If they discovered a potential unborn mage, they would summon a *Hermingild* from the High Temple to assist the mother in concealing the birth of her child, and that child's power would be assessed by the high temple later. The hope was, if they could trick the Empire into waiting long enough before they launched their all-out assault, maybe, just maybe enough magi might be born for us to survive their attack.

"I know that every brave *Hermingild* prays for a stronger mage to take his or her place in the world after they are gone, but none have ever achieved more than Asima did. Your mother's Hermingild ... your grandmother, may very well have saved us all, lad. Her sacrifice will be remembered as long as the land of Afaraon remains, of that you can be certain."

Renn continued to fill in the gaps in Lusam's knowledge for another hour or so, until Alexia and Neala came to join them in the small cosy room. They gave Renn and Lusam an update on the children's condition, and told them everything they had discovered by talking to them earlier. Rebekah and Kayden had already fallen asleep on their makeshift beds, and Neala had secured the main door so no one, or no *thing,* could catch them unawares while they slept that night. Neala and Alexia had been talking with the children most of that day, and the conversation had inevitably turned towards their parents, and what had happened to them. Strangely, Kayden seemed far less affected by their absence than Rebekah, but it soon became clear why. Alexia discovered that Rebekah usually looked after him most of the time anyway, so their absence probably didn't seem so strange to him, yet. Rebekah on the other hand, seemed to understand that her parents were never coming back, but thankfully, she never said as much in front of her little brother. Alexia had explained they were all going to go to Lamuria, and promised that she would take care of them both once they arrived there. It seemed to reduce Rebekah's anxiety a little, but she still insisted that they search for her mother before they left Prystone, just in case she was hiding in their house. Alexia and Neala both readily agreed that they would look for their mother before leaving Prystone the following morning.

Lusam was awoken by a child's laughter. It took him a

moment to realise it was only Kayden and Rebekah in the main temple room. Daylight was just starting to filter through the large window in the office, giving him enough light to see that he was the last one still in bed. Groaning to himself, he sat up and rubbed his tired eyes. To his great surprise, he noticed that the night's sleep had restored much of his magical reserves. He had expected it to take a couple of days at least to regain so much of his magical reserves. The only explanation he could think of, was as his magical reserves had grown, so had his body's own ability to replenish them. He stood up from his chair, and stretched out the knots in his back.

`It's a comfy enough chair to sit in, but using it as a bed leaves a lot to be desired,` he thought to himself, making his way towards the main room. He was pleased to see Kayden looking much brighter and playing with his big sister as he entered the main room.

"Good morning sleepy-head," Neala greeted him with a smile. He quickly realised Renn and Alexia were not in the room.

"Morning," he replied, stifling a yawn. "Where are the others?"

"They went to get the horses ready about twenty minutes ago. Renn didn't want to wake you. He said you needed the extra time to recover your magical reserves," Neala replied.

"I'd never say no to a little extra sleep," Lusam chuckled, "but, maybe we should go meet up with them, now that I am awake. Besides, I can almost smell the contents of that smokehouse from here … I'm starving." Neala rolled her eyes at him, and started to collect her things together.

The cool morning air washed over them as they exited the temple building for the last time. The sky was clear, and it promised to be another warm and pleasant summer's day; perfect for riding. They had only been outside the temple building a moment before Kayden shouted something excitedly, and ran off down the street alone.

"Kayden, come back here," Neala called after him, but

he came to a stop by himself—not too far away—and picked something up off the ground.

"I found it Bekah, I found it!" Kayden said, skipping happily back towards the others, and holding up what looked like a child's wooden spinning top in his hand.

"That's great Kayden, but don't run off like that. There might be more of those monsters out here," Rebekah scolded him. He suddenly looked very nervous, and grabbed tight hold of his sister's hand, pulling her back towards the temple behind them.

"It's okay Kayden, you don't have to be afraid. The monsters are all gone now," Neala promised.

"How do you know? They might be hiding around the next corner," Kayden said, hugging his sister's leg.

"Do you like climbing trees Kayden?" Lusam asked, completely changing the subject.

"Yes, I'm better than Bekah at climbing trees," he said proudly.

"Are not," Rebekah replied sharply. "You only get higher than me because the branches are too thin higher up, and they break if I try to climb on them."

"If we climbed high enough to see there were no monsters hiding, would that make you feel better?" Lusam asked, quickly attempting to defuse the rapidly growing sibling rivalry between them. Kayden looked around the street, then gave Lusam a strange look.

"There are no trees here, silly," Kayden replied, as if Lusam were some kind of simpleton for suggesting it in the first place. Neala almost choked as he said it, and had to turn away to hide her incredible amusement at the boy's statement.

"That's not nice Kay!" Rebekah scolded him.

"Sorry Bekah. But, I'm right, there *are* no trees here," he replied, still looking at Lusam as if he were slightly mad. Lusam couldn't help smiling at the boy's look, and took a step towards him and his big sister.

"Hold my hand, and I'll show you," Lusam said, offering both of them a hand each to hold. He didn't need to hold their hands to levitate them, but he thought they might feel a little safer if they had something to hold on to. Kayden persisted with his strange look as he took Lusam's hand, even Rebekah seemed to be looking at him a little strange now.

"Okay, don't be afraid, you won't fall, I promise," Lusam said, as he lifted them two feet off the ground. Rebekah shrieked at the sudden movement, but Kayden simply giggled. Lusam gave them a moment to get used to the idea, then said, "Shall we go higher, so we can see there are no more monsters?"

"Yes! Up ... up ... up!" Kayden replied excitedly, but his sister only gave a half-hearted nod. Lusam had intended to check the coastline for enemy vessels before leaving Prystone anyway. The last thing they needed was to have another shipload of Empire agents following them while they travelled to Lamuria. Lusam slowly levitated them all to just below roof height, not wanting to openly show their presence if there were any enemy ships nearby. He peeked over the rooftop, towards the ocean beyond, but saw only an empty expanse of water, thankfully devoid of any Empire ships. He continued climbing, until he was high enough to see beyond the cliffs to the south, and was equally relieved to see there were no signs of Empire activity in that direction either. The streets were now far below them, but still clearly visible from their vantage point.

"There, you see, no monsters," Lusam said, wondering if Rebekah would ever open her eyes and look.

"Look Bekah, look how high up we are!" Kayden said excitedly, tugging at his big sister's hand so she would open her eyes. Rebekah opened one of her eyes, and squealed loudly, as she gripped Lusam's hand even tighter than before.

"Okay, I think we better go back down now," Lusam said, beginning to feel sorry for Rebekah.

"Aw! Not yet. Can we go up higher? Please ... Please," Kayden pleaded.

"Not right now Kayden, I don't think your sister likes it very much," Lusam replied.

Kayden looked at his sister for a moment—who still

had her eyes tightly closed—then said, "Can we go down *really* fast then, instead?"

"You wouldn't be trying to scare your big sister, would you?" Lusam asked, knowing exactly what he had in mind. Kayden just gave Lusam a wide toothy grin, confirming he'd just been found out, then turned his attention back to his terrified looking sister. Lusam smiled to himself, as he lowered them all back down to earth, suddenly feeling sorry for Rebekah for an entirely different reason.

"That was great!" Kayden said as soon as their feet touched the ground. "Can we do it again later, please?"

"We'll see," Lusam replied, instantly recognising the phase his grandmother had used on him many times, whenever she didn't want an argument about something.

"Rebekah, are you alright?" Neala asked, concerned by her pale complexion. Rebekah nodded, and immediately swapped Lusam's hand for Neala's. Kayden remained exactly where he was, holding onto Lusam's hand, and beaming his new best friend a smile.

"Boys!" Neala said under her breath and rolling her eyes.

"Can we go look for mother now?" Rebekah asked, starting to look a little more steady on her feet.

"Of course, where would you like to start?" Neala asked, knowing that Rebekah knew the village far batter than she did.

"This way," Rebekah replied, pulling Neala behind her. Kayden remained firmly attached to Lusam, and they both followed Rebekah and Neala towards the far end of the street. Rebekah led them towards the docks, scanning the water for any signs of her father's ship, or the remains of it. All she saw was an empty bay. She was about to leave and check her house, when she noticed the sunlight glint off something on the ground. As soon as she saw it, she knew exactly what it was: her mother's necklace. She let go of Neala's hand and ran towards it, tears forming in her eyes as she picked it up and cradled it in her hands.

"What is it Rebekah?" Neala asked quietly by her side.

"Mother's necklace," she whispered, as tears ran down her cheek.

"May I see it please?" Neala asked. Rebekah hesitated a moment, then offered her it without saying a word. Neala inspected the necklace, and immediately had her fears confirmed. It had been broken, and it wasn't a flimsy construction either. Whatever had happened to her mother, had involved some kind of physical contact, which would suggest she hadn't made it out of here before the initial attack. Neala handed back the necklace to Rebekah, and noticed her tears.

"Don't worry Rebekah, I'm sure your mother only accidentally dropped the necklace here, before she ran away," Neala said, knowing full well that her words were little more than a kind-hearted lie. "Shall we go check your house?" she asked, offering Rebekah her hand. Rebekah nodded, and slowly they headed back towards the village streets. A few minutes later they arrived at what was once Rebekah and Kayden's house. All that remained now, was a burnt out shell. Lusam scanned the inside of the house using his mage-sight, and thankfully found no signs that anyone perished in the fire.

"There's nobody inside," Lusam said out loud, then wished he hadn't when both Rebekah and Kayden started crying.

"It's okay," Neala said, hugging them both tightly. "It's good news that she wasn't here when the fire started. That means she could have run away, and hidden somewhere else. Come on, let's go find Alexia and Renn, shall we? I think they might have found you a horse that you can ride on." Neala knew it wasn't much of a diversion, but it seemed to lift their mood a little, as they headed off to meet up with the others at the paddock.

Ten minutes later they arrived at the large paddock. There was no sign of Renn or Alexia, so Lusam guessed they must be with the horses at the far side of the small hill. Lusam noticed that they had already placed four saddles on the ground, along with two bags of food taken from the smokehouse. Lusam's stomach reminded him loudly that he hadn't eaten breakfast yet, as soon as he thought about the tasty food within the bags. There didn't seem any point taking food back out of the bags. Not when the smokehouse was only a few hundred paces away, so he informed the others that he would go fetch them some breakfast, and headed off in the direction of the smokehouse. On his way there he met Alexia coming the other way.

"I thought you were with Renn," Lusam said.

"I offered to help him, but he was confident he could handle the horses by himself, so I went to explore a bit," Alexia replied.

"Yeah, I got the same speech from him yesterday," Lusam laughed. "Have you eaten yet?"

"Yes thanks. We both had something to eat at the smokehouse earlier, while we filled a couple of bags for the trip."

"Yeah, I saw the two bags of food back there, but I didn't see any point taking food back out of them for our breakfast—not when the smokehouse is so near," Lusam said, then he began to explain what had happened back in the village when they had visited the docks and the children's burnt out house. Alexia looked very concerned for Rebekah and Kayden, and rushed off to meet up with them as soon as Lusam had finished telling her the story.

It wasn't long before Lusam had gathered enough food for their breakfast, and headed back to the paddock to share it out. When he arrived, he noticed Rebekah and Kayden playing together, pretending to ride two of the horse saddles on the ground. Lusam gave each of them some food, then went to join Neala and Alexia at the fence. He handed Neala a share of the food, and then noticed what they were staring at. At the bottom end of the field, Renn was attempting to corner one of the horses, so he could get a rope around its neck. The horse kept rearing up at him, and on two occasions it almost caught him with its front hooves.

"It doesn't look like it wants to be caught," Neala said, in-between mouthfuls of food.

"Don't worry, he said he knew what he was doing," Alexia replied, cringing as he narrowly missed being injured for a third time. Eventually he abandoned that particular horse, and attempted a similar manoeuvre on one of the others, with similar results. This time one of the other horses came up behind him, and lifted him clean off his feet with its nose, sending him crashing to the ground a few feet away. He landed with a loud thud, flat on his back and Lusam burst out laughing at him.

"It's not funny, he might get hurt," Neala scolded him, but not without giggling herself a little first. Alexia was in hysterics by the time Renn managed to get to his feet.

"Lusam, can't you help him?" Neala asked, not taking her eyes off Renn, who was now up, and chasing another horse around the field, trying to get a rope around its neck.

"I suppose I could ... but he told me: *as long as he showed the horse who was the boss, he only needed patience to tame it.* I think by the looks of that, he needs a little longer to convince those horses he's the boss," Lusam replied chuckling.

Alexia managed to stop laughing just long enough to ask, "What could Lusam do anyway?"

"He can talk to the animals. Well, not exactly talk to them, but he could, I'm sure, convince those horses to calm down before Renn gets hurt," Neala replied scowling at Lusam, who was now bent almost double, laughing at Renn's attempts to catch the horse. A moment later Renn managed to finally get the rope around one of the horses' necks, but not before he also managed to get his leg caught in the other end of the rope. The horse reared back, dragging him clean off his feet, then half-galloped across the field, dragging him along behind it. Alexia and Lusam howled with laughter, but Neala didn't see the funny side of it, as he bounced along the field behind the horse.

"Do something!" she shouted at Lusam. He could barely see the horses through his tears of laughter, but he managed to project a calming thought towards them, then coaxed them towards the fence where they were standing.

Even Neala began to see the funny side of it, as Renn was slowly dragged the length of the field in their direction, unable to release his own leg from the rope. Lusam waited until the horses were almost to the fence, then magically severed the rope to free Renn. Six horses were now neatly lined up against the fence, completely ignoring Renn as he tried to remove the remains of the rope from his leg.

"You certainly have a lot of patience Renn ... but I'm not sure you quite convinced them that you were the boss," Lusam said with a straight face. Alexia and Neala almost fell over laughing at his statement, and even Lusam couldn't hold out against the incredulous look on Renn's face.

By the time they all finished laughing at him, Renn had already begun saddling one of the horses without saying a single word. Lusam couldn't decide whether he was angry, or simply embarrassed by the prank. But having felt the flat part of Renn's blade once before on his backside, he decided to give him a wide berth this time, just in case. Eventually he stopped what he was doing, and turned towards Lusam with a puzzled look on his face.

"How did you do that? ... No, wait ... I don't even want to know," Renn said shaking his head and attempting to brush off some of the mud—and other, less pleasant substances from his clothing—which elicited another round of raucous laughter from the others. Eventually everyone calmed down enough to saddle their own horses, and it was time to leave Prystone behind. Rebekah had chosen to ride with Alexia, and Kayden had asked to ride with Lusam.

They barely made it to the edge of the village, before Kayden was asking Lusam if they could fly to Lamuria instead. `It's going to be a long trip,` Lusam thought to himself, as the others began laughing at *his* predicament this time.

Chapter Thirty-Nine

Zedd and Cole spent the first night within Coldmont's walls. It had been late in the day, and far too late to begin their long descent of the mountain. They had refrained from speaking openly about any of their earlier transgressions, fearing that Lord Zelroth had ways of monitoring not only the strange book room, but also Coldmont as a whole. It had been a shock to Zedd when Lord Zelroth had revealed, that they were actually inside the fabled home of the ancient Guardians themselves. He had, of course, read the various history books pertaining to its existence, but as far as he was aware, its precise location still remained a mystery to almost everyone else in the world.

Early the next morning they had begun their long descent of the mountain. They had discussed their route in detail whilst still in Coldmont, and decided not to return directly to Stelgad. Instead they would avoid the strange fog covered valley by descending in a more easterly direction. Once they reached the first town or village, they would procure themselves horses and supplies by whatever means necessary, then head directly to Lamuria.

Zedd had no idea how he would achieve what Lord Zelroth had commanded him to do: take command of all of his forces outside Lamuria. His new rank of *Baliaeter* was sufficient to take command of such a force, but Lord Zelroth had given him no indication of how he was to usurp the current *Baliaeter* already in command there. If he arrived and simply announced that he was taking command of the forces, he would certainly be challenged by the existing *Baliaeter*.

And if that happened, Zedd didn't stand a chance of winning a direct confrontation with him. Although his new rank was of the same level, his magical ability was certainly not—he would have to choose his tactics wisely.

Descending the mountain was far quicker and easier than their trip up it had been. Zedd simply levitated himself and Cole down the almost vertical walls, avoiding the many switchback paths they had been forced to use during their accent. Zedd could tell that Cole was very nervous each time they stepped off the mountainside to levitate down to the next plateau. He obviously thought Zedd would let him fall to his death, knowing that he couldn't levitate himself if he did. It had crossed Zedd's mind to let him fall, but the truth was, Cole was no longer a liability to him. In fact, his strong mental abilities had already been proven beyond doubt against the Darkseed Elite in Coldmont, and Zedd was confident he could make use of them again in the future. Everything Cole knew about Zedd's indiscretions would now almost certainly remain a secret. Cole had already lied to Lord Zelroth, so he could no longer report Zedd's actions to anyone, and it was extremely unlikely that anyone other than Lord Zelroth himself was powerful enough to read his mind directly. So as long as he didn't annoy him too much, Zedd would let him live, for now at least.

It took them a further two days to traverse the foothills of The Elveen Mountains, before they finally emerged from the treeline onto a road. Zedd had no idea where they were, so he decided to head directly south, towards Lamuria. They hadn't eaten anything for almost three days, and were both very relieved to find a copse of fruit trees growing by the side of the road, not far from where they had joined it.

Four hours later they arrived at a small village. Zedd recognised it as one he had passed through on his way to Helveel several months earlier, and if his memory was correct, it would put them about three days north of Stelgad. Zedd's first thought had been to simply destroy the village, kill anyone who got in his way, and take what they needed for their trip south. But once he'd taken a moment to think about it, he came up with a far better plan, one that would not require him to use up most of his dwindling reserves of energy. Neither of them had eaten much for days, nor had they had any meaningful rest in that time. What Zedd *really* needed right now, was a hearty meal and a proper bed for the night. There would be no point at all in arriving exhausted and bedraggled at Lamuria, especially if he *did* end up having to confront the current *Baliaeter* there. No, he wouldn't waste his energy here. Not when he could use Cole's instead.

"We should spend the night at that inn, and recover our strength before we continue," Zedd announced, pointing towards the two storey building across the street.

"Oh, do you have some Afaraon coin?" Cole asked, sounding a little surprised, and hopeful at the same time.

"Of course not, you fool!" Zedd spat at him, making him cringe. "Why would I need their coins, when I have you?" Cole stared at him, not knowing what he meant, and too afraid to ask. Although Lord Zelroth had also promoted him to the rank of *Baliaeter*—meaning Zedd could no longer kill him using his ring—it didn't mean he would survive a direct attack from Zedd.

Zedd sighed loudly, dismayed at his travelling companion's stupidity.

"You have level eight mind control. Use it to get us a bed and a meal," Zedd said slowly and clearly, as if speaking to a dullard. Cole nodded mutely, and stared towards the inn opposite. He had never attempted to control the mind of another person before. Only Inquisitors were allowed to undertake the mind control of another Empire citizen. He knew how to do it in theory, but knowing how to do something, and actually doing it, were two completely different things. Then there was the limiting fact that mind control only worked for a short period of time, depending on the individuals natural resistance. There was no possible way he could maintain that amount of control long enough to achieve what Zedd was suggesting. The more complex the suggestion was to the victim's mind, the more chance there was of him or her discovering the deception.

"I don't think I can do it. I would need to keep control of their mind for far too long. It's just not possible to do," Cole said. Zedd closed his eyes, and tried to calm his anger at the fool standing before him.

"You wouldn't need to keep control of anyone, you idiot. I will ask for what we need, and suggest we pay for it in the morning. All you have to do is make whoever we speak to think that's acceptable. Or is that beyond your ability too?" Zedd replied through gritted teeth. He didn't wait for an answer, he simply strode towards the inn. Either Cole would succeed, or he would kill whoever was inside. It made no difference to him either way.

As it turned out, it didn't become necessary to kill anyone. Cole not only managed to convince the innkeeper to allow them to pay for their food and lodgings the following morning, he actually kept his word, too. After the previous evening's meal, he had *suggested* to a table of wealthy looking traders that he might join their card game, to which of course, they readily agreed. By the time Cole left the card game and retired to his room, the poor traders had little more left than the shirts on their backs. The next morning they didn't even have to steal any horses or supplies, they simply bought them with some of Cole's ill-gotten funds.

"So, how much money did you actually take off those men?" Zedd asked quietly, as they set off south on horseback.

"More than enough so we don't have to sleep rough again, or worry about replacing these horses," Cole replied grinning at Zedd.

"Good. Just remind me never to play cards with you in the future," said Zedd, kicking his horse into a gallop. Cole smiled to himself, knowing that was probably as close to a compliment he was ever likely to hear from Zedd, then he too spurred his horse into a gallop after him.

`If all goes well, we should reach Stelgad in a couple of days at this pace, then Lamuria in another seven or eight,` Zedd thought to himself, glad for a second time that he hadn't killed Cole.

***

As Lord Zelroth entered the large hexagonal shaped room, the chained Netherworld creature shrieked fiercely in the far corner, violently testing its chains and their anchors with its great strength. The *Aznavor* was unique on this side of The Great Rift. It had been captured before the end of The Dragon-Mage Wars, and held captive by several early warlords in Thule, before Lord Zelroth had found it, and bound it in its current prison.

It was deep red in colour with shiny scales, and looked like a strange giant decapitated floating head, with a huge single cat-like eye in the centre of its skull. Its immense mouth was filled with thin razor sharp teeth, each one six inches long and curved inwards. It had no limbs, apart from six long tentacles that sprouted from its head, each one tipped with what appeared to be a blind eye. But Lord Zelroth had discovered their true use many centuries ago. The *Aznavor* was similar to a *Vesdari,* in the sense that it would consume any and all magical energy it came into contact with, but there, the similarities ended. It didn't consume the magical energy as voraciously as a *Vesdari*, nor did it explode when it reached its full capacity. Instead, Lord Zelroth had discovered—by feeding it many prisoners of The Thule Empire—that it slowly bled out its magical energy again over time. At first he believed the magical energy simply re-entered the world at large, but later he discovered the truth: it was sent back to the Netherworld.

After Lord Zelroth realised the magic wasn't being vented locally, he set about proving his new theory, that the energy was being sent back to the Netherworld somehow. He believed that if the energy could enter the Netherworld, then maybe he could force open that conduit and allow his God, Aamon to escape. It took the lives of three of his best Inquisitors before the truth was finally discovered. Each one of them had attempted to form a mind-link with the creature while it vented its magical energy, and each one had ended up fully drained himself. Once the *Aznavor* locked onto an energy source, it would never relinquish that source until it was fully exhausted. It wasn't until the fourth attempt, that they discovered if they fed the *Aznavor* to capacity first—to start the venting process—then gave it another life to feed on during that venting process, the Inquisitor could then safely mind-link with the creature. As long as the mind-link was severed before the prisoner died, the Inquisitor was in no danger. Soon after their initial success, it was confirmed that the energy that the *Aznavor* vented, was indeed being sent back to the Netherworld.

At first, Lord Zelroth attempted to use the energy stream to force open a crack in The Great Rift, but he soon found that no matter what he tried, he could not influence the energy stream in any way, whatsoever. One unintended side effect of all the new magical energy being sent to the Netherworld, had been an accumulation of creatures gathering on the other side of The Great Rift, to feed on it. Eventually, that had attracted the attention of Aamon himself, and he was then able to use the *Aznavor's* energy stream to communicate with the outside world. Ever since then, Lord Zelroth had been communicating and taking his commands directly from his God, Aamon.

There were five prisoners in the room. Each one magically bound and guarded by a Darkseed Elite guard. Most prisoners were usually from the lower classes of society, but they were all magi, and capable of using magic to one degree or another. They were selected at random from a large pool of prisoners, and all knew their possible fate once they entered the *Aznavor* room. Lord Zelroth's method of delivering the prisoners to the *Aznavor* had changed over the years. At first, he had brought only the number of prisoners required for each successful communication. But he soon realised that almost every prisoner wasted a large amount of their magical energy trying to escape, knowing that their death was inevitable when they were fed to the *Aznavor*.

Now he brought more than he needed, selected them at random, and always made sure at least one returned back to the general prison population. Any prisoner who tried to escape, became next in line for the *Aznavor*. It was a simple, and very effective way of controlling the prisoners, without wasting their magical energy in the process. It seemed that even a one in five chance of surviving the trip to the *Aznavor* room was enough to keep most of the prisoners in line.

Lord Zelroth finished his preparations and turned to address the prisoners.

"Good afternoon gentlemen, oh, and lady," he said, inclining his head slightly towards the woman within the group. "I'm sure you already know why you are all here, and what might happen to you within this room. I'm afraid, everything you have heard is true. But I *can* promise you two things. Firstly, not everyone in this room needs to die today. Not unless any of you are foolish enough to try and escape, that is. And secondly, if you *are* selected, I can assure you that no amount of struggling will change the outcome of your fate. All it will do is shorten the amount of time you will have, once the *Aznavor* starts feeding on you. So, you may be asking yourself this question: why shouldn't I fight back, when I'm going to die anyway? Well let me tell you. If you try to fight back and waste your energy reserves, one or more of those people standing next to you, will have to make up that deficit. If that happens, it's quite possible that none of you may live to see tomorrow. Then I would have the hardship, of sending for more prisoners," Lord Zelroth said with a sarcastic smile.

Standing to the side of the room was a single Inquisitor in bright red robes. At a silent command from Lord Zelroth he walked slowly to the centre of the room, stopping briefly in front of each prisoner to assess their magical capabilities on his way. Lord Zelroth turned his back to the prisoners, and began to chant a spell over and over. At first nothing seemed to happen, but after a moment a small silver disc appeared in front of him, floating at about chest height. It seemed to be spinning in mid air, and gradually increased in size, until it was twice the height of Lord Zelroth, and four times as wide. When he finally finished the incantation, the giant disc resembled a pool of silver liquid, rippling and moving as if disturbed by some great unseen force. Lord Zelroth signalled the Inquisitor, and the process began.

The Inquisitor pointed to one of the prisoners, and his legs buckled under him with fear. He pleaded for his life, as the Darkseed Elite dragged him back to his feet, but no one took any notice of him. The other prisoners remained silent and still, not wanting to draw attention to themselves in any way, while their fellow cellmate was dragged towards the waiting *Aznavor*. The creature shrieked with anticipation, knowing it was about to be fed once more. It surged forwards towards the man, straining at its bonds, reaching towards him with its six long tentacles, and opening its huge jaws to reveal the utter blackness within. It seemed to be reaching for the man with every essence of its being, but he remained just out of reach of the creature, whimpering and begging for his life. One push from the Darkseed Elite, and the man came within range of the creature's influence. He froze in place, fighting against the mental control it exerted over him. Every blind-eyed tentacle now pointing directly towards him, and boring its way into his mind. He screamed in absolute terror, when first his left leg took an involuntary step towards the creature, then his right followed it. Each agonizing step took him closer to the creature, and his ultimate death. As he came closer to the creature, its control over his body became absolute, and the man walked right up to it. The *Aznavor* opened its huge jaws, reared up, and swallowed the top half of the man whole, clamping its thin six inch long fangs into his chest. The man screamed in agony, but the *Aznavor* didn't bite deep enough to kill him. Instead, it started to drain his magical energy slowly through its razor sharp fangs.

The silver liquid shimmered, and rippled as the *Aznavor* began to vent its surplus energy back into the Netherworld. Lord Zelroth waited patiently for his God to appear before him, not even noticing when the second prisoner began begging and screaming for his life to be spared. A moment later Aamon's image suddenly appeared within the silver liquid disc. Lord Zelroth fell to his knees, and prostrated himself on the floor before his God.

"Lord, I serve you in all things, as always," Lord Zelroth said reverently.

"Report!" Aamon's booming voice replied.

"Our troops are now massed outside the Deceiver's home city. Soon we will claim their power source, and use it to free you from the Netherworld once more, my Lord."

"And then I will let my new Netherworld army loose to cleanse the world of my siblings' filthy creations once and for all. You have done well my disciple. I will make sure that you are rewarded appropriately when the time comes, of that you can be certain," Aamon said, his image fading away inside the liquid silver disc. Lord Zelroth remained on his knees until the prisoner took his last breath and the *Aznavor* bit him clean in two with frustration at there being no more magical energy forthcoming. The woman screamed, then collapsed onto the floor in a quivering mess, while the other two prisoners shook uncontrollably at the sight they had just witnessed. Lord Zelroth didn't even notice, he simply stood up and left the *Aznavor* room without looking back, leaving the Darkseed Elite guards to return the prisoners to their cells.

Chapter Forty

Every village and town they had passed through, had already shared a similar fate to Prystone. The buildings were burned, livestock slaughtered, and supplies plundered or destroyed. And just like Prystone, the Empire agents had left their hideously damaged undead behind, to cause further heartache and destruction for anyone attempting to return home to their village or town. Each day Lusam's party arrived at a new town or village, killed the undead there, then found themselves a secure place to spend the night. They did sometimes come across survivors of the attacks, but they were few and far between. Twice they had managed to learn of another village on their planned route from those survivors they encountered—ones that were close enough to reach before nightfall, thus enabling them to cover more distance than they might have done otherwise.

They had discussed the possibilities of taking the survivors with them to Lamuria, but had quickly decided against the idea. They simply didn't have the resources to feed them, or indeed, guarantee their safety once they arrived at Lamuria. Lusam had healed any injured villagers they came across, and enchanted each one of them a basic weapon, so they could kill any wandering undead they may encounter later. He explained that the weapons would only kill a certain number of undead before they became useless again, but he felt much better about having to leave them there alone, knowing that they could at least protect themselves once he had gone.

At the beginning of their journey, Rebekah and Kayden

had been terrified of the first undead villager they had encountered outside Prystone. They had panicked, kicking and screaming to be let go, so they could run and hide from the creature. Lusam and Alexia had kept tight hold of them both, and reassured them that they were perfectly safe behind Lusam's magic shield. When the undead villager bumped into Lusam's shield and couldn't get any closer, they began to visibly relax a little. Alexia had explained that the damaged undead-villagers were not really a threat to them, as long as they could see them coming. She had shown Rebekah and Kayden her glowing bow and Renn's sword, explaining how they would always warn them—by glowing brightly—if any undead were nearby. Lusam had suggested that he dispose of the undead-villager by incinerating it, but Alexia said she had a better idea, one that would show the children that they weren't so scary after all.

She had dismounted her horse, leaving Rebekah alone in the saddle, and removed one of her blessed arrows. She asked Lusam to let her pass through the rear of his magical shield, and then winked at Rebekah and Kayden. Once she had left the protection of Lusam's shield, she casually walked around it, towards the front of his barrier, where the undead-villager had still been trying to batter its way inside. When it had finally noticed her, it began shuffling towards her. She had taunted it, by tapping her arrow on the top of its head at arm's length, and then walked slowly in a wide circle, proving to the children how slowly and cumbersome the creature moved. Rebekah had still looked concerned for Alexia's well-being, but Kayden was soon laughing at the pathetic attempts of the creature to catch up with Alexia. Then, after walking around in circles for a while, Alexia had taken one of her arrows and pretended to prick her finger with its tip. She had made a strange face, suggesting that it was sharp, and it had hurt her finger. It had reminded Lusam of a carnival attraction he had seen in Helveel with Neala, where a man had exaggerated his movements to tell a story, but without speaking any words. Alexia then grinned, and pointed to her own buttock with the tip of the arrow, making the same strange face again, before pointing towards the undead-villager's buttock. Rebekah and Kayden both understood the implied suggestion from Alexia, and had cheered their support for it loudly. Kayden had even clapped his hands as if he had been at a carnival watching an actual show. Alexia waited until the undead villager had its back to the others, then she had swiftly moved behind it, letting the children clearly see her gently jab the undead villager's buttock with her arrow. The undead villager fell forward dead, and the children cheered wildly, as if she had been a great heroin, battling a giant foe.

Lusam had felt mixed emotions over that incident. On the one hand, he felt bad for the dignity of the once innocent villager, but on the other hand, if it helped reduce the children's anxiety a little during their journey to Lamuria, he felt it was probably worth the indignity caused.

That had been six days ago, and since then they had cleared eight towns and villages of undead, and were now almost within sight of Lamuria.

"Lamuria is just over this next ridge," Renn announced, as if reading Lusam's own thoughts.

"What do you expect we'll find when we get there?" Lusam asked, hoping they were still in time to help save the city.

"I'm not sure lad..." Renn began to say, suddenly pulling his horse to a stop as they crested the hill. "But certainly *not* that," he said in complete shock.

"Oh, Gods!" Neala whispered loudly, as she too saw the scene before them.

Covering the entire valley floor below them, were tens of thousands of undead. Not the slow moving, damaged kind like they had been killing for the previous six days, but the fully mobile, and deadly kind, like they had faced in The Elveen Mountains.

"Aysha have mercy on us all," Renn whispered. He dismounted his horse, removed his sword and plunged it into the ground, then he immediately fell to his knees in prayer, both hands still gripping his sword tightly. Alexia approached

Renn's side, unable to take her eyes off the valley floor below. Eventually, she too dropped to her knees next to Renn in prayer, asking Aysha to watch over them all, and give them the strength they would need to survive what was about to come. Neala came to stand by Lusam, holding both children by their hands. No words could describe the scene before them. There were so many undead, the entire valley floor seemed to be moving.

Lusam could just about make out several small pockets within the writhing mass of undead below. When he looked again, this time using his mage-sight, he could clearly see the bright blue auras of the paladins, as they hopelessly battled against the insurmountable number of undead. Lusam noticed a single magical-missile arc through the air, and impact close to a group of battling paladins, fortunately killing only the undead it hit. When Lusam checked where missile had come from with his mage-sight, he gasped loudly.

"What is it … what do you see?" asked Neala, sounding very concerned by his sudden outburst. Lusam turned towards her, only now noticing that she was standing so close to him. He slowly turned back towards what he had just seen, trying hard to convince his own mind that it was not actually real, and only a figment of his imagination, but the terrifying sight remained. On the opposite side of the huge valley, high up on the tops of the cliffs, were thousands of magi. Their collective auras burned like a crimson sun. There were so many, it was impossible to count them all, but Lusam guessed there were at least five thousand of them—far more than he could possibly hope to defeat alone. To Lusam, the battle seemed lost before it had even begun.

"Thousands of Empire magi," Lusam replied quietly, pointing towards the far horizon.

"Oh, Gods, no," Neala whispered, scanning the cliff-tops at the far end of the valley.

"Lusam, look..." Neala said breathlessly, pointing towards Lamuria. Lusam looked in the direction she was pointing, and was about to ask her what she was looking at, when she spoke again.

"It's Lamuria!" she said, still pointing at the city below with her mouth open in awe. Lusam looked at her strangely, worried that the sudden shock of what was before them, was to blame for her stating such an obvious thing.

"Are you alright?" he asked, slightly concerned for her state of mind. She frowned when she saw the look of concern on his face, realising he still hadn't made the connection himself.

"Look ... it's Lamuria! The painting on the ceiling in Coldmont ... it's Lamuria!" Neala said excitedly, still pointing at the city below. Lusam turned to look at the city, and truly saw it for the first time. Neala was right, it *was* the city painted on the ceiling of Coldmont, complete with its white marble-clad buildings, huge tower, and massive circular wall that encompassed the whole city.

"You're right, it is," he replied in a whisper.

"You know what that means, don't you?" Neala asked.

"That there is a Guardian book somewhere in Lamuria," Lusam replied, not even noticing Renn and Alexia approach behind them.

"I've already told you lad, there is no Guardian book in Lamuria, or I would know about it," Renn said confidently.

"There *has* to be one here. In Helveel the picture was of Coldmont, and we found one there. And in Coldmont the picture was of Lamuria, so there must be one here too," Lusam replied.

"I'm sorry lad, but there just isn't," Renn replied, genuinely sounding sorry for the answer he gave.

"Then how do you explain that?" Lusam asked, pointing towards Lamuria. The undead were pounding at the walls of the city, and with each strike, the walls shimmered red, just like the ones inside Helveel and Coldmont.

"It's no secret that Lamuria has a magical shield lad. That's the only thing that has kept the Empire at bay for so long. That and its flawed intelligence of how weak we actually are," Renn replied, placing a hand on Lusam's shoulder. Lusam thought for a moment, about what he had read in the journal from Helveel, the Guardian's visit there, and the construction of the book room and its defences.

"No, Renn, you're wrong. There *is* a Guardian's book in Lamuria, I just know it. That shield is exactly the same as the ones in Helveel and Coldmont, and we know for certain that both were constructed by the Guardians. The one in Helveel because it's documented in the journal I found, and Coldmont ... well, it was their main seat of power, so who else would have constructed it. And I know what you're going to say— that you would know if there was one here, but you didn't know about the one in Helveel, or Coldmont, so why would you have been told about the one here? You once told me that the paladins of Aysha were only privy to certain information regarding the workings of the High Temple, just in case they were ever caught and tortured for that information by The Thule Empire. I would certainly imagine the existence of a Guardian book wouldn't be allowed to become common knowledge, even amongst the paladins of Aysha. According to the journal, the location of each Guardian book was to remain a closely guarded secret. Who knows, maybe only the High Priest knows about it, or maybe even he doesn't. Either way, I just *know* there is a book here ... there has to be," Lusam said passionately.

The more Renn thought about Lusam's words, the more it began to ring true. Why else would Lamuria have been given such a shield? It would certainly explain Lord Zelroth's unhealthy interest in Lamuria over the last few centuries. After all, he had already discovered Coldmont, and no doubt seen the painted image of Lamuria there himself. If he too believed there was a Guardian book in Lamuria, that would explain both his single-mindedness in his pursuit of the city, and his reluctance to launch and all-out assault. For all he knew, the High Temple could be filled with powerful magi who had read the Guardian book there, making it an incredibly dangerous place to attack.

Renn knew something must have spurred him into action recently, and he believed that *something* to be Lusam. Lord Zelroth already knew that Lusam had read at least two of the Guardian books, and now that the location of

Coldmont was known, Lord Zelroth could no longer afford to wait. If he did, and those *imaginary* magi in the High Temple read the Guardian book in Coldmont, he would soon be faced with impossible odds. Then the final part of the puzzle fell into place for Renn, as he suddenly remembered that the image painted on the ceiling in the High Temple was that of Irragin, in Mount Nuxvar: Lord Zelroth's seat of power, and another—highly probable—location of a Guardian book.

"I think you might be right lad," Renn said quietly, shaking his head in disbelief. The evidence had been staring him right in the face, and still he hadn't seen it. "If you *are* right, then we need to get you inside the High Temple to read that Guardian book lad, before they decide to launch and all-out assault. The city's shield might stand up to those undead for a while, but it would collapse quickly against an all-out attack from those magi," Renn said, nodding towards the far horizon, indicating that he had already seen the huge number of magi massed at the far end of the valley.

"And just how do you propose we reach the city gates, with all those undead down there?" Neala asked nervously. Renn looked at Lusam and raised his eyebrows, waiting for him to reply. Lusam thought about it for a while, knowing he would only get once chance to reach the gates undetected by the huge number of magi poised to attack. If they even thought it was him trying to enter the city, he had no doubt they would launch a massive assault on both him, and the city —one he knew neither he, nor the city would survive.

"Firstly, we leave the horses here and go on foot. We'll need to blend in as much as possible down there. If those Empire magi even suspect we are anything other than another group of paladins, we are done for. We'll need to stay very close together, so it's not obvious to the watching magi that we are behind a shield. I can alter my shield so it will allow you to freely strike at the undead from inside. But you must be very careful, if any part of your body is outside my shield, and you're grabbed by one of the undead, they could easily pull you out from behind my shield's protection. We will need to keep moving forward too, because I suspect the more of those things we kill, the more scrutiny we will receive from those magi up there. So only kill the ones in front of us, and to the sides. I think if we make it half-way across the valley floor, we should be hidden from the magi by the city walls. I guess once we're no longer visible to the magi, we can kill as many undead as we like," Lusam replied thoughtfully.

"I wouldn't be so sure of that, lad," Renn said. "Most of your plan seems pretty sound, but the magi who are controlling those undead, will also sense their destruction. If too many of them die too quickly, they will no doubt investigate further. They often use their undead minions as extensions to their own ears and eyes, sending them into dangerous situations where they themselves refuse to go. My advice would be to simply get to the gate as quickly as possible lad, and ignore the ones who are not in our way. That way we don't draw any unwanted attention to ourselves." Lusam nodded at his words, knowing that Renn knew far more about the undead than he did.

"I have a question," Alexia said, crouching down, and hugging Rebekah and Kayden close to her. "If we *do* make it to the gate in one piece, how do we get through that shield, and then inside the city?"

"Good point," Neala said with a nervous laugh.

"Don't worry about that, the shield will allow any paladin who is carrying a blessed weapon pass through it, along with anyone else they are in contact with. There is a small wicket gate next to the main one, so we can enter through that. Inside there's an enclosed stone courtyard, and an inner gate. Once they see who we are, they will allow us entry into the city," Renn replied.

"What about my knives?" Neala asked suddenly.

"What about them?" Lusam replied.

"Well, Renn has his blessed sword, and Alexia her blessed arrows, but my knives will soon be useless down there against all those undead. You would spend more time cleansing them, than I would using them," Neala said.

"Hmm, I hadn't thought about that," Lusam replied,

trying to think of a way around the limitations of her knives. A few moments later he had an idea. "Take out one of your knives, and saturate its blade by touching it, please," he said to Neala. She did as he asked, then held out the blade for him to take, but instead of taking her knife he placed his hand on her shoulder. He easily created a link to the blade through Neala's body, and cleansed the blade of all its magic.

"It won't be a problem, I can cleanse your knives constantly, by maintaining physical contact with you. I'll have to keep my shield as small as possible anyway, to avoid detection, so staying close enough to each other shouldn't be a problem either," Lusam said confidently.

"So, while we are cutting down the hordes of undead, and you have a hold of Neala, who will be looking after Rebekah and Kayden?" Alexia asked, still hugging the two frightened children.

"Hey, Kayden," Lusam said after a moment, "I bet you know how to back-ride really well, don't you?" Kayden nodded, but kept his head down on Alexia's shoulder. "There we go then. Kayden can ride on my back, and I'll keep hold of Rebekah with my free hand, while you three carve us a path to that gate."

"You make it sound so easy," Neala laughed, looking down at the tens of thousands of undead moving around below them on the valley floor.

It took quite a while to convince Rebekah and Kayden that everything would be alright, and they would soon be safe inside the city walls, but eventually they agreed to the plan. They left the horses behind, and began the journey down into the valley on foot. Fortunately most of the road was hidden from view by thick trees, as it snaked downwards into the valley below, making it easy to conceal their approach. Renn's sword and Alexia's bow had both started to glow brightly long before they reached the valley floor. Renn was leading the group—as he was the only one familiar with the road they were on—and called a halt to the party, just as the road ahead veered to the left and vanished from view. He carefully climbed a small mound and peered over it to check what lay on the other side, then slid back down to tell the others. They all gathered around Renn to hear what he had to say, but also kept a nervous eye on the road up ahead for any signs of movement.

"Just around that next bend, we'll arrive at the valley floor. From what I could see, most of the undead are facing Lamuria as you might expect. So if were lucky, we can probably get a fair distance before they even notice us coming. I know it will be hard, but I suggest we walk, not run. It's far better that the undead see us a little earlier, than have those magi notice a group of fast moving objects, and decide to investigate us further," Renn whispered. Everyone nodded their agreement, but nobody spoke a word. "Alright, let's get into our formation, and may Aysha watch over us all," Renn whispered. Neala threw her arms around Lusam's neck and gave him a tight hug, then gently kissed his lips.

"Be careful," she whispered in his ear, whilst hugging him again. Lusam nodded and smiled at her.

"It should be *me* telling *you* to be careful. You're the one who'll have their hands outside the protection of my shield. Just make sure none of those things grab you and drag you outside of it," Lusam whispered in her ear, and gave her a gentle kiss.

"The day I start to move slowly enough for one of those things to even get close to me, is the day I'll hang up my knives for good," she replied slightly too defensively. Lusam chuckled at the look on her face: one that said he should already know she was far better than that—and of course, he did.

"When you two lovebirds have done slobbering all over each other, we have a few undead to kill," Alexia said grinning at them both. Neala narrowed her eyes and pouted at her best friend, but took it in good humour.

Soon they were formed up and ready to go, Kayden was riding on Lusam's back, Rebekah holding his free hand, and Renn, Neala and Alexia in front of him. He created a magical shield around them all, and adjusted it so they could freely strike at the undead through it, then they were on their way.

As soon as they reached the bend in the road, the valley floor opened out in front of them. It was a sea of movement as far as they could see, all trying to force their way towards the defensive walls of Lamuria. Weapons at the ready, they moved slowly and silently forward, towards the incredible mass of undead.

Renn was the first to strike, jabbing at the mass of undead through Lusam's shield. They fell like stones before his blessed blade, as he carved a narrow path through the undead army. Alexia jabbed at them with one of her blessed arrows, felling any that got in their way, and Neala followed her example with her enchanted knives, whilst Lusam constantly cleansed her blades of magic. Their progress was painfully slow, as they were forced to climb over the many bodies of the slain undead. Kayden had his face buried in Lusam's back, eyes closed tight against the horrors of what was happening right in front of him. Lusam could feel Rebekah's hand trembling in his own, and gave it several squeezes of encouragement to try and reassure her. At first, she had also kept her eyes closed, but several times she had almost tripped on the undead corpses as they clambered over them. Now she looked down at the ground, trying to ignore the grisly sights beneath her own feet, and far too afraid to look up.

Lusam kept a nervous eye on the huge number of magi at the opposite end of the valley. So far, their presence seemed to have gone undetected by them, but he knew that could change in an instant. If it did, he would need to be ready to channel far more power into his shield to survive a single hit. At the moment his shield was purposely very weak, trying to make it blend in with the natural auras and weapons of what should hopefully appear to be nothing more than a group of paladins on the battlefield. He could see three groups of paladins in the distance, not far from the city gates, and was relieved to see that they appeared to be killing the undead at a faster rate then they were. Hopefully that would be enough to stop the Empire magi investigating their party.

Once they had reached the halfway point, the city walls and buildings began to obscure their view of the Empire magi. Lusam breathed a sigh of relief. He knew they weren't completely safe yet, but he also knew that not being in their direct line of sight, was one less chance of being discovered. It would also be a lot harder to target them accurately with any magical-missile, now they were no longer directly visible. On and on they pressed, killing dozens and dozens of undead as they carved their way through their mass towards the gates of Lamuria. As they approached the city walls, Lusam noticed one group of paladins to their left in serious trouble. Two of the four paladins had been injured and were on the ground, while the remaining two tried desperately to keep the undead hordes at bay. They were not being given the space, or opportunity to lift their fallen comrades from the floor, let alone retreat to the safety of Lamuria with them.

"Renn ... wait a moment," Lusam said, making sure he and the others had stopped moving before focusing his attention on the four paladins.

"Careful lad, you don't want to be announcing your presence just yet," Renn warned.

"I know, I'll be careful," Lusam replied, creating a similar magical shield around the four paladins. It took the two men a few moments to realise that the undead were no longer able to reach them, and they started to look around for the cause of it. When they saw Lusam and his party a few hundred paces away, they raised a cautious hand in greeting. Renn waved back, then shouted his greeting. It was obvious that he recognised at least one of the men, by the use of his familiar tone.

"Friend of yours?" Alexia enquired.

"Yeah, we trained together many years ago, at The Sanctum of Light in Stelgad," Renn replied.

"Should we start to carve them a path?" Neala asked, as she watched the two paladins pick up their fallen comrades and place them over their shoulders.

"Might be a good idea," Renn replied, starting to hack his way towards his fellow paladins. It didn't take them long to meet up with the group, and Lusam was then able to create a single magical shield to encase both parties.

"It's good to see you again Renn," one of the men said, holding out his hand in greeting.

"Likewise Carlos," Renn replied shaking his hand.

"Seems we owe you a debt of gratitude for saving our hides back there," Carlos said, grinning at Renn.

"I'm afraid you'll have to thank Lusam for that one, not me," Renn replied, nodding towards Lusam, "but let's all get inside first before we start celebrating, shall we?" Carlos turned towards Lusam and nodded his thanks, then took his place alongside the others, hacking and jabbing their way towards the gate. Neither Carlos nor the other man seemed the slightest bit encumbered by having another man draped across their shoulders, and soon they were at the small wicket gate. Carlos opened the small gate and entered into the inner courtyard, closely followed by his comrade-in-arms. The undead were still desperately battering at Lusam's shield, but the relief of reaching Lamuria's gate undetected by the Empire magi far outweighed his concern over that. He handed Rebekah over to Alexia, then removed Kayden from his back and passed him over to her too. Once she had hold of their hands, she passed through the city's shield and entered the safety of Lamuria. Renn went next, then held out his hand to Neala so she could cross the barrier, and finally it was Lusam's turn.

Once inside Lusam extinguished his shield and closed the gate firmly behind himself, glad to see the back of the undead hordes outside. The entrance led into a small stone courtyard, surrounded by high stone walls. At the far end was a locked iron gate, guarded by several soldiers dressed in immaculate red and blue uniforms. Lusam guessed that they were part of the regular King's guard, and didn't belong to the paladins of Aysha. The two injured men had been carefully placed on the floor, and Carlos was trying to rouse one of them.

"Let me take a look at them," Lusam offered, walking over to the two injured men. He placed his hand on the closest man's chest and used his mage-sight to determine the extent of his injuries. He quickly discovered that the first man had two broken bones and a severe concussion. He didn't think the man would regain consciousness anytime soon, but just in case, he blocked his ability to feel any pain whilst he reset the bones in his arm. With a loud cracking noise his arm bones realigned themselves—making several of the bystanders wince—then he fused the bones back together before moving on to the next man.

"He'll be fine now. I fixed his arm bones, but he still has a concussion. He just needs a little rest to recover," Lusam said, as he began assessing the second man. His injuries were more extensive, and would have been life threatening if Lusam hadn't intervened. He swifty repaired the damage and informed the other paladins of his condition, then went to wait with the others.

"Is there a problem?" Lusam asked, noticing the iron gate still remained locked.

"No lad, it's standard procedure for any unknown arrivals during a time of war. Someone will have gone to fetch whoever's in command so they can decided whether or not to let us into the city," Renn replied chuckling.

"Oh, I see," Lusam said, noticing for the first time the strange looks that Carlos and his fellow paladin were giving him now.

"How did you do that?" Carlos asked, pointing to the two men on the ground. "You didn't speak any incantation, you just ... did it."

Renn burst out laughing, knowing exactly what must be going through both Carlos' and his fellow paladin's mind right now. "Don't ask lads, it's far too complicated a story. I still don't understand it myself, and I've been trying to get my head around it for months now," he said, still chuckling at the amazed look on both their faces. Just then a familiar voice called out from behind them.

"Renn, is that you in there?" Hershel shouted from behind the locked gate. He was still wearing his full suit of chain mail, just like the last time they had seen him at The

Sanctum of Light, but somehow, he seemed older now,—as if the recent events had taken a high toll on him.

"Aye, you old fox, it's me—and I've brought some old friends along," Renn replied grinning at his old mentor.

"OPEN THE GATES!" Hershel bellowed, and a guard swifty obeyed his command. Renn clasped his arm in greeting, then introduced Rebekah and Kayden to him. Once Lusam, Neala and Alexia had greeted Hershel, they all started walking slowly towards the High Temple building.

"How goes the battle?" Renn asked quietly, suspecting he already knew the answer to his own question.

"Not good I'm afraid, old boy. Best estimates give the city's shield two days at most before its power is fully drained. We have every available mage trying to keep it topped up with their magic, but we simply don't have enough magi available. If those Empire magi attacked right now, it would be over in a matter of minutes," Hershel replied quietly.

"Maybe I can help with that," Lusam suggested, overhearing their conversation.

"Any contribution would certainly help young man, but I doubt even *you* can change the outcome of this war now," Hershel replied, sounding a little deflated.

"I wouldn't count on that if I were you, old friend," Renn said grinning. He checked all around to make sure no one else was in earshot, then still grinning from ear to ear, he said, "Hershel, we found Coldmont."

"You what!" Hershel gasped in disbelief.

"And there's more, but we must speak of it in private, and only inside the High Temple," Renn said cryptically. Hershel nodded, and they all picked up their pace as they headed towards the largest building in the city.

They entered the High Temple through the main paladins' entrance, then veered off to the right, towards a small office. Renn suddenly remembered that Hershel knew nothing about the Guardian book in Helveel, or the fact Lusam had already read it long before meeting him. Renn himself had only learned of it during their trek through the fog-covered valley in The Elveen Mountains, and that was after they had seen Hershel in The Sanctum of Light. He trusted Hershel completely, but for some reason he felt an overwhelming desire to keep the exact location of Helveel's Guardian book a secret from him, and as many other people as possible. Coldmont's Guardian book was already known to Lord Zelroth, as was the one suspected to be somewhere inside the High Temple, but Helveel, ... that must remain a secret, or the entire world would be in danger.

"So tell me all about Coldmont," Hershel asked excitedly, as he closed the door of the office behind them.

"We discovered it high in the Elveen Mountains, it's everything you would expect it to be, and much more, old friend. But that's not what I needed to speak to you about. Hershel ... we found a Guardian book there, and Lusam read it," Renn said grinning at his old friend.

Hershel's mouth fell open at the news Renn had just revealed to him, unable to comprehend the magnitude of it. If anyone else had told him such a thing, he would have dismissed it out of hand. But Aysha herself had spoken to him of Lusam's unique abilities and his future potential for saving Afaraon, and he had already witnessed several of those unique abilities himself.

"Lusam read a Guardian book?" Hershel managed to half-whisper through his utter shock.

"No, actually he read two," Renn replied, his grin now so wide that his jaw began to ache.

"What!" Hershel replied, dropping into his chair with his hand pressed to his forehead. Renn nodded slowly, as if that would legitimise his words further. It took a long time before Hershel spoke again, all he could do was stare at Lusam shaking his head in disbelief. Eventually he found his words.

"So, how powerful is he now?" Hershel asked Renn, as if Lusam wasn't even in the room with them. Renn turned to Lusam and nodded his head. Instinctively Lusam knew that Renn wanted him to reveal his aura to Hershel, so he slowly lowered the shutter around his mind, revealing a blindingly bright aura to him, before concealing once more a moment later. Lusam thought Hershel had looked shocked before, but now his face went way beyond the look of shock. It was quite possibly the most hilarious sight Lusam had ever seen, and no matter how hard he tried, he couldn't help himself grinning at it.

"Seven Gods!" Hershel swore, surprising everyone in the room, most of all himself. "How is that even possible? We need to inform the High Priest at once, this could change everything," Hershel said, jumping to his feet and knocking his chair over in the process.

"Wait old friend, I have even more incredible news to tell you," Renn replied, holding up his hand to his old mentor. "And, if you thought what I just told you was hard to believe, wait until you hear this. Hershel, we have found strong evidence to suggest there is a Guardian book right here, in the High Temple—one that Lusam must be allowed to read, before those Empire magi discover just how weak we truly are, and launch an all-out attack."

"But ... there can't be, or we'd know about it already, surely," Hershel said, mainly to himself.

"That's exactly what I said at first, but the evidence to the contrary is overwhelming. I ask that you trust us on this old friend, and arrange a meeting for us with the High Priest as soon as possible, so we can discuss the matter with him in private. It's quite possible that only he knows of its existence, or maybe even he isn't aware of it himself, either way, we must find it and allow Lusam access to it as soon as possible," Renn replied.

Hershel thought about Renn's words long and hard before he replied, but when he did, it was to Lusam, not Renn he spoke. "Lusam, I know the question I'm about to ask you would sound crazy to anyone else, but having seen your aura I must ask it. Could you defeat those Empire magi outside alone?"

"I'm sure I could kill a large number of them, but no, I couldn't survive against that number of magi alone," Lusam replied shaking his head.

"And if we did find another Guardian book here ... what then?" Hershel asked. Lusam thought about it for a moment, not really knowing the answer to his question. All he could go on was how much more powerful the previous books had made him after reading them.

"Possibly, but I'm not certain. It would depend on what knowledge the Guardian book revealed to me. I would certainly stand more of a chance if it increased the size of my magical reserves the same way the previous books did," Lusam replied honestly.

"That's if he survives reading the next one," Neala said quietly to herself.

"Survive?" Hershel asked curiously.

"Yes, Survive! The last one he read almost killed him. Not to mention the amount of time he might be unconscious if he does survive reading it. After reading the first book it was only about forty minutes, but the second one was more than two hours. Who knows how long he would be unconscious for this time?" Neala said, sounding extremely worried at the prospect of losing him.

"It's okay Neala, I'll be fine," Lusam replied hugging her, and trying to sound more confident than he actually was. He knew he had barely survived reading the last Guardian book, and knew if he had remained unconscious a few more minutes, he probably would never have woken up again. The incredible headache, and the damage it had done to the blood vessels in his head were still vivid in his memory. He pulled back from the hug, forcing a smile onto his face and kissed her gently on the lips. "I *have* to do this Neala. You know I do," He whispered to her. She nodded her head, as a small tear trickled down her cheek.

"So, any more revelations I need to know about?" Hershel asked, obviously trying to lighten the mood a little within the room.

"Actually, yes," Renn replied, taking Hershel by surprise yet again.

"Oh?" he asked, looking slightly overwhelmed.

"Our two young friends over there," Renn said

nodding towards Rebekah and Kayden, who were busy playing a guessing game with Alexia at the back of the small room. "We rescued them in a coastal village called Prystone on the east coast. Their parents are ... missing, but we discovered something incredible about not only *their* village, but apparently several more up and down that area of coastline. I don't know if you've noticed their auras, but I believe with the correct training they could both become capable magi. It seems that the local tradition of giving birth far out to sea has spared them from the Empire's culling of newborn magi. The girl told us that everyone in her village, and the neighbouring towns and villages was born at sea, and have been for generations. Other than our two young friends here, Prystone's population was completely devastated, but maybe, if we're lucky, the other towns and villages were spared. If they were, can you imagine the potential there? It may very well save magic itself in Afaraon, providing of course we survive this attack first."

"Well, you're certainly full of surprises today old boy," Hershel replied, shaking his head slightly whilst checking out Rebekah and Kayden's auras.

"I'm afraid I must ask a favour of you Hershel. I was wondering if your sister still lived here in Lamuria? If she does, do you think she would mind looking after them both for a while, at least until we can find a more permanent home for them. I'm sure the High Temple will be more than happy to offer them both a place at their School of Magic once this is all over. Besides, if we do survive this attack, I fully intend to go back to Prystone myself and search the surrounding villages and towns for any more survivors. Who knows how many potential untrained magi are out there, and if I'm lucky, I might find one of their family members there who can take care of them," Renn said.

"Yes, she still lives here, and I'm sure she wouldn't mind looking after them at all, given the circumstances we're all in at the moment. I'll ask her about it as soon as I get a chance, but for now old boy, I suggest we don't waste any more time and see if we can get this young man an audience with the High Priest," Hershel said looking towards Lusam.

"Of course," Renn replied, knowing he still had other important things to discuss with Hershel, such as the creation of a new female branch to the paladin's order: one that he hoped Alexia would lead someday. The paladins' entrance had only led into the barracks, and not the main part of the High Temple, so they were soon back outside making their way around towards the main front entrance of the High Temple.

Lusam was completely overwhelmed by the sheer scale of the building. It towered high into the sky above them, its white marble-clad walls reflecting the sun's light, making it appear to almost glow against the backdrop of the blue sky behind. The incredible detail carved into every slab of marble took his breath away. *'It must have taken decades, if not centuries to complete the work,'* he thought to himself. Each and every one of the countless windows was a work of art in its own right. The colours were so vibrant and real that Lusam was convinced they must have been created by Aysha herself. Then he noticed it for the first time. High above the tallest tower, floating in what seemed like mid-air, was a massive jewel-like structure. It was barely visible as it reflected the blue of the sky across its multifaceted surface, making it almost invisible against the sky beyond.

"Whoa! What's that?" Lusam gasped looking up at the indescribably beautiful object in the sky above him. He remembered seeing the painted picture of Lamuria on the ceiling in Coldmont. That too had shown a floating gem up above the highest tower, but he had thought it was only an artist's impression of something else, and had never expected it to actually exist.

"You can see that lad?" Renn asked in awe.

"Of course, can't you?" Lusam replied, not taking his eyes off the beautiful object.

"No, I can't lad, and I doubt anyone else here can either," Renn replied confidently.

"What is it?" Lusam repeated.

"It's called *The Heart of the City*. It's what powers the

city's defences. In the past, it was visible to almost everyone, but its power has diminished so much over the past few centuries that some people now believe it to be only a myth. How they think the city is actually shielded I have no idea, but I've found that if people can't see something with their own eyes, they often deny its existence," Renn replied, looking up at the spot where he *knew* it was, even if he couldn't see it himself.

"Shall we?" Hershel said, gesturing towards the huge stone staircase in front of them, one that Lusam hadn't even noticed while he was busy taking in the full splendour of the High Temple building itself. It was nowhere near the scale of the stone staircase in Coldmont, but it was still impressive all the same. The handrails were so ornately carved that he dare not even touch them, in case he somehow damaged them. He couldn't believe they had withstood centuries of daily use, not until he looked at them using his mage-sight, and noticed the subtle enchantment on them: one that had no doubt been used to strengthen them, and still, to this day drew its magic from the city's own power source. Although the handrails were certainly beautiful, it saddened him to think of how many other—unnecessary—things in the city were protected in a similar way, all slowly sapping the city's precious power source. He suspected that when the city had first been built, magic had been an abundant resource, and such frivolous use of it would have been commonplace. But ever since magic became so scarce in Afaraon, those same luxuries had slowly been killing the city.

"Is there a problem lad?" Renn asked, startling Lusam out of his reverie.

"No, sorry," Lusam replied, quickly catching up with the others, who had almost reached the doors of the High Temple. As Lusam approached, he could clearly see that even the doors of the High Temple were enchanted with some kind of spell. Hershel entered first, beckoning the others to follow, with Renn entering last.

"Wait here, I'll go and speak with one of the acolytes and see if we can gain an audience with the High Priest. I won't be long," Hershel said quietly, then headed off to find his acolyte. Inside the High Temple was even more breathtaking beautiful than the outside had been. The stone vaulted ceiling rose high above them, forming a procession of intricate arches running the full-length of the immense building. Huge stone statues of former Kings, Queens and High Priests lined the outer walls, each one many times taller than a man. The incredible stained glass windows which had looked so beautiful from the outside, looked positively divine from the inside as the sunlight streamed through the multicoloured glass, flooding the entire floor of the High Temple with its rainbow of colours. Massive chandeliers hung from the ceilings, each one powered magically, and each one another drain on the city's vastly depleted power source.

A few moments later Hershel reappeared and announced that the High Priest would see them as soon as he had finished dealing with a visiting dignitary—one who had been visiting the King before being trapped in Lamuria by the current Empire's siege. Apparently he had been petitioning for days to the High Temple to allow him to contribute towards the magical reserves of the city—something that only the priesthood and the well-known magi of Lamuria were ever allowed to undertake—and he had just been granted permission to do so by the High Priest himself. `A most unprecedented decision to take` according to Hershel, `but, no doubt one undertaken due to the current dire needs of the city.`

They all waited patiently for what seemed like an awfully long time before the High Priest and his visiting dignitary finally appeared in the main chamber. Lusam had been reading the many inscriptions carved into the stone walls before they arrived. Most of them were about the history and creation of the world, and Lusam recognised many of the stories as the same ones Renn had told him in The Dark Forest. The High Priest had already bid farewell to the visiting dignitary and signalled for Hershel's party to approach. The dignitary casually nodded his greeting to them all as he walked by, and continued towards the main temple doors. Something felt oddly familiar about the man to Lusam, but he couldn't quite put his finger on it. As the man walked slowly away, the coloured sunlight streaming through the windows momentarily glinted off his hand. `No, not his hand ... his ring!` Lusam thought, realising too late why he looked familiar. He slipped into his mage-sight and gasped when he saw the crimson aura. He immediately knew the man was an Empire agent, one no doubt sent to infiltrate the High Temple, and find out how depleted the city's power source actually was. A few more steps and he would be outside the protective walls of Aysha's High Temple and able to communicate with with his brethren outside the city. If that happened, and they learned of the fragile state of the city's defences, they would launch their attack without delay, killing everyone inside the walls of Lamuria, and gaining access to everything the city had, including the Guardian book if it was there. Lusam knew he could not allow that to happen.

"Excuse me sir," Lusam called loudly in the man's direction, whilst moving towards him at a fast walking pace. The man already had one hand on the door, but when he heard Lusam's calls he glanced over his shoulder.

"I'd like to thank you sir, for helping with the city's defences," Lusam said holding out his hand.

"No need, I was happy to help," he replied, turning back to the door.

"No, I insist," Lusam said, finally catching up with him at the door. The man turned to face Lusam and offered him his hand half-heartedly. Lusam took hold of his hand and turned it over so he could see his ring.

"Oh, I have a ring just like that one," Lusam said, surreptitiously removing the dead Empire agent's ring from his pocket.

"I doubt that," the man said arrogantly.

"Actually, I do ... look," Lusam replied, holding out his other hand with the Necromatic ring clearly visible in his palm. The man's eyes widened when he saw the ring in Lusam's hand. He desperately tried to form the words of a spell, but Lusam had already located the man's magical reserves, and a heartbeat later he had drained all but the tiniest amount of magic from the man. The man collapsed unconscious on the floor, and Lusam heard the running footsteps and concerned voices behind him.

Chapter Forty-One

"What have you done?" the High Priest asked sounding extremely concerned as he approached the unconscious man.

"I just saved all our lives, and everyone else's in Lamuria," Lusam replied calmly. "He's an Empire agent, and if I had let him step out of that door he would have contacted his people and reported *exactly* how much power you had left in the city's shield. I'm certain if the Empire had discovered how weak you are, they wouldn't have hesitated to launch everything they had at Lamuria."

Lusam was fully expecting the High Priest to ask him how he could possibly know that he was an Empire agent, but to his great surprise—and relief—he didn't. Instead he smiled at Lusam and offered him his hand.

"You must be Lusam, the one Hershel has told me so much about. He informed me of how you discovered the spy at The Sanctum of Light in Stelgad. I presume you used a similar method here?" the High Priest said pointing towards the unconscious Empire agent. Lusam nodded as he shook his hand in greeting.

"Well, it seems Aysha has delivered you to us safely, just in time to save us all, thank you Lusam. And speaking of our sacred and beloved Aysha, I believe you have had the *great* honour of meeting her not once, but twice in person, as well as receiving her blessing several times before that. I have to admit Lusam, even though it is unseemly for a man in my position to say so, I *am* more than a little envious of you," he said smiling at Lusam.

Lusam didn't really know how to reply to that, and

thankfully Renn broke the awkward silence between them. "How long is he likely to be unconscious?" he asked nodding towards the Empire agent.

"I'm not sure, but probably a couple of hours at least I would say. He won't be in any fit state to be throwing his magic around for a little while longer than that though," Lusam replied, not envying the man's headache when he did finally wake up. Renn then formally introduced the others to the High Priest, explaining briefly how they had rescued Rebekah and Kayden in Prystone, and soon after had noticed their magical potential. He decided not to mention their curious local tradition of giving birth at sea, and how it might mean a new source of magic for Afaraon—if any of the surrounding towns and villages had been spared the fate of Prystone. That was something they could revisit after the current crisis was over, if any of them survived it.

The High Priest signalled for one of his acolytes, who promptly came over to assist him.

"Your Grace?" the acolyte said bowing his head slightly.

"Please inform today's duty officer that we require the immediate removal of this Empire agent. Tell him that the prisoner is currently unconscious and likely to remain that way for some time yet, but to make the necessary preparations for when he regains consciousness so he is unable to use his magic. And under no circumstances is he to be allowed outside the High Temple walls, is that clear?"

"Yes, Your Grace," the acolyte replied bowing once more, then he rushed off to find the duty officer. The High Priest waited until the acolyte had gone before turning back to Lusam.

"Would you mind me asking exactly what you did to render him unconscious before he was able to silence you?" the High Priest asked curiously.

"Their silence spell has never really worked on me ... well, not in the way they intend it to do anyway. All I did was drain most of his magic reserves into my own, which caused him to lose consciousness," Lusam replied, glancing over at the Empire agent. The High Priest's eyes widened in surprise at Lusam's explanation.

"Our teachings tell us that it is impossible to take another's magic by force, Lusam. The only people to ever have shared another's magic were the Guardians themselves, and they only shared it with their bonded dragons. It is, however, understandable given your lack of proper training how you might misinterpret what you just did to that Empire agent. But for now, we must thank Aysha you were able to do whatever you did, before he managed to silence you," he said smiling at Lusam. Renn chuckled quietly to himself, gaining the attention of the High Priest as he did so.

"Do you find some amusement in my words Renn?" the High Priest asked, giving him a stern look.

"Forgive me Your Grace, I meant no disrespect," Renn said bowing his head in deference, "but I'm afraid you have not been made fully aware of Lusam's capabilities yet. May I suggest we speak further in private about this matter, Your Grace." The High Priest gave a curt nod then turned on his heels without saying another word, and headed towards the far end of the main chamber. Lusam noticed a brief look of sympathy on Hershel's face for Renn, but neither of them spoke a word as they all followed the High Priest.

They eventually passed through a large door at the far end of the main chamber and entered a long corridor. Lusam was relieved to see that only normal candles illuminated this part of the High Temple, instead of the magically powered lights that adorned the main chamber. As they walked down the long corridor they could clearly hear children's voices and laughter coming from somewhere up ahead. Rebekah and Kayden were still holding Alexia's hand, but the sounds of other children seemed to pique their interest somewhat. A moment later it became apparent that it was no coincidence the High Priest had chosen that particular route. He stopped outside the door of what they soon discovered was a classroom and knocked quietly, before opening the door.

"Good afternoon, Your Grace" a woman greeted him, and her greeting was quickly echoed by all the children in the classroom.

"Good afternoon, Miss Hiroko ... good afternoon children," he replied smiling at them all.

"Is there something I can help you with, Your Grace?" Miss Hiroko asked curiously.

"Yes, I was hoping you wouldn't mind if our two young guests here took part in your class this afternoon, while I discuss some important matters with their friends."

"No, I don't want to. I want to stay with Alexia," Kayden said hugging her leg tightly.

"It's okay Kayden, it's only for a short while. I promise I'll come back for you very soon. I'm sure you'll have a wonderful time with all the other boys and girls here," Alexia said trying to reassure him.

"We were just about to have some cake and milk if you would like to join us," Miss Hiroko said, holding out a plate of delicious looking cake.

"Do you promise to come back for us later?" Rebekah said quietly to Alexia.

"Yes, of course I do Rebekah. You two go and eat some of that yummy cake and have some fun while we talk about all the boring stuff," Alexia replied winking at her. "Maybe Kayden could show Miss Hiroko how he makes his wooden spinning top move, I'm sure she would like that."

"Oh, I would like to see that very much, Kayden. Could you show me please?" Miss Hiroko said enthusiastically. It was the perfect distraction for Kayden, he was inside the classroom demonstrating his spinning top even before Alexia had the chance to say goodbye to him. Rebekah on the other hand was far less enthusiastic about it, giving Alexia such a sad look when she bid her farewell, that it almost brought her to tears. At first Alexia felt angry that the High Priest had decided to do what he had done without discussing the matter first with her or one of the others, but when she thought about it more, she realised the less Rebekah and Kayden knew about Lusam and the Guardian books, the less danger they would ultimately be in.

The High Priest led them further down the same

corridor, which eventually opened up into a large circular room. Five more corridors led away from the room, each one equally spaced around its perimeter, but it was what Lusam saw in the centre of the room which caught his attention the most. In the middle of the room was a large round table with five chairs, three of which were currently being used by men dressed in priest's robes. On the table in front of each man was what appeared to be a glowing gemstone. Each one was the size of a large apple, and each one glowing to their touch. The two unoccupied places also had gemstones set into the table, but neither of those two were glowing like the others, at least not until Lusam looked at them using his mage-sight, then he had to shield his eyes from the intensity of their blinding light. He instantly recognised them as much smaller versions of the huge floating gem outside the High Temple. The light they emitted seemed very familiar to Lusam, and it took him a moment to realise why. They didn't glow like Renn's blessed sword or Alexia's bow to his mage-sight, instead they reminded Lusam of a person's aura: a very powerful aura.

As he stood there staring at the closest gemstone, he found himself inexplicably questing out towards it with his mind, as if it were calling to him somehow. When his mind came into contact with it, he gasped inwardly at what he sensed. The gemstone was alive ... no, not alive, but definitely sentient, or at least it was in part. It was the strangest feeling Lusam had ever known, and very difficult to describe. He could sense incredible sadness and regret emanating from the object, but by far the strongest emotion he sensed was anger. Not anger directed at him personally, but a more generalised anger, unfocussed anger, anger at the world around it—a world it could no longer truly sense. He tried to communicate with the object, and for a heartbeat he thought he might have gained its attention, but it soon became obvious that whatever it was, or had been, was no longer capable of any kind of logical thought.

"Lusam!" Neala called out, dragging him back to himself. When Lusam once more became aware of his surroundings, he noticed that he had somehow walked over to where the gemstone lay on the table without even realising it, and now Neala was desperately tugging at his hand.

"Are you alright lad?" Renn asked sounding a little concerned.

"Err, yeah, I think so, why?" Lusam replied, feeling a little disorientated.

"We were all at the far end of the corridor by the time we noticed you were missing. When we came back for you, you were standing right there, staring into space. We tried to wake you up, but nothing seemed to work. What happened to you?" Neala said sounding very worried.

"I'm not really sure. I was looking at the gemstone's aura using my mage-sight and it felt like it called out to me, so I reached out to it with my mind. It felt like it was alive somehow, with emotions and feelings, but no true consciousness. It's hard to explain," Lusam replied.

"Aura, what aura?" Renn asked looking at the gemstone.

"You don't see it?" Lusam asked.

"No, all I see is a *Power* Orb lad, or should I say five *Power Orbs*," Renn replied, checking for himself. Lusam checked once more but the aura remained blindingly bright to his mage-sight. He didn't understand why Renn couldn't see it, but by the confused look on Hershel's and the High Priest's face he guessed that they couldn't either.

"What are they? " Lusam asked, still staring at the gemstones.

"They are called *Power Orbs*. We use them to collect the magic from our priests and magi. Then that power is transferred to *The Heart of the City,* which in turn is what provides the power for our city's defences," the High Priest replied. Lusam knew he had to help strengthen the city's defences with his magic, but he felt far less enthusiastic about it now that he knew he would be interacting with those *Power Orbs* again.

"Did you know they were alive,?" Lusam asked,

knowing how crazy the question sounded.

"Of course they are not alive!" the High Priest snapped at Lusam. His vehement denial took Lusam by surprise, and by the reactions of the others, them too. Lusam was sure he knew more than he was admitting, but decided against pursuing the matter further, in case it damaged his chances of finding out if a Guardian book was indeed hidden within the High Temple.

"Would it be alright if I made a donation of magic?" Lusam asked changing the subject. The High Priest's smile reappeared, wiping away all signs of his previous scowl.

"That is a most gracious offer, Lusam, but one I'm afraid I could not risk you undertaking until after your training. We will of course teach you the relevant incantation that will enable you to contribute towards the city's defences in due time, but it may take you a while to perfect it. But even before you attempt a power transfer, you must also learn how to detect when your magic is running low, otherwise the *Power Orbs* could drain you completely. I can see by the strength of your aura that you do not possess a great deal of magic Lusam, so you must be especially careful during the process," he replied smiling at Lusam.

Lusam looked at Hershel, wondering exactly how little he had told the High Priest about his abilities. Even though Hershel hadn't known that Lusam had read a Guardian book when he first met him, he did know about his ability to hide his aura, and the fact that he didn't need to speak any incantations to cast a spell—something he obviously had neglected to inform the High Priest about for some reason. He would have to ask him the reasons why later, but for now, he needed to reveal his abilities to the High Priest. If he didn't, the High Priest would never admit to the existence of any Guardian book in the High Temple, let alone allow him to attempt to read it. Lusam could see how amused Renn and the others were by the High Priest's ignorance of his abilities, but he hoped they wouldn't make it too obvious and jeopardise Lusam's chances of finding out if there actually was a Guardian book there.

Lusam was fairly certain the yearly reports his grandmother had sent to the High Temple must not have contained any reference to his ability to hide his aura. If they had, Renn would have already known about it, and probably found him much sooner than he did. He had already thought about it many times before, and concluded that there had been no advantage for his grandmother to inform the High Temple about his ability. If she had, and the missive had been intercepted, or there had been a spy within the High Temple, the Empire agents would have simply switched their tactics and killed *all* children, not just the newborn magi. Something she would never have allowed to happen.

"I hide the true strength of my aura from people, Your Grace," Lusam said, knowing full well he wouldn't be believed him until he proved it. The High Priest chuckled at Lusam's statement then gave him a sympathetic smile.

"There is no reason to be ashamed of your limited power Lusam. Aysha has blessed you with her gift of magic, something you should rejoice in, and give thanks for," he said, still wearing his sympathetic smile, one that disappeared a moment later when Lusam lowered the shutter on his mind, revealing a blindingly intense aura for everyone in the room to see. The High Priest's eyes widened in shock, and two of the priests still sat at the table gasped out loud at the sight before them. Lusam walked over to the closest *Power Orb*, placed a hand on it, and transferred most of his power into it, resisting the pull on his mind to reach out towards the strange object. The *Power Orb* glowed so brightly that it lit up the entire room, as if a sun had just risen there. As soon as Lusam removed his hand the intense glow lessened greatly, but didn't completely extinguish itself like the other *Power Orbs*.

"Aysha be blessed," the High Priest muttered to himself, still trying to look directly at Lusam's blazing aura. Lusam lowered the shutter once more to conceal his aura, then waited for the High Priest to speak, which took much longer than he had anticipated.

"How ... how is that possible? No one is supposed to

be able to hide their aura. No one ..." the High Priest half-whispered, still looking at Lusam's diminished aura. Then he seemed to notice the glowing *Power Orb* on the table for the first time. His eyes widened again, and his mouth began to move, but no sound came out. Only Hershel remained within sight of the High Priest, the others had moved behind him, so he couldn't see them struggling with their amusement. Neala had wandered off down one of the long corridors, unable to contain her amusement any longer, but Lusam doubted the High Priest would have even noticed if she had stayed. One of the other priests stood up and approached the *Power Orb* Lusam had just used. After giving Lusam a wary look he placed a hand on top of the *Power Orb*, closed his eyes and began an incantation. A moment later his eyes shot open, and he stared open mouthed at Lusam. He then approached the High Priest and whispered something in his ear. Lusam watched as the High Priest duplicated exactly what the other priest had just done, even down to the bulging eyes and open mouthed look after inspecting the *Power Orb*. He turned back to the Power Orb and picked it up very carefully, before turning back to Lusam.

"This *Power orb* was almost fully depleted before you touched it Lusam, now it has more magic contained within it, than it has had in living memory. It would have taken every priest and mage we have weeks to accumulate such a store of magic. How can you possibly be so powerful?" he asked, handing the *Power Orb* carefully back to the other priest, who bowed his head and hurried from the room, no doubt to strengthen the city's defences with it.

"That is one of the many things we need to discuss, Your Grace, but I must insist we do so in private," Hershel said, keeping his voice low so it didn't leave the room.

The High Priest looked at Hershel for a moment, then nodded his head. "Very well, follow me," the High Priest said, heading off down one of the other corridors.

It wasn't long before they arrived at a locked door, and when the High Priest took a key from around his neck and began to unlock it, Hershel spoke again.

"Your Grace, are we to be allowed entry to the inner sanctum?" he asked in a surprised tone.

"What's an inner sanctum?" Neala asked curiously. The High Priest gave her a look that suggested everyone should know what the inner sanctum was, but he allowed Hershel to answer her question all the same.

"The inner sanctum is the most sacred part of the High Temple. Only the High Priest and senior members of the priesthood are allowed to enter it ... usually," Hershel replied.

The door creaked opened to reveal a large rectangular room beyond. The room had very little in the way of furniture inside, just a single writing desk and several basic chairs. One wall of the room was lined with bookshelves that reached almost to the high ceiling, and the other had various portraits of what Lusam assumed were previous High Priests. At the far end of the room was another of the beautifully crafted stain glass windows, one that depicted various images of the world's creation. Once everyone was inside the inner sanctum the High Priest closed the door behind them, then went to sit behind his desk. He didn't speak for quite a while, instead he studied the faces of Lusam, Hershel and Renn, ignoring Neala and Alexia completely.

"I have allowed you all entry to the inner sanctum because this room has certain ... safeguards built into it. Nothing we say in here will be overheard by anyone else, I assure you. First of all, I would like to know how you managed to charge that *Power Orb* without speaking an incantation?" he said looking directly at Lusam.

"I don't need to speak to use my magic, I never have," Lusam replied truthfully.

"Could you show me, please?" he said after a moment's hesitation.

"What would you have me do?" Lusam asked.

"Anything will suffice, thank you. I simply wish to see what I believed impossible only a short time ago," he replied, watching Lusam very carefully, as if he was expecting some trickery or sleight of hand from him.

Lusam had already transferred a good portion of his

power reserves to the *Power Orb*, so he didn't want to do anything too magically strenuous. He hoped the magic he had donated to the city's defences would be sufficient to protect the city long enough for him to read the Guardian book—if there was indeed one there. If there wasn't a Guardian book in Lamuria, he knew he could always reclaim some of his power from the city's shield if he needed to fight, but he also knew that would be a fight he couldn't possibly win. He decided to create a simple light orb, letting it wink out of existence, and then recreating it several times over.

"And you can do that with any spell?" the High priest asked curiously. Lusam nodded, expecting him to ask for further proof, but instead he turned to speak with Hershel.

"You said that you wished to speak to me in private Hershel?"

"Yes, of course," Hershel replied bowing his head. "I have joyous news indeed, Your Grace. Upon their arrival at Lamuria, Renn informed me that his party had discovered the actual location of Coldmont, and what's more, they found one of the lost Guardian books there. Lusam has already read that Guardian book, as well as one other. He informs me that they found strong evidence suggesting the existence of a third Guardian book, here in the High Temple. Your Grace, if that's true, we must allow Lusam access to it without delay. He believes he may be able to defeat the forces outside of Lamuria if he is able to read a third Guardian book, Your Grace."

The High Priest remained silent after Hershel had finished reporting to him. Lusam had expected him to be excited by the discovery of Coldmont and the Guardian book, or at least ask some questions about it, but instead he seemed to be calculating his next move. Lusam knew that the less time they wasted the better, he simply had to know if there was a Guardian book there or not.

"So, *is* there a Guardian book here in Lamuria?" Lusam asked hopefully, watching his face very carefully.

"No, there is not," he said calmly, turning straight back to Hershel as if Lusam had never asked him anything of importance. "Hershel, where is Coldmont?"

"Renn said they discovered it high up in the Elveen Mountains, Your Grace," Hershel replied. The High Priest nodded his head slowly, but instead of questioning Renn about the precise location of Coldmont, he continued questioning Hershel.

"Tell me Hershel, when you first met Lusam in The Sanctum of Light, did he reveal to you his ability to hide his aura, and the fact he could perform magic without speaking any incantations?" the High Priest asked, surprising everyone in the room with his sudden change of topic. Hershel was obliged to answer the High Priest's questions truthfully, and so he did.

"Yes, Your Grace, he did," Hershel said bowing his head.

"Then why did you omit such important information when you reported the captured spy to me?"

"Your Grace, I was warned to keep Lusam's abilities a secret by Aysha herself, I—" he replied, but was cut short by a sudden outburst from the High Priest.

"A secret! I am Aysha's High Priest! Do you think she intended you to keep that information from me, her own High Priest?" he shouted at Hershel.

"I apologise, I meant no disrespect, Your Grace," Hershel replied. Lusam had been wondering why Hershel hadn't already told the High Priest about his abilities, and now he knew.

The High Priest was now standing behind his desk, glaring across it at Hershel.

"So, tell me about the other Guardian book you mentioned," he said in a much calmer voice. Hershel momentarily looked at Renn, realising he had never asked about the second Guardian book.

"I'm sorry Your Grace, I don't know anything about that Guardian Book," Hershel replied truthfully.

"Renn?" the High Priest prompted. Renn was also obliged to report truthfully to the High Priest, but he knew how important it was for the location of the Guardian book in

Helveel to remain a secret. The fewer people who knew of its existence the better. Renn remained silent, torn between his duty to the High Priest and what he believed in his heart to be right.

"I'm waiting Renn," he said impatiently.

"Your Grace, I beg you don't make me reveal the location of the Guardian book, I believe it is in the interest of everyone that its location remains a secret," Renn replied bowing his head.

"I don't care what you believe Renn, you will tell me its location … right now!" the High Priest commanded.

At that instant there was a blindingly bright flash within the room, causing everyone to cover their eyes and look away. When they looked back, they gasped as they saw the incredible sight of Aysha standing before them, with her long silver hair blowing in a breeze that did not exist within the room. Renn and Hershel immediately recognised the beautiful Goddess and fell to their knees, heads bowed before her, quickly followed by Alexia. The High Priest seemed confused by the sudden appearance of Aysha, and it seemed to take him much longer than Lusam would have expected for him to realise who was standing before him. When he did, his eyes went wide with shock and he too fell to his knees, head bowed. When Lusam glanced at Neala, he saw that she too had knelt before Aysha, so he quickly followed her example.

"I am afraid that some secrets must remain just that, even from you Jasper," Aysha said to the High Priest in a heavenly voice.

The High Priest looked mortified at her words. "I beg your forgiveness my lady, I meant no disrespect. I sought only to better protect the Guardian book," he said almost in tears.

"There is nothing to forgive my child, no harm was done," Aysha replied soothingly, then she turned her attention to Renn.

"Renn, my faithful paladin, you were wise indeed to keep the location of the Guardian book a secret. If the location of it is discovered by our enemies, the entire world will be in grave danger. Even though my brother Aamon remains trapped within the Netherworld, I have recently sensed his presence in *our* realm. It seems he has discovered a way to communicate with his followers, even from within the confines of the Netherworld. He has set in motion a plan which, if successful, will tear open The Great Rift into the Netherworld once more, allowing both himself and the vile creatures there to escape into our world. I believe he intends to use Lamuria's *Heart of the City* to achieve his goals, something we cannot allow to happen, or the entire world will perish."

Lusam had so many questions for Aysha, but wasn't sure if he could, or even should ask her anything. After all, he wasn't a priest or paladin, so he had no right to ask her anything, surely.

Aysha turned to face Lusam and fondly smiled down on him. "Of course you may ask me, Lusam," Aysha replied to his unspoken question, startling him somewhat and making his face redden. "What do you wish to ask, my child?"

Lusam thought about which of his many questions he should ask her, but decided most of them boiled down to the same question.

"I was wondering why you haven't filled the *Heart of the City* with your own magic, or simply killed the Empire forces outside Lamuria?" Lusam asked sheepishly, hoping he didn't offend the Goddess. Aysha's smile faded, and was replaced by a look of sadness.

"I wish I could Lusam, but as I told you before, I am bound by an oath to my brother Driden, never to directly interfere with humankind's destiny again. Just as you are able to see the difference in colour between one of my children's auras, and one of the tainted souls from the Empire, so too is Driden able to detect the difference between my magic and yours. If I were to fill the *Heart of the City* with my own magic, either directly or through someone else, he would see it clearly, and the consequences for humankind would be equally catastrophic. More than that, I am unable to say.

"It is ... unfortunate, that the decision was taken to

place the *Heart of the City* in full view of the world. A decision made a long time ago, through arrogance and pride, at a time when Afaraon was powerful and feared no one. If it had been hidden within my walls, where only *I* can see, things would have been very different now. Something I very much regret not enforcing all those years ago, I can assure you."

"I don't understand, you gave me and Renn your blessing before," Lusam said slightly confused.

"When we first met in The Dark Forest, I was responding to the prayers of one of my paladins, something I am still entitled to do within the bounds of my oath. If my actions there had been witnessed by Driden, he would have assumed the same thing. Driden has been rather preoccupied lately with problems of his own, so it wasn't until you read the Guardian book in Coldmont, that he first became aware of you. Once any living creature reaches a certain level of power, the Gods start to take notice of them, especially if it is a human. It is a certainty that Driden's attention will be focused fully on Lamuria right now, so anything I do will be subject to his scrutiny, therefore we must tread very carefully, my child."

Lusam thought about Aysha's words, remembering her regret that the *Heart of the City* was not concealed within the walls of her High Temple, and he suddenly realised something.

"Would I be right in assuming that Coldmont also has a similar power source?" Lusam asked, also wanting to know about Helveel too, but unable to ask openly about it.

"You are correct, my child. Coldmont does indeed have a power source of the same type as Lamuria," Aysha replied.

"Then why doesn't the Empire simply take that one to open The Great Rift? They already know its location and it's completely unprotected," Lusam said.

"I'm sure The Thule Empire has already looked at that possibility, but Coldmont is in a very precarious state. Its power source is the only thing keeping the structure intact. If they were to try and remove it, the entire building would collapse, destroying everything, including the power source. But, enough questions for now my child, let us not waste time we do not have. You came to Lamuria with but a single question, yet curiously you have not asked it," Aysha said smiling divinely at Lusam. She turned to face her High Priest, and he visibly paled under her gaze.

"Your dedication and devotion to your post has pleased me Jasper. You have done well," Aysha said to him.

"I am humbled to hear you say such words my lady. I live only to serve you," the High Priest replied reverently, positivity beaming with pride.

"You will allow Lusam access to the Guardian book without further delay Jasper," Aysha said, making the High Priest squirm slightly.

"My lady, forgive me, but wouldn't he need weeks, if not months of preparation and meditation before he could possibly survive reading a Guardian book?" the High Priest asked averting his eyes from his God.

"If you're trying to suggest he might not survive reading a third Guardian book, I have to say that I share your concerns," Neala said, looking up at Aysha with tears in her eyes.

"Fear not my child, I will ensure Lusam survives reading the Guardian book, that much at least I can do within my own walls. It is for the rest of you that I fear. Even I cannot speed up the process of reading a Guardian book, and during that time Lamuria will be vulnerable. The responsibility of gaining Lusam enough time will fall to you ... all of you. I cannot promise you will all survive the battle to come, but if you fail, not only will Lamuria pay a heavy price, but the entire world.

"I have heard your voice calling to me on many occasions Neala, and I could clearly sense your faith in me, but you keep denying yourself that same faith when it matters most. Let go of your doubts Neala, and you could join Alexia as one of my paladins," Aysha said, waving a hand over Neala's knives. They began to glow an intense blue colour, before fading back to normal a moment later.

"Once, not so long ago in Prystone, you wielded my power Neala. I felt you call out to me, with faith as pure as can be. Open your heart to me again Neala, embrace your faith in me, and your new weapons will become one with me on the battlefield. Then together we will gain Lusam the time he needs to save us all."

Neala bowed her head, overwhelmed that Aysha would grant her such a gift. "Thank you," she whispered through her tears, hoping desperately that she could fulfil Aysha's request. Aysha gave Neala a knowing smile, then turned to face Alexia, who still had not lifted her head since Aysha had first appeared.

"Alexia my child, it gladdens my heart to welcome you as my first female paladin. Rarely do I sense such unerring faith in a person, as I do in you. I see you still have your blessed bow, but few arrows to use with it. I will ensure you find a plentiful supply in the armoury my child, but for now, let me bless your knives as I have Neala's," Aysha said smiling down on Alexia. She raised her hand, and a bright blue light washed over Alexia, making her weapons glow brightly for a brief period of time, before returning back to their normal appearance once more.

"Thank you my lady, I'm honoured that you think me worthy of such gifts and praise," Alexia replied in barely a whisper, her head still bowed.

"You are most welcome my child," Aysha replied turning finally to Hershel. "Hershel, my faithful paladin. Long have you served me, and served me well, but I fear I must ask even more of you now. As their leader, my paladins look to you for guidance on the battlefield. Many will not live to see this day through, but assure them, I *will* be there to greet them if they fall. The odds against you and your paladins will be overwhelming, but you *must* prevail, no matter what the cost. To do otherwise, would mean the destruction of your entire world. I will see to it that every weapon and shield in the armoury is blessed in preparation for the battle to come, but more than that, I can not do to assist you in this fight. It will be down to you … all of you …" Aysha said, fading away before their eyes.

Chapter Forty-Two

Nobody moved within the inner sanctum. The silence was almost palpable, as each person came to terms with what Aysha had just told them. Lusam was the first to stand, closely followed by Neala; the others however, remained knelt in prayer for several more minutes before moving.

Lusam had expected Hershel to look concerned at what Aysha had just told him, but instead he wore a broad smile on his face as he turned to speak with Alexia.

"Congratulations Alexia, and welcome to our order. It will be an honour to have you serve among us," Hershel said offering her his hand. "And also to you, Neala. I hope you take up Aysha's offer and join us too, after all this is over," he said offering her his hand as well.

"Thank you sir," Alexia replied nervously, hoping she had just used the correct form of address for what was now her commanding officer. Neala stayed silent and simply nodded, unsure whether she should commit herself to anything or not.

"Well Alexia, it seems like it's official now. Congratulations, and welcome aboard," Renn said grinning at her, whilst offering her his hand too. "You too, Neala. That was high praise indeed from Aysha, you should be proud of yourself."

"Thanks Renn, I appreciate it. I just hope I don't let anyone down," Alexia replied looking around the room.

"My thoughts exactly," Neala said very quietly to herself, but Hershel still heard what she said.

"If Aysha has faith in your abilities, then so should you.

I'm sure you will do just fine, both of you," Hershel said confidently, then he turned to speak with the High Priest, who had thus far remained silent since Aysha's departure.

"Your Grace, if there is nothing further I beg your leave to withdraw, as I will require time to prepare my paladins for the coming battle," he said respectfully bowing his head. The High Priest seemed to only half-hear his words, and it took a moment for him to respond to Hershel's request.

"Of course, you may attend to your duties Hershel. I will also attend to mine, and show Lusam to the Guardian book. May Aysha bless us all, and watch over you on the battlefield," he said, sounding almost like a different person after his encounter with Aysha. Hershel and Renn nodded their thanks to the High Priest and turned to leave the room, indicating that Alexia should also join them. A moment later only Lusam and Neala remained in the room with the High Priest.

"I'm afraid I can not allow you to accompany us to the Guardian book room Neala," the High Priest said, sounding a little unsure of himself.

"You have to let me go! I need to be with Lusam, to make sure he's alright," she protested, firmly taking hold of Lusam's hand.

"Neala my child, you heard Aysha say that she would take care of Lusam while he read the Guardian book. There is nothing you can do there, that Aysha can not. Aysha also gave you a wonderful gift, and asked that you use it to gain Lusam enough time to read the Guardian book. Surely you can see that Aysha wants you to help Lusam in a different way, other than sitting vigil by his side? Have faith my child, and all will be well."

Lusam hated to think of Neala being in danger while he was unconscious through reading the Guardian book, but he couldn't fault the logic of the High Priest's words. Neither could he deny what he had heard Aysha tell them all: either they won this battle, or the world and everything in it would perish.

"He's right Neala, you should go help the others while I

do this. If we fail, we lose everything. I've seen how well you fight Neala, and I know they could use your skill out there. Just promise me that you'll stay safe, and not take any unnecessary risks. If I lost you, I'm not sure I would care what happens to the world anymore," Lusam said quietly, trying hard to hold back his emotions at the thought of losing her. Neala threw her arms around his neck and pulled him into a tight embrace, tears flowing freely down her cheeks.

"I love you Lusam," she whispered in his ear.

"I love you too," he whispered back, hugging her tightly.

During that long embrace Neala made a promise to herself, that she would gain Lusam the time he needed, no matter what the cost. It was a promise she intended to keep.

***

Lusam felt terrible at having to send Neala away and putting her in harm's way, but he knew if they were to succeed, Hershel would need every fighter he could get on the battlefield. He wished he'd had the opportunity to speak with Renn or Hershel about keeping an eye on her, but he trusted they would do so anyway, knowing how much he cared for her. And if they couldn't for any reason, he was sure Alexia would. Even so, he found himself in silent prayer to Aysha, asking for her to watch over Neala while he was unable to.

The High Priest led him down a series of long corridors before they reached a large oak door. When he unlocked and opened the door, it revealed a wide stone staircase leading down into the darkness below. Lusam created a small light orb, startling the High Priest a little as he did so.

"Sorry," Lusam said smiling at him.

"It's perfectly alright my child. It's going to take me a while to get used to that I'm afraid," the High Priest replied pointing towards Lusam's light orb. Lusam nodded, and let the High Priest lead the way down the stone stairs. When they reached the bottom, Lusam brightened his light orb to reveal a room not dissimilar to the basement in Mr Daffer's book shop. If anything, this room was even larger than the one in Helveel, but it didn't have the numerous corridors leading away from it like that one did. Instead, it had only a single corridor at the far end of the room which disappeared into the darkness beyond.

As they walked through the large chamber Lusam couldn't help himself looking up at the ceiling high above them. It didn't surprise him at all to find another intricately painted image of a temple up there. He created a second light source up near the ceiling and increased its strength to reveal the incredible detail the artist, or artists had painstakingly crafted there. The image was of a large temple, seemingly carved out of the face of a mountainside. Only the front of the building was visible, the rest seemed to be part of the mountain itself. He recognised the image as probably being that of Irragin in Mount Nuxvar, the seat of power for Lord Zelroth and the Thule Empire. He remembered Renn's earlier description of it, but he couldn't help feeling disappointed that it wasn't a picture depicting another, more accessible location of a Guardian book instead.

His circle had come to an end with this image. Helveel had led to Coldmont, and Coldmont to Lamuria, but there was no way he could hope to discover what was painted on the ceiling of Irragin. He just hoped that Lord Zelroth had also failed to discover the whereabouts of that one. Lusam couldn't help smiling to himself, when he thought of how disappointed Lord Zelroth would be if he did indeed win this battle, only to find a picture of his own home painted on the ceiling there.

The High Priest cleared his throat, snapping Lusam's attention back to the present. For a moment he had forgotten the man was standing there as he inspected the great work of art high above him.

"Irragin in Mount Nuxvar," Lusam stated, looking up at the image.

"Yes, you are correct, it is Irragin, but how you would know that I have no idea," the High Priest replied looking at Lusam strangely. Lusam thought about revealing the importance of the image, and decided it couldn't harm if the High Priest knew the truth of what the images represented. After all, he was charged with the safe keeping of this particular Guardian book, and had done a good job of it by all accounts, as had his numerous predecessors.

"It is the location of another one of the Guardian books," Lusam said causing the High Priest to gasp out loud. "At the place where I first discovered a Guardian book there was an image of Coldmont painted on the ceiling. In Coldmont the image was of Lamuria, and here it is of Irragin."

The High Priest took only a moment to realise the implications of Lusam's words. "Then that would mean Lord Zelroth has read a Guardian book within Irragin," he said sounding slightly shocked at the prospect.

"Yes, and also the one in Coldmont I'm afraid," Lusam replied, still inspecting the image high above them. The High Priest muttered something under his breath, but Lusam couldn't tell what.

"If you are correct, then he must suspect that there is a Guardian book here in Lamuria."

"Yes, I believe that's why he has been so interested in Lamuria for as long as he has. I think stealing *The Heart of the City* is secondary to him wanting to read the Guardian book here, and also discover what you have painted on this ceiling. I think he would be very disappointed to discover it was a picture of his own temple," Lusam replied smiling at the High Priest.

"I agree child, but let us hope that we never have to find out. If you will follow me, I will show you to the book room," the High Priest said, gesturing for them to continue on their way. Lusam nodded and followed the High Priest towards the darkened corridor up ahead, extinguishing his light orb near the ceiling, and sending the other one further in front of them to illuminate the way. The corridor wasn't very long, and Lusam soon found himself standing outside a familiar stone door, with a five pointed star carved into it. He slipped into his mage-sight and could clearly see the five indentations on the walls, ceiling and floor that needed to be magically connected to each other to open the door.

"The incantation to open the door is quite complex. If you give me a few minutes to prepare I will open it for you," the High Priest said beginning his preparations. Lusam hoped it was not some kind of sacred rite to open the door. The last thing he wanted to do was offend the High Priest, but he needed to get inside as soon as possible. The more time they wasted, the higher their probability of failure.

"Allow me," Lusam said, instantly creating an unbroken line of power between the five indentations, even before the High Priest had the chance to reply. The door made a sudden grinding noise, and started its slow opening process. Lusam expected the High Priest to protest, or at least ask him how he had created the spell so fast, but he didn't, he simply watched Lusam, as Lusam watched the door slowly open.

Once the door had opened far enough to allow him access, Lusam approached it. He carefully stepped across the invisible boundary into the room, and just as it had done in Helveel and Coldmont, the interior of the room burst into light, revealing an identical circular room. In the centre stood a familiar looking pedestal, and on that pedestal a Guardian book.

The first thing Lusam noticed about the Guardian book was the word *Transcendence* written on the front of it in large golden letters. He remembered the one in Helveel had the word *Freedom* written on it, and the one in Coldmont had *Absolution* on its cover. None of the words meant anything of significance to him, either alone or combined. He decided he would ponder over their meaning at a later date, when he had more time to do so.

One other curious thing he noticed, was the fact that the green lines-of-power he had seen in Coldmont, and later in Helveel were absent from the pedestal in this room. So too were the words associated with their relevant destinations. He then remembered that both the green lines-of-power, and the words on the pedestal had only become visible to him *after* he had read the Guardian book in Coldmont. Once he had thought about it for a moment, he realised that any mage who wished to use the pedestals to teleport from location to location, must need to have already read the Guardian books at each of those locations for it to work. If he was right, both the names and the green lines-of-power would become visible to him after he had read this Guardian book.

Lusam stepped up to the pedestal ready to open the Guardian book, but paused before he touched it. He had an idea which may, or may not prove to be of importance, but he decided to take a gamble anyway.

"Your Grace, I need to ask you to do something for me, but please, don't ask me why, as I'm unable to answer that question," Lusam said cryptically.

"What would you ask of me child?" the High Priest said.

"I would like you to bring me one of the Power orbs and leave it inside this room, for when I regain consciousness," Lusam replied. The High Priest agreed to his request, assuring him it would be there waiting for him when he regained consciousness. He thanked the High Priest, turned back to the Guardian book, and opened its cover. He was instantly enveloped by a blindingly bright light that burst forth from inside the book, freezing him in time before it. The High Priest watched him for a few more minutes, then turned to leave the room. If he had stayed a few moments longer, he would have witnessed the pulses of Aysha's light washing over Lusam, as she watched over him.

Chapter Forty-Three

Hershel had all of his men fully assembled for battle by the time Neala caught up with him in the barracks. She guessed the men must have already been on high alert given the current situation outside, but it was still an impressive sight to see so many paladins all in one place ready for battle. Alexia entered the room a moment later carrying what looked like several bundles of arrows.

"I thought you were staying with Lusam?" Alexia said, unwrapping the bundles of arrows on the floor.

"Yeah me too, but I figured I couldn't let you have all the fun without me," she replied, grinning at her old friend. "Besides, Aysha gave me these blessed knives, so I guess she wants me to help you fight."

"*Fun*, probably isn't the word I'd use to describe what's out there," Alexia replied in a serious voice.

"Oh, come on, you're not scared of a few thousand undead are you?" Neala said with a nervous laugh.

"The undead ... no. It's the thousands of Empire magi that are making me slightly nervous," Alexia replied, grinning up at her friend. She noticed Neala seemed unusually anxious about the coming battle, but didn't know exactly why. She had fought alongside Neala many times in the past, and never had she seen her so unsure of herself. Alexia knew very well how good she was with a blade. No one that Alexia had ever seen her fight, had even come close to beating her in the past. So why she would suddenly be afraid of fighting the undead outside Lamuria was confusing to her. Then she suddenly realised the problem. It wasn't her faith in her own ability to fight that she was questioning, it was her faith in Aysha: if she failed to wield her new blessed weapons, she would be defenceless on the battlefield. She simply couldn't allow her best friend to enter battle with doubts like that, or she would never survive out there.

Alexia stood up and took hold of both of Neala's hands. She looked her straight in the eyes, and said, "Neala, listen to me. I can see you're having doubts about whether or not you'll be able to use those blessed weapons that Aysha gave you. You just need to put your faith in her, and she will *not* let you down out there, I promise you. Open your heart to her fully, and let her in Neala. Think about it, she would never have given you those blessed knives, if she didn't *know* you were capable of using them them Neala."

Neala smiled and nodded at her words of encouragement, but Alexia could tell she hadn't managed to erase all her doubts, and knew that could be very dangerous for her out there. A few moments later Alexia noticed Hershel heading back towards the armoury, and hurried to catch him up. Her excuse to Neala was that she was needed there to help with the equipment distribution, but really she wanted a quiet word with Hershel about Neala's frame of mind.

"Sir, may I have a quiet word," Alexia called after him. He stopped in his tracks and waited for her to catch up to him.

"Is there a problem Alexia? If any of the men are giving you a hard time just let me know their names, and I'll sort them out. I'm sorry they aren't used to having female company in the barracks—" Hershel said, but was cut short by Alexia.

"No Sir, the men have been no trouble, but thank you. I needed to speak with you about Neala. She's having doubts about the upcoming battle. I tried to talk to her about it, but I'm not sure I made any difference."

"Everyone has their doubts before going into battle Alexia, it's perfectly natural," Hershel replied.

"No sir, you don't understand. She doesn't doubt her ability to fight, she is doubting her ability to use the blessed weapons Aysha gave her. She is doubting whether or not she will have the faith to use them in battle."

"Oh, I see. That could be a big problem for her out there with all those undead walking around. I don't suppose we could convince her to stay inside the city could we?" he asked hopefully.

"I doubt it, she believes Aysha gave her the knives so she could help Lusam, and she's probably right. I was wondering if there was any way we could keep an eye on her out there, so she doesn't go and get herself killed?"

"Leave it with me, I'll think of something," Hershel said, "and by the way, you don't have to call me sir when we're out of earshot of the men. After all, once this is all over, you will most likely be in command of the new female branch of Aysha's paladins."

"Me? ... But I don't know anything about being a paladin myself yet, how can I possibly lead others?" Alexia asked, shocked by what Hershel had just said.

"Well, you're the most senior female paladin we currently have, and you were ordained by Aysha herself. I'd also bet a month's wage, that by the end of today you'll know plenty about being a paladin," Hershel replied grinning at her, but also noticing how apprehensive she'd just become. "Don't worry too much Alexia, I'm sure it won't happen overnight. We still need to find more women willing to join up first, so you should have plenty of time to learn how we operate before then. Besides, most of a paladin's training revolves around cultivating their faith in Aysha—so they are able to use their blessed weapon—and I would say you've already scored top marks in that regard. Then there's weapon's mastery, which by all accounts, it seems you score pretty highly there too, according to Renn. Which only leaves you with the history of our order and that of the High Temple's to learn, and I'm sure I can help you with that."

Alexia was about to respond, when they were interrupted by one of Hershel's men bursting into the room.

"Sir, there's movement on the southern edge of the valley. It looks like they are preparing to attack the city," the paladin said. Hershel swore under his breath, he had been hoping for more time, but knew it had finally run out.

"Thank you Captain Garett, I'll be right there," Hershel replied dismissing the man. He waited until Captain Garret was out of earshot before turning back to Alexia.

"I don't suppose you know how long it will take Lusam to read that Guardian book do you?" he asked hopefully.

"No idea, sorry. I'm not sure anyone does to be honest. All I know is that he was unconscious for about two hours when he read the one in Coldmont. Which apparently, was more than double the amount of time it took him to recover from the first book he read, according to Neala," Alexia replied, knowing it wasn't much help.

"I see," Hershel replied, lost deep in thought. "We better hope and pray that he wakes up much sooner than four of five hours, or it won't just be female paladins we'll be short of."

Over two hundred paladins stood in formation waiting patiently for Hershel to address them. The atmosphere was one of quiet resignation and reflection. Each man knew the insurmountable odds they faced once outside the gates of Lamuria. Their concern was not for the massive numbers of undead, but for the thousands of Empire magi massed at the southern end of the valley. The undead were easily dispatched by the paladin's blessed weapons, but the magi, that was a different matter entirely. The Empire magi had the advantage of the high ground, and also the vast range from which they could attack. The paladins would only be effective at close quarters against them, and that would be impossible when they were massed along the cliff-tops as they were. The paladins knew that if they tried to circumnavigate the cliff-tops and attack the magi directly, it would take them far too long to reach their position. The magi would see them coming with plenty of time to react, and the general consensus was, that the Empire would launch everything they had at the city before the paladins arrived. If that happened, the shield would fail quickly, and the undead would be free to wreak havoc within the city, killing everyone inside.

The men knew how precarious the city's magical defences were, and knew their mission was ultimately a hopeless one. They believed they were simply buying Lamuria's citizens extra time with their lives, and all were prepared to do so without question or regret. If they could clear enough of the undead, it might enable many of the citizens of Lamuria to escape with their lives before the city was completely destroyed. They knew nothing of Lusam, or the Guardian book in the High Temple.

Rumours had circulated throughout the barracks of a powerful young mage who had recently arrived in the city. One who had saved a group of paladins and healed their injured comrades. There was even speculation it was the same mage responsible for healing two men at The Sanctum of Light in Lamuria several months earlier. All of the rumours however, were tainted by the unbelievable tale of the same mage being able perform magic without having to speak any incantations—something no sane man could possibly believe.

Hershel silently paced back and forth in front of his men. Men he had known in some cases for many years, and shed blood with on numerous occasions. Others, he had only recently being in charge of training a few short weeks earlier in Stelgad. He knew, as well as they did, that many of them would die on the battlefield before the day was through. He could see the acceptance of it in all their faces, as he met each man's eyes in the formation before him. They had lost all hope, and now clung only to their faith in Aysha, that she would deliver them from this life as swiftly and painlessly as possible when their time came.

Hershel knew from experience that when a man had lost all hope even before stepping foot on the battlefield, they would often quickly fall. He needed to somehow give them their hope back, or this battle would be over before it had even begun. They needed something to believe in. Something that would sustain them possibly for hours on the battlefield when all else looked lost, and that something *had* to be Lusam. He knew every man before him knew the story of the Guardians and their books, and if anything could bring them hope, it was that. He stopped pacing, and turned to face his men.

"Gentlemen, I will not lie to you, the odds are overwhelming against us, and many of us will not live through this day. But for those of you who do fall upon the battlefield, know this ... Aysha *will* be there to greet you. I *know* this to be true, because she told me herself this very day, of that I swear to you in her name. When I look at your faces, I see all hope has fled from your eyes. I see only resignation, that death will soon claim you, and that our sacred High Temple will soon fall into the hands of the Empire. Well, I'm here to tell you, that is *not* true. We do have hope. In fact, we have more than hope, we have a *real* chance of winning this battle." Hershel paused for a moment, letting his men digest what he had just told them, then he continued.

"How? I hear you ask. Well, let me tell you. I'm certain by now that most of you have heard the rumours of a powerful young mage arriving in Lamuria. Well I can confirm those rumours are true—"

"Sorry sir, but what use is one mage going to be against that army of Empire magi?" one of the men said, cutting Hershel off mid-sentence. Hershel nodded his head at the man, then continued.

"You're right, of course son. One mage against that army would be no use at all, but he is not *just* a mage. Before arriving in Lamuria with Renn and his friends, Alexia and Neala here," Hershel said gesturing towards each in turn, "they did something that no one has been able to achieve in over two thousand years. They discovered the location of the fabled temple of the Guardians ... Coldmont."

Everyone looked towards Renn for confirmation of Hershel's words, unable to comprehend what he had just told them all, and what the implications were for the battle to come. Hershel continued over the top of the men's murmurings.

"Gentlemen, that is only part of the incredible news I must share with you. Whilst they were there, they discovered one of the lost Guardian books, and what's more, the young mage read it," Hershel said, as the crowd of men erupted in excited chatter. He held up his hand to quieten the men, and a moment later they fell silent once more.

"What's even more incredible, is the fact that the Guardian book they discovered in Coldmont, was not the first Guardian book he had read, but the second."

The men seemed to forget where they were as they excitedly discussed the news between themselves, and Hershel allowed them the freedom to do so. He was already aware that the Empire knew the location of Coldmont, and the existence of the Guardian book there, so there seemed no harm in revealing the information to his men. The same applied to the High Temple, and its Guardian book. He knew full well that if he failed to rally his men enough before they entered battle, Lusam would never have enough time to complete his task, and as a result the city would fall, as would the entire world. He needed to give his men something solid to hold onto during the coming hours of battle. Something that would sustain them through the hardships of what they were about to face.

Hershel was fully aware that Lusam had been unable to give any assurances as to whether or not he could defeat the Empire forces, even after he had read the Guardian book. But he knew he couldn't tell his men that. He had never lied to his men before, and regretted having to do so now, but if he didn't give them something to fight for, everything would be lost. He said a silent prayer to Aysha, asking her to forgive him for his lie, then took a deep breath. He held up his hand, and waited until his men settled down again, then he addressed his men once more.

"As you would imagine, after reading two Guardian books our young mage is already extremely powerful, but unfortunately, he's *not* powerful enough to defeat that army of Empire magi out there ... yet," Hershel said pointing towards the southern cliffs, then he paused again, letting his men absorb what he had just said.

"The more astute amongst you will notice that I said

the word `yet`, and I meant it, wholeheartedly. For not only did our young mage discover the location of Coldmont, and the two Guardian books, he also discovered the whereabouts of a third Guardian book. That third Guardian book, Gentlemen, is right here in Lamuria, and he is reading it right now as I speak. Our mission, is to gain him the time he needs to complete his reading of it. If we succeed, he will emerge powerful enough to crush the Empire forces outside Lamuria. His name … is Lusam."

The men's cheers were so loud Hershel felt sure the Empire magi would have heard them on top of their cliff, at the far end of the valley. He saw the fresh new hope in each of his men's eyes, and knew he had achieved what he needed to do. Now, it would be up to them.

"That was a bold move, old friend," Renn said quietly by Hershel's ear. Hershel simply nodded, knowing exactly what he was referring to. Then he remembered what Alexia had asked of him a few minutes earlier.

"Renn, I'm going to assign you a special task. I need you to keep the gate area clear of undead. We're bound to have a high number of casualties, and the easier it is to get back inside Lamuria, the better their chances of survival will be. I want you to take Neala and another man with you, but keep an eye on her, apparently she's having some faith issues at the moment," Hershel said quietly.

"I take it she wants to go out there then?" Renn asked quietly.

"So it would seem. She believes Aysha gave her the blessed knives so she could help Lusam, and she's determined to do just that by the looks of it, old boy," Hershel replied.

"Well, far be it from me to try and change a woman's mind," Renn said chuckling. "Don't worry, I'll keep an eye on her out there."

"Thanks, I'd hate to have to be the one to tell Lusam that she was killed trying to help him," Hershel said quietly. Renn nodded, imagining the conversation and grimacing at the thought of it.

"Good luck out there, old friend," Renn said, clasping

arms with his old mentor.

"You too, old boy. May Aysha bless and watch over us all," Hershel replied, turning back to his men. He nodded his head to Captain Garret, and he in turn bellowed an order for the men to fall in. A moment later every man was standing to attention, and silence filled the air once more.

"Okay men, listen up. I want every man with a shield standing to the left, and every man without standing to right. Now!" Hershel commanded. The men quickly separated into two groups of about equal numbers, half with shields, and half without. Hershel gave a quick prayer of thanks to Aysha for blessing their armoury earlier that day, knowing that the new shields could make a huge difference to the outcome of the fight.

"We will form up in groups of ten men. Five with shields, and five without. The five men with shields will remain at the front of each group. You will be responsible for intercepting any magical-missiles coming from the Empire magi. The five men without shields will be responsible for protecting the shield bearers. Keep your formations tight out there gentlemen, don't give them a target any bigger than it needs to be. Our primary mission is to become the Empire's main focus of attack, so the city's shield survives. If we lose the shield, we lose the battle. Kill enough of those undead, and they *will* take notice of you. Remember, we are playing for time out there, so stay alive. Good luck gentlemen, and may Aysha watch over you," Hershel said, removing his glowing sword and dropping to one knee in prayer. Each and every paladin followed his example, including Alexia and Neala.

A few moments later, the first magical-missile struck the city's shield.

Chapter Forty-Four

"Morgan, you're with me," Renn said as he passed by one of the paladins.

"Yes, sir," Morgan replied, looking genuinely pleased that he'd been chosen.

"You too, Neala."

"What's going on?" Neala asked, as she watched all the others begin to file out of the gate.

"We have different orders from the others. We're to keep the gate area clear of undead, so the injured men can be brought back for treatment easier," Renn replied.

"Oh, I see, and who's idea was that, I wonder?" Neala said sarcastically, as she watched Alexia vanish through the gate with the others. Renn chuckled to himself when he saw the acid look she gave Alexia, and didn't envy her one bit the next time they met up. He knew Alexia's intentions were good, and decided to try and cover for her a little.

"Actually, it was my idea," Renn said, trying to keep a straight face.

"Yeah, sure it was," Neala said, obviously not believing a word of it.

Renn ignored the comment and introduced her to Morgan instead. Morgan was an affable man in his early thirties, with dark hair and a pale complexion. Most of the men affectionately referred to him as `Beany`, due to him being so tall and thin like one of the locally grown bean plants. Renn had first met him more than ten years earlier, during his training at The Sanctum of Light. Morgan had arrived there as a fresh recruit only one year before Renn had completed his own training there, and Renn had been assigned as his group commander for that first year. He had proven to be a very capable soldier, apart for the numerous times he had ended up in front of a commanding officer for his various pranks: everything from placing foul smelling crystals inside the officers candles, to coating the outhouse seat with tree resin. The latter, Hershel was still making him pay for to that day, having left almost every hair he had stuck to the outhouse seat when he peeled himself free of it. Renn swore he could still hear Hershel's screams of pain when he closed his eyes and thought about it sometimes.

"So, shall we go?" Neala asked impatiently, as the last of the paladins left the small stone courtyard.

"Actually, I think we should wait here for a while, lass. It will take time for each group to fight their way further into the valley. They'll need to be well spread out from each other, so the Empire can't target any one large group of fighters. If we give them a few more minutes before we leave, the gate area should be pretty clear for us. It should be a lot easier keeping it clear, if we don't have to fight with our backs against the wall," Renn replied, as he watched the city's shield take another hammering from all the magical-missiles.

"How long do you think the city's shield will last?" Neala asked, noticing the worried look on Renn's face.

"Not long, I would imagine. Especially if they keep hitting it with that intensity. I suppose it all depends on how much power Lusam was able to put into it earlier, but I doubt even that will keep it up for too much longer. We better just hope the others manage to draw the Empire's fire-power away from it, or it will never last until Lusam has finished reading that book," Renn replied.

***

Alexia had requested to join Hershel's group of men before leaving the small stone courtyard, and was now helping defend the shield bearers alongside the other paladins. She had soon found that her bow was of little use against the undead at such close quarters, so she had switched to using her blessed daggers instead. They had slowly fought their way to the centre of the valley over the first few hours, leaving a wide trail of destroyed undead in their wake, but Alexia was now beginning to wonder if she had made a mistake bringing all the blessed arrows with her, as all they were doing was weighing her down.

They were still within sight of several other groups of paladins, each group laying waste to large numbers of undead as they spread out across the valley floor. So far they had not succeeded in drawing much fire—if any—away from the city's shield, and Hershel was beginning to wonder if his plan would work at all. The Empire magi obviously didn't consider the paladins a threat down in the valley bottom, and continued their assault on the city's shield unabated.

Fortunately, not all the Empire magi were attacking the city's shield. For some reason, most of the Empire magi were content to simply watch and wait, as if expecting some kind of large scale retaliation from Lamuria. Hershel knew that their tactics only made sense if they believed that Lamuria still had a hidden magi attack force of its own, which of course, it didn't. He also knew that once they realised that, they would immediately order a full scale attack on the city, which would collapse the shield in a matter of minutes.

Far too many of the paladins on the battlefield had not yet completed their full training for Hershel's liking, and it was now starting to show in the number who were beginning to lose their lives. It wasn't through their lack of fighting ability, as the paladin's of Aysha only ever accepted the very best men from the regular King's guard. It was through their lack of spiritual training, which often took years before they were able to successfully wield a blessed weapon in the heat of combat. He had protested loudly when the High Temple had ordered him to send every available man to help defend Lamuria, but his objections had gone mostly unheeded.

The power of a blessed weapon had to be channelled from Aysha herself, which required the paladin to open themselves up to her fully, both in body and mind, and at all times. Most recruits expected this to be easy, especially the ones who came from a religious background, but Hershel knew better. Of course, it was easy enough to hold one's faith whilst things were going well, but the moment it looked like you might be losing a fight, that was when your faith was tested most. It was one of the hardest things to do: to keep your faith when you think your next breath might be your last. The thing was, if you didn't, and your weapon failed to channel Aysha's power, it probably *would* be your last breath —especially against the undead or a Netherworld creature.

Shortly after leaving the city gate, Hershel had watched helplessly as one of his own group had been torn apart by the undead. A momentary lapse in his faith had transformed his blessed weapon back into a regular sword, making it useless against the attacking undead. That one moment of doubt had cost him his life, as an undead creature pulled him out of Hershel's tight group and into the waiting mass of undead. There had been nothing Hershel could do about it, as it was all over far too quickly for the poor man. Fortunately, Hershel had noticed another of his men's momentary lapse in faith, just in time to save him from a similar fate. He couldn't blame him for it, as Hershel knew he had been friends with the dead man, and witnessing something like that happen would shake the faith of most men, no matter how religious they were. But *that* was the difference between a man, and a true paladin of Aysha.

The ground vibrated underfoot with every impact on the city's shield. The Empire magi had gradually ramped up their attack over the last half hour, and were now also attacking the paladins closest to them. Hershel's plan of five shield bearers in each group of ten paladins seemed to be working well for the time being. As the magical-missiles rained down on the forward groups of paladins, they simply raised their shield to intercept them, whilst continuing to attack the undead in front with their blessed swords, and the others defended their flanks. It was slow going, and Hershel guessed that at least four hours had passed since the battle had begun. He had no way of knowing the exact number of casualties his men had suffered, but he could estimate that they had dispatched around a quarter of the undead already —something the Empire magi had also noticed, judging by the ever increasing amount of magical-missiles heading their way.

Hershel's group of paladins were one of the most forward groups on the battlefield, and they were now close enough for the Empire magi to start hitting them with far more accuracy. It didn't take the Empire magi much time to realise the same thing, and soon the number of magical-missiles increased again. Hershel watched as dozens of magical-missiles headed towards them and the other groups of paladins on the front lines, more than half now finding their targets. One of the missiles however, landed just in front of the group of paladins closest to their left, hitting a large group of undead instead. The undead were blown apart by the impact, sending them flying through the air in all directions. One of the undead was propelled through the air, landing directly in the midst of the paladins. Hershel watched helplessly as the undead creature grabbed two of the men's ankles and shattered them with its immense strength. The forward facing shield bearers seemed unaware of what was unfolding directly behind them, as they continued to stab past their shields at the advancing undead. One of the men tried to come to the aid of his fellow paladins, stabbing the undead creature with his glowing sword, but a heartbeat later, he was dragged screaming from the group by several undead who had managed to slip past their weakened defences. Hershel watched in dismay as two of the remaining paladin's blessed weapons winked out, as their faith momentarily faltered. It was more than enough time for the undead to end their lives, along with one of the injured men on the floor.

Hershel had decided to distribute the blessed shields to the more seasoned men, and men he believed would more likely hold their nerve during the battle—a decision he was thankful for, as he watched the five shield bearers reform into a tight protective circle around the injured man on the floor. Shields held high to protect against the incoming magical-missiles, they stabbed furiously at the advancing undead, but were unable to assist their fallen comrade without exposing themselves to the undead.

"Hershel—" Alexia began to say, whilst taking down another two undead.

"Yes, I see them," Hershel replied, trying to keep an eye on them and maintain his defensive position at the same time.

"We have to go help them, they can't move with that injured man on the floor like that. If those Empire magi notice them, they'll become sitting targets," Alexia said.

"I agree, so we better start making our way over there, before those Empire magi *do* notice them," Hershel said loud enough for everyone to hear. They all changed direction, and began to fight their way towards the stranded paladins. The two groups had almost merged, when it finally happened: the city's shield failed.

"Oh, Gods no!" Alexia swore, as the first explosion erupted from within Lamuria. The cheer from the cliff-tops was audible from where they were, as thousands of Empire magi roared at their success. The Empire magi immediately ceased their attacks on the paladins, and concentrated all their fire on Lamuria. Alexia watched stunned as thousands of missiles arced through the air on their way to devastate Lamuria. Several hundred hit the High Temple itself, winking out of existence as soon as they touched its blessed walls.

"May Aysha have mercy on their souls," Hershel whispered, as dozens of buildings exploded within the walls of Lamuria, sending debris high into the air. Plumes of thick black smoke rose from within the city's walls, darkening the afternoon sky above them. Huge chunks of masonry rained down within the city, blasted away from every building within range of the Empire magi. Thousands upon thousands of missiles fell on the unprotected city, turning it into a giant inferno.

The undead now all but ignored the paladins, and as one, headed towards the city gates. Alexia watched as every group of paladins tried to retreat and defend the gates from the undead. If they broke through the gates, the entire city would be lost and everyone in it. She knew it was the paladins standing orders, if the city's shield failed, regroup and defend the gates at all costs.

It took the Empire magi only a matter of minutes to completely destroy the parts of Lamuria within their range. Then they did something no one expected. They attacked the outer wall of the city.

"Seven Gods!" Hershel swore, watching as huge chunks of stone were blown away from the city's wall. The wall was huge by any comparisons, standing as high as thirty men, and fifty paces wide at its base, but it wouldn't survive long against the onslaught now being rained down upon it. Alexia knew it was too soon for Lusam to have finished reading the Guardian book yet.

He needed more time.

They needed to somehow regain the attention of the Empire magi, but now that the city's shield was down, she knew that no matter how many undead they killed, they still wouldn't divert their attention away from the city wall. Then she had an idea.

"Hershel, get me closer to those Empire magi, then maybe I can gain their attention for a while," Alexia said, removing her bow. Hershel knew she intended to to try and shoot them with her bow, but the cliff was far too high for them to be in range of her bow shot.

"They will be well outside your range Alexia," Hershel replied, looking up at the cliff-tops high above.

"No ... they won't, trust me. Lusam has enchanted my bow so it shoots much further than a regular bow. If you can get me a little closer, I can hit them," Alexia said confidently. She knew she only had three of the enchanted arrows left, and wished she had thought about asking Lusam to enchant the rest of the newly blessed arrows before he had left to read the Guardian book. She knew those three arrows would find their targets for sure, but given the concentrated number of Empire magi on the cliff-tops, she doubted many of the blessed arrows would miss anyway, so she decided to keep the enchanted arrows in reserve. She was also painfully aware that as soon as the first group of magi were killed, her party would immediately become their main target. There was no way they could survive such an assault, and everyone knew it, even if they didn't say so.

As they moved closer to the cliff face, Alexia found herself thinking about the time when they were running through the large gorge, just before they entered the mist covered valley in The Elveen Mountains. Lusam had been under intense fire from the pursuing Empire magi, and was struggling to maintain his magical shield. His solution had been to bring down a large part of the rock face to block their pursuers line of sight, so they couldn't fire directly at them, and it had worked perfectly. She knew, of course, that any large boulders on the valley floor would be of little use to them when the Empire magi were firing on them from directly above. The fact that the Empire magi had taken the high ground, had been causing them difficulties ever since the battle begun, but now, Alexia had a plan to turn their advantage against them.

"Is this close enough?" Hershel asked, knowing that any closer and Alexia wouldn't be able to see her targets on the cliff-tops.

"No, I want to be almost at the cliff face. If they can't see us, they can't attack us ... well, not with any accuracy anyway," Alexia replied. Hershel grinned at her, knowing their chances of surviving had just increased dramatically. All the undead were now moving towards the gates of Lamuria, leaving Hershel's group free to position themselves at the base of the cliff face.

"Good luck," Hershel said, as Alexia drew back her bow. She nodded and released the first arrow into the sky above, quickly followed by several more. The death pulses came almost immediately, as one after another of the blessed arrows rained down on the magi above. Dozens of the undead fell to the ground throughout the valley as their masters died and their tenuous links were severed. The assault on the city's wall quickly faltered, as confusion began to mount as to where the attacks were coming from. Alexia varied the angles of her shots, making sure to cover as wide an area as possible on the cliff-tops. The Empire magi dropped fireballs blindly over the cliff edge, hoping to hit someone below, but only twice did the shield bearers have to intercept any.

After a few minutes the firing ceased, as did the death pulses from Alexia's arrows. Everyone held their breath, wondering what their next move would be.

"What do you think they're up to?" Alexia asked quietly.

"I'm not sure, but as long as they aren't attacking the wall it doesn't really matter I guess," Hershel whispered back. After another couple of minutes, he seemed to have a change of heart.

"Give me your shield, I'll go check what they are doing," Hershel said to one of the paladins.

"Be careful out there, if they see you, they'll all fire on you," Alexia said, as if he didn't already know. He took the shield and ran off along the base of the cliff several hundred paces, before moving slowly out into the open. He walked slowly backwards with his shield at the ready, scanning the cliff-tops for any signs of the Empire magi. They saw each other almost simultaneously, several hundred magical-missiles were launched towards him. He didn't even consider trying to block any of them, instead he ran as fast as he could back towards the cliff face, cutting off their line of sight as fast as possible. As soon as he was within hailing distance he shouted to Alexia.

"They've moved back a couple of hundred paces," he said, gesticulating towards the cliff-tops above. Alexia nodded, moved away from the base of the cliff, and sent ten arrows towards the location Hershel had just described. Six found their targets, with six powerful death pulses confirming the fact.

Alexia removed one of her three enchanted arrows and nocked it ready to fire. If she was right, the Empire would send a scout to pinpoint their location before making their next move. Putting herself in their position, she would do the same, then once their location had been determined, either collapse the cliff on top of them, or concentrate their fire on that position. Neither of which appealed to her much.

"Be ready to move," she said, not elaborating any further. Each man nodded, but she was too busy scanning the cliff-tops to notice, then she saw him. A single Empire mage stuck his head out over the cliff edge to spot them below. She loosed her arrow as he scuttled back out of sight, but it was already too late for him. The arrow homed in on its target, killing him almost instantly.

"Oh! Nice shot," Hershel said genuinely impressed.

"As much as I'd like to take credit for it, I can't. That was one of Lusam's special enchanted arrows. As long as I get them anywhere near, they will find their own target. It's just a shame I only have two of them left now," she said, nocking another enchanted arrow.

"Fortunately, *they* don't know that," Hershel replied grinning at her. Alexia didn't have chance to reply before she loosed her second enchanted arrow. This time the Empire mage had remained on his feet, and at the first sight of her, turn and run a zigzag course away from the cliff edge. It didn't help him. Another large death pulse rippled through the valley.

Alexia didn't think they would send another scout after seeing the enchanted arrow zigzag after the last one, but just in case she nocked her final enchanted arrow.

Another twenty minutes passed before they discovered the Empire's next move.

"Aysha have mercy on us," Hershel whispered to himself, as he noticed every remaining undead in the valley heading their way.

Chapter Forty-Five

Renn had waited another ten minutes before leading them out through the gate. The corpses of the undead littered the ground outside, but as Renn had predicted, the immediate area around the gate had been mostly clear of any potential danger. After despatching the dozen or so undead still lurking nearby, Renn and Morgan had begun moving the corpses. Renn had put Neala on look-out duty, while they stacked the corpses into a makeshift barricade. The idea was to leave a single entry point to funnel any returning undead through, making it easier to despatch them. Even if they chose to climb over the barricade, they should be slowed down enough to be dealt with more easily, or at least that was the hope.

Most of the fighting was obscured to them now by the city walls, but from what little Neala could see, the paladins were making decent enough headway against the large number of undead. It soon became apparent however, that the few paladins she could see, didn't seem to be attracting the attention of the Empire magi as they had hoped. The relentless bombardment of the city's shield continued without pause, making Neala wonder just how much longer it could possibly survive. Thankfully it didn't appear that all of the Empire magi were attacking the city's shield. She suspected that maybe the paladins closer to the front line— where she couldn't see— were being more effective at drawing their fire away from the shield, after all.

After three hours Neala had still to make her first kill. Every undead that came close enough was quickly despatched by Renn or Morgan, and added to their ever growing barricade. Renn and Morgan had even resorted to whistling loudly to try and attract more undead their way. On four occasions during that time injured men had been brought back to the gate, and each time a handful of undead had followed them, providing yet more building materials for Renn and Morgan.

Neala was beginning to become more than a little restless. She had been given a set of blessed knives, and therefore a job to do by Aysha herself, but here she was, doing nothing more than reporting the movements of the undead to two men who could spot them perfectly well themselves. Part of her yearned to be out there, doing her part against the enemy forces, but another part of her secretly feared what would happen if she tried. She had never been a particularly religious person, and even though she had now come face to face with Aysha, she still found it difficult to resolve her own issues regarding her faith. She knew that most people went through their entire lives without ever seeing or hearing from Aysha, yet they were still able to hold firm to their faith somehow, something Neala envied greatly about them.

Neala removed two of her knives from her belt and inspected them. Neither of them glowed like Renn's or Morgan's sword. She tried to reassure herself that it was because she was slightly further away from the undead than they were, but deep down she knew that wasn't really the case. She offered a prayer to Aysha, asking for her help in using the blessed weapons, but it changed nothing; the knives still remained the same. She replaced the knives in her belt, and tried to convince herself that she *would* have enough faith to use them, if she really needed to.

Over the next hour, the bombardment of the city's shield increased steadily. Fewer and fewer of the undead had come within range of them, and only one other injured man had been carried to the safety of the city gates. Neala hoped that was because of fewer injuries, rather than higher fatalities on the battlefield. They could no longer see any signs of either the paladins, or undead on the battlefield.

Everything that was unfolding now, was taking place further south along the valley floor, where they could no longer see due to the city's wall.

Neala was about to ask if she could go see what was happening on the battlefield, when it finally happened: the city's shield collapsed.

Neala ducked her head involuntarily as an enormous explosion came from within the city walls. A massive plume of fire and smoke, almost as tall as the High Temple, mushroomed into the sky above the city. For a moment after the initial explosion all seemed still, and she swore she could hear the cheers of the Empire magi coming from the far end of the valley.

Then all seven-hells seemed to break loose.

Thousands upon thousands of missiles arced through the sky towards Lamuria. She thought she heard Renn say something to himself, but she was far too stunned at the sight to ask him what he'd said. Dozens of buildings exploded within the city, sending debris and flames high into the sky. She watched helplessly as hundreds of magical-missiles headed straight for the walls of the High Temple. She expected the High Temple to be utterly devastated, but amazingly the magical-missiles simply winked out of existence as they made contact with its walls. It was then she remembered what had happened in Stelgad at The Sanctum of Light, when Lusam had rescued her and Alexia from the Hawks` guild, and they had been chased by the Empire agents there. Hershel had explained to them that the walls were blessed by Aysha, and therefore impervious to magic. She thanked Aysha in a silent prayer for the blessed walls protecting Lusam, and asked once more for help in using her blessed weapons, so she too could help protect him.

Everything within range of the Empire magi was completely destroyed within a few short minutes, only the High Temple remained untouched. Thick black smoke filled the sky above the city, and the acrid smell of burning hung thick in the air. Shortly afterwards the bombardment of the city ceased abruptly, and was replaced by what appeared to be a more focused attack on southern side of the city a few moments later. Neala watched as Renn scrambled up his makeshift barricade to get a better vantage point.

"Oh Gods! They're trying to break through the south wall," Renn said, watching helplessly as huge chunks of the city's wall were blown away by the Empire magi. He knew if they managed to breach the wall, the city would fall within a matter of minutes. Renn's orders were to protect the city gates, but it seemed pointless doing that when the enemy seemed intent on entering the city elsewhere. He knew if they were to gain Lusam the time he needed to finish reading the Guardian book, they must stop the undead from entering the city. Renn felt sure the Empire magi would have already moved their undead army away from the city wall before attacking it. If they hadn't, they would be destroying their own army as well as the wall.

Although Renn couldn't see what was happening on the battlefield, it made tactical sense to him that the paladins would now be regrouping by the wall, to try and stop the undead from entering the city—at any cost. Both he and Morgan had blessed shields and could be of use there, but Neala on the other hand would stand little chance against the Empire magi attacks.

"Neala, we have to go and help protect the south wall. I know you're not going to like it, but I can't take you with us. It will be safer if you stay inside the city, and—" Renn said, but was cut off by Neala's snort of laughter.

"If you think I'm going to hide behind the city walls and do nothing, while you all risk your lives for Lusam, you're crazy," she said, moving towards the break in the barricade. "Let's go!"

"I can't let you go out there Neala," Renn said, stepping in front of her. Neala stopped mid-stride and took a deep steadying breath, before looking into his eyes.

"Renn, I appreciate what you're trying to do, but nothing you can say or do will stop me from going out there and doing my part to help Lusam. And if you think you're capable of stopping me, I'd think again. I would hate it if you forced me to do something I'll regret later," Neala said in a calm voice.

Morgan whistled at her words. "She's a feisty one," he said smirking at Renn.

Neala gave him a threatening look: one that said she was about to show him just how feisty she was if he said another word.

"Enough!" Renn boomed out. "We're not here to fight each other. The fight is out there," he said lifting an arm towards the battlefield. "If you insist on coming with us, just make sure you stay close enough so we can protect you with our shields."

"Fair enough," Neala said, still looking at Morgan menacingly. Her look must have made him feel a little uncomfortable, because he was the first one to head off towards the battlefield without another word. They all broke into a jog, but Morgan seemed keener than the others to join the fight, as he was a good fifty paces in front by the time he reached the end of the wall.

"Don't go running off Morgan," Renn shouted after him. Morgan turned his head and gave Renn a mischievous grin as he disappeared around the corner of the wall. He had barely vanished from sight before he reappeared again, but this time he was flying backwards through the air, and landed hard on the ground with a loud thud. Renn and Neala sprinted towards him, but even before they reached his location the first undead appeared around the corner of the wall. Neala's mouth fell open at the sight before them: thousands upon thousands of undead were moving towards them. Renn had already drawn his glowing sword and was cutting down the first group of undead to come within his range.

"Morgan, get up man!" Renn shouted desperately, but he didn't stir. Renn even nudged him with his boot between sword swings, but he seemed to be out cold. Whatever had hit him, had hit him hard. Neala stepped in front of Renn and began killing the undead.

"Get him back to the barricade," she shouted, knowing

that she wouldn't be able to lift him and run at the same time. Renn didn't hesitate, he picked Morgan up and threw him over his shoulder, then started back towards the barricade. Neala's first set of knives were saturated with magic almost immediately, and she narrowly avoided being injured by one of the undead. Switching to a second set of knives, she began to retreat towards the scant safety of the barricade, praying that her blessed knives would start glowing. She pleaded silently with Aysha to allow her to wield her weapons, but they remained unchanged.

Renn dropped Morgan at the gate and rushed back to aid Neala. She had almost made it back to the barricade by the time he reached her.

"Whatever happens we must hold them here! If they get past us, they'll break through the gate and into the city," Renn said desperately, as he swung his glowing sword in a large arc, cutting down more than a dozen undead in one swing. Neala stood by his side with her final set of enchanted knives, praying as hard as she could that they would start to glow like Renn's sword. Neala knew if she failed to wield her blessed weapons, the undead would break through the city gates and it would all be over. The High Temple's walls may well be protected against magical attacks, but its doors would soon be destroyed by the strength of the undead. Twice before she had witnessed how vulnerable Lusam was at the moment he was released by the Guardian book's magic, and had no doubt he would be killed at that point if she failed now. She screamed in frustration as her final set of knives became saturated with magic. An image of Lusam flashed before her eyes, just as the undead-minion struck her across the face and sent her sprawling to the ground well inside the barricade.

"Neala!" Renn called out, but he was unable to come to her aid. He moved to his right to better block the barricade entrance, but not before two undead had got past his guard. There was no way he could leave his defensive position to help Neala now, or the undead would flood in behind the barricade.

"Neala, get up!" Renn yelled desperately.

Neala heard his voice, but it seemed so far away. She watched as two sets of feet slowly shuffled towards her, her mind unable to make any sense of it. Then she seemed to suddenly become aware of her surroundings again. Realisation of what was about to happen to her sharpened her reactions. She sprang to her feet as adrenaline flooded through her body, and watched helplessly as the two undead closed in on her. She was forced to back up further and further until her back was against the grisly barricade. She had nowhere else to go. Even if she climbed over the barricade, there would be thousands of undead waiting for her at the other side. Her time was up. This was where she would finally die, having failed the only person she had ever loved in her entire life. And that hurt far more than anything these two undead could ever do to her. She closed her eyes and prayed. Not for herself, but for Lusam, Renn and everyone else she was about to leave behind. For all the people who would die and suffer because she had failed to have enough faith to wield her blessed weapons.

As the cold hand of the first undead creature touched her, it felt like a veil being lifted from before her eyes. She suddenly knew with absolute certainty that Aysha would be there for her, and everyone else who fell that day. She smiled, knowing that everything would be alright now, and opened her eyes to see the world for the last time in this life. She felt a strange pulse, and the two undead-minions suddenly slumped to the ground in front of her. Tears of joy filled her eyes as she looked down on the two unmoving corpses and saw four glowing knives in her own belt. She had finally opened her heart to Aysha, and it felt like all her fears and doubts had been washed away. She noticed her other two knives on the ground where she had been knocked down, and went to retrieve them. As she picked them up, they too began to glow brightly in her hand. She had nothing to fear any more, she could feel Aysha within her, and she would take *her* into battle with her.

With a battle cry that would still the hearts of most

men, she rejoined Renn. Her hands moved so fast they were barely visible. Whereas Renn had barely managed to hold back the tide of undead, Neala was cutting a path through them like a scythe through wheat. Within seconds she had created a pocket of space amongst them, and that space grew rapidly. Renn could see several groups of paladins desperately trying to fight their way back to help protect the gates, but there were simply too many undead between them and the gate. Neala must have also seen them struggling, as she started to carve her way through the undead army towards them. The undead tried to close in on her, but she was simply too fast. The slightest touch of her blessed blades was enough to end them, and end them she did, in unbelievable numbers. Renn had never seen anyone fight like that in his entire life, and knew with absolute conviction that Aysha was with her as she fought.

When Neala finally reached the groups of paladins, she simply reversed her course and carved them a path back towards the gates. By now she was covered in so much blood and gore that Renn wouldn't have been surprised if the paladins had mistaken her for one of the undead, but they too seemed mesmerised by her deadly speed and grace on the battlefield.

Renn was suddenly startled by a movement behind him, and almost ran Morgan through with his sword, thinking he was one of the undead that had somehow managed to get over the barricade.

"Seven Gods!" Morgan swore, as he saw Neala cutting through the army of undead in front of him.

"Yeah, I bet you're glad you didn't upset her any more than you did earlier," Renn said, chuckling at the look of astonishment on his face. He just nodded open-mouthed and continued to stab at any undead that came within range from behind his shield.

Neala had created another large pocket of space within the undead, and continued to destroy them at an incredible rate. Many of the paladins she had gone to help were now within hailing distance of Renn, but many of them were too busy watching Neala to even notice. Neala didn't even slow down when the undead turned and started walking back the way they had come. She continued to destroy every undead that came within her range, and that range increased dramatically when she removed her other four knives and sent them flying through the air towards the retreating undead. Four more hit the floor never to move again.

"I know I took a big knock to the head, but did I just see thousands of undead run away from her?" Morgan asked. Renn didn't really know if he was joking or not, but by the look on his face he would have guessed not.

"Well, wouldn't you run away from her, having seen that?" Renn said grinning, and nodding towards the corpse littered battlefield.

"Seven Gods yes! But I doubt I'd get very far," he said shaking his head and watching Neala retrieve her knives.

"I agree, so I'd be nice to her if I were you," Renn replied, chuckling to himself. Morgan simply nodded as he watched her approach.

Around forty paladins watched silently in awe as Neala slowly walked back towards the barricade. Her knives had lost their glow just like everyone else's weapon, but Renn had no doubt it would return the next time she was in battle. And he could tell by her new found confidence, that she no longer had any doubts either.

When Neala reached the barricade she stopped directly in front of Morgan and met his eyes, then after watching him squirm for a moment she grinned at him.

"That's going to be a nice shiner you have there," she said, pointing to his rapidly blacking eye. Renn burst out laughing at the look on his face, then watched as Neala went to find something to clean off all the blood and gore with.

After a moment Renn noticed that the bombardment of the city's wall had stopped. His heart sank as he realised the Empire magi must have already broken through the south wall, and that would also explain why the undead had been recalled by their masters. He sprinted towards the far end of the wall so he could see for himself, shouting for all his fellow paladins to follow him so they could help defend the breach.

When he reached the end of the wall, he breathed a sigh of relief. Although the city's wall had been badly damaged, it thankfully remained intact enough to prevent the undead from entering the city. He had expected to see the remaining paladins near the wall attempting to protect it, but strangely they were nowhere near it. Even stranger was the sight of the undead army ignoring the wall altogether, and instead retreating towards the south cliffs where the Empire magi were massed.

Then he saw the reason why. Directly at the base of the cliffs were a group of paladins. The Empire magi had retreated well away from the edge of the cliffs for some reason, but one of them broke away from the rest and came slowly forward to peer over the edge. Renn watched curiously as the man quickly looked over the edge, then turned and ran as fast as he could. A bright blue flash streaked upwards from the base of the cliffs towards the fleeing man. He took no more than five strides before he fell to the ground, and his death-pulse washed over Renn and the others in the valley below.

It all began to make perfect sense to Renn. It seemed that Alexia had somehow achieved the impossible, and forced the Empire magi to retreat out of range of the city walls. The Empire's response had been to recall their undead army to attack her and the paladins with her. But from what Renn could see, it looked like she had little more than a single group of paladins with her, and that would never be enough to defend against what was now heading her way. Renn knew they would never make it to her group in time, but they had to at least try.

Chapter Forty-Six

Lusam collapsed to the floor in a crumpled heap as the Guardian book released him from its magical grip. His vision blurred with the incredible pain inside his head, made all the worse by the intense white light within the room. He felt, rather than saw the blue pulse-of-light wash over him as he lay next to the book pedestal, curled into a tight ball against the searing pain in his head. As the blue light washed over him, his pain eased considerably, and he was once again able to think more clearly. Remembering the severe damage that had been caused to the blood vessels inside his head when he read the Guardian book in Coldmont, he quickly began to search out any new life threatening injuries, but found none. He felt certain there had been many, but somehow knew he had just been healed by Aysha's light. She had given Neala her word that she would look after him whilst he read the Guardian book, and it would seem she had kept that promise, much to Lusam's relief.

Lusam felt like he could throw up at any moment, and it took him much longer than the previous times to recover his composure. When he did finally manage to stand up, he was pleased to see that the High Priest had done as he had asked, and brought him one of the Power Orbs. He attempted to bend over and pick it up, and immediately regretted it, as his head began to spin wildly once more. As he stood there, willing his world to stop spinning again, he checked to see how much the Guardian book had increased his capacity to hold magic. He was stunned by what he found. His magical capacity had grown so much, he doubted that any mage alive even came close to his level of power, including Lord Zelroth himself. The small amount of power he had left himself after charging the city's shield earlier, was now barely even noticeable within his massive new magical reservoir.

Lusam placed his hand on the wall to steady himself before attempting to pick up the Power orb again. As he did so, he could feel distinct vibrations coming through the wall with his hand. His head was still trying to sort itself out from reading the Guardian book, as if the new information it had given him was fighting with itself to find a place within his mind to permanently reside. It was difficult to think clearly while it was going on, but as the fog in his mind began to clear he became aware of the distant sounds associated with the vibrations. He strained to hear the distant sounds, and as he did so, his hearing became far more sensitive to the world around him. He wasn't sure if it was a new ability from this Guardian book, or one of the others, but it was a very strange sensation. He could hear people's voices and their footfalls as they hurried around the High Temple above him. He could also hear the distant thuds that were causing the vibrations in the wall, but he couldn't tell where they were coming from.

As the new information from the Guardian book established itself within his mind, more and more of that information became clear to him. The Guardian book in Coldmont had increased his understanding of how all things were connected to each other magically, and he had used that information on several occasions since. But now, his understanding of it took on a whole new dimension. The information this Guardian book had bestowed on him far outweighed the one in Coldmont. It was as if each piece of information was a part of a much larger puzzle, and now that puzzle was complete. When he opened his mage-sight to the world, he could see lines-of-power everywhere he looked. Everything was connected to everything else, either by physical touch, or by lines-of-power running through them. He could even see for the first time the magic within the air he breathed. It entered his body with every breath he took, and at first he thought that must be how the magi regained their magical reserves, but when he saw the same magic released back into the world again as he exhaled, he knew that not to be the case.

He reached out with his magical senses and searched for the true source of his power, and found it almost effortlessly. He could clearly see the magic that was being drawn towards his body and entering his upper torso, at the exact point where his heart was beating within his chest. It finally made perfect sense to him; the human heart was where a magi drew his or her power from, and that was also why a death-pulse was released whenever a mage died, as the heart released its stored power back to the world at large.

He sent out his magical senses through his hand and into the wall he still touched, through the countless layers of stone and mortar, and reached for the city's power source. He was shocked when he finally linked to it and found it completely drained of power. His mind entered the vast empty power crystal that once powered the whole city, and he felt a strange feeling of unimaginable loss and sadness. He couldn't explain why he felt that way, but it felt like he had suddenly lost someone very close to him. Somehow he knew the crystal could be recharged again, but he also knew that something within the crystal was now lost to the world forever, and could never be regained. What that *something* was, he did not know, but he felt a keen sense of loss, the likes of which he had not felt since his grandmother had died several years before.

From within the power crystal he sent out his magical senses once more, riding the lines-of-power which stretched out forever before him. It was a strange sensation seeing the world through its own magic. It was not like using his normal eyes, where he could see the shapes and colours of things, this was very different. All he could see was the magic of the world, and how it was all bound together. He could see the immense glow of the Empire magi on top of the southern cliffs, and the almost imperceivable amount of magic within the undead in the valley below. He could see the groups of paladins as they battled against the undead, and the bright magical-missiles as they arced towards the city. He could see the magic within several people caught in the bombardment all wink out of existence below, as they were struck and killed by various objects, and how the magic within them was also released back into the world around them.

Lusam watched the world from his strange new perspective without care. He felt almost free of concern for what was unfolding before him. As if it no longer mattered what happened in the real world. Only this new world mattered now, because this *was* the real world, not the one he had been blindly living his life in for so long.

He glanced down to his left and vaguely recognised a familiar glow of power. At first his mind couldn't make the connection between the image and that of the old world, but then he realised what it was: it was Neala's aura. He frowned to himself, knowing that she was somehow important to him, but he couldn't quite remember why that was. Slowly, he sent out his consciousness along the lines-of-power towards her location, so he could see for himself who she was.

He could see that she was stealing the magic from the ones who barely had any, and then they went completely dark to his new sight. As she took their magic, it seemed to become contained within her hands. No, not her hands, it was something else, in her hands. He watched as she moved quickly towards two brighter glows of power, then stopped to face the thousands with barely any power advancing on her position. He watched as she continued to steal the power from the … what were they? He knew he should know what they were, but he seemed to be having great difficulty focusing on anything. He watched impassively as the girl suddenly moved backwards, as if someone had suddenly picked her up and thrown her. He felt that he should be concerned, but he didn't know why as he watched the scene unfold before him. Two of the weak ones moved slowly towards the girl … no her name was Neala, he remembered. Neala was moving now, but the weak ones were also following her. He knew they wanted to steal all of her power, and he knew that was bad. He found a strand of power which led to the one called Neala and followed it. He entered her being and found himself looking out from behind her eyes at the old world. He could sense her thoughts like a gentle whisper on the wind. A name, over and over in her mind. One that meant so much to her, and she felt she had let down so badly. The name was ... Lusam.

It was like a bolt of lightning to his mind. The mere mention of his name brought him back to himself. He pulled the countless threads of his being towards his own consciousness, trying desperately to remember who he was, and what he was. Neala ... now he remembered who she was, she was part of him, an important part of him, and the weak ones were about to steal all of her power.

Neala closed her eyes, but it didn't stop Lusam from being able to see what was happening. One of the weak ones touched her shoulder ready to steal her power, but Lusam sent out his consciousness through the connection and stole its power first, then he jumped across another line of power and did the same to the other weak one. Four incredibly bright objects suddenly appeared in front of him and bathed him in their light. It was like a veil being lifted from his eyes, as a voice more beautiful than anything he had ever heard spoke to him within his mind.

"Lusam, you must go back now. You are not ready for this step yet my child. Follow my light."

He turned and followed the glowing light, back to what, he could no longer remember. He looked back again at the girl one last time, but her name was now gone from his mind. *"Never mind,"* he thought to himself, as he followed the beautiful bright light to wherever it led.

Lusam woke gasping for air on the floor of the book room. His whole body shook uncontrollably as if he had massively overexerted himself physically, but he knew he had never left the room. Or at least his body hadn't. As his mind began to clear, the memories of what had just happened began to reassert themselves.

"Neala!" he gasped, remembering the thousands of undead about to swamp her position.

"*There is no need for you to be concerned for Neala's safety my child, all will be well. She has opened her heart to me, and now wields my power upon the battlefield, but she fights for the love of you, Lusam. My faithful paladins are always a potent foe when they hold to their faith in me, but in Neala, that faith has been amplified by her love for you. Never have I seen a warrior fight with such passion and single-mindedness upon the battlefield. Her deeds here today will be remembered for as long as anyone draws breath in this world,*" Aysha said in his mind, her voice fading away with her final words. Relief flooded through Lusam at Aysha's words, and he thanked her for both sharing the information with him, and her own power with Neala.

Eventually, Lusam managed to get to his knees and reach out to grab the Power Orb. He could feel the pull of the Power Orb on his mind, but now he was much more able to resist it somehow. Once he had regained his feet again, he turned to face the book pedestal. It seemed that he had been correct in his earlier assumption, because now he could see the two green lines-of-power leading away from the book pedestal. It confirmed his theory, that to use one pedestal to reach another pedestal, you must first have read the Guardian books at both of those locations. Now he could clearly see the words *Freedom* and *Absolution* carved into the upright of the book pedestal, each with a green line of power emanating from it.

He reached his hand towards the green line of power coming from the side of the book pedestal marked *Freedom*, and a bright light flashed before his eyes. He felt the now familiar falling sensation, and a moment later found himself within the book room of Helveel. The room's bright light was activated the instant it sensed his presence within, and the familiar Guardian book marked with *Freedom* sat on the pedestal where he expected it to be. He glanced down and breathed a small sigh of relief when he saw not one, but two names now on the book pedestal, *Absolution* for Coldmont, and *Transcendence* for Lamuria.

Lusam quickly located the five indentations and connected their points together with his magic as he had done before, then waited for the door to slowly open. Once he could squeeze through the gap, he created a small light orb and jogged towards the large chamber. He really wished he had time to say hello to Mr Daffer and Lucy whilst he was there, but he knew full well he didn't.

Even before he had read the new Guardian book in the High Temple, he had fully intended to go to Helveel and recharge his own power reserves there, as well as one of the Power Orbs, by using the walls of the underground chamber. He knew he could not have tried to drain any power from Coldmont without risking its complete destruction, not to mention the possibility of bumping into Lord Zelroth again. So here he was in Helveel—again. He made a promise to himself, and to Aysha, that he would return later and replenish all the magic he took. He just hoped there was enough magic within the walls to fill both his, and the Power Orb's reserves.

When he reached the huge chamber he placed his hand on the warm stone wall, then paused a moment. He didn't want to drain any power from the wall until he was sure it held enough not only to meet his needs, but also enough to maintain the shield around the Guardian book room afterwards. The last thing the world needed was for Lord Zelroth to discover the location of another Guardian book. He sent out his new magical sense into the wall to search for the power source which powered it. He immediately felt the same intense pull on his mind that he had suffered when he first encountered the Power Orb, only this time it was far stronger than before.

It seemed to understand what he had come for: to steal the magic that was protecting the Guardian book. It seized his mind in its iron grip and threatened to drag him under. Whatever it was, it was immensely powerful. Lusam struggled desperately to free himself, but to no avail. He could feel the mind of another being crawling through his own, searching and clawing for information, and no matter what Lusam did, he could not stop it. As the entity pulled him in further and further, he began to sense the huge power reserves it had. He need not have worried about draining it. It could have filled his power reserves a hundred times over, and then some.

"Please, stop! I have to get back to protect the Guardian book in Lamuria," Lusam shouted desperately with his mind. The incessant pulling at Lusam's mind lessened slightly, as his words were digested by the hidden entity. Whatever had hold of him didn't let go, but it didn't pull him in any further either. Lusam knew it was waiting for him to speak again, but he also knew that whatever he chose to say next had better be exactly what the entity wanted to hear. Whatever the entity was, Lusam had to assume it was there to protect the Guardian book above all else, and therefore it too had a vested interest in keeping them *all* safe, or at least he hoped.

"The power source has been completely depleted in Lamuria. I need to take some power from here to recharge it, so we can get the city's magical shield back up. There are thousands of Empire magi attacking the city, I must be allowed to get back and defend it, or the entire world will be in danger," Lusam said with his mind. He immediately felt the entity searching through his mind for the truth in his words, so he allowed it free access to his thoughts. Not that he considered for one moment he could have prevented it, even if he had tried.

The entity sent out an incredibly powerful wave of emotion that stunned and dizzied Lusam. At first Lusam thought it was anger, and expected to be pulled in further at any moment, but it was anguish he felt from the entity, not anger. Anguish at being unable to change what had already happened, and anguish at not being able to do more now to help. The anguish was eventually replaced by a deep feeling of sorrow and loss, almost mirroring what Lusam himself had felt when he had discovered the power crystal had been depleted in Lamuria.

"I know you can read my mind, so you must already

know that I'm their last hope to save the Guardian book. Please ... help me! I give you my word that if I survive I will return the power I take from you," Lusam mentally pleaded. The voice that came back was like nothing Lusam had ever heard before. It wasn't a human voice. It was as if the entity struggled to form each unfamiliar word with great difficulty, with a mouth that was never intended for speech at all. Its voice boomed so loud in Lusam's head, he was glad he hadn't been forced to hear it with his normal ears, or he felt sure he would have been completely deaf now.

"BLOOD RECOGNISES BLOOD," the entity said, and suddenly released Lusam from its iron grip. As Lusam retreated away from the entity, it let out a piercing war cry that chilled him to the very bone.

Lusam had no idea what the entity had meant by its strange statement, but he felt sure it had something to do with why he was still alive. He hesitated as he reached his hand out towards the wall again to take his fill of magic, but decided if the entity had wanted to kill him, he would already be dead. The magic flooded into his body, like an ice lake breaking through its glacial barrier. He filled the Power Orb from his new reserves, and was amazed to find that his was almost empty again by the time it was full. It pulsed brightly in his hand, tugging at his mind like an untrained juvenile version of the entity within the wall. Lusam filled his own reserves once more from the wall, then turned back towards the book room.

The door to the book room had long since closed, so Lusam was forced to wait for it to open once more. When he stepped inside the room, the bright light burst into life, and he quickly walked over to the book pedestal. Making sure he was standing in the right spot, he reached out and touched the green line of power that emanated from the word *Transcendence*. The room flashed brightly, and once again he felt the strange falling sensation as the pedestal sent him to his destination.

A moment later he was standing in the book room in Lamuria, still clutching the fully charged Power Orb. He felt a little queasy and disorientated, but it didn't last long, and he guessed it was down to the fact he had travelled twice through the pedestal in a relatively short space of time.

Lusam didn't know how the priests recharged the city's power crystal, and he didn't have the time to find out either. He placed a hand on the wall of the book room and traced a route directly to the main power crystal above the city. Once he had secured a line of power to it, he channelled the magic from the Power Orb directly into the city's power crystal. He could sense the city's power crystal burst into life above the High Temple. What he didn't know, was how brightly it now glowed in the late afternoon sky, as he made his way out of the book room, and towards the waiting battle outside.

Chapter Forty-Seven

Zedd and Cole finally arrived at Lamuria with a small army of their own. When they had reached Stelgad seven days earlier, they had found more than twenty Empire agents still patrolling the general area there. Some had been on their way to Stelgad before the order to move to Lamuria had been issued, others were simply out of communication range when that order had been given. Zedd had immediately taken them all under his command, then set off towards Lamuria without further delay. Each of the seven villages and towns they had passed through on their way to Lamuria had suffered the same grisly fate, and by the time they reached Lamuria, they arrived with an undead army of hundreds.

When they first arrived at Lamuria Zedd and Cole had reported to the *Baliaeter* in charge there, and Zedd had immediately been forced to concede the command of his men and their undead-minions over to him, much to Zedd's annoyance. *Baliaeter* Varorde was a powerful man, both in magic and physical strength, and Zedd knew without doubt he would lose a direct confrontation with him.

Lord Zelroth had commanded Zedd to take charge of his army whilst in Coldmont, but had refused to suggest how he could accomplish that goal. It put Zedd in a very precarious position indeed, because if he confronted *Baliaeter* Varorde with Lord Zelroth's orders without any written proof, he would likely be challenged to a duel for command; as was standard practice in the Empire when two magi of equal rank confronted one another. If that happened, Zedd had no doubt about the outcome of that battle, but neither did he doubt the outcome of failing to follow Lord Zelroth's orders.

He decided for now, that he would simply bide his time and watch for an opening to present itself. If *Baliaeter* Varorde actually won the battle and took control of Lamuria, he hoped that Lord Zelroth wouldn't even remember his name, let alone pursue him. If on the other hand *Baliaeter* Varorde failed to claim Lamuria and the Deceiver's High Temple, Zedd knew that he and Cole were as good as dead if they ever tried to return back home to Thule.

Baliaeter Varorde's second in command was *Vintenar* Nahau, a man who had served under his command for many years. It had been this man that Zedd had first met when he arrived at Lamuria, and he had taken an instant disliking to the man. He had been extremely arrogant, and had openly questioned both Zedd and Cole's legitimacy of being a *Baliaeter* due to their lack of magical prowess. Even though *Vintenar* Nahau was more powerful than Zedd, he still outranked him, and as such he could easily have killed the *Vintenar* using his Necromatic ring, something he was about to do, until Cole communicated silently to him that he had read the *Vintenar's* mind, and found that he was a close friend of the *Baliaeter* in charge. So instead, Zedd had swallowed his pride and tried to ignore the man's derogatory comments.

Baliaeter Varorde used his Necromatic ring to issue his battle orders, silently communicating with everyone in his army simultaneously. They were only to use their undead-minions to weaken the city's shield and keep the Deceiver's paladins busy, until his spy reported back to him from within Lamuria. Once the true strength of Lamuria's shield was known, he would then issue further orders.

The time for the spy to report came and went, and it soon became obvious that he had failed in his mission. It had taken years for the spy to gain the trust of a key member of the Afaraon Royal Family, and now it all seemed like it had been for naught. For decades the Empire had tried to gain access to the inner workings of the Deceiver's High Temple without success. Either the spies were discovered, or they simply failed the priesthood selection process for no apparent reason. *Baliaeter* Varorde felt sure it must be the interference of the Deceiver Goddess Aysha herself, because each time a potential spy failed, the next one adjusted their tactics accordingly, but the end results always remained the same. This time the Empire had chosen a different tactic, and had slowly cultivated a close friendship with one of the Afaraon Royal Family. The Empire had hoped that the legitimacy that came with a recommendation from a member of The Royal Family, would be enough to gain their spy access to the inner workings of the Deceiver's High Temple, but it seemed they were wrong.

Baliaeter Varorde was a naturally suspicious man. He suspected the Deceiver's High Temple held many hidden magi, all waiting to take advantage of a weakened Empire army, and so he based his attack strategy on that flawed assumption. He believed that if he ordered an all-out attack on the city's shield and it failed to collapse, he would be left with an army of heavily depleted magi. If that happened, and the Deceiver's High Temple did indeed hold an army of powerful magi, he would be handing them an easy victory—something he was not prepared to do.

Baliaeter Varorde always led his men from the front. He refused to cower on the rear lines of battle like many of his fellow *Baliaeter* within the Empire, and that he believed, was why Lord Zelroth had chosen him to lead his army during this crucial battle. Their undead-minions were strong, and given enough time, they would vastly deplete the city's shield of its power, but time was not something he had in abundance. The Deceiver's paladins were slowly but surely killing them, and eventually their numbers would be so low as to be ineffective at keeping them occupied in the valley below. *Baliaeter* Varorde knew only too well how effective the Deceiver's paladins could be against his magi, especially when they had blessed shields like many of the ones below.

He needed to speed up the destruction of the city's shield, but not at the cost of exposing his entire army to any hidden magi within the Deceiver's High Temple. He ordered a small contingent of around a hundred magi to attack Lamuria's shield, and then cycled through different groups of magi every few minutes, so as not to deplete their magic too much. Any groups of paladins that were in range also became a focused target, but the vast majority of his forces simply waited, and conserved their magic.

When the first magical-missile breached the city's shield it took everyone by complete surprise. The short time it took everyone to realise they had achieved their goal, felt like an eternity. As one, the magi let out a huge cheer that echoed the length and breadth of the entire valley, then *Baliaeter* Varorde ordered everyone to open fire on the city. The air around them sizzled and crackled with power as thousands upon thousands of magical-missiles arced through the air towards Lamuria, devastating it in seconds. Every building within their range exploded violently, sending plumes of fire and black smoke high into the sky above the city.

Baliaeter Varorde then ordered every magi to send their undead-minions to attack the gates of Lamuria. He knew that once the city's gates were breached it would be over quickly, and the city would be his. He had dreamed of this day. A day when he took the Deceiver's holy city for the Empire. A day he could return home as a hero to his people.

He watched as the paladins desperately tried to retreat towards the city gates and defend them, but there were thousands of undead between them and the gates now, making it impossible for them to get back in time. *Baliaeter* Varorde wasn't a man who liked taking unnecessary risks, so just in case they did manage to somehow thwart his plans and defend the gates, he issued new orders: to destroy a section of the south wall.

"One way or another, my army of undead will enter Lamuria," he thought to himself. He smiled as he watched huge chunks of the city's wall being blown away far below him. Massive pieces of stone crumbled under the intense barrage from a wall that had stood for more than a millennia.

Zedd had sent his own undead-minions towards the city gates long before *Baliaeter* Varorde had ordered everyone else to do the same. He had also communicated silently with Cole to follow his example, even though he only controlled a handful of undead compared to the number Zedd controlled. He wanted to be the first to see what treasures the Deceiver's High Temple held when the gates were finally breached, and if his minions were the ones to kill the High Priest, it would go a long way towards redeeming him in the eyes of Lord Zelroth—or at least he hoped it would.

Zedd and Cole were standing in front of the Empire army, impassively watching as the buildings in Lamuria exploded before them. *Baliaeter* Varorde was even closer to the cliff-tops, with the ever present *Vintenar* Nahau by his side.

"You see, that's how a real *Baliaeter* gets things done," *Vintenar* Nahau shouted to the men, but did so whilst looking directly at Zedd. His intended insult infuriated Zedd so much, that his face turned purple as he resisted the urge to end the man's life with a single thought. Zedd's thoughts of revenge were interrupted by a sudden flash of blue light, quickly followed by several strong death-pulses. At first no one knew what was happening. They all stopped firing on the city and paladins below so they could try and determine where the sudden attack had come from. It was then that Zedd noticed the arrow protruding from the top of *Baliaeter* Varorde's head, only a heartbeat before he fell face first into the dirt ... dead.

Vintenar Nahau's mouth worked wordlessly as he saw his long time commander and friend drop dead before him. He glanced back nervously towards Zedd, who was now wearing a predatory smile and looking directly at him. Zedd and Cole were now the highest ranking magi there, but it would be Zedd who took command of the army. Zedd had to give *Vintenar* Nahau credit for what he did next, instead of cowering before Zedd's stare, he attempted to take command of the army from under him.

"They're at the bottom of the cliffs. FIRE!" he shouted to the men. A dozen or so men dropped fireballs blindly over the edge of the cliff before Zedd bellowed his orders to cease fire.

"You are *not* in command here *Vintenar*, I am. The men take their orders from me now, not you. Do you understand?" Zedd said, daring the man to argue with him. It was the face of *Vintenar* Nahau which turned purple this time, but he managed to control his emotions enough and bow his head in deference, much to Zedd's disappointment.

"Yes, *Baliaeter*. Of course, please forgive me," he said through gritted teeth. Zedd wanted nothing more than to kill the man, but not in front of thousands of witnesses. Instead he fought against his natural urges and simply nodded his head to the *Vintenar's* subservience. Zedd knew as soon as he saw the arrow exactly who it was below them, and he knew how accurate she was with her weapon. He had already had the misfortune of losing men to this female paladin, and he didn't intend to lose any more than he had to now. He gave the order to move back two hundred paces away from the cliff-top, whilst he thought of a plan to end the threat from below.

A moment later a fresh volley of arrows sailed high into the air, but came down harmlessly in the now open space before them. If he had not already moved his men, more of them would have certainly died. His mind raced at what to do next. He tried to put himself in the position of the enemy, and asked himself what he would do next. It seemed obvious to him; they would want to know why their latest volley of arrows failed to hit anything.

"*I want every man on the front row ready to fire. They will send a scout out into the open to see why their last volley of arrows failed to hit anything. When they do, fire on them,*" Zedd silently commanded through his Necromatic ring to his new army. They waited several more minutes before Zedd was proven correct, and over a hundred magi opened fire on a paladin as he emerged out into the open. The paladin managed to narrowly avoid being struck by a number of the missiles, before disappearing once more behind the cover of the cliff-tops.

Zedd realised too late the implications of the paladin seeing where they were, as another volley of arrows emerged from below the cliff-tops to claim another six of his men's lives. Zedd roared in anger and frustration. He didn't care about the men's lives, but he wouldn't be denied his victory by a single girl. Again, he ordered his men to retreat another hundred paces. He decided he would collapse a section of the cliff on top of her, but first he needed to know exactly where she was.

"You!" Zedd commanded, pointing to a man at the front. He came running over to stand in front of Zedd.

"Yes, sir?" the man replied standing to attention.

"Go take a look over the edge of the cliff-top and see where those arrows are coming from."

"Yes, sir," the man repeated, and set off towards the edge of the cliff-tops. Once he was close enough to the edge, he dropped down to his hands and knees and peered over at the enemy below. It was the last thing he ever did. A heartbeat later his death-pulse was felt by all, and he slumped to the ground where he was, never to move again.

Zedd turned back towards his army and pointed to another man. "You! Go take a look," he said. The man's face visibly paled, and he hesitated a moment too long for Zedd's liking. Zedd reached towards the man's Necromatic ring with his mind, and drained every drop of magic from the man instantly. He dropped like a sack of coal to the ground, and his death-pulse was felt by all on the cliff-top.

Zedd knew that if he was to gain the men's unquestioning loyalty, he had to show them that he could not be trifled with. Sure enough, the next man Zedd pointed to carried out his orders without hesitation. He reached the edge of the cliff and peered over the edge, then he turned and started to run a zigzag course back towards Zedd's position. Everyone watched in utter astonishment as a glowing arrow crested the cliff-top, then followed the man's zigzag retreat precisely, before striking him cleanly through the heart from behind. The man stood still for a moment looking down at the arrow protruding from his chest, then looked up at Zedd in sheer bewilderment, before finally falling forward. His death-pulse was felt before he even hit the floor.

Zedd was beginning to become more and more infuriated by the unfolding events, and he had to remind himself that he had already won this battle. The city's shield had already been destroyed, as had most of the southern part of Lamuria. There was no longer any reason to engage this female paladin at the bottom of the cliffs on her terms. Soon the gates of the city would be breached, or they would simply destroy the wall and enter that way. Either way, Zedd and his men would soon be making their way into the valley bottom to claim the city, and they could deal with the paladins then.

Regardless that he no longer felt it necessary to check the position of the female paladin, Zedd still contemplated sending *Vintenar* Nahau to take a look, but decided against it. Instead, he would let him live, knowing that every day of his life he would be reminded of how Zedd had stolen this victory away from his friend *Baliaeter* Varorde. It would be Zedd's name that was remembered throughout history, not *Baliaeter* Varorde's, and certainly not *Vintenar* Nahau's.

Zedd was already aware that the only way down to Lamuria was at the far end of the valley. He knew there were several single file tracks leading down into the valley at his end, but they would leave his men extremely exposed to attack, and it would take far too long to get them all down into the valley below. The problem was, since *Baliaeter* Varorde had ordered all of the undead-minions to attack the city gates, it had also had the added effect of concentrating all of the paladins towards that end of the valley too.

After a moment he realised there might be a way to potentially solve three problems at once. If he recalled all of the undead to attack the paladins at the base of the cliff, then they began to attack the wall again once the paladins were dead, it would draw the other paladins towards his end of the valley. That would hopefully take them away from both the city gates, and the road leading down into the valley. Once the paladins had taken the bait, he could leave several hundred of his men in full view to keep the paladins busy, while he secretly took the rest of his force and circled around to the north end of the valley. If his plan succeeded, they would emerge undetected at the far end of the valley with an almost unrestricted path to the city gates. A few well placed magical-missiles and the gates would yield without much of a problem now the city's shield was down. More importantly, if they caught the paladins unaware, and launched a sudden massive attack from their rear, they could devastate their numbers before they even knew what had hit them.

Zedd issued his new orders, recalling all of the undead army to attack the paladins at the base of the cliff, then he patiently waited for them to arrive. He left his own undead-minions at the far end of the valley, as well as Cole's, making sure he would have them as additional protection when he arrived there later.

The undead army had not made it halfway across the valley floor, before a bright flash in the sky caught Zedd's attention. His jaw hung slack at the sight before him. Where there had been only empty sky above the Deceiver's High Temple a moment earlier, now there was a giant glowing crystal. It hovered motionless in the sky, pulsing with a bright blue light against the late afternoon sky.

Zedd formed a small fireball in his right hand, and sent it towards the strange object in the sky. He watched as it arced through the air towards the strange object in the sky, then gasped loudly when his missile impacted harmlessly on the city's invisible shield.

"No!" he screamed at the sky. Filled with rage he ordered every magi to open fire of the city's shield. Then he watched open-mouthed as a single figure emerged from within the Deceiver's High Temple, one with an aura so bright it was impossible to look directly at it. He knew instantly it was the boy-mage, and he also knew it was time to leave.

Chapter Forty-Eight

Lusam emerged from the High Temple into the late afternoon sun. He no longer shuttered away his aura from view, but instead, he let the full power of it be seen by all. The new magical knowledge the Guardian book had imbued him with, had now become much clearer to him. He knew the Empire magi no longer posed a threat to him or the city, and he wanted to give them every opportunity to retreat by revealing his true magical strength to them. Even though he knew they almost certainly wouldn't.

Lusam could feel the pulse of the city's power source above him now, and when he looked up, he was surprised to see it glowing incredibly brightly, not only to his mage-sight, but also to his regular sight.

As he walked towards the city wall, the utter devastation the Empire magi had wreaked on the southern part of Lamuria became evident. Everything had been destroyed. Not a single building or structure remained standing. He scanned the remains of the buildings with his mage-sight for any signs of life, but found none.

Lusam levitated himself onto the top of the city wall in full view of the Empire magi above. He could see the thousands of undead on the battlefield below him, all connected to their masters on the cliff-tops above by a thin strand-of-power. Instantly he knew the reason why necromancy had never been used during the Dragon-Mage Wars. He remembered how Renn had told him that the vile art of necromancy had been created by the dark God Aamon, and how it had been used before the Great Rift had been torn open to raise vast undead armies. But after the Guardians had been created, it suddenly vanished from use again. It was not used again until much later in the Empire's history, long after the Guardians had vanished from the world. The reason for this was now glaringly obvious to Lusam; necromancy had an inherently fatal flaw. A flaw that left the users of it vulnerable and exposed to anyone powerful enough to detect and manipulate those tenuous magical connections.

Lusam quickly appraised the battlefield below. He could clearly see that most of the remaining paladins were towards the rear of the undead army, and pursuing them towards the base of the southern cliffs. Then he noticed a small group of about fifteen paladins trapped between the cliffs and the advancing undead army. He watched as the undead army surrounded the paladins, forcing them into an ever tightening group behind their own shields. He immediately recognised two of the paladins as Alexia and Hershel, and breathed a sigh of relief at seeing them both still alive and well.

With a single thought, Lusam created a magical barrier around the group of stranded paladins, then expanded it explosively. The surrounding undead army were scattered across the battlefield like chaff to the wind. It only took the paladins a moment to notice Lusam standing on the city wall, and the cheer they gave was audible even to him. Lusam gently levitated the group of paladins within the safety of his magical barrier, and tightly skirted the base of the cliffs with them. He knew he would have to expose his magical barrier to the attacks of the Empire magi for a short period of time—while he crossed the open area between the base of the cliffs and the city wall—but he was not unduly concerned about it. Most of the Empire magi were already focusing their fire on his position, so when the group of paladins suddenly emerged from behind the cover of the cliffs, only a handful of missiles struck his magical barrier before he brought them within the safety of the city's shield.

It saddened Lusam greatly that revealing his aura to the Empire magi had done little to dissuade their attack on

Lamuria. He didn't want to kill all those men, but they seemed to be leaving him with little choice. He simply knew he had to stop them. He said a silent prayer to Aysha, asking her for the strength to do what must be done, and for her to take the souls of the men he was about to kill into her care. He knew they didn't worship Aysha, but they were still men— they were still *her* creation.

"Lusam!" Alexia called out excitedly as she sprinted up to him, closely followed by Hershel and the rest of his group.

"Please, tell us you have some good news," Hershel said, looking a little worried.

Using his mage-sight, Lusam looked out over the battlefield at the tens of thousands of undead, all clearly linked to their masters above on the cliff-tops.

"Tell me Hershel, do the history books tell us why necromancy stopped being used after the Guardians were created?" Lusam asked quietly. Hershel thought for a moment before he replied.

"No, they don't, only that the Guardian's easily destroyed the undead armies of Aamon's followers, but nobody knows for certain how they did it," Hershel replied.

"I do," Lusam said, stepping off the city wall.

Even before he had stepped outside the protection of the city's shield, Lusam had already tapped into thousands of lines-of-power leading back to the magi on the cliff-tops. He levitated himself quickly to the valley floor below, absorbing the impact of hundreds of missiles as he did so. Once he became a stationary target, those numbers increased dramatically, but it was already too late for the Empire magi.

Lusam expanded his shield to make contact with thousands of the undead on the battlefield, and tapped directly into the tenuous connections they had with their masters on the cliff-tops above. He forced open those tiny power conduits, and drained the power directly from the Empire magi to feed his own magical shield. Every impact on his shield drained more and more power from the Empire magi above.

The first massive barrage of magical-missiles that

struck his shield claimed the lives of hundreds of Empire magi. The death-pulses were so numerous and frequent, it was impossible to count them all. The undead fell in their thousands on the battlefield, as the connection to their masters ended with their deaths.

The paladins at the north end of the valley were no longer fighting, or even pursuing the undead. Instead, they watched in complete awe, as Lusam single handedly took on not one, but two armies simultaneously. The Empire magi had now massed their entire force of undead around Lusam, and no longer seemed interested in the paladins at all.

Lusam expanded his shield further and further, incorporating more and more of the undead into his web of power. As he did so, the power requirement to maintain the ever growing shield also increased, draining the Empire magi even more quickly than before. He watched, as thousands of lines-of-power winked out of existence, as the Empire magi died above him in greater and greater numbers.

The bombardment on Lusam's shield suddenly lessened considerably, even though several thousand Empire magi still remained. He suspected their commander had called a ceasefire to try and determine why his men were dying in such large numbers. Even though Lusam had no desire to kill so many people, he knew he could not allow a force of that size to remain within Afaraon. If he did, the death and destruction they would cause would be incredible. Lusam also knew that if he allowed them to leave, they would simply return again in the future, and in even greater numbers to attack Lamuria. But more importantly, if they realised how they had been defeated—by using their own undead-minions against them—the next time might not be such a one-sided battle.

The lines-of-power linking the undead to the Empire magi were like a gigantic glittering spider's web to Lusam's mage-sight. Each strand criss-crossed each other as they made their way towards the cliff-tops above. He reached out with his new senses, searching each strand in turn, until he found the one he was looking for; the one that led to their commander. Lusam seized that delicate line-of-power and forced it wide open, then he turned to face the city behind him. He traced a second line-of-power to the city's power crystal, and used himself to create a new link between the two. Then he began to let the power flow through him, slowly at first, then increasing its flow gradually, so as not to catch the Empire commander unawares and kill him.

Lusam levitated himself high above the height of the cliff-tops, so he could clearly see the Empire army below him. As he increased his power-drain on the Empire commander, he noticed hundreds of new lines-of-power materialise below him—each one linking the Empire commander to another man under his command, as he desperately tried to remain alive by taking their magic through his own Necromatic ring.

Hundreds of men fell where they stood, as they were completely drained of magic by their own commander. Lusam steadily increased the flow of magic, and channelled it all into the city's power crystal. Lusam watched as hundreds and hundreds of auras winked out of existence below him, each quickly followed by a powerful death-pulse. The undead collapsed in their thousands on the battlefield below, as either their masters died, or they abandoned them to try and save themselves.

But nothing could save them now.

Less than five minutes later, and it was all over. Every Empire magi had been completely drained of their power, and every undead-minion stilled forever on the battlefield below. All, that is, apart from a handful of undead that remained at the opposite end of the valley. Lusam traced their tenuous lines-of-power off into the distance, where he saw two men fleeing in the opposite direction. He reached for the glittering lines-of-power—ready to drain the two remaining magi—but as he did so, they suddenly released their hold over their undead-minions, and the lines-of-power vanished. As Lusam watched them disappear over the crest of a hill, he felt certain he saw at least one other strong aura in the distance, but he couldn't be sure.

Lusam couldn't believe the number of corpses that

littered the ground below him, both in the valley, and on the cliff-tops. It was a truly apocalyptic scene. Thousands upon thousands as far as the eye could see lay motionless on the ground. The feelings of guilt he felt were indescribable. It felt as if his insides were being torn out by some invisible force. How he could ever reconcile what he had just done—he had no idea. Then Aysha's light suddenly washed over him, taking him from the depths of despair, to the heights of euphoria in less than a heartbeat.

"Despair not my child. Know, what you have done here this day will save countless lives in the future. If you had failed, and the Great Rift to the Netherworld reopened, those men would have still perished, along with everyone else in this world," Aysha's voice said in his mind, her final words fading away to nothing.

Long after Aysha's voice had faded from his mind, Lusam realised he was still levitating in mid-air, high above the valley floor. Slowly, he turned back towards the city, and was astonished by what he saw there. Thousands of people were now lining the streets, and all were looking directly at him. Not knowing what else to do, he calmly levitated himself back down towards the city's wall, then onto the street below.

The utter silence of the crowd was truly palpable. Not a single person moved or spoke a word. Not a cough, sneeze or whisper was to he heard from any amongst them. Only the late afternoon breeze made any sounds whatsoever, as it blew gently through the trees that lined the city's paved streets. Every eye of the crowd was unflinchingly locked onto Lusam, and it made him feel extremely uncomfortable. He couldn't tell if they pitied him, or feared him. Then he heard the clanging of a metal gate in the distance, followed by a cacophony of excited voices. He was glad of the sudden distraction, as the crowd turned to face the direction from which the noise was coming.

Lusam's heart jumped in his chest when he saw who it was. Heading up the street towards him were more than a hundred paladins, all led by Renn. Lusam was extremely relieved to see that Renn had survived the battle seemingly unscathed, but the one thing that filled his heart with joy more than anything else, was the incredible sight of Neala. She wasn't walking with the paladins, she was being carried on their shoulders as they playfully jostled her around between them in celebration. It seemed she had suddenly become very popular amongst the paladins, and Lusam had to admit feeling more than a little jealous by all the attention she was receiving from the men.

As soon as she noticed Lusam watching her in the distance, she squealed and wriggled to be let down, then sprinted up the street towards him. She almost knocked him clean off his feet when she launched herself at him, and enveloped him in a tight hug. Lusam was sure she hadn't even noticed the massive crowd silently watching their every move only a few paces away, but he wasn't about to ruin the moment by pointing it out to her.

The voices grew louder as the large group of paladins drew closer to them. Lusam could clearly hear the men recounting their battlefield prowess to one another—as he was sure soldiers often did when a battle had been won—but he could also hear the relief in their voices that it was now over.

"Seven Gods lad," Renn swore as he reached them, "how in Aysha's name did you do that?"

Lusam thought he was referring to the battle, but when he looked over Neala's shoulder at Renn, he saw him staring up into the sky above the High Temple with his mouth hanging open. Lusam kissed Neala on the forehead and tried to gently break their embrace, but she was having none of it, and held on firmly. Lusam didn't really need to see what Renn was looking at, and by the ever increasing whispers coming from the crowd, they too had now spotted it.

"It's a long story, but suffice to say I used the magic from the Empire magi to recharge the city's power crystal," Lusam replied quietly.

"The Heart of the City hasn't been visible like that for over two centuries lad. It's just ... incredible," Renn replied in a whisper, never taking his eyes from the glowing object in the sky.

"Neala!" Alexia called out, as she and Hershel pushed their way through the dense crowds towards them. She hadn't seen her best friend since the battle had first begun, and she had been extremely concerned about Neala's state of mind regarding her faith in Aysha, and therefore her ability to use her new blessed weapons.

Neala gave Lusam a gentle kiss on the cheek, and whispered into his ear that she loved him, before finally breaking their embrace. She quickly turned towards Alexia's voice, but stopped mid-stride when she finally noticed the large crowd of people that were taking so much interest in them. Alexia took her by the shoulders at arms length and looked into her eyes.

"Well?" she asked, knowing that Neala would understand exactly what she meant. Neala smiled and nodded her head, as a tear of joy ran down her cheek. She had done it. She had found her faith in Aysha, and knew she would never lose it again, no matter what happened in the future. Alexia pulled her into a friendly hug.

"I knew you could do it Neala ... I just knew it," Alexia whispered through tears of her own. Neither of them had long to dwell on it, as both of them were hauled back onto the shoulders of the celebrating paladins, both now heroes in their own right.

***

The late afternoon light faded slowly into darkness as the news of their victory spread throughout the city. It created a strange atmosphere amongst the population of Lamuria, one of great joy and sadness in equal measures. It was estimated that almost a hundred thousand citizens of Afaraon had lost their lives to the Empire invasion; almost five percent of its population. Many of the bodies would never be found, but the ones that now littered the valley floor outside Lamuria would be given the dignity in death they deserved.

The King had ordered his regular troops to prepare funeral pyres for the countless dead, and they were soon joined by every able man and woman willing to help. By the time full darkness fell, an eerie orange glow filled the sky beyond the city walls. Lusam knew it would burn well into the early hours of the following morning, and probably for much longer than that.

The High Priest had requested a private meeting with Lusam later that evening, to thank him for what he had done for Lamuria and the High Temple, and to discover whether or not he intended to stay in the city for the longer term. Lusam guessed what he truly wanted to know, and promised he would add more of his magic to the city's power crystal later, but not before he had first repaid a debt he already owed. Lusam asked to borrow one of the Power Orbs again, and the High Priest was more than happy to oblige him. He refilled the Power Orb with magic from the city's power crystal, knowing he would be able to replenish it easily enough over the next few days, then he set off towards the Guardian book room with the High Priest.

Lusam returned the borrowed magic to the entity in Helveel as he had promised he would, and informed it of their victory in Lamuria. Although it didn't speak directly to him this time, it did radiate several very strong emotions towards him, including satisfaction and pride—which Lusam decided to take as a good sign. He briefly considered trying to communicate directly with the entity again, but quickly decided against it. He told himself that if the entity had wished to communicate with him, it would have already done so. The last thing he wanted to do, was to anger the entity and find himself back within its clutches again, so he decided to leave it be, and simply return to Lamuria. To his credit, the High Priest never asked where Lusam had gone after he vanished through the book pedestal right in front of him, only to reappear several minutes later; something Lusam was very relieved about.

By the time Lusam had returned to Lamuria, King Theodore had already declared seven days of mourning for the dead, which was to be followed by seven days of celebrations for the living. Apparently, Lusam was to be the special guest of honour at a grand banquet celebrating his auspicious victory over the Empire's army. The banquet would be held at the Royal Palace on the final day of the celebrations, and would be attended by all the noble families of Afaraon, along with many lesser dignitaries. Upon hearing the news, Lusam felt certain he would prefer to face another three Empire armies, than what might await him at the Royal Palace. There was also a statue to be commissioned of him, one that would stand for all time in the halls of the High Temple, alongside the other great names in Afaraon's history.

After the period of mourning had ended, Alexia was finally reunited with Rebekah and Kayden. Ever since the battle had been won, Rebekah and Kayden had been staying with Hershel's sister, Darcie. Apparently she loved having the children there, and had already offered to look after them on a permanent basis, something the children seemed very keen on too—as long as Alexia promised to visit them regularly, of course.

Both Rebekah and Kayden had already been accepted into the High Temple's school of magic, due to their teacher's strong recommendations. Miss Hiroko had been so impressed by their abilities after only a single day in her class, that she had gone personally to speak with the High Priest on their behalf.

Renn had been good to his word, and almost as soon as the battle was over he had requisitioned six men to accompany him back to Prystone and its surrounding towns and villages, to search for any possible survivors. None of the men had been happy about missing out on the city's celebrations, but a promise of a week's furlough upon their return did much to ease their grumblings. Renn asked Alexia if she would like to join his expedition, but surprisingly she had refused, stating rather cryptically that she had *'something to do in Lamuria, and would prefer to remain there if he didn't mind,'* but she refused to elaborate any further on the matter.

Neala and Alexia had both become almost living legends amongst the paladins who had fought alongside them that day. Alexia, for single-handedly holding back an entire army of magi with her bow, and Neala for feats on the battlefield which simply dumbfounded everyone who saw them. Lusam heard various accounts of what Neala had done that day, and had it been anyone else, he would have discounted them quickly. But he had seen Neala fight in the past, and he could only imagine what she would be capable of against the undead with a pair of blessed knives.

The celebrations seemed to stretch on and on in Lamuria, and Lusam had done his best to avoid as many of the celebratory events as he possibly could. Neala had berated him for it on several occasions, telling him in no uncertain terms, that the people deserved the chance to meet him and express their thanks openly for what he had done for them, but he paid little attention to her words. It wasn't that he was ungrateful for their efforts on his behalf, quite the contrary in fact, but he had never felt comfortable amongst large crowds of people. He had spent his entire life trying to be as inconspicuous as possible, so now, to suddenly be amongst crowds of hundreds, if not thousands of people, all wanting to speak with him or shake his hand felt daunting, to say the least. He knew it would be hard for Neala to understand how he felt because she grew up amongst a large group of people, but *he* had only had his grandmother, then later only himself as company as he grew up. He knew he only needed more time to adjust, but that time was fast running out, as the day of the grand banquet loomed ever closer.

The King had insisted that Lusam stay as an honoured guest at the Royal Palace during his stay in Lamuria, and no matter how long he intended to remain within the city, he would always be welcome there. At first Lusam had tried to politely refuse the King's offer, but it soon became apparent to him that it was more than a simple request. The best he managed to salvage from the situation, was to request that

Neala be allowed to join him there, to which the King readily agreed. He wasn't sure if Neala would be angry with him or not, but it soon became apparent that she was overjoyed at the chance to spend some time in the Royal Palace—especially with all its treasures.

The King had assigned Lusam and Neala over a dozen servants to attend to their every need, and by the second day within the Royal Palace Lusam felt like he was suffocating with their constant overzealous attentions. Lusam was sure he had never spent as much time in an outhouse as he did that week in the Royal Palace, not because he needed to be there, but because it was the only place the servants didn't follow him. But even then, whenever they seemed to feel he had been in there for too long, they would ask through the closed door if he was alright, and enquire if they needed to send for an apothecary to ease any upset stomach he might have.

He never thought he would, but he actually looked forward to his daily meetings with the High Priest, when he helped to recharge the city's power crystal. At least he got the chance to leave the Royal Palace and spend some time alone, even if it *was* only for the short walk to and from the High Temple.

During one particularly annoying session, both he and Neala were forced to remain almost motionless for the best part of three hours, while various tailors and seamstresses took a multitude of measurements and pinned numerous lengths of multicoloured cloth to them both. Apparently the clothes they were wearing were less than suitable for the grand banquet, and something more `appropriate` would be made for them to wear in time for the big event.

"You'd think they'd just be happy you saved the city," Neala grumbled under her breath, shortly before being stuck by yet another pin. Lusam chuckled, but was also rewarded by a sharp pin prick.

"Please try to remain still sir," the tailor said, without a hint of an apology.

"I'd be careful if were you, he turned the last person

who drew blood from him into a toad," Neala said with a perfectly straight face. The tailor's face instantly paled as he looked between Neala and Lusam for any signs of humour, and when he didn't find any he took a step back, as if to assess his own work.

"Yes ... yes, I think we have enough here to work with, sir," he said out loud, quickly dismantling his creation, and being very careful not to prick Lusam with any of the pins he removed. There were no words exchanged between the tailor and the seamstress, but she too had her multicoloured reams of cloth and silks dismantled and stowed away even before the tailor had finished his own. With little more than a perfunctory bow, they both disappeared through the door, closing it firmly behind themselves.

"That was very mean of you," Lusam said, grinning widely.

"Not as mean as what I was about to do to her if she stuck me with another one of her pins," Neala replied, grinning right back at him. Lusam glanced at the door, almost feeling sorry for them, then he realised—they were finally alone. Four strides later he was at the door, the key turned with a slight clicking sound locking out the rest of the world on the other side. It was the first time in weeks he had been alone with Neala, and he wasn't about to waste a moment of it. He turned back towards her with an even wider grin on his face, and saw her brandishing one of the seamstress' pins menacingly at him like a miniature sword.

"If that's supposed to scare me away, you should know that I once had a beautiful blonde girl stab me through the foot with her knife, and that didn't work either," he said grinning and slowly stalking towards her.

"I did not!" she squealed, dropping the pin and attempting to slap his arm. He caught her hand and pulled her into a tight embrace, kissing her passionately as they both fell to the floor in each others arms—neither of them responding to the later knocks at their door.

The day of the grand banquet had finally arrived.

Lusam found himself wide awake even before the sun had fully crested the high cliffs, so he decided to go early and make his magical contribution to the city's power crystal. He had trouble sleeping all that night, and knew there was no point in trying to go back to sleep whilst his mind raced with all the possibilities of what was to come later that day.

Until a few days ago, he knew nothing about the political complexities of Afaraon, let alone how to act in the presence of Royalty, or even the lesser nobles that would be attending the grand banquet. During one of his early visits to the High Temple however, the High Priest had struck up a conversation with him regarding the Royal Palace. At first he had kept the conversations simple, mostly enquiring about how his stay at the Royal Palace was going, and had he met this person or that yet?

By the third day Lusam had begun to become a little suspicious of the High Priest's real motives for asking all of his questions, and decided to confront him over the matter. If he was honest, Lusam didn't much care for the High Priest. Up until that point Lusam had thought of him as a slightly conceited, self-important man who liked to revel in his own lofty position. But after he confronted him about his earlier questions, Lusam's opinion of the man began to change considerably. It quickly became apparent that the High Priest had Lusam's best interests at heart, and had been simply trying to comprehend the level of understanding Lusam had about the political system of Afaraon, before being '*thrown into the lion pit with them,*' as he described it.

Lusam had already been nervous about the grand banquet, but by the end of that first day discussing it with the High Priest, he was positively terrified. He was warned that he would be used as a tool—or even a weapon if they could— between various warring noble houses. They would stop at nothing to gain his trust, and that of his closest friends. For anyone to even be seen speaking with him at the grand banquet, would gain them favour amongst the other noble houses. Friendships, were apparently traded like commodities amongst the nobles—even perceived friendships—therefore he should be very careful not to spend too much time talking with any one person there. He should expect to be showered with expensive gifts from the various noble houses, each one trying to outdo the others. He should accept the gifts graciously, but show no preference to which was his personal favourite, even if asked directly—which he surely would be, many times over.

By the end of the first day speaking with the High Priest, Lusam's mind reeled with all of the implications. On the second day, the High Priest insisted that they held their '*discussions*' within the inner sanctum, where they could not possibly be overheard by anyone. Apparently, he felt that even his own position within the High Temple was vulnerable to the politics of Afaraon, should he be discovered giving Lusam any guidance in the matter. One of the biggest shocks Lusam had, was when the High Priest pointed out the King's own gift to him; the statue. No noble in the land could offer such a gift, and by doing so, the King sought to gain the loyalty of Lusam above all others. The High Priest had even suggested that Lusam should single out the King's gift as his favourite during his speech to the gathered nobles and dignitaries. Lusam almost choked when he heard he would have to stand up in front of everyone and make a speech, but the High Priest said he would help him prepare for it, and for that Lusam was very grateful.

For each of the six days Lusam went to speak with the High Priest, he always expected him to ask for something in return—but he never did. And as Lusam got to know him more and more, he actually began to like the man. He could clearly see how he relaxed as soon as they entered the inner sanctum, and how his official bearing returned as soon as they left it again. Lusam began to understand why he had to be as he was—two men; one who fulfilled his official duty as the High Priest, and the real man who was hidden beneath, and unable to show himself in public.

Lusam took his usual route from the Royal Palace to the High Temple that morning. He hadn't expected to see many people on the streets at that time of day, but he was surprised at the number of people there actually were. It was positively buzzing with activity around the Palace grounds, with various tradesmen and deliveries being made for the upcoming event. The streets quietened down again the further from the Royal Palace Lusam travelled, and it wasn't until he was nearer the High Temple that it began to get busy again.

Lusam had heard rumours that ever since *The Heart of the City* had become visible in the sky again—after over two centuries of absence—people had begun to gather there at first light, to appreciate the incredible spectacle as the first rays of sunlight hit it each morning, and it seemed the rumours were true. Dozens of people lined the street, all looking up at the beautifully glowing crystal as it caught the first rays of light from the morning sun as it crested the high cliff-tops. Lusam tried his best to remain unnoticed as he walked past the crowds of people, but he only got a few short strides before the whispers started. Lusam lowered his head and continued walking towards the High Temple, pretending not to notice the whispers coming from the growing crowd.

"Sir ... sir. Excuse me sir," a woman's voice said from the crowd. Lusam glanced in the direction of the voice and saw a young woman holding a small baby in her arms. Lusam paused for only moment, but it was long enough for the woman to step away from the crowd towards him. He met her eyes, and saw fear within them, but it didn't stop her advancing towards him, her baby clutched tightly in her arms. By the time she reached Lusam, he could clearly see her trembling with fear, and when she spoke, he could also hear it in her voice.

"Sir, I'd like to thank you for what you did for us. For all of us," she said turning towards the other people in the crowd. "May I ask your name, sir? So I may tell my daughter who it was that saved her life when she is older." The crowd became deathly silent, all waiting for Lusam's reply, and the woman's trembling seemed to increase with every heartbeat he didn't respond. He smiled at the young woman, hoping to ease her anxiousness, even though he was feeling more than a little anxious himself.

"My name is Lusam, and you don't need to be scared of me," Lusam replied to the young woman, placing a hand gently on her shoulder. She flinched as he raised his hand towards her, but to her credit she never moved. Lusam could feel her trembling under his touch, and he felt very guilty for causing such a reaction, even though he had done nothing to warrant it as far as he knew. She managed a nervous smile at him, then averted her eyes and bowed her head.

"Sir, may I beg a Guardian's blessing for my child?" she half whispered through her fear. Lusam suddenly realised why the people of Lamuria looked at him the way they did; they believed him to be an actual Guardian.

He knew the Guardian's of old had been practically revered amongst the people of Afaraon. They had held almost godlike status amongst the population back then, and their legend had only grown since. Most people never got to see Aysha in their lifetimes, but everyone was able to see the Guardians back then. Renn's words echoed in Lusam's mind, about people believing in only what they could see, and wondered exactly what was going through the minds of these people, as well as everyone else's in Lamuria right now. He needed to stop these rumours, and quickly, before they took a firm hold within the population.

"What's your name?" Lusam asked the woman softly.

"Ella, sir," she replied, still averting her eyes from Lusam's.

"Please, look at me Ella," Lusam said, and waited until she raised her eyes to meet his. "I am not a Guardian, do you understand?"

"But, sir ... I don't understand, we all saw what you did out there to that Empire army," Ella said, looking towards the southern wall of the city and the valley beyond.

"That was only my magic," Lusam replied, as if that would be enough to explain away the things he had done.

"Forgive me sir, but everyone knows that all magic comes from the grace of Aysha herself, and those she favoured the most were once the Guardians. That was why they held such incredible power, just as you do now sir," Ella replied, once more averting her eyes from Lusam's. Lusam took a deep breath and held it for a moment, before sighing it out again. There was no way he could explain to these people that he held only a fraction of the power of a true Guardian, let alone how he acquired that power. He thought the best thing he could do right now, was to continue denying he was a Guardian, and hope that once they eventually left Lamuria behind, life would once again return to normal—something he was beginning to doubt would ever be possible again.

"I am not a Guardian," he repeated, slightly louder so the crowd would hear his words. Ella simply bowed her head, but Lusam knew he had not convinced her or a single person in the crowd, let alone the rest of the city who had not even heard his words. He turned away from the young woman without another word, and continued walking towards the huge doors of the High Temple.

Chapter Forty-Nine

It was less than three hours until the grand banquet would commence, and a package containing their new clothes was finally delivered to their room by a palace servant. Neala excitedly peeled open the corner of one of the packages to check which was hers, and once she was certain she had the right one, she gave Lusam a quick kiss on the cheek and headed for the door.

"Where're you going?" Lusam asked.

"I'm going to Hershel's sister's house to get ready there. Alexia is there with the children, and she promised to help fix my hair for the banquet. Oh ... don't look so grumpy," she teased him, "I'll see you at the banquet, don't worry." Neala winked at him as she disappeared through the door, clutching her brown paper package tightly.

Lusam walked over to the door and collected his own package of clothes from the floor, then closed the door behind her.

Reluctantly, Lusam opened the package, and immediately wished he hadn't. He wasn't sure if it was the tailor's idea of bad joke, or the current style for such events, but either way he was mortified by what he saw. Before him was a peach coloured knee-length jacket, with golden embroidery that ran all the way around the collar and down the front of the opening. The cuffs were turned up, and they had the same garish golden embroidery around them too. A pair of knee-length trousers in the same design and colour, as well as a waistcoat and a pair of long white woollen stockings that completed the outfit. There was also a pair of very shiny black shoes in the package, which wouldn't have been so bad if they hadn't been so long and pointy. Lusam wondered if he would even be able to walk in them without falling over his own feet.

Lusam stood looking at the piles of clothes not knowing where to begin, when he was startled by a knock at his door.

"Come in," he called out. The door opened and in stepped Shannon, the head servant assigned to Lusam and Neala.

"Ah, excellent. I see that your new clothes have already arrived. Would sir like me to arrange for some hot water to brought up for you to bathe, before I assist you in getting dressed?" Shannon asked. Normally Lusam would have been aghast if anyone had suggested helping him dress, but having seen the complexity of the outfit, with its countless buttons and fastenings, he was more than happy to accept the offered help.

"That would be fine, thank you," Lusam replied, still staring at the garish clothes on the bed.

By the time Lusam had emerged from his bath, Shannon had also added several undergarments to the pile of clothes, as well as a white silk cravat. Lusam couldn't believe how long it took him to get dressed in the new clothes, and by the time he was done, he felt like he could barely breathe. Even when he had lived rough on the streets of Helveel, he had never worn as many layers of clothing as he did now.

When he was finally dressed, and Shannon had finished trying to—unsuccessfully—get a comb through his unruly hair, he stood before the full-length mirror to inspect the results. He didn't even recognise his own reflection in the mirror, and he felt sure the tailor was indeed exacting his revenge over what Neala had said to him earlier. At that point there was one thing he knew for certain; if it *had* been within his power to turn the man into a toad, he would be hopping and croaking around his tailor's shop right now.

Shannon fussed around him a little more, and even gave his hair another attempt, before finally leaving him in peace with little more than an hour remaining before the banquet started.

The High Priest had been true to his word, and had prepared Lusam with a speech for the grand banquet. After carefully reading it through several times, Lusam could barely believe that such a long speech could actually contain so little. It expertly avoided everything from his origins to his current abilities, and instead focused on thanking the King for his gracious gifts, and offered promises of a brighter future for all of Afaraon now that the Empire's invasion had been defeated. There was no mention of the estimated one hundred thousand citizens of Afaraon that had lost their lives at the hands of the Empire, and when Lusam had asked the High Priest why, his answer seemed less than satisfactory to Lusam. Apparently talk of the dead was limited only to the time of mourning, but during the time of celebrations, no mention was allowed of such things, which somehow seemed very wrong to Lusam.

Lusam spent the final hour before the grand banquet nervously reading over his speech, trying to make sure he knew its contents well enough not to make a fool of himself later that evening. The High Priest had asked Lusam to rewrite the words in his own handwriting, then burn the original copy, so as not to implicate him in its creation. He also suggested that Lusam should request some writing implements to be brought to his room, and rewrite it there, instead of at the High Temple. That way it would add credence to his own writing of the speech, should anyone enquire later.

Lusam was already thoroughly tired of all the political undercurrents of Afaraon's high society, and he hadn't even met a single person from one of the noble houses yet. He knew he wouldn't have to wait too much longer for that to happen though, as a moment later he heard the knock at his door, and the call that he was expected in the main banqueting hall shortly. Taking a deep calming breath, he carefully folded up his speech and put it away in his inside jacket pocket for later.

He already knew his way to the main banqueting hall, because Shannon had shown him the way there a few days earlier. Shannon had also explained that he must remain outside the banqueting hall doors until he was formally called to enter, and also exactly what he should do when he did enter. Apparently, as the guest of honour he would be the last person to enter the room. That way everyone in the room could see him enter and greet him accordingly. Something that made Lusam feel both sick, and weak to his knees.

There were two Royal Guards stationed outside the large double doors leading into the banqueting hall, each one dressed in his pristine bright red and blue uniform. As Lusam approached, they both simultaneously drew their shining sabres and saluted Lusam, making him momentarily pause mid-stride. A finely dressed servant stepped out from the shadows, and silently ushered Lusam towards the grandly designed doors of the banqueting hall. Lusam's heart thundered in his chest, as he tried desperately to appear relaxed to anyone who would see him once the doors opened.

The servant pulled on a small rope by the side of the left door, but Lusam heard no bell. He guessed it must control some kind of visual marker on the inside of the room, one that would indicate his presence outside the doors to anyone watching for it on the inside. Almost immediately the music inside the banqueting hall stopped, and was replaced by a very loud voice.

"Your Royal Highness', Lords, Ladies and gentlemen. It is my great privilege to introduce to you, our guest of honour this evening. The new saviour of Lamuria, and of all Afaraon ... LUSAM."

Lusam just about managed to take a steadying breath, before the large doors swung open to reveal a packed banqueting hall beyond. Hundreds of people suddenly applauded as he stepped into the huge banqueting hall. The noise was almost deafening. He forced a smile onto his face and nodded in random directions as he had been instructed to do, but he met no one's eyes as he did it. He followed the finely dressed servant to where he would be seated at the King's table, and almost gasped in horror when he realised he would be sitting by himself at the opposite end to the King, and not with Neala as he had expected.

Desperately, he scanned the room for Neala, and his heart almost melted when he finally saw her. She was one of the most beautiful sights he had ever seen. The sleeveless dress she wore was made from a delicate blue silk. It hugged her figure tightly, then flowed out from her waist to the floor in wave after wave of silk layers. Her blonde hair had been made into an intricate bun on the top of her head, using both plaits and delicate silver chains. And when she smiled at him, his heart seemed to skip a beat in his chest. He had always thought she was beautiful, but tonight, she was simply breathtaking.

"Sir?" a voice said over his shoulder, jolting him back to the present. Lusam turned his body towards the voice, leaving his gaze locked on Neala as long as he could before looking away.

"Yes?" Lusam asked absent-mindedly.

"Your chair sir," the servant said, indicating that he should take his seat.

"Oh ... yes, thank you," Lusam replied, taking his seat whilst the applause began to die down again. That was the last time Lusam managed to see Neala for several hours.

The King's table was in the centre of the enormous room, with dozens of tables arranged around the outside—three or four deep. Lusam guessed that Neala had been seated at one of the many tables behind him, but due to the continuous questions coming from the occupants of his own table, he barely had time to chew and swallow his food, let alone search out Neala's whereabouts in the room.

The meal seemed like it went on forever, with course after course of food served, most of which, Lusam had no idea what it was. Many of the dishes were made to resemble something they weren't, like pieces of fruit that turned out to be sweet cakes instead, or savoury pastries shaped like a fish or a chicken. `Just one more strange thing to add to the *growing list,*` Lusam thought to himself, as he bit into another oddity of food.

When the meal and all the toasts were finally over, the speeches began in earnest. The King was first to speak, and he wasted no time at all reminding everyone in the room of his unique gift to Lusam; a statue that would stand for all time amongst the greatest men and women ever to have lived in Afaraon. Then he invited anyone else wishing to bestow their own gifts upon Lusam to come forward and do so, which they did, in their droves.

Within minutes Lusam was almost buried alive by all of their gifts, and if it hadn't been for the vigilant servant recording each one as it arrived, Lusam wouldn't have had a clue who had sent what by the end of the evening. After the hordes of people had finished delivering their gifts, the same servant quietly informed Lusam that they would all be sent to his room, along with a copy of the list so he could see who had gifted what later. Lusam nodded and thanked the man, wishing privately that he too could return to his room along with the gifts, or even without them for that matter, he didn't care much which.

For almost an hour Lusam listened to speech after speech, all concerning him in one way or another. It seemed incredible to Lusam how much these people—who he had never met before—presumed to know about him. Almost every speech hinted at some fanciful friendship he had—or would have—with that particular person or noble family in the future, and how they would somehow work together to make Afaraon great again. Even though the High Priest had already warned him what to expect, the shallowness and insincerity of those people almost made him feel ill.

By the time it came to his own speech, he cared very little for what the people in the room thought of him any more, so he simply read it out as if reciting a passage from a well known book. Although he was still a little nervous speaking in front of so many people, his lack of enthusiasm seemed to go completely unnoticed by his audience, and they still applauded him loudly when he had finally finished.

Soon the food and the tables began to be cleared away, and the musicians started to play once more. People began to congregate in smaller groups, and others danced to the music with their partners. Lusam soon spotted Neala towards the back of the large room, and had already started making his way towards her, but every second step he took was blocked by one noble or another, each enquiring how he was, or more predictably, which gift did he like the best?

On his way to Neala, Lusam was passed by Alexia as she made her way towards the area of the room now allocated for dancing. She too looked stunning in her new bright red dress, and she gave Lusam a wink and cheeky grin as she passed him by, dragging along a startled looking young paladin behind her, in his pristine dress uniform. Lusam didn't know whether to envy or pity the young paladin, but felt sure he would have learned more than a few new dance steps come the morning.

"Hello handsome," Neala teased, as her eyes ran over his new attire. Lusam had almost forgotten he was wearing the ridiculous outfit, and his face flushed at her comments.

"You look absolutely incredible," he said quietly as he came close to her. This time it was Neala's turn to blush, something he hadn't often see her do.

"Thank you. So do you," she replied, trying to keep a straight face. Lusam raised his eyebrows at her statement, and it was enough to send her into fits of giggles at his expense.

"So, who was that with Alexia?" Lusam asked, trying to change the subject. It almost worked too, until Neala glanced down at his ridiculous shoes, and once again almost fell over laughing at him. He waited patiently for her to recover herself.

"I'm sorry, it's just that you look ..." Neala started to say.

"Ridiculous! Yes, I know," Lusam finished for her. "Trust me, if I ever see that tailor again, being turned into a toad will be the least of his worries." Neala burst out laughing again at his words. Lusam couldn't help smiling back at her, he loved seeing her so happy—even if it was at his expense.

"What's so funny?" a young voice asked by his side. When Lusam looked down, he saw Kayden standing by his side looking up at them both, with a huge piece of cake in his hand, and sticky jam all around his mouth.

"Oh, there you are, thank the Gods" a woman's voice called out from behind them. Lusam turned to see Darcie and Rebekah coming across the room towards them, with Hershel not far behind.

"Where have you been Kayden? I've been looking everywhere for you," Darcie said, sounding a little distressed.

"I was up there," Kayden replied innocently, pointing to one of the two wide staircases that curved towards a large viewing gallery and outside balcony above.

"What in Aysha's name were you doing up there child?" Darcie asked.

Kayden shrugged his shoulders, then replied, "Eating cake. And looking at the stars in the sky outside."

"Kay, you really shouldn't wander off like that. Poor Darcie has been worried sick about you," Rebekah scolded him.

"Sorry Bekah ... I was only eating cake," Kayden replied quietly, looking at his own feet.

"It's not me you should be saying sorry to," Rebekah said.

"Sorry Darcie," Kayden sobbed, with his head still down.

"Oh, don't be getting all upset now, there's no harm done. Come now, let's go and get you cleaned up, and maybe you can show me where you got that delicious looking cake from," Darcie said, holding out her hand to Kayden. He sobbed again, then nodded his head before taking hold of her hand. Lusam thought he was genuinely upset at being scolded, but as he was being led away, he turned his head back towards his sister and gave her such a mischievous grin, that he knew immediately it had all been a ruse.

"I'm not sure your sister knows what she's getting herself into there," Lusam said jokingly, nodding towards the departing pair.

"She will do, soon enough," Rebekah answered before Hershel could.

"Aye, I think you might be right there, but I'm not going to be the one to tell her," Hershel said chuckling to himself, as he watched his sister being led away by a very astute five-year-old boy.

"I take it Renn isn't back from Prystone yet?" Lusam asked.

"No, not yet I'm afraid. I expect he'll be another week at least, but knowing Renn, it might take him even longer than that. I was surprised to hear that Alexia had requested not to go with him though. Apparently she said she had something important to do here in Lamuria instead," Hershel replied, taking a drink of his wine.

"Yeah, now we can *all* see exactly what she had to `do` here in Lamuria," Neala said jokingly, as she watched her best friend dance with her new man. Her words generated a new round of laughter, but no one there begrudged Alexia her chance of happiness.

"I suppose we better go and see if Darcie is coping alright with her small friend," Hershel said, grinning at Rebekah.

"If it's okay, I'd like to stay here for a while. I need to ask Lusam something, but I'll come and find you all later, don't worry," Rebekah replied, sounding much older than she actually was. Hershel didn't reply to her request at first, but instead looked at Lusam and Neala for guidance.

"It's okay, she can stay with us for a while. I'll bring her right back to you when she's ready," Neala promised. Hershel nodded his acceptance, and after a quick farewell, went off to find his sister again.

"Thanks," Rebekah said, taking hold of Neala's hand. She looked very pretty in her red velvet dress and open-toed sandals, and Neala couldn't help wishing that she had owned a dress like that when she was her age, instead of the bland clothes she had always been made to wear back then.

"What would you like to talk to me about?" Lusam

asked, breaking Neala out of her reverie. Rebekah looked up at Lusam momentarily, then turned her gaze away again, as if too afraid to speak.

"It's alright Rebekah, he's not as mean as he looks," Neala said grinning at Lusam, and giving Rebekah's hand a small squeeze, "you can ask him whatever it is you need to ask."

Rebekah took a moment before she found her words, but when she did, they came flooding out. "Before those men attacked my village, they attacked my father's ship and destroyed it. I was with my mother on the dockside, and we watched it happen right in front of us. I haven't told Kayden yet, but I know our father died on his ship that day. If he hadn't, he would have come to find us after the men left … but he didn't.

"I took Kayden and we ran away to hide before the men could see us, but my mother … she just kept staring at where my father's ship had been in the water, and she wouldn't come with us. I don't know what happened to her. I don't know if those men killed her, or if they took her somewhere, or if she ran away that day," Rebekah said, with tears rolling freely down her cheeks at the painful memories.

"I really like Darcie, I do, and I know Kayden does too. But I really need to know if our mother is still alive. I was hoping you could use your magic to help me find her again. Please help me, please," she begged.

Lusam felt terribly saddened by her story. No one should have to see the things she had seen, and certainly not someone as young as she was. He understood far too well the pain of losing someone very close to him, but not to know if they were alive or dead—that must be even worse. He knew the necklace around Rebekah's neck once belonged to her mother, and felt sure he could use it to track her mother's location if she was still alive. But he didn't want to attempt it in front of all these people.

Lusam had noticed several groups of nobles slowly edging their way towards his position ever since he had joined Neala at the back of the room. They seemed to be stealthily competing between themselves for the best position to pounce on Lusam whenever he decided to move from his current spot, but none of them as yet had approached him directly—something he was sure would change soon enough.

"Rebekah, I'll try to locate your mother for you with my magic, but I can't promise it will work. If it doesn't work, that doesn't mean you should give up hope of ever finding her. Do you understand?" Lusam said quietly. He didn't want to give her any false hope where there was none, but he also didn't want to bring her world crashing down with the knowledge of her mother's death either. He remembered one of his grandmother's sayings: *wherever there was hope, there was life.* And he didn't want to end her hope, or ruin her life with the information he gave her.

Rebekah looked up at Lusam and nodded her head, tears still filling her eyes.

"We can't attempt to do it here though. Maybe we should find that quiet spot your brother found earlier," Lusam suggested. "The trouble is, I think all those people want to speak with me, and they will likely follow us upstairs too."

Rebekah casually glanced over her shoulder at the growing number of nobles gathered only a few strides away from where they stood, then turned back to Lusam and smiled. "My brother showed me a way to get through the busy crowds on market day. Trust me, they will move out of our way, and they won't follow us either," she said confidently, with a grin that resembled her brother's so entirely, that Lusam had to look again to make sure Kayden hadn't just taken his sister's place somehow when he wasn't looking.

"I think I'm going to throw up, maybe you should take me outside for some fresh air," Rebekah suggested, putting her hand to her mouth, hunching over, and heading directly towards the growing crowd of nobles, whilst visibly and dramatically retching. Lusam and Neala placed a hand on each of her shoulders and quickly followed her. The crowd parted before them like magic, as each person scrambled to get clear of the retching girl, just in case they were caught in the aftermath. Unsurprisingly, not a single noble attempted to stall Lusam's progress with conversation, and a few moments later they were outside on the balcony in the cool evening air.

"Oh, I'm really starting to like your little brother," Lusam said, chuckling to himself.

"That's because you don't know him well enough yet," Rebekah replied in her big sister voice, making him chuckle once more.

The large balcony overlooked the Royal Gardens, and Lusam knew the view in daylight must have been quite spectacular, especially at that time of year. It was a clear night with almost a full moon in the sky, which gave them plenty of light by which to see each other. Lusam sat himself down on a long stone bench, and was quickly joined by Neala and Rebekah.

"I'll need to use your mother's necklace to try and find her," Lusam said to Rebekah. She removed the necklace and handed it to Lusam without saying a word.

Since reading the third Guardian book in Lamuria, Lusam's understanding of magic had increased dramatically. He now knew that items belonging to someone for a long period of time would often absorb some of their magic, like a fabric did with a scent. He hoped he could use that small amount of magic to search out its original source; Rebekah's mother. It wasn't too dissimilar to what he had done when using the enchanted knives to find Neala after her abduction, but he knew this would only work if her mother was still alive.

Lusam placed the necklace in the palm of his hand, then sent out his mage-sight to inspect the tiny amount of magic contained within it. Once he had located it, he concentrated on finding its original source, but saw and felt nothing. He tried several different methods, including trying to make it point in the direction of Rebekah's mother, but nothing worked. She simply was not there.

Lusam kept his eyes closed long after he had abandoned his attempts at finding Rebekah's mother. He was trying to think of the best thing to tell her. He had always been taught that the truth was best, but in this case, he wasn't so sure. He knew that time healed the raw feelings of loss, even if it didn't erase them entirely, and he believed Rebekah deserved that time to adjust to her new life in Lamuria. If she felt compelled to search out her mother later in life, only to then fail, what was that when measured against a full and happy childhood?

Lusam opened his eyes to find both Rebekah and Neala looking at him intently.

"I'm sorry Rebekah, it didn't work. Maybe the necklace has been away from her for too long," Lusam lied. A grim smile flickered across Rebekah's face, one that told him she fully understood what he really meant.

"So, she's dead then," Rebekah said quietly.

"I didn't say that she was dead," Lusam replied.

"It's okay, I expected as much. At least now I know," she said, as Neala pulled her into a hug.

"Oh, Rebekah, I'm so sorry," Neala said hugging her tightly. "I know no one can ever replace your real parents, but maybe we can be your new family now, if you'll let us. I know Darcie loves you both very much, and I'm sure you'll be very happy living there with her, she seems such a lovely lady."

"She is, and we are happy," Rebekah said through her tears, "I just wish I had a chance to say goodbye to them both, that's all."

After a few minutes Rebekah seemed to recover herself incredibly well, and asked Neala if she would take her back to meet up with Darcie. Lusam suspected she would grieve in her own time, when the full impact of it all had finally hit her. But for now, she seemed as happy as someone in her situation ever could be, and he marvelled at her resilience.

Lusam knew as soon as the nobles downstairs noticed Neala and Rebekah returning, they would be heading in his direction to seek him out. He badly needed some time alone, and it was almost as if Neala had read his mind, when she told him that she would be with Darcie and Hershel whenever he was ready to rejoin her.

He thought about blocking the door with one of his magical barriers to avoid speaking with the nobles, but it seemed such a petty thing to do. Instead, he levitated himself off the balcony and up onto the roof of the palace, where he soon found a deserted rooftop garden. Several stone benches identical to the one on the balcony below were distributed throughout the garden, and he soon chose one to lie down on.

The cool night air was a welcome relief to Lusam in his thick, tight fitting clothes, and he dreaded having to return to the stuffy heat inside the Royal Palace, let alone confront all those intolerable nobles seeking his attention. Staring up at the twinkling stars above, he absent-mindedly started to loosen his tight cravat, when his fingers caught on something underneath it; his own mother's crystal amulet.

He realised it had been a long time since he had even thought about his own mother, and felt a strange kind of guilt over that. He had never known his mother, nor very much about her. In fact, the only connection he had ever had with his mother, was owning her crystal amulet. It was then that he realised, that for the first time in his life he might actually be able to touch a real part of his mother; her magic. But only if the crystal amulet still contained any of her power after so long.

Lusam sent out his mage-sight into the crystal amulet, and immediately found what he was looking for, but it was no small amount of power that he found there. Whatever material the amulet was made from, it seemed capable of holding a large amount of magic for its small size.

He spent several blissful moments immersing himself in the remnants of his mother's magic contained within the amulet, before beginning to wonder exactly what had happened to her on the day she had died.

It was like a bolt of lightning.

The incredible image of a soaring dragon flashed before his eyes, then his vision suddenly shifted, and he raced across vast areas of land and sea. It moved so fast that he could not see any of the detail below him as it flew by. A moment later he was in a darkened room, looking down into what looked like several dirty prison cells. He could see two people asleep there, a man in one cell, and a woman in another. But it was the woman he was hovering over. It was then that he saw a fine strand-of-power linking her to his amulet. She seemed to somehow sense his presence there, and suddenly sat bolt upright, staring straight at him. She mouthed a single soundless word.

"*Son!*"

"Mother!" Lusam gasped, as he was slammed violently back into his own body a heartbeat later by some incredible magical force. A distant voice rang in his ears, one that he instantly recognised as Lord Zelroth's, but the meaning of the words were lost to him, as his vision faded to black and he slipped into unconsciousness.

*****

Chapter Fifty

Zedd watched in absolute terror as the second man was selected to be fed to the *Aznavor* by the Inquisitor. The large floating disc now rippled like a pool of quicksilver in front of Lord Zelroth, made even larger by the previous victim's sacrifice. The man screamed in sheer terror as the Inquisitor took control of his body, and slowly walked him towards his certain death. The *Aznavor* shrieked and strained at its bonds, trying its best to mentally reach the condemned man. Its six long tentacles groping towards him as he came ever closer. Just before he came within range of the creature's influence, the Inquisitor broke off his own connection with the man, and one of the Darkseed Elite pushed the man forward. The *Aznavor* instantly gripped the man's mind, taking control of his every movement for itself. The man begged and pleaded for his life, but it was already far too late for him, as he was forced to unwillingly walk towards his own end. The creature's huge jaws opened wide, revealing its wicked curved black fangs, each one longer than a man's hand. Inside its gaping mouth only blackness could be seen, as if all light from the outside world feared to enter. As the screaming man came closer, it reared up above him, then striking with the speed of a viper, it swallowed him almost to his waist. The man screamed in agony, as it bit down onto him with its enormous jaws and began to drain him of his magic, just like it had done with the first man Zedd had seen die.

Soon it would be his and Cole's turn to fuel the creature's link to the Netherworld, so that Lord Zelroth could report his failure at securing Lamuria's power source to their

God, Aamon.

After fleeing the disastrous outcome of the battle at Lamuria, Zedd and Cole had quickly been intercepted by *Baliaeter* Chaol—the most powerful *Baliaeter* in the Thule Empire. Apparently, Lord Zelroth had commanded him to travel to Afaraon and take control of his army outside Lamuria, even before he had instructed Zedd and Cole to do the same at Coldmont.

Baliaeter Chaol's magical strength was very well know within the Thule Empire, and it was believed that only his battlefield prowess had prevented him from becoming one of Lord Zelroth's Darkseed Elite. When he had discovered Zedd and Cole fleeing the battlefield, he had at first believed them deserters, and treated them accordingly. He almost executed them on the spot, but for Cole's subtle intervention within his mind suggesting he should ask more questions first.

Upon hearing that Lord Zelroth had personally ordered that Zedd and Cole take charge of the army at Lamuria, he quickly had the two Inquisitors travelling with him verify their story. Unlike Cole, Zedd had no way to resist the mind probe of the Inquisitors, and neither did he try. Instead, he willingly revealed the full details of their meeting with Lord Zelroth at Coldmont, knowing that was his best chance of surviving the situation.

Zedd had known full well, that Lord Zelroth would kill them both for their failure once they returned to the Empire —something he was very keen to avoid, by escaping during their long trip back home. He knew if he did, his family would be held responsible and made destitute within the Empire— but at least he would survive, and maybe he could rescue his family at a later date.

Unfortunately, he never got the chance.

Baliaeter Chaol was a shrewd man, and had both Zedd and Cole dosed with large amounts of Calligray root for their whole journey back to the Empire. Calligray root only grew in the hot southern deserts of Thule, and was used to incapacitate a person from using any magic whatsoever. It was often used within the Thule Empire to control its prisoners, and prevent their escape; their food dosed with it daily. Once taken, it took several days before that person was able to perform any kind of magic again.

It had been two weeks since they had arrived back in the Thule Empire and delivered directly to Lord Zelroth, along with the news of their failure. Lord Zelroth had descended into a fit of rage, the likes of which Zedd and Cole had never seen before. Several unsuspecting servants who just happened to be in the room at the time paid with their lives, as Lord Zelroth lashed out violently at the people around him. Zedd and Cole both thought their lives would end at any moment, and in the following days, they both wished they had.

Lord Zelroth ordered Zedd and Cole to be taken by the Darkseed Elite and tortured, and the days that followed were beyond any pain imaginable. Their bodies were broken beyond recognition, only to be healed again, and then the process repeated over. No amount of screaming or pleading helped, and no respite was given. By the end of the first day, Zedd would have gladly taken his own life a dozen times over to end his own suffering. By the end of the second day, he prayed to be freely allowed to enter the gates of the seven-hells for all eternity, rather than be made to suffer more of what he had.

Often Lord Zelroth would come and watch their torture, gleefully adding his own form of mental torture to that of the physical type being ministered. He revealed his twisted plans for Zedd's family and property, and promised him much more pain to come.

Apparently, it had all been a sick joke of Lord Zelroth's, and he had never expected Zedd or Cole to survive challenging *Baliaeter* Varorde for control over his army at Lamuria. *Baliaeter* Chaol had already been sent to Lamuria to take command of the army, even before Lord Zelroth had met Zedd or Cole at Coldmont. He had been sent to take *Baliaeter* Varorde into custody for alleged treasonous acts committed against the Empire during a recent campaign in the southern badlands.

Lord Zelroth went to great lengths to explain how insignificant both Zedd and Cole were to him, but unfortunately, the results of their actions had not been. It wasn't the fact they had failed to carry out his orders—or even attempt to—it was what Lord Zelroth had been forced to do since their return. The location of Coldmont was a closely guarded secret by Lord Zelroth, with only a handful of his most trusted Darkseed Elite and Inquisitors knowing of its existence. Unfortunately, neither *Baliaeter* Chaol, nor the Inquisitors travelling with him were among those trusted few, and Lord Zelroth had been forced to execute them all due to Zedd and Cole's actions—something that Lord Zelroth had promised them excruciating pain for as recompense, and he certainly didn't disappoint. He also promised that it would be their lives that would be used to form the link to the Netherworld, so he could inform Aamon of his failure to release him.

As the doomed man continued his helpless screaming within the *Aznavor's* jaws, an image of Aamon suddenly flickered into existence at the centre of the shimmering silver disc. Lord Zelroth fell to the ground, prostrating himself in front of his God.

"Might I presume by my continued imprisonment within the Netherworld that you have failed me?" Aamon said in an otherworldly voice.

"Please, I beg your forgiveness sire. Our forces were taken completely unawares by a powerful young mage who emerged from the Deceiver's Temple. From the information I have obtained about the battle, it appears that he used a form of Guardian magic to destroy our forces, similar to what is recorded in our ancient sacred texts. Sire, if the Deceiver has once again allied herself with Driden and his dragons—"

"SILENCE!" Aamon commanded. "There is no new alliance, and there will be no resurrection of the Guardians either. Even here, in the Netherworld, I sensed the disruption in the fabric of magic caused by the emergence of this new mage. He *is* powerful—but he is *no* Guardian. Without a dragon, such a feat is impossible.

"I know my brother, and so I know that Driden will never forgive the treacherous acts of my sister. I may be trapped within the Netherworld, but the outside world is not beyond my sight. I have seen Aysha's creations proudly mount the stolen dragon heart above her High Temple, and rest assured, so has Driden. I have felt his rage at her betrayal over the countless centuries whilst I have been imprisoned here, and now that the dragon heart at Coldmont has become visible to him, his fury has only grown stronger. He believed that she had only stolen one of his sacred creations, but now he knows the truth—or at least part of it. I am confident that once I am set free from the Netherworld, and Driden learns the full truth of our sister's treachery, that he will be more than willing to form an alliance with me against her, and her vile creations."

"Sire, I regret to report that the dragon heart at Lamuria has already been partly regenerated, and is now protected by their powerful new mage. I know of the weakness he exploited, and the same mistakes will not be repeated—but it will take us time to wear down their defences again."

"Fortunately for you, that will not be necessary. During our recent communications I have begun to sense the existence of another dragon heart in your world. At first, I thought it to be the one at Coldmont, but realised its location was much closer than that. As you know, any dragon that dies in your world is immediately taken back to Nerroth by its brethren. Its heart is removed there, and the knowledge within is shared amongst their kind for all time.

"The soul of a dragon lives on in its heart after death, and all of its life experiences along with it. Their final resting place is a well guarded secret, and very well protected. I know of its existence, but even I am unable to penetrate the powerful magic protecting its location, or sense the dragon hearts within. It is Driden's equivalent to a High Temple, and as such, carries all the safeguards associated with it. So knowing all of that, I could not understand why I was able to detect a dragon heart at first—one that had not been recovered by its kind and returned to Nerroth—then I began to understand; it was because the other dragons could not see it. I believe it remains hidden somewhere in The Dark Forest of Afaraon, somewhere close enough to The Great Rift for it to be hidden from the senses of both dragons and Gods, and somewhere it has remained since the time I was first imprisoned here. You will use the power of that dragon heart to finally free me from this prison ..." Aamon's image began to shimmer and fade, as the last remnants of power was drained from the dying man by the *Aznavor*.

"Another one—quickly!" Lord Zelroth said, snapping his fingers at the Inquisitor. Zedd's legs went weak as his bonds were suddenly released, and his mind seized by the Inquisitor. His legs began moving independently of his mind, taking him one step at a time towards the waiting *Aznavor*, and his impending doom. He tried desperately to break the Inquisitor's control over him, but his body still suffered the effects of the Calligray root, and no matter how hard he tried, any form of magic was beyond his ability. He had promised himself that he wouldn't plead for his life, nor would he give Lord Zelroth the satisfaction of hearing him scream, but now, he wasn't so sure.

As Zedd came almost within range of the creature's influence, he suddenly realised why Aamon's words had sounded so familiar to him. During his own trek through The Dark Forest in Afaraon, he had seen a pile of ancient dragon bones through the eyes of the *Vesdari* he was controlling, and they had glowed with power to its hungry eyes.

"WAIT!" Zedd screamed. "I know where the dragon heart is."

Lord Zelroth held up his hand to the Inquisitor only a single footstep outside the range of the shrieking *Aznavor*.

"If you are lying to me, I will have you tortured for the rest of your natural life," Lord Zelroth said menacingly to Zedd.

"I'm not. I swear it. We discovered the dragon remains when we travelled through The Dark Forest in pursuit of the boy-mage and his paladin friend. I summoned a *Vesdari*, and it stumbled across the dragon remains whilst it hunted for them. I saw it myself, through the creature's own eyes," Zedd said desperately, knowing that one more step would be his last.

Lord Zelroth locked eyes with Zedd, pointed to his Inquisitor, then to the final prisoner still chained next to Cole. The man's bonds fell away, and he began to scream in terror as the slow walk to his death began.

Zedd breathed a sigh of relief, smiling inwardly at the prospect of surviving another close encounter with death. He would try and convince Lord Zelroth of Cole's value, but whatever the outcome, at least *he* would survive this day.

***

Acknowledgements

Thank you for reading **LUSAM – The Dragon Mage Wars – Book Three**. I hope you enjoyed reading the book as much as I enjoyed writing it, and I very much hope you will join Lusam and the others again in the next thrilling instalment.

So, it seems my pet cockroach Zedd escaped with his hide intact once again. I think an email I received from a Mr Michael B. sums it up perfectly: *Zedd would make a great politician*.

Be honest, did you remember the pile of ancient dragon bones from the second book? Well done if you did!

Although I will not give specific details that will spoil the plot, I can assure you that the action in book four will really `hot up` (if I may use a local colloquialism of mine). Obviously Lusam will attempt to rescue his mother, putting him on a direct collision course with Lord Zelroth, and the Great Rift will feature heavily, as will the Netherworld—more than that, I can not say.

If you enjoyed reading my books, please, please leave me a review. It really does help stabilize my sales whilst I write the next book in the series for you, and it means I won't be knocking on your door asking if I can wash your car for a dollar.

Joking aside, I really would love to hear your

thoughts about the series of books, because you, the reader, are the most important person to any author, and without you, there simply would be no point in us writing anything at all.

Once again, thank you for your support.

www.deancadman.com